MW01504716

ACTUS

MY BEST FRIEND IS AN

ELDRITCH HORROR

BOOK FOUR: VOIDWALKER

aethonbooks.com

VOIDWALKER
©2023 ACTUS

Aethon Books
www.aethonbooks.com

Print and eBook formatting by Josh Hayes. Cover art provided by Cyan Gorilla. Typography by Steve Beaulieu.

Published by Aethon Books LLC.

Aethon Books is not responsible for websites (or their content) that are not owned by the publisher.

ALSO BY ACTUS

A BRIEF REFRESHER

Damien's first year at Blackmist was anything but what he'd expected. His greatest problems had gone from trying to find a door that worked for his room to keeping the Void and the Corruption—two deadly forces that have been warring over the Cycle for countless eons—from ripping the mortal plane to shreds.

After Delph and Dredd mistakenly freed It Who Stills the Seas, one of the bound Void creatures, from its containment, Damien and Sylph finally got a chance to explain just how bad the situation was to someone over the age of twenty.

They proceeded to spend the rest of the summer hunting the Corruption, then returned to the school just in time to absolutely dominate the Kingsfront interschool tournament. During it, they butted heads with Second once more, only surviving the encounter due to intervention from Moon, a strange man with an uncomfortable obsession with Damien.

With their second summer finally upon them, Damien and Sylph have earned a break. Sylph joins Damien in finally visiting his hometown. What could possibly go wrong?

CHAPTER

ONE

Damien and Sylph staggered out of the portal, and it snapped shut behind them. A wave of nausea slammed into Damien, and he staggered, repressing a grimace. It was the worst reaction to a teleportation he'd had for quite some time, but he still managed to keep himself from retching.

"I think this counts as kidnapping," Sylph said, but she couldn't keep the small smile from her face.

"You'll live," Damien replied. "Besides, my mom always makes too many pancakes. You can spare me from gaining ten pounds of fat."

Sylph shifted her stance and glanced nervously up at the city on the hill before them. The wooden walls were aged from years in the sun, and the chirp of birds filled the air. There were no clouds in the brilliant blue sky, and the sun shone with just a little too much heat for comfort.

"Come on," Damien said, starting toward Ardenford. "I don't want to get cooked out here."

"You never mentioned your hometown before," Sylph said, keeping pace with him.

"There isn't very much interesting here," Damien replied. "It's just farmland, really. Not much point talking about that in a mage college."

There were no guards at the gate when they arrived. A young boy Damien didn't recognize ran past them, giggling as an old woman chased after him, waving a spoon in the air. The woman paused as she spotted Damien and squinted at him.

"Damien?"

"Hello, Mrs. Hubbard," Damien said. "You're looking lively today. It looks like that hole in the school fence has still yet to be patched."

"Bah, everyone's always too busy, and my back would never forgive me if I tried it myself," Mrs. Hubbard said, a small smile cracking her stern expression. "You've gotten so tall. And thin. Is there an occasion for the visit?"

"Nothing bad," Damien promised, and her features relaxed even more. "I'm just visiting, I guess. Got sent on vacation."

"Vacation is good. You need to take care of your mind, and your mother was unhappy when you didn't return last summer," Mrs. Hubbard said. "I'd love to talk more, but Jeremy is going to get into the stables again. Please, excuse me, and make sure to drop by the school again before you leave. I'd love for you to teach some of my students just how useful Rune Crafting is."

"I'll do that," Damien promised.

Mrs. Hubbard nodded and ran off after the little boy again.

"Come on," Damien said, starting back toward his house. "If my mom finds out I didn't head right home after we got here, she's going to be sad."

Sylph nodded mutely, following a few steps behind him and taking in Ardenford with wide eyes.

They reached Damien's house a few minutes later. The two-story building looked just as Damien remembered it, but it still somehow managed to come off as foreign. It had been so long since he'd gone home that coming back felt strange.

"Don't tell me you're scared," Henry said, giving him a mental prod. "Come on."

If I recall correctly, you were the one who was scared of her. You thought she'd kill both of us for the sake of humanity.

"It's not my fault you were a dirty little liar."

"Are you talking to Henry?" Sylph asked.

"Yeah, sorry." Damien shook his head and approached the door, knocking twice on the wood. A few seconds passed with no response. He went to knock on the door again, but it swung open before his hand could make contact.

His mother stared at him for a moment, her eyes widening in recognition. She didn't look like she'd aged a day. Her hands were covered in flour, and she wore an apron. "Damien!"

She swept forward, pulling him into a tight hug and holding it for a few seconds too long. Damien gently extracted himself from his mother's grip and felt a flush rise to his cheeks.

"Hi, Mom. I'm sorry I couldn't visit earlier. I was...busy, I guess."

"That's what all the teenagers say," Hilla said irritably. "I did the same thing when I was your age. Nobody wants to come home to their boring old mother."

"It really was important!" Damien exclaimed. "Blame my teacher, not me. He's the one who wouldn't let me leave."

"Good move," Henry said. "Pass the problem onto Delph. Maybe your mom will beat him up for us."

Shush.

Henry cackled and faded back into Damien's head. Hilla finally took a step back and noticed Sylph standing awkwardly a few feet behind them. She glanced back at Damien, then brushed her hands off on her apron and grinned sheepishly.

"I'm sorry, I didn't notice you there. I blame Damien for not keeping in contact enough. A mother has to worry, you know."

"Mom, this is Sylph," Damien said. "I was hoping she could stay with us for a week."

"Of course, she can! It's a pleasure to meet you, Sylph. I'm Hilla. Are you one of Damien's friends from school?"

"I'm his roommate," Sylph said, shifting from foot to foot. "I'm sorry for intruding."

"Nonsense," Hilla said, dragging them both inside. "If you've managed to bring Damien home, the very least I could do is put a roof over your head. Have you eaten yet?"

Sylph started to stammer out a response, but Hilla didn't give her a chance to finish. She led them to a table and pushed the two into chairs.

"I'm making pancakes," Hilla said. "I didn't realize I'd be having company, but I'll have some extra if you give me a few moments."

She darted back to the kitchen, leaving Damien and Sylph at the table.

"Sorry," Damien whispered. "She's a bit over the top sometimes."

"No, it's fine," Sylph said. "She's much...happier than I expected."

"Yeah," Henry added. "For someone who broods so much, you don't feel related to her at all."

Shut up.

Henry let out a snort of laughter.

"Henry seems talkative today," Sylph observed.

"Is it still that obvious when I'm talking to him?"

"You've gotten better at not zoning off and staring into space," Sylph admitted, "but I've gotten pretty used to it by now, so I can spot it. Your eye kind of twitches a bit."

Hilla swept out of the kitchen carrying two plates each bearing a single pancake. She slid them in front of Damien and Sylph, then grabbed a glass jar of syrup from the counter and put it down in front of them.

"Would you like some butter or blueberries?" she asked. "I'll have more pancakes out in a few minutes."

"She'll take the blueberries," Damien said before Sylph could refuse. Sylph glared at Damien once his mother returned to the kitchen. He shrugged in response.

"Are you telling me you didn't want the blueberries?"

"Well, no," Sylph admitted. "But I don't want to take advantage of your mother's kindness."

"She's probably not going to give you much choice," Damien said. "You'd better just brace yourself for it and go with the flow."

Hilla emerged from the kitchen a few minutes later with a huge bowl of blueberries. She plopped it down in front of Sylph, then returned to grab several plates piled high with pancakes.

"You're both still growing, so you must be very hungry," she said, sitting down across from them. "Please, eat as much as you like."

"Thank you," Sylph said, glancing at the bowl of the blueberries like it was about to fight back. She carefully took a small spoonful from the top.

Damien carved off a piece of pancake and stuffed it into his mouth to hide a grin as Hilla took the spoon and added nearly half of the blueberries to Sylph's pancakes, completely burying them. Sylph shot a pleading glance at Damien, but he just shrugged and dug into his meal.

Once all the food had been finished, Hila grabbed the plates and brought them to the kitchen. She adamantly refused Sylph's offers to help do the dishes and banished them to

Damien's room, forcing him to promise to show Sylph around the town once they got settled in.

"Your mom is intense," Sylph whispered once they'd left the room. "Is she always like this?"

"Pretty much. You'll get used to it. I think she was disappointed when I stopped bringing friends over."

"Why?" Sylph asked.

"After Henry, I kind of pulled back," Damien said. He led her through a hallway and toward his room. "It was hard to have any sort of relationship with people when there was a Void creature trying to end the world hitching a ride in my head."

Damien's shadow twitched as Henry commandeered it. It lengthened, rising up on the wall and growing a mouth and two purple eyes. "I'll have you know that Damien was a terrible host. He kept trying to wake me up while I was asleep."

"You slept for four years!" Damien snapped. "And is it really wise to reveal yourself like that?"

"It's fine," Henry said. "You'll notice this isn't my normal form. I've been working on a normal manifestation for you. There's no trace of Void energy when I'm like this."

"Ah," Damien said. "Cool."

"You see?" Henry asked Sylph. "I had to deal with this for years."

"I'm sorry for your loss," Sylph stated. Damien glared at her, and she smirked in return.

Damien pulled his door open. A wave of nostalgia washed over him. His room was as plain as he'd left it. A single bed rested underneath his window, across from his desk. He walked over to it and pulled a drawer open. There were still sheaves of paper stored in it.

"I forgot how boring your room was," Henry said. "At least your place in the mountain still has some character. You could at least put a drawing of me up on the walls."

"Henry, are you literally just here to make fun of me?"

"Pretty much," Henry said. "I was getting bored in your head, and this felt like a good place to practice my manifestation."

"And you've got nothing better to do other than hover over me and critique the stylistic sense I had when I was thirteen?"

"Well, now that you mention it," Henry drawled, a grin tugging on his mouth. "Maybe I'll take a look around town. See if there's anything more interesting than your boring room."

He pulled away from Damien's feet and shot through the window, vanishing into the dimming daylight.

"Wait!" Damien hissed, running up to the window. "You've got my shadow, you bugger! What if somebody sees?"

There was no response. Damien rolled his eyes and flopped onto his bed. Sylph sat down beside him.

"It's not that bad," she said after a few moments.

"Huh?"

"Your room," Sylph clarified.

"Oh, thanks," Damien said, rubbing the back of his head. "I really didn't think about decorating much because I was so worried about my magic and Henry."

He blinked, then slapped himself in the forehead. "Shit, I wasn't thinking, was I? You had much bigger things to worry about in the forest than I did."

"I don't know if I'd say that," Sylph said, twisting to look out the window. "More urgent, maybe. But not bigger."

"Were you really just going to camp out at your old place?" Damien asked. "Alone?"

"I wasn't sure what else to do, I figured they wouldn't have torn the house down even if he was dead. The only people who know about it are the ones from Blackmist, and they should know I don't have anywhere else to go."

"That's not true," Damien said. "You can come back with

me whenever you want. Unless you'd prefer to go alone, of course. I don't want to force you—"

"I definitely prefer coming with you," Sylph said, cutting him off and giving him a small smile. "The forest doesn't hold any good memories for me."

"That makes sense," Damien said, desperately searching around for another topic to talk about. Words suddenly evaded him like fish in water, and he became vividly aware of the fact that he was sitting alone on his bed with Sylph. It wasn't that different from what they'd done in Blackmist, but it *felt* different.

He glanced at Sylph out of the corner of his eye. Her cheeks had the faintest spots of red on them, which only served to make his heart beat even faster in his chest.

"I, uh—"

The window flew open, and Henry shot inside, giggling like a child. "Have you ever tried scaring a goat? I knew they play dead when under threat, but it's so much more fun doing it in person!"

He paused, glancing from Damien to Sylph. "Am I interrupting something?"

"No," Damien said quickly. "And what did you do to the goats?"

"Nothing," Henry said defensively. "Nothing lasting, at least."

Damien sighed and rubbed his forehead. He wasn't sure if he was angry or relieved Henry had interrupted them. "Just please don't get caught. I'd rather not get chased out of my own town with torches and pitchforks."

"They don't know of my true nature," Henry reminded him. "It would probably just be pitchforks, given I might have scared one of the goats away from the herd."

There was a polite knock on the door.

"Can I come inside?" Hilla called.

"Sure," Damien replied, sending a sharp glance at his companion. Henry shot back into Damien's feet, giving back his shadow.

Hilla slipped in. "I've got a town hall meeting in a few minutes, so I'm going to have to head off. I just wanted to make sure you knew before I left."

"Are you on a town council?" Sylph asked.

"Something like that," Hilla said with a small grin. "I'm pretty sure they only invited me to try to get Damien's father on board, but I suspect they regret that now. They want to remove more funding from the school and invest it in funding the useless properties Mayor Shindal owns."

"They're still trying to do that?" Damien asked. "Isn't that what the council was doing before I left for Blackmist?"

"And it's what I've been stopping for the past few years," Hilla said. "Don't worry about it. There's nothing they can do about it. I'm happy enough that you've come back. The mayor has been strutting around that his kid came back early and rubbing it in my face a bit."

"Joey?" Damien asked after a moment of digging around for a name. "He went to college a few years ago, right?"

"He graduated from Greenvalley," she confirmed. "And Shindal is setting him up to become the next mayor. Enough of this, though. I didn't come to complain, I just wanted to let you know I'd be off for a little. If you want to go into town, use the back entrance so I can lock the front door."

"I will," Damien promised. "Are you sure you don't need help at the council or something?"

Hilla snorted. "It's just a bunch of old geezers whining, Damien. Don't you worry about it. Now, stop being an ungracious host and show Sylph around the town. I'm sure she'd love to see where you grew up."

She headed out of the room and down the hall, grabbing her coat from a chair and slinging it over her shoulders before disappearing from view.

CHAPTER
TWO

Damien cleared his throat. "I guess I could show you around, if you'd like."

"Sure," Sylph said, rising to her feet.

Damien led her out of the house and into town. There were a fair number of people out, but it took him longer than he would have thought to recognize them. It was hard to match the faces he saw with the ones in his memory, even though it had only been a little over a year.

"That's the school," Damien said, nodding at a large group of flat buildings surrounded by a fence. Several students milled about between them, playing various games and laughing. "I think I spent most of my time there, actually."

"You didn't strike me as the type that ran around and played games a lot," Sylph said, a smile tugging at her lips.

"Well, I might have spent most of my time *inside* the buildings," Damien admitted. "The teachers didn't have a lot of students that actually liked Rune Crafting, so that worked a lot in my favor. And don't even get me started on the number of books I read about summoning companions. I thought I was an expert."

"It turned out well in the end," Sylph said. "I couldn't imagine what would have happened if you didn't get Henry. For one, I'd probably be dead or crippled."

"That's true," Damien said, his face brightening. "Even if he is an insufferable idiot."

"Hey!" Henry snapped.

Don't even get me started. You just scared a bunch of goats half to death.

"Half?"

Damien groaned and pushed Henry back. The Void creature laughed the entire way.

"I wish I could do that," Sylph said.

"Huh? Speak with Henry?"

"Not specifically with Henry," Sylph said. "My companion. I can send general desires, but it's not the same. You have perfect communication with Henry. The more communication a mage has with their companion, the stronger they can be."

"I'm sure you'll learn to communicate with yours pretty soon," Damien stated. "You've had your companion for way less time than everyone else, and you're already using their powers really well. That wind armor is pretty strong."

"It's an endless struggle to keep up with you," Sylph said, flicking Damien in the forehead. "Let's get back to you showing me around unless you want the teachers to start wondering why we're standing outside the fence."

"Oh, right," Damien said, flushing. "Let's go more into town. There are a few interesting stores."

Sylph followed him down the road and toward a dense cluster of buildings around a fountain that had long since stopped running. There were several wagons along the outside of the town circle with tables laid out before them. Wares of every type covered them.

"Traveling merchants," Damien explained when he noticed

Sylph examining them. "They come by every week or so with stuff they've bought from other cities. It can occasionally be pretty cool, but it's usually overpriced."

They walked up to one of the tables, where a tall man in multicolored robes watched them approach with a wide grin.

"Ah, you have seen the quality of my wares and wish to partake, yes?" he asked, a heavy accent placing his origin from somewhere in the north.

"We're mostly just looking," Damien said diplomatically. "Is there anything of particular interest we should check out?"

"It depends what you seek," the man replied, rubbing his hands together. "You are students coming home from school?"

"Mages," Damien confirmed. "And I've studied Rune Crafting."

"Then, I fear many of my wares will be below your standard," the merchant said reluctantly. "I am not foolish enough to try to sell a runed item to someone with knowledge of the field. Most don't spend their time or effort on it. However, I do have a few pieces of art and jewelry sure to catch your eye."

He reached under the table and took out a small wooden box. Placing it before them, the merchant popped the cover off to reveal several rows of beautiful rings, necklaces, and brooches. They ranged from plain silver bands to gaudy pieces covered with so many gems that there was no way a normal merchant could have afforded them—if they were real.

"Please, feel free to take a look," the merchant encouraged. "Some of them have some basic runework as well."

"Like what?" Damien asked, intrigued as Sylph picked up a ring and examined it. "Shields or weaponry?"

"Nothing so advanced. Some of them can generate light or store a very small amount of Ether. Not enough to make any real difference, but it can be a fun little party trick. They interfere with each other if you have too many, so stick to one or two. Many couples get matching storage rings and infuse it with a type of Ether that the other can't control."

"Why?" Sylph asked. "It's not like someone could use a different type of Ether if it was in their ring, could they?"

"It's about the thought," the merchant defended. "You can't use Ether if it isn't one of the types you can see, but it's like carrying a part of your lover around even if they aren't there with you."

Henry let out a mental snort. "It's like carrying around someone else's fingernail. Gross."

I'm this close to telling you to go find more goats to torture.

"Please, do. An excuse is all I'd need to go scare a few more of those moronic creatures. It's the most fun I've had since coming onto the Mortal Plane."

Damien shook his head and brought himself back to the present. The merchant eyed him warily, his hands hovering near the box of jewelry.

"He zones out sometimes," Sylph explained. "It's nothing to worry about."

"Ah, of course," the merchant said. "Is there anything else I can get you?"

"I think we're good." Thank you."

The merchant nodded, and Sylph grabbed Damien's hand, pulling him away from the merchant before the man could get any more suspicious.

"Sorry about that," Damien said. "Henry distracted me. Do you want to check out the local bakery? If I remember correctly, it's better than a lot of the food in the mess hall."

"It's fine," Sylph said with a grin. "And that sounds great."

The bakery wasn't hard to find, even for someone who hadn't ever been to Ardenford before. All they had to do to follow the scent of freshly baked bread and warm spice. A small crowd sat amongst a dozen tables scattered around an open-fronted shop.

"Oh, shoot." Sylph paused and glanced over her shoulder. "Give me one second, I forgot something."

Before Damien could respond, she shot off. No more than a minute later, she jogged back over, her cheeks slightly red.

"What did you forget?" Damien asked.

"Nothing, I just checked the wrong pocket. Sorry."

Damien shrugged, and they headed into the bakery.

A large man wearing a stained white apron and a floppy chef's hat stood on the other side of a counter, kneading dough with enough force to shake the table he worked on. He turned as Damien and Sylph entered the shop, a kind grin crossing his face.

"Well, I'll be! Damien is back from college!" he boomed. "And he's brought a girl with 'im."

"This is my *roommate*, Sylph," Damien said, stressing the word and doing his best to keep his cheeks from heating. "Sylph, this is Bael. He's a great chef."

"Hmm," Bael rumbled, setting his dough down and brushing his hands off on his flour-stained apron. He walked over to the counter and peered over it, examining them. "Sure, whatever you say. You got one of them fancy band things that shows off how cool you are? Lemme see it."

Damien laughed and pressed his hand to the band around his wrist. It struck him that it had been a long time since he'd checked it. As far as he was concerned, it was quickly going to become outdated. With Henry hiding his power from the band, there was only so much it could accurately read about him.

Damien Vale
Blackmist College
Year Three

Major: Battle Mage
Minor: Dredd's Apprentice
Companion: [Null]
Magical Strength: 12.1
Magical Control: 3.8
Magical Energy: 29.2
Physical Strength: 1.3
Endurance: 4.2

Minor is Dredd's Apprentice? Seriously? Did he change that right before we left for summer? And that's not even a minor.

Henry chuckled in his mind. "Your physical strength is finally over one now, and your endurance is also getting a little respectable. The stupid little band is actually getting a bit complementary. I wonder what would happen if we let it have a taste of my real strength."

Let's not wonder that, or you might get curious.

"College has treated you well, Damien. You've gained some muscle," Bael said, letting out a low whistle. "We were all starting to think you were bored of ol' Ardenford, though. Glad to see you still remember us."

"Thanks," Damien said with an embarrassed grin. "And we were just delayed. I had no intention of staying away this long."

"We, huh?" Bael asked. He grinned as Damien started to sputter, then knelt to reach inside a small display case. He pulled out two large triangular pastries and set them on a small plate. "I've got your favorite here. Kept making them just for my favorite customer."

"Those are everyone's favorite," Damien accused. "And everyone is your favorite customer."

"Shh, don't say it so loud," Bael said. "One of my other favorite customers might overhear and get cross with me."

Damien rolled his eyes and pulled a few coins out of his

travel bag. He slid them across the counter and took the plate. "These are filled with apple. Did you want to try something else, Sylph?"

"Apple sounds good to me," Sylph said.

"Of course, it does," Bael rumbled. "Apple is delicious. Then again, everything I make is. When you get hungry again, come back and try my cherry turnovers next."

"We'll do that." Damien fully meant it. He hadn't realized how much he'd missed Bael's Bakery until the smell had reached his nostrils. They sat at a table outside the store, and he handed Sylph one of the pastries before taking a large bite out of his own.

The food didn't last long after that. Both pastries disappeared down their gullets in record time. Damien licked his lips and used more than a little self-control to stop himself from running back into the bakery and buying more. If he showed back up to school shaped like a sphere, he didn't think Delph would be very pleased.

"That was fantastic," Sylph said. "It might have been the best pastry I've ever eaten. Not that I've had a lot."

"Bael knows what he's doing," Damien agreed. "I don't know why he sticks around. He could make a crazy amount of money in one of the larger cities or a college campus."

"I just like it here," Bael yelled at them from within the shop.

"He's got good hearing," Sylph muttered.

Damien shrugged. "He worked as a mage before he became a baker."

Bael snorted.

"Stop eavesdropping on your customers," Damien said. "You're going to scare everyone away."

"To where?" Bael asked with a laugh. "I don't see any other bakers in Ardenford."

"He's got a point," Sylph said. "And some very dangerous pastries. Delph will have our heads if we spend too much time here."

"I was thinking the same thing," Damien said, sending a longing glance back at the bakery. "There are a few more interesting things in Ardenford. Now that we've had something to eat, we can go check them out. I bet Bael can't hear us there."

"Don't be so sure," Bael said with an evil chuckle. "Not that I want to hear everything that two college kids are doing. I think I'll keep my attention within the vicinity of my bakery, thank you very much."

Several people chuckled, and Damien rolled his eyes. He and Sylph left the bakery and headed past the buildings toward the edge of town.

"Ardenford is built near a pretty large waterfall," Damien said as they walked. "It's the only thing out here other than grassland, but it's impressive enough."

"Where is it?" Sylph asked, glancing around. "It looks like we're mostly surrounded by small hills and grasslands. Not much room for a waterfall."

"Underground," Damien replied. "Come on, I'll show you."

They wrapped around the side of the town. A second hill rose across from them, creating a small valley. Damien led Sylph into it, then into a large group of boulders that housed a cave entrance just large enough for them to walk through.

The sound of rushing water in the distance greeted them as they headed into the tunnel. Small patches of moss grew on the walls, and the air smelled fresh and earthy. The path wound into the earth for a few minutes before opening above a sprawling cavern.

A rushing waterfall fell from the opposite side of the cavern, cascading into a pool of crystal blue water far below it. The area was large enough that the dull roar of the water, while present, wasn't so much that Damien couldn't hear.

Rays of light entered the room from several thin holes in the ceiling, illuminating portions of the cavern and leaving others in the shadows.

"Wow," Sylph breathed as they walked out onto the ledge and sat a few feet away from the drop. "This is incredible. I never would have thought that something like this would be out here."

"It's pretty impressive," Damien agreed. "Most of the town has an agreement not to share any information about the waterfall with outsiders so we don't get overwhelmed with tourists. It's not law or anything, but don't go telling other people."

"I won't," Sylph promised, not taking her gaze from the water. "I've never seen something like this. It would be a crime to let it be ruined. There wasn't much in the way of waterfalls in the woods."

"Did you really never leave them? I don't mean any disrespect, but you're much more eloquent than Mark."

"My old master was very insistent that I maintain every skill I could in the best shape possible," Sylph said, her face darkening. "He taught me a lot about the outside world, and the mages brought me up to speed on anything he missed when I joined Blackmist."

"Oh," Damien said with a wince. "I'm sorry. I didn't mean to bring up bad memories."

"No, it's fine." Sylph shook her head. "I've been meaning to tell you anyway."

"Tell me what?"

"About my life before Blackmist. You've already told me just about every one of your secrets, so it's time for me to do the same, so long as you'd like to hear."

Damien just nodded, not wanting to interrupt her. Sylph drew a deep breath before starting.

"I was raised to be an assassin. I had multiple teachers, but the main one is the one I referred to as my master. They wanted to make me into a weapon that could kill powerful mages. My first memories are learning to become a killer, and I was never allowed to be anything else. A control rune was put on my chest when I was just a kid. They used it to make sure I could never rebel against them, even in my own thoughts."

"I'd guessed a bit of that," Damien admitted. "But who would need an assassin like that? The queen?"

"No," Sylph replied, her voice grim. "She could crush just about anyone she wanted to with brute force. I was supposed to be for a different purpose, but that all came apart when they realized I barely had any magical power. Without their training, I would have amounted to nothing. A mage college probably wouldn't have even accepted me. My Core wasn't even big enough to summon a companion. My master implanted an artifact in me as a last-ditch effort to save his investment."

Damien remained silent, allowing Sylph to continue to speak unimpeded.

"They knew I would never be as powerful as they originally wanted, but it didn't matter. I only had to take on a single mission," Sylph said. "So, they went even harder on my training. The other teachers left and gave my master full control. He wouldn't let me sleep in the house and forced me to learn how to survive in the forest, saying it would make me stronger."

Sylph paused for a moment to gather herself. "I once told you that I killed my master. That wasn't entirely true. He was actually killed by someone else. A few months before the mission they'd been preparing me for, someone found my master's house. One of the queen's inquisitors. They got into a fight with my master, and I distracted him by trying to break the control seal. It was enough for the inquisitor to kill him."

"So, the inquisitor saved you?"

Sylph let out a bitter laugh. "For a little, I guess. He was kind, but he brought me back to the other inquisitors when he realized who I was and my relationship to my master. They tried to figure out if they could use me as an assassin. They tried to figure out if I was a threat to the queen or if I could be used as a weapon. Eventually, they decided I wasn't up to standard. It was bad, but nothing compared to what I was used to. I managed to hide the true extent of what I could do, and my lack of magic made me pretty pathetic anyway. They let me go and pulled a few strings so I could get into Blackmist as if that would make up for things."

Damien put a hand over Sylph's. She stiffened but didn't pull away.

"I'm sorry," he said, at a lack for better words. "I had no idea. It's disgraceful that the queen's men would act like that. They're supposed to protect the kingdom not torture its people. It must have been hard to stand face to face with the princess and act polite."

Sylph's lips twitched. "You have no idea. But I can't entirely blame them. After all, they were largely right."

"What do you mean?"

"The mission my master had been training me for was to assassinate the princess. I have no idea why his group wanted to get rid of her. I wasn't privy to that. All I knew was that she was my target. If the inquisitors figured that out, I doubt I would have walked out of there alive, even though I was being controlled."

"Eight Planes," Damien muttered. "I'm glad they didn't figure it out."

Sylph examined him closely. "That's it? You don't care that I was going to kill the kingdom's princess?"

"I mean, not really," Damien admitted. "It wasn't you. You were being used as a tool. I could see some idiot blaming you for it, but it wasn't your fault. Even if you'd succeeded, it wouldn't have been your fault. I do see why you hate the idea of anyone controlling you so vehemently, though. How long was the control rune on you?"

"At least ten years," Sylph said. "I don't know the exact amount."

Damien shuddered. "You're stronger than I am. I don't know if I'd be fully sane if I'd had to go through that for ten years."

"You sure know what to say to comfort someone." Sylph burst into laughter.

Damien sputtered an apology, but it got caught in his throat as she scooted closer to him and leaned against his chest. After a moment, he wrapped an arm around her shoulder and pulled her closer.

"I'm glad I went to Blackmist," Sylph said. "I'd just planned to go to the college to see what other people did for a year, then drop out when my low magical energy became a hinderance. I could never have imagined life would be so...interesting."

"Henry has a way of making things interesting."

"What makes you think I was talking about that?" Sylph asked coyly. Damien opened his mouth, then snapped it closed when he realized Sylph was smirking.

He opted to say nothing. Damien didn't know how long they remained there, listening to the sound of the waterfall, nor did he care to find out.

Somewhat predictably, the moment was interrupted by Henry. Damien's shadow peeled away from his feet and unfurled before them. Henry leaned against a wall and covered a fake yawn with a shadowy hand.

"I took the liberty of restricting the sound while you two blathered," he said, leaning in close. "Sylph, I wouldn't speak about anything you said here again. Damien and I have spent too long making sure that we didn't end up alienating the kingdom, and I'd rather not have to go on the run after all that."

"They wouldn't go after Damien if they found out," Sylph said, glancing up at Henry without moving.

"Probably not," Henry admitted. "But the moron would go with you. Honestly, it might make a few things easier if we could stop wasting time at the college, but he'd probably complain to me anyway."

"Sorry, Henry," Sylph said with a laugh. "I won't mention it again."

"Just keep it to Damien's mindscape," Henry said. "Keeping secrets can weaken your soul. Trust me, I'd know. Just make sure you don't reveal them to the wrong people."

"An Eldritch creature is giving advice about opening yourself up to people?" Sylph asked, raising an eyebrow. "If you don't mind me asking, where'd you learn that? It doesn't seem to fall in line with what one would normally expect someone like you to believe."

"Even idiots occasionally have a point," Henry said with a grunt. "It was Damien who taught me. Wipe that smug grin off your face, you little brat. If your head gets any bigger, it might pop."

"Thanks for the advice, Henry." Sylph said. "I appreciate you looking out for us."

"I'm just protecting my own interests," Henry grumbled. "There's one more thing. There's someone in another part of the cave. His magic is pathetic, but I put up a weak barrier to stop him from getting closer just in case."

Damien groaned. Sylph slipped to her feet, and Damien followed her up, mentally cursing the intruder. He knew the waterfall was hardly his own property, but that didn't make him feel any happier with the interruption.

"Hold on," Sylph said, digging through her pockets and pulling out two rings—the ones the merchant had been selling. Her cheeks reddened slightly, and she held one of them out. "I, uh, thought they looked kind of nice. I put some of my Ether in this one. You don't have to take it if —"

Damien took the ring, feeling his own face get equally as red as Sylph's. He touched the other ring in her hand, sending a mote of Space Ether into it. Clearing his throat, he slipped the ring onto a finger. "Thank you, Sylph. I really appreciate it."

She just nodded, sliding her own ring on. Henry tapped a shadowy foot on the ground impatiently. "Are you done being gross yet?"

"For now," Damien replied, almost grateful to his insolent companion. Judging by the look on Sylph's face, she was, too. "Who's the assailant?"

"Are they trying to get closer to us?" Sylph asked.

"Nah, he's scribbling some runes on the wall," Henry said. "Not the best work I've ever seen. Reminds me of Damien when he was younger."

"There aren't a ton of people here who actually like Rune Crafting," Damien muttered. "Is he practicing? Or actually trying to draw something?"

"Last I checked, he was drawing in chalk and erasing it a bit later," Henry said. "Looked like practice to me."

"Well, he's not bothering anyone," Damien decided. "No reason to get in his way. He didn't hear anything, right?"

"Nothing," Henry confirmed. "But he did mention someone named Shindal pretty angrily under his breath. That's the mayor your mom didn't like if I'm not mistaken."

Damien sighed and rubbed the bridge of his nose. "Let's go find out what his problem is."

Henry smirked. "Thought so. Just head back out, he's in your way anyway. Not sure why he chose the middle of a tunnel to complain, but it certainly makes things easier for us."

He shrank, reconnecting Damien's shadow. Sylph and Damien exchanged a glance, then headed down the tunnel. Damien heard the angry muttering nearly a minute before they actually saw its owner.

A short, mousey boy with unkept hair sat in front of a wall, drawing runes with sharp, aggressive lines on the walls. His chalk clicked with each stroke. The boy was so engrossed in his work that he didn't even notice Damien and Sylph until they were nearly upon him.

He leapt, dropping his chalk and scrambling back on all fours as his eyes went wide. Damien knelt, picking the piece of chalk up and offering it back to the boy. He didn't recognize the kid, who looked to be a few years younger than he was. "Sorry to interrupt."

The boy eyed Damien, then slowly reached out and took the chalk back. "I didn't think anyone else was here."

"Don't trust your thinking until you're good at it," Damien said automatically, quoting Delph during one of their less productive sessions. He immediately winced. "Sorry, my teacher's words coming out before I can think."

"Maybe they were more apt than you give him credit for," Sylph said with a smirk. "We're sorry for interrupting you, though."

Damien scrunched his nose and examined the runes on the wall. His eyebrow rose incrementally. The pattern wasn't the best he'd ever seen, but it looked similar to the ones he used on his flame papers. There were a few errors that would make it dangerous—both for the person activating it and anyone in the area.

"You shouldn't draw runes like this," Damien said, nodding

at the wall. "You need to be calm when you work. If you misdraw something, you can seriously hurt yourself or someone else."

"Why do you care?" the boy asked. "Who are you, anyway?"

"I'm Damien," he replied. "Hilla Vale is my mom. I got a week off college, so I came back to visit."

The boy's eyes widened. "Mrs. Hubbard talked about you. You love runes, right?"

"Love is a strong word," Damien said slowly, "but I use them a fair amount, I suppose. They're powerful and interesting. I didn't realize Mrs. Hubbard remembered me that well."

"Nobody likes runes," the boy muttered. "Real magic is way cooler. She remembers everyone who actually paid attention in her classes. It's not hard when you can count them on one hand."

Sylph snorted. Unbeknownst to her, Henry did the exact same thing.

"If nobody likes them, why are you drawing them on the walls?" Damien asked.

"Mayor Shindal made Mrs. Hubbard stop teaching us runes so she could do work in his big stupid house. We only learn runes three days a week now. Mayor Shindal said that runes aren't as useful as preparing for real magic. He hired Mister Joey and wants to get rid of Mrs. Hubbard, but she's way nicer than he is, and I don't want her to go so I'm trying to practice runes and get good at them, but I kept messing up so I came down here to practice on my own and —"

"Whoa," Damien said, his head spinning. "Slow down for a moment. Shindal wants to fire Mrs. Hubbard?"

"Yeah. So she can work more on his house, I think," the boy said.

"He's replacing her with his own kid? Does he even have qualifications?" Sylph asked.

The boy shrugged. "He's stupid."

"All right," Damien said, squatting to be at face level in front of the kid. "I don't know if we can do anything to help, but I like Mrs. Hubbard. I'd like to help her if I can. What's your name?"

"Tim."

"Okay, Tim," Damien said, rising and holding out a hand. "Is there anyone else who feels like you, or are you the only one who wants to help?"

"My friends do, too," Tim said, wiping his nose with the back of his sleeve before accepting Damien's hand. "But their parents don't want to make Mayor Shindal angry."

"How about you take me to Mrs. Hubbard?" Damien suggested. He pulled Tim to his feet and wiped the bad runes on the wall away so nobody would activate them. "I'd like to get a better understanding of what's going on."

"Are you going to kill Mister Joey?"

"What? No!" Damien exclaimed, nearly choking. "I'm just going to try to help out a bit. Can you just take me to Mrs. Hubbard?"

"Okay," Tim said, nodding. "But I still think you should kill him. I was gonna blow him up with the runes, but you'd probably be better at it than I am."

Henry howled with laughter.

"Ah, what a kid," Henry said gleefully. "Isn't that a refreshing take? If everyone thought like that, the world would be a lot more fun."

Shut up, Henry.

"Don't take that attitude with me," Henry said. "I just blocked out the latter half of the day so I didn't have to dodge all the horrid thoughts bouncing around your head. You should be thanking me for not eavesdropping."

Damien rolled his eyes, ignoring Henry's snicker as they fell in behind Tim and headed out of the cave.

THREE

Tim led them to the school and through an old metal gate that had seen better days. It felt simultaneously familiar and completely foreign to Damien as they walked past the short buildings and entered a tiny square room at the edge of the campus.

Mrs. Hubbard sat at a table, hunched over a stack of papers. An old quill rested on the table beside a splotch of ink, and her head was in her hands. She jerked upright as they entered, adjusting her glasses and pushing the hair out of her tired face. "I'm sorry, I wasn't expecting company. I see you've met Damien, Tim."

"He's going to help me kill Joey," Tim proclaimed.

"I absolutely am not," Damien said sharply as Mrs. Hubbard's eyes widened. "Tim let me know there was something going on with the school, and I wanted to find out what it was myself."

The elderly teacher frowned and let out a slow sigh. She stood and walked around the desk to kneel before Tim. "Honey, please go home for today. I'm sure Damien will find some time to hang out with you later, but the grown-ups have to talk for a little now."

Tim nodded empathetically. "Right. No witnesses so you can have dena—dehna—how do you say it?"

"Deniability?" Sylph provided.

"Yeah," Tim said. "That."

"That is absolutely not the case," Mrs. Hubbard said.

"Yeah," Tim repeated, giving her an exaggerated wink that was really more of a blink. "I didn't hear *anything*."

He darted out of the door, pulling it shut behind him. Mrs. Hubbard sighed again and ran a hand through her hair. "I'm sorry about him. He's gotten a little excitable as of late. He's a good kid at heart."

"I gathered," Damien said, hiding the grin tugging at his lips. "Could you tell me a little bit about what's going on? Tim said Mayor Shindal is trying to shut the school down. Why would he do that?"

"Hold on, Damien," Mrs. Hubbard said, crossing her arms as a flicker of steel passed through her features. "You haven't introduced me to your friend. I know I taught you more than just runes, and I'm pretty sure manners was covered in my class."

"Whoops, sorry," Damien said, rubbing the back of his head. "This is Sylph. She's my roommate at Blackmist. She's visiting for the week."

"It's nice to meet you, Sylph," Mrs. Hubbard said, inclining her head. Sylph returned the gesture. "I'm sorry you've gotten wrapped up in my mess. Damien should have known better than to drag you into this."

"It's quite all right," Sylph said with a small grin. "We've dealt with a lot worse. Education is important."

"If only everyone shared that opinion," Mrs. Hubbard said, chewing her lower lip. "Mayor Shindal wants to phase out a large portion of the Rune Crafting classes, I'm afraid. He's set on hiring Joey as a teacher, but Joey doesn't know any Rune Crafting—and he refuses to learn it. I'm about ready for retirement, so I would have been happy to pass on enough knowledge for Joey to continue the school without me, but..."

She shrugged helplessly. "The kid will barely talk to me. It's as if he's *trying* to be antagonistic. He interrupts my classes and undermines my authority with the kids. He used to be such a nice lad. I don't know what's gotten into him."

"My mom mentioned something about Shindal trying to set Joey up as the next mayor and taking funds from the school for his own properties. Could this have something to do with it?" Damien wondered.

"I really don't know, I'm afraid," Mrs. Hubbard said. "Honestly, I shouldn't be bringing you into this at all. You're still in college, Damien. Problems like these should be left to the adults. There are still a few years for you to run around and have fun before you have to deal with the underbelly of the world. You should enjoy them."

Damien exchanged a glance before bursting into laughter. Mrs. Hubbard blinked.

"I'm sorry, Mrs. Hubbard," Damien said, composing himself. "Sylph and I have been involved in some pretty intense after school activities with our professors. We've both fought for our lives more times than I can count. Something like this isn't even on our danger charts."

"Is there anything we could do to get some pressure off you?" Sylph asked. "Surely, the mayor needs to be able to prove that Rune classes aren't useful, right? This isn't a dictatorship."

"Well, yes. He can make small changes, but he needs half the town council for any major changes," Mrs. Hubbard said. "But he's got nearly half of them on his side already. One or two votes would be enough to sway him."

"So, if we were to convince the council that he's an idiot or that Rune Crafting is clearly important, you'd be fine?" Damien asked.

"I suppose." But how could you do that? As much as I love the kids, I don't have any exemplary students as of late. There just isn't much interest in Rune Crafting. The mayor does pay a fair amount for me to do other work. It might just be time for things to move on.".

"Maybe, but maybe not," Damien said, tapping a finger on his leg. "We'll look into things a bit without stepping on any toes. I hate to see such an important class fade away just because nobody respects how useful Rune Crafting can be."

He and Sylph bid farewell to Mrs. Hubbard and headed out into Ardenford.

"Is there really anything we can do?" Sylph asked as they headed toward a large house that overlooked the town. "Aside from making him disappear, of course. Actually, that wouldn't be too hard."

"Let's avoid that for now," Damien said, choosing his words carefully. After what Sylph had told him about her past, a few things about some of her suggestions made more sense. "We may just be able to talk some sense into Mayor Shindal. After all, I wouldn't have gotten anywhere without Rune Crafting. Henry wouldn't have ever bonded with me."

"You can't exactly show someone Henry," Sylph pointed out. "I'll follow your lead, though. I don't want to get you in trouble in your town."

Damien nodded appreciatively, and they reached the mayor's house a few minutes later. He approached the large wooden door and knocked before stepping back. A few moments later, an elderly butler pulled it open.

"Mayor Shindal just got back from his town hall meeting,"

the man said. "If you're looking for him, you'll have to wait a little."

"We don't mind waiting," Damien said, digging around for the butler's name.

"You may wait inside, then," the man said, stepping aside and gesturing for them to enter.

Henry mentally pulled the memory of the man's name up. "Thank you, Mr. Jones."

He and Sylph headed into the large building. Mr. Jones closed the door gently behind them and led them over to a long wooden table with a dozen red cushioned seats along it. They sat down near the end and a light blinked on automatically above them.

"I'll get some snacks for you both," Mr. Jones said. A door opened itself for him, revealing a kitchen for a few moments before it shut in his wake.

"There sure are a lot of runes here," Sylph muttered. "Automatic lights and doors? Seems a bit excessive."

"It isn't that hard if you've got a Rune Crafter on retainer," Damien whispered back. "Or a lot of money. From what it sounds like, he's got the latter and is working on getting the former."

Mr. Jones came out of the kitchen a few minutes later bearing a tray piled high with cheese, crackers, and fruit. He set it in front of them and inclined his head. "I've informed Mayor Shindal that you've come back from college to visit. He should be down to meet you in a few minutes."

"He was in the kitchen?" Damien asked.

"No, there is communication between every room in the house," Mr. Jones said with a small smile. "Mayor Shindal has been improving the town with magic. It makes many tasks much easier."

"He's done more than just his house?"

"He's begun it," Mr. Jones said, rubbing his beard. "The work he's having done is very intricate. I don't know the full extent of it. I'm sure he'd be happy to tell you, though. It's all he's spoken of recently."

A door on the other end of the room opened and Mayor Shindal entered the dining room. He'd aged a fair bit since Damien had last seen him. His cheeks sagged slightly, and lines of stress built up beneath his eyes. The mayor had put on more than a few pounds and his graying hairline had started to recede.

He walked over to the table and pulled out a chair across from Damien and Sylph, sitting down and snagging a grape. Mr. Jones made his escape through the kitchen door before the mayor could start talking.

"It's been quite some time, Damien," Shindal said. "I was honestly a little concerned for you when you went off to Blackmist. You'd changed a lot in the years before you left, but I'm glad to see you've turned out so well. We're a bit out of the way, but I heard you've done pretty well for yourself. You won a tournament, didn't you?"

"That was Sylph, actually," Damien said, nodding to her. "I've been enjoying Blackmist though."

"You managed to place well though, right?" Shindal pressed, not addressing Sylph. "How did you match the training and skill of the noble students, though? Some of them should have already had experience in both fighting and with their companions."

"Mrs. Hubbard's Rune Crafting class," Damien said, latching onto the opportunity to steer the conversation to his goal. "Most people didn't know how to fight with runes, so that knowledge was a huge benefit."

Shindal pursed his lips. "I see. You've spoken with Mrs. Hubbard, then."

"I have," Damien said, seeing no reason to lie. "She didn't want me to interfere, but I don't know why you would want to get rid of such an important class. Rune Crafting isn't the most exciting field, but it's very important. You clearly think so, too, considering that your house is full of runes."

"I'm well aware it's important," Shindal said, crossing his arms and leaning back. "And, contrary to popular opinion, I don't want to get rid of Rune Crafting because I dislike it. The problem is that we are not getting results, and Ardenford is not rich."

"What do you mean by that?"

"Rune Crafting requires both supplies and time," Shindal said, ticking the points off on his fingers as he spoke. "But every year, fewer and fewer students perform in the class. We spend a significant portion of this town's resources trying to train new Rune Crafters, but the students don't actually go into the field. The ones who have talent for magic join a Mage College and take a more interesting career, and the ones who don't just have no reason to bother with Rune Crafting. Mrs. Hubbard is a very talented woman, and her abilities are much more useful improving the town."

Damien frowned, spotting the kernel of truth in the mayor's words. He couldn't very well argue as he was exactly who the mayor was talking about. Damien had no plans of sticking around the town, offering Rune Crafting services to the people. Of course, his situation was a little different, but the mayor had no way to know that.

"It's still an important subject, though," Damien said. "If you remove it, kids won't even have a chance to learn. It might not be the most popular field, but it's still useful to have an understanding of it. Is the town really hemorrhaging money that badly?"

"That's more my problem to worry about than yours," Mayor Shindal reprimanded.

"Couldn't you just teach the theory and keep the resources for students who are actually interested," Sylph asked, interrupting them.

Shindal's brow lowered. "We could, but it would still be a waste of Mrs. Hubbard's time and money. Students interested in Rune Crafting can seek instruction when they go to a higher learning institution. That isn't the concern of the town. We just need to make sure money is being spent appropriately."

"So, why'd you hire your son to be a teacher?" Damien asked. "That's a big new expense since you've got to pay both him and Mrs. Hubbard, isn't it?"

"You're far too much like your mother," Shindal said irritably. "I hired him because he was a good teacher who will help transition things to the new set of lessons."

"Are you sure it isn't because he's your son?" Sylph asked.

"Control your mouth, young woman," Shindal snapped. "Are you accusing me of hiring someone simply because they are related to me rather than on merit?"

"Yes."

Shindal blinked, put off balance for a moment by her blunt answer. He gathered himself and stood up in a huff. "This isn't the concern of children, especially ones who aren't even from Ardenford. If it helps you sleep at night, I have no plans of permanently relieving Mrs. Hubbard of her teaching job. Joey will fully take over for a few moments so she can bring the town up to some standards, and then she can have her usual role back. Supplies will be much more limited, but teaching won't stop entirely. Now, it's getting rather late. You should be getting home. Mr. Jones?"

The butler emerged from the kitchen. They rose, and the butler took them out of the house. Damien cast a glance back at

Shindal as they left. The mayor's face was twisted in a mixture of annoyance and what might have been worry.

"What now?" Sylph asked. "He's clearly hiding something."

"You think?" Damien replied, only half-joking. "I mean, he did say he was going to give Mrs. Hubbard her job back later. Maybe he really does just want to fix the town up a bit? It *is* a little outdated."

Sylph scoffed. "He didn't strike me as the type of man who did anything for free, Damien. Was he a kind mayor before you left for school?"

"I'm not sure. I really never spoke to him all that much. My mom did most of that, and I don't think she was ever much of a fan."

"Then, that should probably tell you all you need to know," Sylph said. They headed back through the town, passing the bakery on the way back to Damien's house. "But he's aiming for something. If you want to help your mom, we should probably figure out what it is."

"Maybe she knows," Damien said. They came to a stop at his front door a few minutes later. His mother pulled it open before he could even knock. She gave them a wide grin and ushered the two in.

"You were out late," Hilla said. "Do anything fun?"

"A lot of things, actually," Damien replied. "Most of them were fun."

"Most?" Hilla's eyes narrowed. "What did you do, Damien Vale?"

"Why do you assume I did something wrong?"

"You summoned a companion when you were thirteen. When I found you, you were covered with blood and trapped inside your own rune circle," Hilla said, crossing her arms.

Damien groaned. "Are you ever going to let me live that one down? It was five years ago now!"

She ignored him and turned to Sylph. "Did Damien ever tell you how he got his companion?"

"Parts of it," Sylph said, hiding a grin. "I knew he summoned one when he was young, but that was most of it."

"He was a right terror." Hilla clicked her tongue and shepherded them toward the dinner table without asking if anyone was hungry. "He stole the Summoner's Almanac from a locked cabinet by memorizing the password when I got money out of it, then waited until I left for a town council meeting to summon his companion. Then, after all that, he refused to show me what he summoned. In fact, I still don't know!"

They both turned an accusatory glare against him. Damien raised his hands. He automatically reached out to Henry for help, but his companion was gone. With a start, Damien realized Henry wasn't in his mindscape. "Hey, I haven't been back. It isn't my fault."

"You could have at least written a letter," his mom said, crossing her arms. "Does Sylph know what your companion is?"

"Well, yes. But—"

"Maybe I have to ask her, then," Hilla said. "Sylph, since Damien won't let me know what I've been worrying about for the past few years, could you help this old lady out? He'll probably keep forgetting or avoiding the topic until he's old enough to move out."

Sylph glanced at Damien, but she didn't say anything. Hilla's eyebrow's twitched upward. A moment passed in silence. Then, she shook her head. "I'm glad Damien has a friend like you, Sylph. I was a bit scared he'd hole himself up in Blackmist and not talk to anybody, but your loyalty to keeping his secrets, even from me, is very admirable."

Damien snapped out of his reverie. He'd been so focused on thinking about Mayor Shindal that the conversation had gotten completely sidetracked. Henry's sudden disappearance only exacerbated the problem. "Mom, I'm not trying to keep secrets from you. Well, okay, maybe I was—am. But you don't have to make it into a big deal. My companion's name is Henry."

"Henry? What kind of companion is called Henry? That sounds like a human name. An intelligent companion, then?"

A shadow flickered across the room and re-entered Damien. He felt Henry's familiar presence return.

"Henry, could you come out? And slowly, please. I don't want Mom accidentally blowing the house up out of surprise."

His shadow shifted. A portion of it bubbled up and floated into the air, forming a sphere around the size of Damien's head. Three tentacles sprouted from the base of the sphere, and purple energy filled it. Eyes and a long, sharp toothed mouth followed after. Henry topped his appearance off with two tiny horns.

"Hello," he said cheerfully. "I'm Damien's babysitter."

All three of them stared at Henry in shock.

"What? Is something wrong?"

"I've never seen a companion like you," Hilla said, squinting at him suspiciously. "What are you? What plane are you from?"

"The Plane of Darkness," Henry replied. "And I'm a demon. Of sorts."

"No demon I recognize." Hilla walked in a circle around him. "Damien, did you discover a new species of companion?"

"It's part of the reason why I had to stay at school over summer," Damien said. "And yeah, Henry is pretty unique."

"Demons can be quite tricky, though," Hilla said. "He hasn't been offering you any dangerous deals or trying to trick you into signing your soul away, is he?"

"I know how demons work, mom," Damien said with an exasperated sigh. He pointedly avoided the question about if Henry had goaded him into any deals. He'd told enough lies already, and when they eventually came down, the more truth he said the better.

She harrumphed. "It's my job to worry, you know. There's not much else for me to do here other than argue with that pompous fool Shindal. I'm sorry for doing this while you were here, Sylph. It was inappropriate of me."

"It's fine," Sylph said. "I'm intruding on your family after all. You shouldn't have to censor yourselves because I'm here."

"Oh, you aren't intruding at all," Hilla said. "Now, please, sit. I've made dinner, and it must all be eaten before it goes cold."

She pulled a metal cover off a large plate in the center of the table. It was laden with steak, potatoes, and several green vegetables Damien didn't recognize. Henry floated down to the food and snagged a potato with one of his tendrils, bringing it up to his mouth and popping it in.

"You can eat?" Damien asked. "Have you ever done that before?"

"I have recently developed rudimentary taste buds," Henry replied. "Last night, actually. Did you know goats taste like cheese?"

"No, I don't think they do," Damien said. "And when did you get a chance to taste cheese?"

"When did you get a chance to taste goats?" Hilla asked, squinting at Henry.

"Yesterdayish," Henry replied, not offering further clarification. His voice sounded a little slurred. "These tubers are tasty. I've never looked much into nonmagical herbs, but I suspect they are aiding in my experience."

"Uhh, Henry? You sound a bit weird," Damien said.

"He sounds drunk," Hilla said. "Hold on."

She walked into the kitchen and knelt to peer inside one of

the cupboards. A laugh slipped through her lips. "Damien, your companion ate half a bottle of alcohol."

"Ate?" Sylph asked.

Hilla carefully lifted the jagged bottom half of a glass bottle. The top was completely missing.

"Ah. Ate."

"Henry!" Damien snapped. "Really? You were out of my body for what, a few seconds?"

"You can't blame me," Henry said. "I'm doing this for you, after all. Taste buds are absolutely vital to making a Full Manifestation."

"Did you really have to include the ability to get drunk?"

"I was curious," Henry defended. A vibration ran through his body, starting at the tentacles and working up. When it faded, his eyes had sharpened. "And I could get rid of the effect whenever I wanted to."

"Fascinating," Hilla said. "You're a very interesting companion, Henry. How are you doing things without Damien's permission?"

"He gave me rein to run around a bit so long as I don't cause any trouble." Henry glanced at Damien out of the corner of his eyes. "Stealing bottles of angry water doesn't count. "Can I have another potato?"

"Help yourself," Hilla said, slowly sitting back down. "Everyone, please eat. I don't want the food to grow cold."

Her words left no room for argument, and Damien was starting to get a little hungry anyway. Their conversation petered off as everyone helped themselves to the food, although Henry stuck to exclusively potatoes.

After they finished and everyone, including Henry, had thanked Hilla for the meal, Damien took the opportunity to get back to the original subject he'd wanted to talk about.

"Mom, do you know what Mayor Shindal is trying to do

with the school? People seem to think he's trying to get Mrs. Hubbard to retire."

"How'd you find out about that? Did Mrs. Hubbard tell you?"

"Well, not really. I was showing Sylph the underground waterfall, and we saw a boy called Tim drawing runes when we were leaving. He was pretty angry at Joey."

"I can't blame him," Hilla said with a sigh. "Joey is a horrible teacher. I dropped by a few of his classes to see if he was as good as Shindal said. The boy doesn't have an understanding bone in his body."

"Then, why does Shindal want him to teach? I don't get it."

"Because Joey isn't a very good mage," his mom replied with a shrug. "He can't get a job anywhere else. Shindal is hoping that having this on Joey's experience will help him get hired somewhere else, but I doubt it. All he's doing is screwing over the school. I've been trying to stop him, but Shindal is buying the council over by getting their houses upgraded with runes."

"So, what happens when Joey can't get another job?"

"He probably stays as a schoolteacher and makes a whole generation of students hate a topic," Hilla said, scrunching her nose in annoyance. "Hopefully, I can keep the council seeing reason, though. If your father came home, he'd talk some sense into those idiots."

"Why can't you do it yourself?" Sylph asked. "From what I can gather, you're an influential member of the council, aren't you?"

"Oh, I am," Hilla said with a laugh. "They respect me. But they *fear* Damien's dad. I don't have the power or temper to level Ardenford, and they know it. I've been trying to take care of things diplomatically. I'm just hoping Joey does something stupid and makes it easier for me to convince people he's incompetent. If anyone else in this stupid village actually knew Rune Crafting, it would be a lot easier."

"What about me?" Damien asked.

"That wouldn't work. You're my son. They aren't going to believe anything you say. Joey would have to make a very clear demonstration of his incompetence, and Shindal would never let that happen."

Damien grunted. That had given him a few ideas, but none that he cared to voice out loud yet. There was still a fair amount of time until Delph came to pick them up, so there was no point rushing things.

Hilla rose to her feet with a contented sigh. "I'm stuffed, and my old age is getting to me. I need to get some sleep. Damien, there's a spare mattress in the closet, but I'm too tired to get it out right now."

Damien nodded absentmindedly. "Thanks for dinner, Mom. It was good. We'll get the mattress when we go to bed."

Hilla considered them for a moment, then turned, a small smile on her face as she headed into her room and pulled the door shut behind her.

"I could eat Joey," Henry offered. "Shindal, too. Solve the problem, and I'd get to find out if humans also taste like cheese."

"No," Damien said. "And you should probably fix your taste buds if you plan on using them. Goats are not supposed to taste like cheese."

Henry harrumphed. "We'll see about that."

He shot back into Damien's shadow.

"That sounded vaguely ominous," Sylph observed.

"I'm just going to ignore it and pretend it isn't a problem," Damien decided. He covered a yawn and stood up. "Probably time for bed, though."

"I need to meditate first," Sylph said. "But that won't take long, and I can do it on the mattress."

"Oh, you can use my bed," Damien replied as he walked through the hall, stopping before a door that led into the closet. "You're the guest, after all."

He pulled the closet open and peered inside. Dust flew out, and he sneezed, wiping his nose with the back of a hand and grimacing. Sylph poked her head over his shoulder and peered in as well.

"I don't see a mattress."

"Neither do I," Damien said. "She can be a bit bad at putting things away. She probably forgot it somewhere. I'll ask her."

He walked up to her door, then paused as he heard loud snores.

"Already?" Sylph asked. "That was fast."

Damien sighed and shook his head. "I don't remember her falling asleep that fast before, but she's always been quick to it. She works a lot."

They wandered back over to his room, and he pulled the door shut behind them to avoid bothering his mother.

"I can just sleep on the floor," Damien offered. "We can figure out what happened to the mattress tomorrow."

"I'm not going to sleep in a bed if you're on the ground," Sylph said, crossing her arms. "That isn't fair to you."

Damien's shadow rippled before he could respond. Henry rose up from it bearing his normal, humanoid form.

"I'm going to stop you right there," Henry said. "I do *not* want to be here for this. Especially not in Damien's head. Just share the bed, you morons. You've done it before, and it isn't that small. You can both fit without so much as touching each other. I'm going to go bother the neighbor's goats now. Enjoy."

He flickered, launching through the window and vanishing

from sight in the darkening sky. Damien and Sylph exchanged a glance.

"I guess we could—"

"Yeah."

They stared at the bed for a few seconds. Damien was the first to move, pulling the covers back and sliding all the way to the far side until he was pressed against the wall. "Is there enough room for you to meditate?"

"Yeah," Sylph said, sitting down beside him. Damien stared at the wall, well aware this was barely any different from what they'd done in the past. Dull motes of magical energy swam overhead, gathering around Sylph.

Damien watched them for a few minutes, then turned over to his side and faced the wall to give her at least a little privacy. Sylph finished meditating a short while later—much faster than she usually did—and slipped under the covers as well.

Henry had been right—the bed was easily large enough for both of them. Damien wasn't sure if he was relieved or disappointed about that, but he didn't get much time to consider it.

Sylph shuffled under the covers until her back was just barely touching his. He stiffened for a moment, then shifted so they were pressed against each other. A small smile crossed his face, but no coherent thought formed in his mind.

A few minutes later, they were both asleep.

CHAPTER
FOUR

Damien woke up the next morning feeling more rested than he had in a long time. As much as he didn't want to admit it, Delph had been right about needing a break. Now that he'd actually paused for a little, he realized just how exhausted he'd actually been.

His bed was warmer than he was used to, and he didn't even feel like opening his eyes. It was also a fair bit warmer than he recalled. His mind, which had still been half asleep, finally caught up to the present, and he realized that he'd turned over in his sleep.

Sylph was snuggled against him, her head pressed against his chest. One of his arms was slung over her shoulders. He froze, unsure of what to do. To his later shame, the first thought that came to his mind was that he was glad Henry didn't seem to currently be watching.

He considered moving his arm before Sylph noticed it, but another thought struck him. She never woke up after him. Damien shifted his gaze down without moving. Sylph's head twitched and glanced up, meeting his gaze for a moment. She closed her eyes and lowered her head again. Damien decided that his hand was fine where it was.

They remained there for nearly another hour before Damien heard footsteps outside from around the kitchen. He and Sylph moved at the same time, both sitting up and glancing at the door in unison.

"I, uh—" Damien started, a stammer worming into his speech.

"Not now," Sylph said. She squeezed his hand briefly, then slipped to her feet. "Where's the bathroom? I should take a shower."

"The door right outside my room," Damien replied, sounding slightly lost. Sylph flashed him a grin and slipped out of the room, pulling the door shut behind him.

A few minutes later, a shadow slipped through his window. Henry unfurled to his normal shadowy form and flopped onto Damien's bed, crossing his hands behind his head in a remarkably human expression.

"What's with that dumb grin on your face?" Henry asked. "I'm not going back into your head until you wipe it off. I don't even want to consider what disgusting little human things might be dancing around in there."

Even Henry's complaints weren't enough to get rid of Damien's smile. "It's nothing. What were you doing last night?"

"I believe I already mentioned," Henry said. "Your neighbor's goats will never be the same. What amusing little creatures. The more scared they are, the longer they don't move. Did you know that?"

"I never measured it," Damien said suspiciously. "What exactly did you do?"

"I stacked goats," Henry replied. "My highest goat tower was four. Pretty decent, if you think about it. Might be a world record. Tomorrow I'll aim for five. Those stupid little bastards were terrified, but I'm sure I could do better."

Damien racked his memories to see if he could remember who had goats, but he came up blank. They must have been a relatively new acquisition.

"Just don't get caught. Especially now that we're trying to help Mrs. Hubbard out, we don't need people thinking I'm working against the town or something."

"Bah. Any self-respecting person would trust someone who could stack four goats on top of each other. By the way, you were right."

"About what?"

"Goats don't taste like cheese at all," Henry said. "I double checked after a few modifications based off information in your memory. They taste more like cooked beans."

"That's...still completely wrong," Damien said. "I'm not sure they could be much farther from that, actually. Then again, it's closer than cheese. I guess."

"Are you sure?" Henry asked, squinting at him with several dozen eyes. "I'm pretty sure it was beans."

"Yes, I'm— Wait. How are you tasting goats without killing them?"

"Tiny nibbles."

"Just to make sure, would you classify the bite you took out of my mom's alcohol bottle as big?"

"Bah. I just wanted to see what it tasted like," Henry said. "The glass felt like it might provide some interesting texture. Frankly, it tasted better than the stuff inside the bottle. I also tried to simulate what I expected an oversaturation of alcohol would do to a human, but I can't say it was very enjoyable. Why do humans like it?"

"Don't ask me," Damien replied. "I've never drank. Mom

wouldn't let me, and now I just don't feel any need to. Getting drunk wouldn't be terribly conducive to relaxing or training."

Henry grunted. "I don't understand how you see an experience you've never had and don't feel any desire to try it. Novelty is fascinating."

"Maybe I will if I get to your age," Damien said with a chuckle. "I just hope my sense of humor evolves with me."

"Hey!" Henry snapped. He started to form a reply but stopped mid-sentence and shot back into Damien's shadow.

A moment later, Sylph pulled the door open. Her wet hair hung low past her shoulders. She raised an eyebrow. Damien cleared his throat and grabbed a change of clothes.

"My turn," he said, slipping past her. Damien took a moment to appreciate the fact that this bathroom didn't have any rug inside the shower before washing up and heading back outside.

"Good morning, Damien," Hilla said cheerfully. "I'm making pancakes. There's some fruit and milk on the table already."

"Thanks, Mom," he said. Sylph was already seated at the table, but she'd yet to take any food. Damien sat down beside her, trying to keep the flush from his cheeks. He was pretty sure he did a decent job at it, too.

"Stop that," Henry complained in his mind. "I amend my earlier statement. There *are* some things I don't want to experience."

Damien gave him a mental flick and claimed some berries for himself. Sylph followed suit a moment later.

"So, what are your plans today?" Hilla asked.

"There are still a few places around town that I haven't shown Sylph," Damien said. "We'll probably drop by those. We've also got to go on a run and make sure we don't get too out of shape. Delph wouldn't be happy if we did."

His mom paused. She glanced back at them, an unreadable expression on her face. "Who?"

"Our teacher, Delph" Damien said. "Why?"

"Oh," Hilla said, shaking her head. She slid a pancake out of her pan and onto a large plate, which she brought over to the table. "I misheard you. I used to know somebody with a similar name."

"In the town?"

"No, one of your father and my acquaintances while we were on the frontlines together," Hilla replied. "I haven't heard anything about him in a long time, though. He was part of a pretty specialized unit that certainly wouldn't have been spending time teaching at a college."

"The inquisitors?" Sylph asked. Her voice barely shifted tone, but it was enough for Damien to notice.

"No, not them," Hilla replied. She sat down and set the large stack of pancakes down in the center of the table. "I don't know if they even had a name, but they reported directly to the queen. Scary people. Their job was retrieving artifacts that were very far beyond the frontlines. They were some of the best mages I ever knew."

"Better than Dad?" Damien asked, serving himself a pancake as Sylph relaxed slightly.

A smile played across Hilla's face. "Some of them were, but he used to place pretty well amongst them. They sparred frequently. I haven't seen him fight seriously in a long time, though. Who knows how things would stack up now."

The conversation trailed off as they all polished off the food on the table. Damien and Sylph thanked his mom once they'd finished and helped wash the dishes.

"No town council meeting today, so I'll just be doing chores around the house," Hilla said. "Make sure not to come home too late, okay? I don't want you getting hurt. And don't antagonize the mayor too much. He'll accuse me of sending you after him or something."

"We won't," Damien promised. "Not too much, anyway."

Hilla sighed, but she gave them a wry grin. "Well, so long as you aren't traced back to me and don't leave any bodies lying around..."

"We're not going to kill him, Mom!"

"Just go have fun," Hilla said with a laugh, putting one hand on one of his shoulders and another on Sylph before pushing them toward the door. "You really shouldn't be worrying about your mom's problems while you're on vacation. If things get to the point where words are no longer working, I'll ask your father to drop by. That should take care of everything in an instant."

Damien nodded and waved goodbye. He and Sylph started down the road toward Ardenford.

"Just who is your dad?" Sylph asked. "Is he really that strong? I'm not an expert of sensing magical energy, but I'm good enough to know that your mom is a pretty strong mage."

"She is," Damien said. "And honestly, I don't know how strong my dad is. I haven't seen him in years, and he never really did magic in front of me beyond small tricks. He works for the queen, though, so he's got to be up there."

"Huh," Sylph said. "That's interesting. I wonder who he is. Someone that strong must be at least a little well known."

"His name is Derrod, if that means anything to you."

Sylph shook her head. "Nothing. He must go under a different name while he works."

"Speaking of different names," Damien said, slowing to a stop at a wooden bench at a small outcropping along the hill. It overlooked the majority of Ardenford. He and Sylph sat down in it. "Do you think that my mom knows Delph? Going out and collecting artifacts...that sounds exactly what he did."

"It would be just like him to use a slightly different name, wouldn't it?" Sylph asked. "Either that or Delph *is* the slightly different name."

"I wonder if he knows my parents," Damien mused. "That would be weird. He's never given me any indication that he knew who I was."

"He's a good liar," Sylph pointed out. "You can try asking when he shows up to pick us up. I know what tells to look for when someone lies. If he does, I might be able to spot it."

"Good idea," Damien said. There was a short pause as the conversation ran out of topics. Damien's mind drifted back to the morning.

"Stop it!" Henry hissed, poking him with a mental finger. "How would you like it if I slung sludge around your room?"

Just stay in my mental space or something! I've seen you change things in there.

"It's more comfortable in your normal head, so long as you don't do weird things. Oh, look, you're doing it again."

"Talking to Henry again?" Sylph asked with a smirk.

"Yeah," Damien said, rubbing the back of his head. "My, uh, I'm a bit distracted. He's just overreacting."

A tiny mouth sprouted from Damien's shadow. "I most certainly am not. If you had to live with someone else's weird thoughts assaulting you while you tried to relax, you'd be mad, too!"

Damien squished the mouth with a finger.

"About this morning," he hedged.

Sylph raised an eyebrow. The tiny grin tugging at the corner of her mouth told Damien she was enjoying this. "What about it?"

"Are we dating?" he finally managed, forcing the words out before his nerves could stop him.

"Do you want to be?" Sylph asked, the smile fading away as

her tone turned serious. "I've never done anything like this before. I like you, but I've got a lot of baggage as well. Do you want to get any more involved in that?"

"I think I'm carrying around at least a bit of baggage myself, and he's a sarcastic asshole that wants to destroy the world," Damien said, finding a bit of confidence with her confirmation. "And I like you, too."

Henry rose from Damien's shadow, taking on his three-tentacled spherical form. "Perfect. It's done now, right? So, please—"

Sylph reached out and tapped Henry. He vanished with a *pop*, banished back into Damien's mind.

"Sorry, Henry," Sylph said. "I owe you my life and then some, but please give me a little more personal time with Damien. My Corruption antimagic works on that manifestation you make since it's using Dark magic. I know you don't like listening to this, so we'll make it quick, okay?"

Henry let out a mental grumble and sank deeper into Damien's mind, letting out the faintest sense of agreement.

"Did he agree?" Sylph asked.

"Yeah, actually," Damien said. "I'm a little surprised that worked."

"I think he just likes talking," Sylph said. "It's too bad the other Void creatures are less reasonable than him. You could collect them and give him something to do other than ride around in your head all the time. It probably gets boring."

"I honestly didn't think about it," Damien said, a frown crossing his face as he put himself in Henry's place. "I guess I should probably go get him a bunch of books to read, at the minimum."

"That can wait," Sylph said. "I bargained for a little time without him, so we're not wasting it on that."

"I'm not sure you can call that a bargain—"

Sylph leaned in, cutting his words off midsentence as she slipped under his arm and rested her head on his shoulder. Damien relaxed, letting the words die on his lips as he pulled her closer and let his eyes close.

They were still sitting there about thirty minutes later, when Princess Yui strode up the road toward them, flanked by Gaves and Bella and with a determined expression on her face.

She stopped a few feet away and cleared her throat. Damien and Sylph both sat bolt upright, flushing.

"Princess Yui?" Damien exclaimed. "What are you doing here?"

Henry, why didn't you tell me she was coming?

"I was giving you privacy," Henry replied with a smug laugh. "You *did* ask for it, you know."

He couldn't argue with that. Damien tried to force the red from his cheeks, but judging by Gaves' bemused expression, it wasn't working.

"Do you have any idea how hard it was to track you down?" Yui asked, shaking her head. "I tried to find you after the tournament at Blackmist, but you'd gone off on vacation in the middle of the school year."

"It was mandated by our professor," Damien defended. "But why were you looking for me?"

"It's of private nature," Yui said, her lips thinning. "I was originally looking for your professor on suggestion of my mother, but he said you'd be more appropriate to help me since he was busy."

"Anything you tell me you can tell Sylph," Damien said flatly.

"Oh, I gathered as much," Yui said. "But we're in the middle of your city. We really need somewhere a little more secluded. This is not something that we can have floating around in rumors."

"Oh," Damien said. "Well, we can go to my house, I guess. There's a shed in the back that's pretty secluded, and I can put up a sound ward."

"That works," Yui said. "Please, lead the way."

Damien and Sylph rose and headed back toward their house with Yui and her associates in tow.

If they were looking for Delph, does that mean the Corruption?

"Or the Void," Henry said. "It Who Stills the Seas is out there, and a fair amount of time has passed. It may have begun preparations. I haven't noticed anything, but my senses are far from what they once were."

Damien bit his lower lip. Sylph shot him a concerned glance, and he gave a one-shouldered shrug in response. He wasn't about to tell Yui anything she didn't know. She was polite, but who knows what her true goals were or how she'd take knowing that he was carrying a Void creature around inside him.

They reached the shed a few minutes later. Damien pulled open the door and was greeted with stale air and darkness. Yui raised her hand behind him, summoning a small sphere of fire in her palm to illuminate the room.

Everyone stepped inside, and a strange sense of nostalgia washed over Damien. He hadn't been back in the shed since he'd first summoned Henry. His mother had cleaned out the bloodstains and chalk, but it felt as if nothing else had changed.

Gaves shut the door behind him. "The sound ward, please."

Damien shrugged and sent the request to Henry. A ripple of purple energy spread out from his body, reflecting against the walls of the shed and filling it with faint purple light.

"There, nobody should be able to hear what we say in here," Damien said. "What's so important that you needed to find us?"

"A strange monster turned up near Goldsilk during the

tournament," Yui said. "It bled green acid and was almost completely immune to normal forms of attacks. It just healed from everything the mages fighting it tried. These monsters have been popping up around the kingdom for some time now, and Mage Delph has been hunting them according to my mother. Unfortunately, there are too many monsters for him to handle at once."

"Okay," Damien said. "So, he sent you to us?"

"He said he taught you how to fight them while you trained over summer," Yui explained. "Since he had too many monsters to fight, he said you could show us how to deal with them. You wouldn't actually have to fight any yourself, don't worry. Your teacher was pretty strict about keeping you and Sylph from any actual fights."

Damien rubbed the back of his head. "I guess we could help. It's mostly mental energy. You need a fair bit of it, though."

There was a knock on the door before Yui could respond. They all paused, turning toward it. Ether sparked in Gaves' hand as the door swung open, revealing Nolan.

"Damien! There was a group looking for you in Blackmist. You need to get out of here before—"

The words died on his lips as he spotted Yui and her attendants a few feet behind him. "Ah. I see I'm late."

Henry let the sound ward fall.

"Hello, Nolan," Yui said with a bemused grin. "I didn't expect to see you here. Did you think I meant Damien and Sylph ill?"

"Of course not, Princess," Nolan replied. "I never saw who was looking for him. I just came over here to warn him in case it was someone with bad intentions. It's a relief to know it was you."

"An understandable mistake," Yui said. "Although traveling

all this way just because someone was looking for Damien seems a little excessive, doesn't it?"

"Better safe than sorry, Princess."

"I've told you to call me Yui," she said.

"More importantly, how did you find us?" Gaves asked. "There should have been a ward blocking out the sound from within the building."

"I asked Damien's mom after I had a teacher at Blackmist teleport me here," Nolan replied. "She saw him heading into the shed but neglected to mention there were more people than just Sylph with him."

"Thanks for coming to try to warn me," Damien said. "The thought is appreciated. Have you eaten? The least I could do is get you a meal."

"Ah, I have not," Nolan said. "That would be fantastic."

"Hold on," Gaves said. "We aren't done here."

"Do you expect me to teach you everything now?" Damien asked. "It takes practice. There's no immediate rush, is there?"

"The sooner this task is accomplished, the better," Bella said, speaking up for the first time that day. "But not all of us are present. We have to retrieve a few more people, so a short delay would not be a major problem."

Gaves clicked his tongue and dismissed the magic in his hands.

"It's fine, Gaves," Yui said. "We don't want to impose, so we'll go get the last few people who need to learn how to fight these monsters and meet you at your house. Does that sound okay with you?"

"That works," Damien confirmed. He and Sylph left, heading into the house with Nolan.

"Did something happen at Blackmist?" Damien asked as soon as they were inside.

"I saw the princess asking around for you," Nolan said. "She never looks for people unless she needs something from them, so I asked Auntie to teleport me to where you lived so I could warn you before she got here. Clearly, the princess got here first. Do you need to make a run for it?"

"I think we should be fine," Damien said. "She came here because Delph sent her. He taught me and Sylph some magic that she needs to know on command of the queen. It should only take a day or two, and I don't think Sylph or I are in any danger."

"Oh," Nolan said, rubbing the back of his head. "That's awkward. I thought— Ah, never mind. Just be careful around the princess. She's very polite, but she carries enormous political power. I've seen her at the courts when I was younger, and she's every bit as ruthless as her mother. She'll make a great queen, but you should be wary of her."

"Thank you, Nolan," Damien said, grabbing some fruit and setting it out on the table. "We'll keep that in mind. By the way, aren't you supposed to be on a quest right now with Reena?"

"We got our quests done already," Nolan replied. "My father pulled some strings to let us access a few extra ones over summer so we wouldn't have to worry about it during the school year. Reena is back home."

"Well, we appreciate your help," Sylph said. "Even if Yui beat you here, your attempt speaks a lot for you."

"Thanks," Nolan said with a wry smile. He took a berry from the plate of fruit that Damien had set out and popped it into his mouth. "Uh, so are you two...?"

"Yeah," Damien said, reddening. "But how did you know?"

"Well, aside from it being obvious for the past year or so? Your mom told me. She's a nice lady. Said she saw you sitting together on the bench through the window."

Damien slapped himself on the forehead. "I forgot you

could see it from here. Eig- Ah, Seven Planes, that's embarrassing."

"Not as embarrassing as Yui walking up on us while we were there," Sylph muttered.

Nolan burst into laughter. "She did? That's rich. I wonder if she was jealous."

"Jealous?" Damien asked. "Why?"

"She isn't allowed to have any sort of romantic relationship," Nolan replied. "Not until she takes the crown. The queen ruled it to keep her focused on her studies, supposedly. All the major noble houses were informed to keep anyone from trying to pursue her."

"Supposedly?" Sylph asked. "Are you sure the queen didn't just say that to keep a bunch of sleazy nobles off her back until she was actually interested in someone?"

"It's possible," Nolan admitted. "But unlikely. She's already got a betrothed, actually. Their marriage just isn't ratified until she becomes queen."

"That sucks," Damien said, and Sylph nodded empathetically. "I'd hate to be forced into something like that."

"It's no matter," Nolan said. "I'm glad that things weren't as bad as I thought."

"Well, now that you're here, you might as well join in on the training we're going to give Yui," Damien suggested. "There's a fair chance you'll need it sooner rather than later."

Nolan cocked his head. "Now that's ominous. Sure, I'll stay. More training couldn't hurt, although I do wonder why Delph can't just teach us himself."

"It's Delph," Damien said. "That's probably explanation enough. He's also busy hunting the monsters that he wants me to teach you how to fight against, so he probably doesn't have time to do anything else."

"It's a little concerning that the problem has gotten so bad that other people are getting involved, though," Sylph said, lowering her voice.

"We'll have to talk with him when he gets back," Damien agreed. Someone knocked on the door, interrupting their conversation.

"That's probably Yui," Damien said walking over and pulling it open. Yui and her companions stood outside. She'd been joined by Viv, Elania, and Eve. The three Goldsilk girls were covered in small cuts and wore hardened leather clothing instead of their school colors.

"Hello again, Damien," Viv said. "I hope we aren't intruding too much."

"It's fine," Damien said, shaking off his surprise. Yui had mentioned that the problem had been near Goldsilk, but he hadn't expected to see these three again anytime soon. "I don't think the table is big enough for everyone, but I guess you should come in."

They followed him inside. Yui sat down at the table and her attendants took up position behind her. There were just enough chairs for the Goldsilk girls to sit down. Elania eyed the fruit.

"Please, feel free to eat," Damien said. "It looks like you've been traveling for a while."

"Only a day or two," Viv said, but Elania eagerly grabbed a fistful of berries and started shoveling them into her mouth.

"Why are you all here instead of fully fledged mages?" Sylph asked. "Wouldn't it be better to send them against the monsters?"

"They're mostly all already fighting or caught up in something," Viv replied. "The assault on the frontlines has been intensifying as of late, so a lot of teachers have had to leave the school to keep the monsters from pushing through. The remaining ones are stretched between protecting the schools, hunting monsters, or teaching students. We were supposed to get someone called Professor Delph to teach us how to fight the monsters since he's got experience with them, but he told us to find you instead."

"So, Yui has told me," Damien said. "But why are you all cut up? Did you get attacked?"

Elania flushed. "No. When we dropped by Blackmist, we took turns sparring with Mark. Princess Yui told us that we had to go through a portal to find you, and we didn't have a chance to see a healer first. None of the injuries were serious, so it wasn't worth wasting time."

Viv's nose wrinkled in amusement, but she didn't say anything to contradict the other girl.

"Well, we'll do our best to live up to your expectations. I'm not exactly a teacher," Damien said.

His parent's bedroom door swung open, and Hilla stepped out, pulling a coat around her shoulders. She froze mid-step, her eyes widening as she took in all the people sitting around the table.

"Oh my. Damien, you have so many friends! Why didn't you tell me they were coming over? I would have made pancakes."

Damien bit back a groan. "Uh, I didn't actually know they were coming. It was a bit of a surprise."

Nolan rose smoothly from the table and inclined his head. "A pleasure to meet you, Mrs. Vale. I'm Nolan Gray."

Hilla's eyebrows twitched. "Gray? You're far from Kingsfront, Nolan. I hope my son has been appropriately hospitable. You've come a long way."

"More than I could ask for," Nolan said. "I'm sorry we're all imposing on your hospitality, Mrs. Vale."

"Nonsense," Hilla said. "Damien has been a loner for too long. It's good to see him socializing a little more."

She turned to the others, starting with Yui.

"And what's your name, young lady?" Hilla extended a hand

to the princess. Gaves and Bella both stiffened, and a tiny flicker of Ether sprung to Gaves' hand. Before anyone could react, a band of white light snapped around his hand, canceling the spell and squeezing his fingers together.

"No magic in the house," Hilla said, piercing Gaves with a flat stare.

"Gaves!" Yui snapped. "She is our *host*. Show some respect."

"My apologies," Gaves said. "I was startled by the sudden motion."

The band of light released him, and Yui took Hilla's hand. "I'm Yui. I'm terribly sorry about that. Gaves is a little overzealous."

"Oh, it's fine," Hilla said with an easygoing smile. "I knew a lot of people just like him. If he's here long enough, he'll learn. Just like they did."

She then went around, introducing herself to all of the Goldsilk girls. Once she'd finished, she told them that she'd return for dinner and make enough for all of them to eat before heading out.

"You've got an interesting mom, Damien," Nolan observed once she'd left. "That was some crazy fast casting."

"She's a strong mage," Damien agreed, still watching Gaves warily. "I don't know if we've got enough food here for everyone to eat. You guys should go check out the bakery. Sylph and I need to figure out just how we're going to teach this, so come back in an hour or so."

Yui nodded her understanding. She rose from the chair and gestured for the others to follow her as she headed out the door. Gaves, Bella, and the Goldsilk girls followed her out of the house.

FIVE

Damien ran a hand through his hair and flopped down into a chair. "What in the Eight Planes is going on? This is just weird."

"Eight Planes?" Nolan asked.

Damien cursed inwardly. "Got mixed up. I haven't thought about the Planes in a while. I meant seven."

It wasn't the most convincing argument, but Nolan grunted his understanding and let the matter drop.

"I think I'm missing a few key pieces of information," Nolan said. "So, I can't help you there. Do you actually need time to figure out how to teach us this secret magic?"

"Not really," Damien admitted. "It's pretty much brute force. All you have to do is use your mental energy to disconnect the lines of Ether from the Corruption."

"Corruption?" Nolan asked.

"Ah, that's what the weird monsters are called," Damien said. "They consume the Ether around them, draining the environment until it's almost completely devoid of it. You can't kill them while they're connected to the Ether, since they have an incredible regeneration rate. You've got to split them off, then kill them."

"Interesting," Nolan said. "Is separating the lines connecting someone to the Ether really that easy, though? I'd have thought that would be a common fighting technique if it was."

"It seems borderline impossible on people," Sylph said. "I gave it a shot once we figured out the technique. My mental energy is unfortunately low, so I can't do the technique. I did ask Delph, and he reported similar results, though."

"So, something about the Corruption makes them easier to split off?" Nolan asked. "Interesting. It's like they're not properly connected to the Ether at all. Are these monsters artificial?"

"We don't know," Damien admitted honestly. "They're... something, and it isn't good. The easiest way to fight them is with at least two people. Have one person disconnect them from the Ether and have the other finish them off."

"I see," Nolan said. "In that case, I have another question. Why did you send the princess and everyone else off? If you didn't need time to prepare, couldn't you have just taught them now and have been done with it?"

"Well, it's easier in concept than it is in practice," Damien said, snagging a berry. He went to eat it, then paused and handed it to Sylph. She took it with a grin, and Damien claimed another berry for himself. "It'll probably take some time for everyone to master it, and there's no real way to practice beyond actually fighting the Corruption, so it'll be a lot of theory. But for your first question, I sent them away because I need to figure out if we can somehow use them to solve a problem I've got."

"A problem? What is it?"

"Nothing quite as important as the Corruption," Damien admitted. "It's a political problem. The mayor here, Shindal, is trying to get rid of the old teacher and trying to install his kid in her place. He's claiming that Rune Crafting isn't worth teaching, and her talents would be better put to use elsewhere."

"What?" Nolan exclaimed. "Rune Crafting is incredible! I'm still not particularly good at it, but there are so many applications both in and out of combat. It's incredibly important for people to at least get a taste of it."

"That's the problem," Damien said. "I'm pretty sure the mayor's kid just can't get a job so he's trying to get him here at the cost of people's educations. We're trying to figure out a good way to help the teacher keep her job."

"Ah," Nolan said, his eyes lighting up. "I see what you're getting at. You want Yui to step in?"

"It's the least she could do," Damien said with a wry grin. "It's not like the mayor can ignore a direct request from the princess."

"You're not wrong, but the mayor is probably going to know exactly who asked Yui to step in," Nolan warned. "Rumor moves fast in small towns, and he'll absolutely hold this against you."

"Does that really matter? He probably wouldn't go back on his word with a princess," Damien said. "And I'll be back at Blackmist soon enough. I don't have any plans of living in Ardenford forever, so if the mayor doesn't like me, it hardly matters."

"That's true, but your mom is still here. Couldn't he cause her difficulties?"

"I guess it's possible," Damien said with a frown. "I didn't think about that. Honestly, I don't think he could do much to her. She's a council member, and my dad is pretty influential—when he's actually around. The most he could do is annoy her, and I don't think she'd mind that in exchange for letting Mrs. Hubbard keep her job."

"Then, it can't hurt to ask," Nolan said. "Everyone who

came here asking to get trained essentially owes you a favor, anyway."

"Wait, what? Why?"

"That's how things work with nobles," Sylph answered before Nolan could speak. "And all the people we're about to train are nobles. That means they all owe you a favor. If they didn't, they'd be indebted to you, and that could cause issues down the road if other people found out and accused them of not paying back what they've been given."

"You know a lot about nobles," Nolan said, raising an eyebrow. "I didn't realize."

"I picked up a thing or two," Sylph replied with a shrug. Damien briefly wondered how much her training had forced her to learn about noble society. He repressed a grimace and the desire to ask Henry if it was possible to dig up someone's soul just to drop kick it off the Planes.

"Wait, if they owe us a favor, is this really the best thing to use it on?" Damien asked.

"With Princess Yui? Absolutely," Nolan said. "You want to get rid of that as quickly as possible. Trust me, you want to limit any ties you have with her. Having favors from minor and major nobles is great, but the crown is different altogether. That gets you wrapped up in the real politics. You don't want to be anywhere near that."

"It sounds like you're speaking from experience," Damien said, offering Nolan a grape. He accepted it and sighed.

"I am," Nolan said. "Please, don't ask more than that. I don't want to speak about it, but I'd answer if you did. I promise it isn't very important to what we're doing right now."

Damien shrugged. "Sure, you don't have to talk about it if you don't want to. It's not a surprise to either of us that we have secrets. But you say you'd answer if I asked—is that because you feel like you owe me a favor?"

Nolan's mouth quirked up. "Perhaps."

"I— You know what, never mind. I don't think I'm ever going to fully understand nobles," Damien admitted. "But I do appreciate you as a friend, favors or not."

Nolan blinked, then gave Damien a small grin. "And I likewise. You've taught me more than I think you realize."

"Now, more importantly," Sylph said, "wouldn't it be funny if we made everyone run laps until they were exhausted before we started training?"

Yui and the others returned about an hour later. As tempting as Sylph's suggestion was, they instead opted to return to the shed to begin training. Damien wanted to minimize the amount of time he had to spend training so he could get back to doing just about anything else.

"All right," he said. "First off, you can't actually beat the Corruption on your own, so you'll need to partner up. This is a two person job."

"Corruption?" Yui asked.

"There are only three of us," Gaves said.

"There are six," Damien corrected, nodding at the Goldsilk girls. "One of you can partner with one of them. And the Corruption is the name of the monsters that we're fighting against. If you want to know why, ask Delph."

They shrugged, although Gaves didn't look particularly pleased.

"Why do we need two people?" Eve asked, her voice so quiet that Damien barely heard her. "Delph is on his own."

"Because it's too dangerous for one of us," Damien replied. "I don't know what Delph is doing, and I was under the impression he was working with another professor. Regardless, he's a professor, and we aren't. To fight the Corruption, you first need to understand how it works."

Damien spent a few minutes explaining the Corruption's regeneration and how they consumed the Ether in an area the longer a fight went on.

"So, that means if you fight this Corruption too long, or if you just fight a lot in the same area, you could end up draining the magic away?" Elania asked.

"If you fight incorrectly, yeah," Damien said. "Which is why it's vital that you don't. The Corruption's power is tied to siphoning away the Ether from the surrounding area. Unlike normal people, it looks like they can be split off from their magic using mental energy. Once you do that, they still regenerate a little, but they're much weaker. You can attack them until they turn to stone and eventually die."

"So, that's why you need two people," Viv mused. "One person has to concentrate on splitting the Corruption off from the Ether, and the other one kills it and protects the mental energy user."

"Exactly," Damien said. "So, split up. One person in each group should be at least competent with magical energy, since I know all of you are at least semi-capable fighters. Nolan will just have to partner up with me or Sylph since we're short one person."

"What's that supposed to mean?" Gaves asked, cocking an eyebrow.

"We fought the Corruption for an entire summer," Sylph said, stepping to meet his gaze. "And both of us have nearly died multiple times, even with Delph's help. We don't need to argue with you about this. Either do what we say or leave."

Gaves glowered but inclined his head.

"Gaves, partner with Bella, she's got a good grasp of mental energy," Yui said. "I'll partner with Viv, if that's okay with her. I'm decent at using both mental energy and Ether."

"That's fine, Princess Yui," Viv replied, walking to stand beside her. "Elania is very talented at using mental energy herself, so these parings should work."

"Perfect," Damien said. "I'll go over how to properly use your mental energy to split it off from the Corruption together with Bella, Elania, and Viv. Sylph, can you go over some strategies to fight the Corruption with everyone else? Nolan can watch whichever he'd prefer."

Sylph nodded and waved for Yui and Gaves to follow her outside. Nolan strode after them. Once they'd left, Damien gathered his Ether. He channeled it into his hand, then shifted its form to look like a lasso.

"You can't actually see my mental energy, so I'll just use Ether to demonstrate," Damien said. "You need to make some way to grab a large number of Ether strands. I don't think it matters what method you use, but it can't just be one strand at a time. If there's even one still connected to the Corruption, it won't die."

The lasso morphed into a dozen tendrils. "If you can control multiple probes at once, then that's probably the most effective way to do it. You need a lot of mental energy for that, though. Most people don't use much at once, so it wouldn't surprise me if this seems a bit foreign to you."

"How many strands of Ether are normally connected to the Corruption?" Viv asked.

"I don't think it's the same every time," Damien said, scratching the back of his head. "Expect anywhere from ten to a few dozen. Maybe more, but most of them had around that. If there are too many for you to handle, then let your partner know and just retreat."

Elania screwed her eyes shut in concentration. A moment

later, a confident grin crossed her face. "Can we just collect them all with one or two tendrils?"

"Yeah, that works. Just make sure you don't lose hold of them. It gets harder when you try to hold a lot at once."

"I can tell," Elania admitted. "I'm holding a few right now without drawing from them. I couldn't hold this for long, especially if there were a lot more."

"Which is why coordination is very important for this. Most people don't have enough energy to hold the Ether indefinitely, so you'll have to work with your partner closely. For now, everyone should practice and figure out what method works best for you."

He leaned against the wall of the shed and watched as the other students closed their eyes and got to work.

"I bet if you walked over and pushed one of them, they'd fall on their face before they realized what happened," Henry mused. "They're so unaware of their surroundings when they close their eyes like that. Humans are more like goats than they think."

We're not doing that.

"*You're* not doing that," Henry corrected with a gleeful laugh. "Bets are off for what I do at night, unless you want me sticking around."

Damien didn't have a good response to that. He was pretty sure setting Henry loose on an innocent farmer's goats in exchange for time with Sylph was at least a little evil, but he wasn't about to say no.

"I think I've got a basic grasp of it," Bella said after a few minutes.

"As do I," Viv added. "But eight strands of Ether are my max and, even with that few, I wouldn't be able to hold on for more than a few seconds. How did you manage to do it for a few dozen?"

"I have naturally high mental energy," Damien admitted. "But a good portion of it was also practice. A lot of my spells use a ton of it, so I've just had more time than you to get good with it. Don't worry, it's much easier to train than new spells. You'll probably be seeing results by the end of today."

Henry laughed in his mind. "We'll see about that."

Henry's assessment was right. They practiced through the day and until the light coming into the shed started to fade. Moving into the yard bought them another hour, but the sun was soon completely gone.

In that time, the only one that managed to grab ten strands of Ether at once was Viv, and even she could only hold it for a second. Damien tried everything to explain methods, but everything pointed toward their problem not being technique but practice.

"I don't think I can do another second of this," Elania groaned, rubbing her head. "My head is going to split open."

"As much as I hate to admit it, she's right," Viv said. Her lips were pressed thin, and she was doing an admirable job of keeping the pain from her face. "I don't think I can go much longer without hurting myself."

"I guess we'll stop then," Damien said reluctantly. He'd been hoping that they could finish today, but that was clearly not going to happen. Within him, he felt Henry's smug energy. The Void creature was clearly taking pleasure in something, Damien just wasn't sure if it was watching the girls struggle or proving him wrong.

"Are you lot finally done?" Hilla asked, poking her head out of a window. "I've got dinner ready, so why don't you come in and have some dinner?"

"We need to get Sylph, too," Damien replied.

"Oh, I've already called her in. She and your other friends are already inside."

"Lucky," Elania muttered under her breath. Damien rolled his eyes.

"All right, thanks, Mom," Damien said before nodding to his trainees for the day. "Let's go, then. The headache will get better once you stop trying to use mental energy and let it relax for a bit."

They all headed inside. Hilla had added several new chairs to the table so that everyone had a spot to sit. Damien wasn't entirely sure where she'd found that many extra chairs, but it wasn't important enough to ask.

Like Hilla had said, Sylph and her group had beaten them back. Sylph was sitting in her chair. On the far end of the table, as far away from her as they could get, was Gaves, Nolan, Eve, and Yui.

Of the lot, Gaves looked the best—but that wasn't saying much. All four of them were pale and matted with sweat. They sported a multitude of thin wounds, and all looked about an inch from falling asleep where they sat.

"I take it back," Elania muttered. "What did Sylph do to them?"

"We started training," Sylph replied. "The Corruption isn't going to go easy on you, and it's important to be able to fight against them without magic if things go poorly. After you get a grasp of what Damien is teaching you, you should probably join in with me to get an understanding of what your partners are dealing with."

"And if you don't get a grasp on it, maybe we'll just try swapping you with someone on Sylph's side," Damien put in with an evil grin. "Maybe they'll take to it faster."

The girls shuddered, and they all sat down. Damien claimed his spot beside Sylph, and his mom emerged from the kitchen with a plate bearing a huge stuffed and roasted bird. It was nearly as large as a pig.

"Please, eat up! You all clearly need to keep up your strength," Hilla said with a smile. "I won't stick around to bother you. I've already eaten. I trust you've all got places to stay? I'm afraid we don't nearly have enough room to house all of you."

"We'll stay at the inn," Nolan promised. "We don't want to be any more of a burden than we already are. Thank you very much for the meal, Mrs. Vale."

"Of course," Hilla replied. "Any good host would provide food for their guests."

Elania took a carving knife from the plate and sliced off a large portion of the golden-brown bird. She took a large bite out of it, and her eyes widened. "This is amazing!"

That was the end of the conversation at the table. It was the politest mad scramble that Damien had ever seen. Even Princess Yui, who he would have thought would remain prim and proper no matter the situation, still impatiently grabbed for the knife when Gaves took a little too long cutting off a piece.

The food lasted all of ten minutes. They all leaned back, contented expressions on their faces.

"Your mom is a brilliant cook, Damien," Sylph said.

"Can you cook like this, too?" Viv asked. "Nolan is right, that was amazing. It was better than anything I've had at Goldsilk by a wide margin."

"No," Damien and Sylph replied at the exact same time. Damien reddened. "We've got some basic cookware set up in our room. I'm...not very good."

"Can't be good at everything," Nolan said with a relieved sigh.

"The food really is good, but I bet part of the reason it tastes this great is because of how tired we are," Bella said.

Gaves grunted in agreement. "I haven't worked like that in

ages. I didn't realize how far behind I'd gotten relying on my magic."

They traded a few more niceties before Yui rose from the table and inclined her head. "Thank you for your hospitality and training today. We should be off to get enough sleep to prepare for tomorrow. What time will you be ready for us?"

"An hour before sunrise," Damien replied. "We have a lot of progress to make."

"Agreed," Yui said. "Until tomorrow, then."

She and the others bid farewell, heading out the door and leaving Damien and Sylph alone once more. They gathered the dishes up and brought them to the sink.

"What did you make them do?" Damien asked as he washed a plate. "I thought for sure my group would be exhausted, but they looked spry compared to yours."

"A lot of laps," Sylph replied. "And then a lot of fighting without magic. If the Corruption manages to drain all the Ether in an area, they need to be able to kill the monsters without magic."

"Not an easy task for people who have been using magic most of their life," Damien observed. "How were they?"

"Not good," Sylph said. "Gaves and Eve had some skill, but the others were worthless. Yui is fit, but she's never fought without magic. I suppose Nolan was okay as well, but he relies too much on magical techniques as well. How did things go on your end?"

"Not much better," Damien admitted. "None of them are very good with mental energy. They've got a lot of practice ahead of them."

He finished up the dishes and beat Sylph to the shower. She took his place once he'd finished, and he returned to his room. Damien slipped under the covers, and Henry pulled away from his shadow, escaping from the other side of the bed.

"It's goat time," Henry proclaimed. "And I might pay a visit to your fellow students along the way. I'm curious about a few things."

"Try not to get into any actual trouble," Damien said. "And what are you curious about? Do you think they've got ulterior motives or something?"

"Everyone has ulterior motives," Henry said dismissively. "I don't care about stupid mortal politics. You can deal with that so long as it doesn't actually involve any danger to us."

"Then, why are you observing them?"

Henry's dark eyes sparkled. "No reason at all. Don't get into any trouble while I'm gone."

He shot through the window with a cackle, vanishing into the night before Damien could respond. Damien rolled his eyes and pulled the window shut behind Henry so the crisp air wouldn't chill his room.

"Goats again?" Sylph asked, pulling the door shut behind her.

"Among other things," Damien said. "Nolan and the others might be in for an interesting night."

"Henry's come a long way from making sure he stays hidden from anyone and everyone." Sylph nudged Damien out of the way and climbed into bed.

"He's pretty confident in his new form, I think," Damien said.

"That's good. Maybe you'll have your full manifestation soon," Sylph said with a sly grin.

"Hey, it's not like you've got one! You've just got a battle manifestation."

"For now. I'm making progress with my companion. Give me a few weeks, and we'll see how things look."

She pulled the covers higher and snuggled against Damien's

chest. He put an arm over her, more than happy to let the conversation fade, and slowly drifted off to sleep.

A rattle woke Damien. He was just barely able to make out Henry slipping through the window out of the corner of his eye. His companion was in the three-tentacled orb form. Damien sat up with a sigh.

"Ah, you're awake," Henry said. "Good."

Sylph rose as well. She pushed the hair out of her eyes, then raised an eyebrow. "Did you manage to beat your record with the goats?"

"Five of them this time," Henry said proudly. "And in case you were wondering, just about all your friends are convinced the inn is haunted. Don't worry, I waited until just a few minutes ago to bother them, so they'll have gotten all the sleep they need."

"Of course, they are," Damien said with a sigh. "You weren't seen, I hope?"

"Nope," Henry replied. "Also, Princess Yui sleeps with a little fuzzy yellow hat."

"Right, we don't need to know that," Damien said. "Wait. What did you do with her hat, Henry?"

"The goats were hungry." Henry snickered. "I believe that is what most people refer to as comedy."

"No, that's just called being a dick," Damien corrected him. "You wouldn't like if someone took your hat, would you?"

"I don't have a hat."

"Well, presume you had one."

"Then, I wouldn't let someone pluck it off my head," Henry replied, crossing two of his tentacles like arms.

"Maybe stick to bothering goats," Sylph suggested. "You don't want to accidentally mess up something someone actually cares about."

Henry made a face. "Fine. It might be problematic if

someone caught onto me anyway. Not like they'll ever find that hat. The goats didn't leave much of it behind."

He darted under the covers and merged with Damien.

"It's like he's going through the phases of growing up in reverse," Damien said with a sigh. "I think pranks usually come before snarky attitude."

"I wouldn't know. That wasn't something I covered in my studies," Sylph said, rubbing her chin. "I'll take your word for it, but we should probably get ready for now. Henry has clearly gotten everyone up."

Damien nodded, and they hopped out of bed, setting out to meet the others when they arrived. None of them mentioned anything about the previous night, so they split off into their groups and set off once more.

The next three days fell into a routine. They would train through the day, only stopping to eat, and then go back to bed and start it again the following morning. Everyone started to show varying degrees of progress, although it was faster for Damien's group than Sylph's.

Viv was the first one to be able to grab twenty four strands of Ether at once, and the others weren't far behind her. They couldn't hold it for long, and more than once someone passed out mid-practice, but Damien took what he could get. They still couldn't hold it nearly long enough, but at least they were almost at the point they needed to be.

Damien warned them that, even once they figured out how to fight against the Corruption, he had no way to teach them how to actually *locate* it. He wasn't about to reveal Henry's secrets, so he told them that responsibility fell to Delph.

On the fourth day after Nolan and the others had arrived, Damien pulled Yui aside before dinner.

"Delph should be dropping by pretty soon to pick me and Sylph up," Damien said. "Before we leave, there's a small thing I need to take care of here. It's not exactly my field of expertise, so I was hoping you might be able to help me."

"Of course," Yui said smoothly. "What is it?"

"The mayor of Ardenford is trying to replace the Rune Crafting teacher," Damien replied. "He wants to hire his son as a replacement, but —"

Yui raised a hand. "Damien, I'm going to do you a favor."

He blinked. "I'm sorry?"

"I know you're new to dealing with nobles, and while Nolan has clearly done a lot to try and inform you, there's much you need to learn. When a noble owes you a favor, you don't explain why you want something. You just tell them what you want. Oversharing is dangerous, and people will use the extra information you give them against you in the future."

"I'm not trying to be a noble, though."

"But you deal with them regardless," Yui said. "Look at the company you keep. Nolan is in debt to you, and you keep company with the princess of the kingdom. If you were to enter conflict with someone, it is not unreasonable for multiple noble houses to get dragged in along with you."

"Nolan is my friend," Damien said firmly. "But I didn't look at things like that. Could that much drama really come from me misspeaking?"

"Probably not," Yui admitted. "But it is still possible. Now, reword your request."

Damien thought for a few moments. "I want you to stop Mayor Shindal from removing the current schoolteacher, Mrs. Hubbard, from her job."

"Very good," Yui said, a grin stretching across her lips. "It will be done, but it does not cancel out the debt I owe you. The information I seek is greater than the service you request."

Nolan's warning ran through Damien's mind, and he pursed his lips, searching for a way to cancel out Yui's debt.

"Then, I'd like to spend the rest of what you feel that you owe me on information that I would find important," Damien said.

"You learn fast," Yui praised. "Deal. Here's your information —I'm well aware that Nolan didn't do the runes on my staff. You did. I don't mind, of course. But Nolan's father is growing impatient to choose an heir between him and Reena, and Nolan's talent with runes is tipping the scales in his favor. I do not believe Nolan wishes to be chosen as heir, nor does he know about his father's thoughts. Do with that as you will."

Yui inclined her head and headed inside, joining the others and leaving Damien outside, a worried frown crossing his face.

CHAPTER
SIX

The following morning, Mayor Shindal resigned from his post via a letter on his chair in the council meeting room. By the time anyone found it, his house was empty, and there was no sign of him or his family.

His house had been thoroughly cleaned out of any valuables and abandoned like trash at the side of the road. According to his note, he'd decided to leave for the east side of the kingdom for an unexpected job opportunity that had opened up.

Hilla relayed all of that to Damien and the others over dinner that day. It was strange, but there was nothing to be done aside from begin preparing to elect a new mayor over the next few weeks.

Yui caught Damien staring at her and gave him a slight nod, her expression not changing in the slightest. Nobody other than Nolan noticed the exchange.

The rest of the week passed quickly, as there was nothing to do but train. Henry continued leaving at night to bother the goats, but he swore he left the other students alone. Damien and Sylph had swapped students a few times, just to make sure everyone had an understanding of what they would be dealing with.

On the seventh day, everyone had gotten to the point where Damien was hopeful they could hold their own against a normal Corrupted monster. They still weren't at the point where he felt they could kill it, but at least they wouldn't instantly die. Everyone gathered in front of his house one last time.

"Delph should be coming by to bring us back to Blackmist soon," Damien said. "I think we can count this week as a success, though. You've got a pretty good chance of standing against the Corruption if you work together."

"Just stay aware of what you're dealing with," Sylph warned. "You can probably handle the normal Corruption, but the Seeds are on a completely different level. They're much more powerful, and from what I know, usually much larger as well. If you run into a Seed, just run and pray that someone stronger arrives."

"Have you fought a seed?" Gaves asked. "It sounds like you're talking with firsthand experience."

"No," Damien lied. "But it took an entire high-ranking mage party to take down a half-dead one. You know how we mentioned that the Corruption turns to stone as it loses its connection to the Ether? It was like that, but it was so strong that even in its stone form, it was still healing. We fought one of its clones that crumbled apart as soon as the main one died, and that nearly killed us."

"But you're strong enough to actually take the normal Corruption on," Gaves pressed. "Can you show me your band? I want to know how far off I am."

Damien considered the question a moment, then shrugged and brought up the information from the wristband, pushing it forward into the air with mental energy so that Gaves could see it.

Damien Vale
Blackmist College
Year Three
Major: Battle Mage
Minor: Dredd's Apprentice
Companion: [Null]
Magical Strength: 12.3
Magical Control: 3.9
Magical Energy: 29.9
Physical Strength: 1.4
Endurance: 4.2

"What in the Seven Planes is that Magical Energy?" Gaves asked, his eyes widening in shock. "No wonder you can fight these things. You just bury them under a mountain of magic."

Damien dismissed the numbers with a shrug. "It's not the only way. Sylph fights them, too. It's just practice."

"Right," Elania said. "And running away from any Corruption that isn't a pushover."

They all laughed, but it was equal parts amusement and nervousness. The group milled about the front of Damien's house, relaxing as they waited for Delph to arrive.

About half an hour later, the air crackled. Everyone scrambled to their feet as a sparking blue line carved through the air in front of them, hissing and popping with energy.

"That's not Delph's portal," Sylph warned, her hand lowering to the daggers at her hip.

The portal widened, opening like the maw of a great beast until it was nearly ten feet tall and flooding the area with brilliant light. Lightning crackled along its edges and the shadow of a large figure formed within it.

A man stepped out from the portal, his eyes burning with faint traces of magic. He was clean shaven and wore heavily runed metal armor with pauldrons that curved to points above his shoulders. Two curved blades rested at his hips, and his gear was unblemished and practically glowed. It was about as close to a polar opposite of Delph as one could get. Sylph stiffened.

"This is quite the surprise," Yui said. "Sentinel Stormsword, what are you doing here? I hope my mother hasn't sent you just to get me."

"Princess Yui, I didn't expect to see you here. I'm afraid that I'm off duty and currently carrying out some other business," the man said, his voice a smooth baritone. "So, please, no titles. Out in Ardenford, I just go by Mr. Vale or Derrod."

"Dad!" Damien exclaimed, finally snapping out of his stupor. "What are you doing here?"

"You're looking well, Damien," Derrod, said, stepping up and ruffling Damien's hair. "I'm helping an old friend out. But look at how much you've grown! Before we get any further, I'm going to go say hi to your mother. I'll be back shortly."

He raised a hand without waiting for a response and strode up to the house, closing the door behind himself. Everyone stared at where he'd left in mute shock.

"*He's* your dad?" Gaves asked, aghast.

It took Damien a few moments to pick his jaw up off the floor. "Uh...yeah. It's been a long time since I've seen him, though."

"He seemed a little impersonal," Elania observed. "I would have thought he'd be more excited to see you than that."

"Elania!" Viv snapped.

"Sorry," Elania muttered.

"It's fine," Damien said, shaking his head. "That's just how he is. But what is he doing here? He said he's helping a friend—does that mean Delph?"

"They were both on the frontlines," Yui mused. "It's possible they know each other. But I never knew you were Stormsword's kid, Damien."

"You keep saying that name, but he never used it around me. I didn't even know he was that important. I thought he was just a field agent or something," Damien said. "Did you talk with my dad much? It seems like you know him."

"He was around the castle pretty frequently," Yui replied. "I spoke to him every month or so if I had to guess. Not a lot, but he was always kind. He's very important, though. Stormsword is essentially my mother's right hand. He executes her will around the realm. He's one of the strongest mages in our army."

"And he never mentioned anything about his family?" Elania asked.

"He mentioned he had a son, but he played his cards very close to chest," Yui replied with a bitter smile. "Trust me, I tried multiple times to figure information out about him. It was almost something of a game. I never won. He's better at it than most nobles are."

"Does that mean Damien wins, even though he wasn't playing?" Viv asked, laughing. "After all, he's the reason you got the information."

Yui scrunched her nose. "I suppose it does. Seven Planes, that's mildly annoying."

"Tell me about it," Damien said, his eyebrows lowering. He was finding it hard to line up the Stormsword that Yui was talking about with his father. Then again, he met the man so infrequently that he supposed anything was possible. "You spent more time with my dad than I did."

"What's this emotion you're feeling?" Henry asked. "I don't like it."

I believe that would be called bitterness.

It struck Damien that Sylph had yet to say anything, which was vastly more important to him than the appearance of his father. He nudged her gently with his foot. "Sylph? Are you okay?"

She blinked. "Oh. Yeah, I'm fine."

"I don't think she's fine," Henry observed.

You don't say. She recognized him.

He wanted to press Sylph on it, but it clearly wasn't the time, so he resolved to wait until they were in private. Sylph clearly had something she didn't want to share with everyone else. A few minutes later, Derrod strode out of the house, a lazy grin on his face.

"Sorry to keep you waiting, kids. It's been some time, huh, Damien? I can sense a fair bit of magical energy around you now. You end up dropping those runes for combat magic?"

"I'm kind of doing both, but more combat than anything," Damien admitted, peering at Derrod as if he weren't convinced the man was really there. He didn't much feel like small talk. "You mentioned you were doing a favor for your friend. Did you mean..."

"Dove," Derrod said. "But he said he's been going as Delph around you."

"Wait," Nolan said, raising a hand and speaking for the first time since Derrod had arrived. His eyes were wide in adoration and awe. "I'm sorry to interrupt, but...Damien, your dad is Stormsword?"

"It's news to me as well," Damien said, glaring at his dad accusingly. "I've never heard of it, either. I guess *Stormsword* is too busy with his job to let me know what he's actually doing."

"I did tell you I was working for the queen," Derrod said with a chuckle. "I like to keep my work separate from my home life, so I avoided mentioning any specifics beyond that."

Damien's mouth worked, searching for the right words, but he settled for a sigh. "So, what do you even do? Yui said you were the queen's right-hand or something?"

"Ah, can't say more than that. Even to you, kiddo. Sorry," Derrod replied. "You don't do jobs for the queen, and then go chatting about them. If you ever end up employed by her, maybe I'll fill you in. How have you been doing at school?"

Figures. He dodges and goes for even more small talk.

"Uh, good. I guess."

"He's underselling himself, Mr. Vale," Nolan interjected. "He placed third in Blackmist's ranking tournament last year and second in the intermural."

"Did you, now?" Derrod asked, his eyes sparkling. "That's my boy. I wish I could have kept up a bit more with you these past few years, now more than ever. Unfortunately, things on the frontlines only seem to be picking up."

He sighed, scratching his chin for a moment before shaking his head. "Let's not get into that. Introduce me to your friends. I already know Princess Yui, of course. I'd love to hear how you met."

"That would be because of Nolan," Damien said, nodding to the noble. "It was mostly an accident, though."

"A pleasure to meet you. I'm Nolan Gray," Nolan said, inclining his head. "I never thought I'd be personally talking to Stormsword."

"The Gray house?" Derrod asked. "I fought together with your father a few times. He was a good mage. Who's everyone else?"

Damien introduced everyone else, leaving Sylph for last. She hadn't moved an inch since his father had arrived.

"And this is Sylph," Damien said, pausing a moment to find the right words. "My girlfriend."

"Is she now?" Derrod asked, his mouth crinkling. Damien

watched his eyes closely, but his father's face was completely unreadable. "Fascinating. A pleasure, Sylph."

"It's nice to meet you, too, Mr. Vale." Sylph's voice was flat and emotionless.

"Are you here to take us back to Blackmist?" Damien asked, sending a worried glance at Sylph. Something was *definitely* wrong, and his dad was at fault in some way. "Or are you just dropping by before Delph comes?"

"The former. Delph asked me to pick you up since he was busy dealing with some new artifact. Typical, but I was headed in the direction anyway, so it wasn't much trouble. It didn't hurt that I got a chance to see you again after all this time. I really do need to start taking more time off my work before I blink and find that you've already graduated.

Damien was pretty sure Derrod had said that the last few times he'd visited, and those were all before he'd gone to Blackmist.

"You know, you pretty much did the same thing to your mom," Henry pointed out. "Not that I really care either way. I would never."

That's different. I was fighting the Corruption!

"How do you know that isn't what your dad was doing?"

Damien scrunched his nose and mentally pushed Henry back. His companion might have had a point, which made it all the more annoying.

"Delph did say he doesn't need you back quite yet, so I've got no mind to waste what little time we do have," Derrod said.

"What do you mean?" Damien asked.

"Oh, as much as I'd like to steal you away for a few days, we don't have quite that much time—maybe an hour or two. How about you show me a bit of what you've learned? I'm sure your friends would love to see your old man breaking a sweat."

"You want to spar me?"

"Don't worry," his dad chuckled. "I know how to pull my punches. But what better way to trade true words than fighting? Our fists tell stories .our mouths never could."

Damien's mind finally caught up with the present, although he couldn't shake the feeling that he was somehow asleep. "I don't want to make everyone else wait. We've got a lot of stuff to do, and it wouldn't be fair to make everyone sit around."

"Sit around? We'd love to wait," Nolan exclaimed. The others—Sylph excluded—nodded. "You're one of the greatest mages of your generation! Most people never get a chance to see someone of your caliber fight. I still can't believe you're Damien's dad."

"He's like a child overdosing on sugar," Henry said, returning from Damien's banishment. "I don't think I've ever seen him like that."

At least one of us is excited that my dad is here. I wish Delph had just come like he was supposed to. If Sylph knows my dad, that means he had something to do with her past.

"Well, don't blame Damien for it," Derrod said with a chuckle, breaking Damien's thoughts. "Until today, I'd kept my work pretty separate from my normal life. Anyway, why don't you show me what you've got, Damien? Let's see if this old man can keep up with the youth."

Damien sent another look at Sylph. She gave him a reassuring nod, and everyone moved a few paces back, giving him and Derrod room.

"What are the rules?" Damien asked. "We shouldn't waste too much time."

"Let's see—I want to keep things fair for you," his dad mused. "I won't attack to start. I need to gauge your strength so I don't mistakenly hurt you. Your mom has healing magic, but I'd be living out of the shed for the next year if I injured you. For the first round, let's see if you can land a blow on me."

Henry let out an angry murmur within Damien's mind. "Land a hit? I think he's underestimating us a little."

Now's as good a time as any to find out.

"Then, let's see what kind of power he's throwing around," Henry said. "I've got a few things of my own that should make things a bit more interesting. You'd be surprised what you learn from goats."

"Wake up, Damien," Derrod said. "You're staring off into space. Do that on a battlefield and you'll be dead before you know it."

"So long as you don't show up after being missing for a few years, this wouldn't happen on a battlefield," Damien countered, gathering himself. He pushed his emotions away as he cast out his mental net and started to draw Ether into himself.

As the energy traveled through his body and gathered in his palms, Henry slid into Damien's mage armor, activating his combat manifestation.

"Oh, you've got a combat form!" Derrod exclaimed, pleased. "Well done! What can it do?"

Damien cast Warp Step, teleporting behind Derrod and driving a Gravity Sphere into his back. An instant before the spell struck, his father's body shifted. Derrod twirled like a dancer, slipping past Damien's strike effortlessly without wasting a single inch of space.

Henry lashed out with several tendrils, grabbing at Derrod's arms and legs. Derrod dodged out of the way, batting them away before they could touch him.

Ether stormed around Damien, and he sent it through both his feet as well as his hands. He thrust two Gravity Spheres at his father, then kicked another one up while Derrod was avoiding the first two.

Damien teleported before seeing the result, appearing to his dad's left and sending a roundhouse kick at his chest.

Magic detonated around them, but Damien had kept the Ether low enough to avoid damaging himself with his own magic in close range. Derrod managed to dodge every single attack, but he let out a gleeful laugh as he grabbed Damien's shin before the kick could land.

"Not bad, son," Derrod said. "Space magic is impressive. But your attacks need a little more vari—"

The Gravity Sphere Damien had channeled at the tip of his foot shot out, cutting Derrod off before he could finish speaking. Damien twisted, using the momentum to yank his foot out of his father's grip moments before the spell went off.

Derrod blurred, appearing several paces to the side, unharmed. Damien formed multiple Enlarge spells, storing them on the dirt beneath their feet. Derrod lowered into a fighting stance, giving Damien a respectful nod.

Three pillars shot out from the ground. Derrod dodged the first two and used the third to vault himself into the air.

"New rules, Damien!" Derrod called. "We're playing tag, and I'm the chaser."

Damien teleported back, narrowly avoiding his dad. Before he could gather himself, Derrod was before him again. Damien's eyes widened, and he teleported himself into the air, forming a Gravity Lance and teleporting back down.

He slung the spell at Derrod, who sent a tiny spark of blue lightning out from his fingers to meet it. The spells struck each other and fizzled out with a hiss. Derrod blurred, and Damien teleported preemptively.

Despite his fast response, he still felt wind brush past his neck.

"Good block," Derrod said. "I didn't realize your battle manifestation was that fast. How did you see me behind you? Or did you just guess?"

Damien didn't even know what he was talking about until

he realized that Henry must have blocked his dad's hand with the tendrils from the mage armor.

"A mixture," Damien replied.

"You're better than I expected. Very good," Derrod said. "I'm going to start fighting back a bit. I'll be pulling my punches, but don't let your guard down or your mother is going to be very cross."

Blue lightning crackled across Derrod's body. It gathered around his feet, and he vanished. Damien instinctively teleported, but electricity still prickled across his skin. He teleported twice more, but the feeling of growing danger didn't leave.

Damien cast the spell one more time, launching himself far into the air.

Eight Planes, is he following my teleports?

"He is. I think he's watching the minute movements your body makes right before you teleport, then using his speed to catch you right as you get there," Henry said.

"What do you think, Damien?" Derrod asked, launching into the sky beside him. Damien teleported back several feet, avoiding a punch that would have caught him in the stomach, and then cast four Gravity Spheres in rapid succession, throwing them out around himself and forcing Derrod to fly back to avoid getting caught in the blasts.

"Absolutely terrifying," Damien said, teleporting to the ground. Despite himself, he was impressed. Derrod's magic was incredible, and he got the sense his dad was holding nearly all of it back. "Are you actually reading my movements that well?"

Derrod let out a booming laugh. "Figured it out already? Delph is a fantastic teacher. I'm using lightning magic to accelerate the speed that my brain runs at. It gives me a lot more time to analyze what you're doing, and as fast as your Space magic is..."

A hand settled on Damien's shoulder, sending a sharp jolt through his body and making him jump.

"I'm faster," Derrod said, a wide grin stretching across his features.

"Seven Planes, that was amazing," Nolan said. "I didn't realize storm magic had any way to teleport."

"It does," Derrod replied. "But I don't use it in combat. It's not very efficient. What you saw was just speed not teleportation. In fact, Damien's magic is much the same if I'm not mistaken."

Damien nodded reluctantly. "I'm folding space, so I'm not technically teleporting when I use Warp Step. I'm just making the area I pass through a lot smaller."

"A good technique," Derrod said approvingly. "But your face and body give your intentions away. You'll have to work on that or get a mask if you ever get to more dangerous opponents."

"I think he did pretty well," Viv said. "He's only a third-year student, but it looked like he nearly landed a few spells on you."

"It wasn't a bad showing," Derrod agreed. "I'm actually curious to try my hand against a few more of you kids, but my wife is already peeved that I'm fighting at home. She's glaring at us through the window."

Hilla, who was indeed at the window, gave them all a wide smile when she realized she'd been spotted.

"I suppose I should take you all back to Delph, then," Derrod said with a sigh. "If I stay here much longer, word is going to get out that I'm home and half of Ardenford's council will be knocking at my door."

"Don't you want to spar with Damien more or something?" Yui asked. "You only get to see him once in a while."

"I think we've said enough to each other with our fight," Derrod said. "And I think I'll be around the Blackmist area a little more than normal in the foreseeable future. We'll have more than enough time to catch up when all of you aren't waiting on us."

Derrod drew one of the swords from his side and drew a line down through the air, leaving behind a trial of crackling blue energy. When the blade reached the floor, the line split open and formed into a square portal. The energy it put off was enough to make Damien's hair stand on end.

"Go on through," Derrod said. "This'll take you right to Blackmist's obsidian courtyard. I've got a few more things to take care of here, so I won't be following."

"Thanks," Damien said, more than happy to head through the portal. He turned back and waved in the direction of his house. "Bye, Mom!"

Hilla pushed the window open. "Don't wait so long to visit next time, or I'll come find you at Blackmist myself!"

"I won't," Damien promised, then stepped through the portal. Magic tickled his skin as the world went blue. The world twisted around him, warping and swirling like a whirlpool. His foot hit solid ground and the obsidian floor of Blackmist's portal courtyard greeted him.

A wave of vertigo washed over Damien, but he pushed it down and managed to collect himself in time to stagger away from the portal before anyone else could come through. Sylph was the next one through, and Nolan emerged a second later.

To Damien's surprise, the portal didn't close. Elania, Viv, and Eve popped out from within it. Following them was Yui and her attendants.

"Uh...I think my dad forgot to change the location of the portal for you," Damien said. "You might want to go back through before he closes it and tell him he messed up."

"No, this is the right location," Yui said. "We'll be visiting Blackmist for a while, and we won't be the first. That artifact you and Sylph brought back from the Crypt turned out to be quite important, and my mother is buying it off Blackmist."

"I didn't get the impression Whisp or Delph were willing to sell it," Damien said, cocking his head. "Whisp was dead set on getting her hands on it."

A grin tugged at a corner of Yui's lips. "I don't think she's giving them much of a choice. In exchange, Blackmist will get access to a portal that leads beyond the frontlines and into the ancient city of Forsad."

"Forsad?" Damien asked. "I've never heard of it. I didn't realize we had access to anywhere beyond the frontlines. Even if we can get there, aren't the monsters too strong?"

"That's the thing," Yui replied. "Forsad's barriers are still active, even though the city was destroyed. The strongest monsters can't get there, but there's supposedly a huge amount of Ether in the area. It's a great training area with a fair bit of lost magic, so Blackmist will be bringing a bunch of their students as well as those from any colleges able to buy a spot from them on a training mission."

"You've already bought a spot, then?" Nolan asked, not sounding particularly happy about it.

"It was part of the deal my mother struck," Yui said. "Goldsilk bought three spots as soon as they heard."

"And how have they heard already?" Sylph asked. "Was it announced while we were at Ardenford?"

"It hasn't been announced yet, but Goldsilk has more than enough favors to cash in and learn about anything of import happening," Yui said with a shrug. "Everyone wants a chance to make their top students look better, especially after a rather humiliating defeat at the intermural. I'm sure there's a fair bit of interest as to what Blackmist has changed in their teaching methods."

Damien grunted. "It sounds like the Crypt again. Why doesn't everyone always train at this place, then?"

"Activating the portal is incredibly difficult. My mother herself has to do it, and it leaves her weak for a while after activation. Don't you worry—we've had soldiers search the city for years. There shouldn't be anything ground shaking left over, but we might find a trinket or two."

"And when would this be happening, since you already seem to know everything about it?" Nolan asked.

"Probably a month or two from now at the earliest," Yui replied. "Blackmist will have to announce it, choose what students are going, and then see if they want to sell any more spots to other schools. Of course, if things with the Corruption get too bad, it might not happen at all."

"But, long story short, we'll be hanging around for a while," Viv said. "We already got some rooms set up when we first visited."

"We'll have to meet up again for dinner, then," Damien said. "You'll have to excuse me and Sylph, though. We've got a fair bit of work to do now that we're back since we were technically skipping out on school for the past week. Delph isn't going to let us off easy."

"Is Mark going to come?" Elania asked. Viv shot her a sharp glance, and Elania cleared her throat. "Dinner it is. Thanks for the invite."

Damien hid a laugh and waved farewell to the others before he and Sylph headed through the portal and continued up to their room on the mountain. Once they'd gotten back, Damien sat down on his bed across from Sylph.

"What happened with my dad, Sylph? How do you know him?"

Henry slipped from Damien's shadow unbidden. He sent a pulse of purple energy around them, stopping the sound waves from leaving the room so that nobody could overhear their conversation.

"I'm not sure I should say," Sylph said slowly. "I don't even know for sure that I recognized him. It could have been someone that just looked similar. The person I'm thinking of didn't go by Stormsword. I mean...he's your dad."

"Barely," Damien said with a scoff. "I see him like once or twice a year. Sure, he's really busy with the work the queen gives him, but I don't even know what that is. I don't know the guy in any meaningful way. My mom is the one who raised me."

Sylph studied his expression, then nodded. "I think he was the head inquisitor in charge of trying to figure out if they could make me into a weapon for the queen."

"Eight Planes," Damien said. "Did he..."

"Nothing that bad," Sylph said, shaking her head. "He was always kind, I suppose. When I was released, he was also the one who pulled the strings to get me into Blackmist without a real companion. He was still responsible for keeping me locked up, though. The whole thing ended as soon as he decided I wasn't worth the effort."

Damien's hands clenched. "I'm sorry, Sylph. I had no idea."

"I know," Sylph said. "And I don't hold you or your mother responsible for his actions. He and the inquisitors are technically responsible for my release, I suppose."

"They also kept you locked up afterwards," Damien said. "That doesn't excuse them."

"People do a lot of things when asked to by their leaders. Honestly, I'm not totally convinced it was even your dad. He didn't seem like he recognized me."

"I was watching for that as well," Damien admitted. "But he might have been hiding it. If he works for the queen, he's got to have a pretty good game face. He clearly had me fooled. I never knew he was some bigshot agent, going around and kidnapping teenagers."

Sylph laughed and shook her head. "I was just worried he would try to take me back or something. There's no point losing sleep over it now, I guess. Your dad is crazy strong, both in magic and political position. He could do just about whatever he wanted and face no repercussions for it. If he wanted to do something to me, he could have done it there, and not even Yui would have been able to stop him. I just didn't expect to see him, and it brought back emotions that I thought I'd buried."

"I guess that's good," Damien said with a frown. "But I'll make sure he stays away from you as much as possible—not like that'll be very difficult. He mentioned he'll be in the Black-mist area, and I bet that's got something to do with that Forsad city that Yui was talking about. We probably won't see him until then."

Henry's body flickered and condensed, changing into his spherical form. "You've got company at the door. I'm dropping the sound ward."

Damien and Sylph both turned to the door in surprise as it swung open, and Delph strode inside, his cloak rippling behind him.

"I see you two have enjoyed your vacation," Delph said, letting the door close behind him. His cloak didn't stop rippling, even though there was no longer any wind. He flicked it irritably. "Havel, stop it."

The cloak froze.

"Why'd you send my dad to get us if you weren't hunting monsters?" Damien asked, crossing his arms.

"That's an odd question. I thought you'd want to see him." Delph raised an eyebrow. He glanced from Damien from Sylph, taking in the mood. "Ah. Daddy issues, then."

"They aren't daddy issues!" Damien snapped, but Sylph couldn't keep a snort of laughter from escaping.

"It was probably a bad idea, but not for the reasons you're thinking," Sylph said. "I have to say, Dove is a very pretty name."

"Seven Planes, that pompous piece of flaming shit," Delph growled. "He told you my name?"

"And here I thought you liked him," Damien said, then paused as a thought struck him. "Wait a minute. Did you send my dad just to give him extra work?"

The look on Delph's face answered Damien's question without any words, but he confirmed it anyway.

"It might be a possibility," Delph admitted. "If it helps, I didn't know you were his kid when I started teaching you. He was pretty uptight with his home life when we worked together."

"You do know him, then," Damien said. "Can you tell me more?"

"I probably shouldn't," Delph replied. "But that's never stopped me before. Anything you want to know in particular? Stormsword isn't someone you can summarize easily."

"Maybe start with how you learned he was my dad?"

"That's an easy one. The queen told me a few days ago. She's the only one he doesn't keep secrets from."

"How did you meet him?" Sylph asked.

"On the frontlines. He's a strong warrior and a terrific mage. Terrible dinner guest, though. Don't ask more than that, I won't say."

"Why not?" Damien asked. "Did the queen order it or something?"

"Nope. That bit is personal. I'm happy to share information that will inconvenience Stormsword, but not anything that bothers me. You get one more question, I don't want to spend all day here."

Damien couldn't keep himself from laughing. "Fair enough. Then, one more question. What kind of person is he? I know you more than him, and I don't know what to think."

Delph's lips thinned. "He's reliable. When he makes a promise, he keeps it, but only if he promised. Stormsword is ruthless in his service to the queen, and he values nothing more in his life. If he had to choose between anyone and her, he'd choose her. Does that answer your question?"

Damien was tempted to press further, but the look on his professor's face stopped him.

"Yes. It does."

"I've got one unrelated to Stormsword," Sylph said, then nodded at Delph's cloak. "Who's Havel?"

"Stupid little bugger. I told him to be still," Delph muttered, but Damien didn't get the sense he was talking to them. "Havel, you might as well come out. There are enough secrets flying around this room already, one more won't hurt."

As he spoke, gray light washed over him in a similar manner to Henry's sound ward. Delph's cloak twisted around his side and flipped onto his shoulder, detaching from him and folding into the shape of a small man.

"It's good to meet you both face to face, boss mans," Havel said, dropping into a small bow. "I'm Delph's unpaid slave."

"He's my companion," Delph said irritably. "And he's recently gotten into the notion he should be paid for his work."

"I should!"

"What would you even use the money for? It's worthless to you!"

"It's about the principal," Havel said, crossing his tattered cloth arms."

Delph's eyes narrowed. "Was that a pun? I told you about what would happen if you said any puns in my presence."

"You should maintain your decorum in front of students," Havel said quickly, hopping off Delph's shoulder and scurrying over to Sylph. "A professor shouldn't lose his cool."

Delph's eye twitched. "As you can tell, my companion is a bit of a handful."

"I've never seen one like Havel," Damien said. "Nor have I read about one. What is he?"

"An artifact," Delph replied. "A very old one."

Sylph's eyes widened. "Your companion is an artifact?"

"Yes, just like you used to have," Delph said, waving his hand dismissively. "You're lucky yours was inanimate. Havel is a pain in the ass."

Havel turned his nose up. "Your students treat their companions better than you do."

"Hardly." Henry scoffed. "Damien barely lets me stack goats, and he made me break Sylph's original companion."

Havel drew in an affronted breath. "That's horrible."

"That's enough, I think," Delph said. "I'll not have our companions start plotting against us."

Havel let out an amused chatter and unfurled, fluttering through the air and attaching back to Delph's neck.

"Any more ill-advised questions?" Delph asked. "Maybe you'd like to know about my dating life as well?"

"Well, if you're offering..."

"I am not," Delph said. "And, believe it or not, I came here to get a few things accomplished."

"We aren't stopping you," Sylph said with a grin.

"I'd like to see you try. You'll both be resuming your training tomorrow. I expect to see a full manifestation from both of you in the coming month. In addition, it's time to start learning more powerful spells. Aside from Warp Step, your magic isn't up to the level we need to fight the Corruption."

He reached into a pocket and pulled out a small book he tossed to Sylph.

"Nothing for me?" Damien asked.

"Your companion has clearly been teaching you magic," Delph said. "Nothing I have is better than what it knows, but Sylph is now using a mixture of dark and air, so she needs help."

"Smartest thing you've said today. I'm a genius," Henry said.

Delph ignored the Void creature. "There are a few more things to cover, but they can wait. For now, I've got the reward Whisp promised you for getting the artifact, even if it has been commandeered by the queen. You'll get them tomorrow, when you meet me for personal training."

"Two hours before sunrise?" Damien asked.

A small smile tugged at Delph's lips. "Two hours before sunrise."

SEVEN

Damien and Sylph arrived at the arena three hours before sunrise. Delph was already there waiting for them despite their attempt to arrive early.

"You're late," Delph said, pushing away from the wall.

"We came an hour early," Damien pointed out.

"And yet I still beat you to it," Delph replied. "That makes you late in my book."

Damien rolled his eyes. "Fine. What are we doing today, then, professor?"

"You know, I liked it a lot better when you were scared of me," Delph said, rubbing his chin. "Well, then, since you're feeling snappy today, why don't you show me what you can do? I'd like to see just how badly this vacation rusted your skills."

Damien rolled his neck and Henry took over his mage armor. Inky black darkness enveloped his clothing and tendrils emerged from the unfurling cloak behind him.

"How serious are we taking this?" Damien asked.

"As if you could afford to take things as anything but life and death when you're up against me," Delph scoffed. "Come at me with everything you have, but no cheating with your companion's real power. I don't need Whisp breathing down my neck."

Damien locked a Gravity Sphere in place where he stood, then teleported behind Delph. The professor snapped his fingers and a ripple of compressed air shot out around him, forcing Damien to teleport again to avoid getting caught within it.

He cast Enlarge on the sand through his foot, launching a pillar in Delph's direction. The older man raised a hand, and the air warped before it. Damien's pillar evaporated as Delph's spell shredded it apart.

"Somewhat disappointing," Delph said. "Is this really all you can do?"

Damien Warp Stepped directly before Delph, and three tendrils shot out for him. A ripple of magic arced across the air before Delph, slicing the tendrils in half. Without missing a beat, new ones grew from the cloak and shot out once more, wrapping around behind Delph.

While Delph was preoccupied stopping Henry's assault, Damien threw a Gravity Sphere at Delph's chest. He formed two more of the spells, throwing them as well before teleporting back just in time to avoid a spatial red that split the air where he'd been standing.

A blade of twisted magic shot from beneath Delph's cloak, carving all three of Damien's spells in twain.

"Better, but still lacking variety," Delph said. "More, Damien."

Mental pain barrier, please.

"Make it quick," Henry warned.

Damien Warp-Stepped in rapid succession, forming a ring of Devour spells around Delph before stopping a short distance away from him. Gravity Spheres formed in his hands and at his feet.

"Ah. You used this one in the tournament," Delph said idly. "But it's got a glaring flaw. Why do you assume I'm going to stay inside the circle?"

"*Freeze,*" Damien commanded. Ether swirled around him, surging to obey his order. The air shimmered around Delph as the gravity surged, pressing down on the professor. Delph fell to one knee. The effects of the spell didn't spare Damien either, and he was pulled down as well.

"Catching yourself in your own magic. That's not a good look," Delph said, his voice slightly strained.

Damien responded by launching the Gravity Spheres into the black circles of magic behind him. He threw several more into them, then used Expunge to send them flying back at Delph in all directions.

Delph's cloak whipped around him and vanished in a puff of gray light. Damien swore, Warp-Stepping backward. A flash of the fight with Derrod flickered through Damien's memories, and he teleported once more.

"Good reaction timing," Delph said approvingly.

Damien let the ring of spells drop before the draw became too heavy and turned back to face Delph. The professor hadn't been hit by a single attack.

"My dad did something just like that when we fought," Damien replied. "You're showing a lack of originality."

"Don't you turn my words against me, you little brat," Delph growled. "Let's turn the heat up a little. Wake up, Havel."

Delph drove his foot into the ground. A loud explosion shook the arena, throwing sand into the air and blocking him from view. Henry's tentacles whipped out, striking the ground and launching Damien to the side.

A blur severed the tentacles, and a blast of wind knocked the sand away, revealing Delph as he pulled a gray broadsword from the ground. His cloak was gone from its position on his back.

"Hey, that's no fair," Damien complained. "Is that your combat manifestation?"

"No," Delph said with a snort. "This is just Havel pretending to be a sword. You wouldn't last a second against my combat manifestation."

He flicked the sword. A ripple of warped magic shot through the air, forcing Damien to teleport to avoid it. Delph followed after him, initiating a game of cat and mouse. He constantly remained just a half-second slower than Damien, never giving him a chance to do anything but dodge.

"You're using a lot of magic," Henry warned. "I'm holding the strain off, but you're running out of time."

"*Freeze,*" Damien commanded, teleporting to avoid Delph's latest strike and his own spell. Delph slammed to the ground and Damien formed a Gravity Lance with all the Ether he could muster. A streak of black magic screamed out of his hand.

"*Erase,*" Delph said. The spell shattered, falling to the ground like pieces of broken glass. He rose to his feet, brushing the sand off his knees, and cocked an eyebrow. "Still no variation, but at least you've got raw power. If I didn't have about ten ways to counter that, it might have posed a slight issue."

Damien bent over, putting his hands on his knees and breathing heavily as he gathered his breath and tried to repress the growing headache forming at the back of his head. He didn't take his eyes off Delph for a second.

"How many of those ways did I manage to keep you from using?" he asked between pants.

"About two," Delph replied. "For a starting Year Three, that's nothing to scoff at. For what you need to be able to do, though...well, tell your all-powerful companion that it needs to stop being lazy and teach you some new forms of magic. All of your attacks involve throwing something that goes boom and hoping it connects."

Damien opened his mouth, then closed it with a snap. Delph wasn't wrong.

"Is the fight over, then?"

"For now," Delph replied. "Come on, Sylph. Let's see what you can do with that new companion of yours."

Damien flopped onto the sand and leaned against the cool stone wall of the arena. He gave Sylph a weak grin as she stood and paced over to Delph, thin lines of wind whipping up around her.

Twin black daggers formed in her hands and Sylph flickered, fading out of view. Delph clicked his tongue, and Havel unfurled from his sword shape, returning to a cape on the professor's back.

He stomped on the ground, sending out a spray of sand and revealing Sylph's position to his side. She dropped the camouflage with a wry grin.

"I guess that isn't going to work on you."

"It isn't going to work on anyone who's seen it countered before," Delph admonished. "Come on, now. I expect more from you."

Sylph leapt at Delph. He flicked a hand into the air, sending a ripple of energy hurtling at her. She twirled out of the way and flicked one of her daggers at Delph. He knocked it away with his armored forearm.

The wind around Sylph surged, and she accelerated, arriving before Delph with startling speed and thrusting her remaining blade for a gap in his armor. Energy flared around Delph, picking Sylph off the ground and throwing her across the arena.

She spun midair, and a thin disk of air appeared beneath her feet. She launched off it, shooting back at Delph as two more blades formed in her hands.

"Don't you have any magic other than whatever this weird stuff is?" Sylph called.

Delph thrust a hand in her direction, throwing Sylph back again before she could even get close to him. "Yup. Are you really asking for me to make this harder?"

Sylph smirked and flicked two more daggers at Delph as she closed the distance between them once more. Delph snapped his fingers, and a bolt of black energy leapt from them, streaking toward Sylph.

She raised a hand, and the spell vanished with a *pop* as it neared her palm. Delph's eyes twitched in surprise, but he didn't have time to speak before she was upon him. He twisted, taking a strike that would have hit his exposed underarm on his shoulder plate.

Havel lashed out, forming a hammer and striking Sylph in the side. Wind condensed in front of Sylph right before the attack struck her, cushioning the blow. It still sent Sylph tumbling back across the sand, but she hopped back to her feet, no worse for the wear.

"Now, that's more interesting," Delph mused. "You ate my Ether. That explains why you wanted me to use different types of magic. But how many can you absorb?"

Delph snapped his fingers. A scarlet flower bloomed in his hand. Streaks of fire launched out of it, curving and darting toward Sylph. She threw herself out of the way, but the spells twisted to follow her.

Sylph threw several blades of wind into Delph's fireballs, blowing them apart before they could reach her. She skipped back, putting more distance between herself and Delph.

"Not bad," Delph said. "But it doesn't look like you can deal with fire. Is it just dark magic, then?"

"Light as well," Sylph replied.

"Impressive," Delph said. "Limited use, of course. But it could be instrumental in the right situation. Unfortunately, you're going to need more tools that have general purpose applications. It looks like you're already nearly out of Ether."

Sylph pursed her lips and drew the daggers from her waist. "I've still got these."

She dashed at him, but a wall of force shot out from Delph, knocking her back before she could even get close.

"Not a bad idea," Delph said approvingly. "But I already know you're more than capable with physical combat. I've got no need to test you there. Why aren't you using that black gauntlet you pulled out in the tournament?"

"It wouldn't help me here," Sylph replied. "You're too fast, and it takes a lot of Ether. If I used it, I'd just open myself up to a counterattack or just end up wasting energy."

"Then, I believe you see your current deficiencies," Delph said. "Damien needs more magic that can be used optimally in specific situations, while you need to expand your repertoire of magic that can be used in most fights. Essentially, he needs a way to finish fights while you need a way to extend them."

"There isn't much I can do other than end fights," Sylph said, lowering her daggers. "My Core evolution gave me extra Ether to work with, but my Core is still significantly smaller than everyone else's. I can't match anyone on Ether output or regeneration. The only way I can win is to end the fight before it can really begin."

"That's not a bad strategy, but it isn't always going to be possible," Delph replied. "Stronger enemies can't be killed that easily. Especially the Corruption. It's unlikely you'll be able to catch them off guard since we're almost always fighting on their terms. You just need to use spells that are much more Ether efficient than normal. The book I gave you should have a few, and I'll look into seeing if I can locate more if those aren't to your taste."

What do you think, Henry? Do you have a spell that might help me diversify my fighting style a bit more, or should I go to the library?

"Who do you think you're talking to?" Henry asked irritably. "Of course, I have spells that would work. We've just been focusing on giving you the basics so far. I still think Delph is trying to move a bit too fast. You still haven't gotten a perfect grasp over the magic you're using, but I suppose you don't have an eternity to master it."

"It looks like you're both thinking," Delph said. "That's good. As much as I'd like to smack you both around for a little longer, it'll be more beneficial if you get to work figuring out some new magic."

He turned and started toward the exit.

"Hold on," Damien called. "What about our reward from Whisp?"

"You can get that once you land a hit on me," Delph replied, raising a hand in farewell. "It won't do you any good until then anyway."

His cloak swirled around him, twisting into a point and taking him with it until nothing was left. Damien and Sylph watched the spot where he'd vanished in disbelief.

"Did he just steal our reward?" Damien asked.

"I think he'd probably refer to it as an extended borrow, but yes," Sylph said, scrunching her nose. "And what does he mean by it wouldn't do us any good? I'm pretty sure gold is gold."

"He's probably just betting with it," Damien muttered. "Whatever. We better land that hit on him sooner than later because I get the feeling he'll end up using all our money if we take too long."

They both took a turn in the shower and broke off to the

training rooms. Sylph took Delph's book, and Damien called on Henry once they were alone.

"Well?" Damien asked. "Care to share your all-knowing thoughts?"

His shadow twisted, breaking away and forming into a tiny sphere that sprouted three tentacles. Henry's sharp-toothed face formed upon it, followed by two eyes and a pair of amusingly small wings.

"I think about a lot of fascinating things," Henry said. "But on the topic of new spells, I have more than you could possibly learn. What we need to consider is not the strongest spell, but the one that would suit your style of fighting the best. It's about time for you to start specializing."

"Wouldn't it be better to be good at everything?" Damien asked.

"Sure, if you had a thousand years to practice," Henry said with a laugh. "And that would only be by human standards, not those of the Void or the Corruption. No, we don't nearly have that much time."

"Fair enough," Damien said. "So, what do you mean by specialize? I'm already mostly doing Space magic. I could just keep doing that."

"That's just limiting your options," Henry corrected. "Specialization isn't the nature of the magic you use, although that can still tie into things. It's the way you fight. Look at Sylph. She's an assassin through and through. She has a few tools outside of that skillset like that black gauntlet, but her magic is either fast, stealthy, or survivability. The Corruption isn't exactly something she chose, so we can't count that."

"I see what you're getting at," Damien said, rubbing his chin. "I don't think I'm an assassin. That seems neat, and I could see myself fighting like that with Warp Step, but it doesn't feel right. Space magic, particularly gravity, is really destructive. I've taken to it quite a bit."

"That might be because you haven't learned much outside of the field," Henry pointed out. "But I agree with your first point. While you could learn to fight like Sylph, your talents could be used better elsewhere. You should be in the thick of the fight throwing Ether everywhere, not saving your energy for key moments."

"I thought I was supposed to decide this," Damien grumbled.

"Do you disagree with me? I'm only coming to that conclusion by reading your surface thoughts."

"Well, no," Damien admitted. "That sounds about right to me. But isn't that kind of what I'm already doing? You control my mage armor, which gives me defense, and the Gravity Spheres and lances do a lot of damage in a large area."

"They're also slow and easy to avoid if you know what you're doing," Henry said, floating back and forth as if he were pacing. "Delph is right. You're too predictable, and your repertoire is too...flat. To my displeasure, I've come to realize my own fighting style is partially at fault for this. For a Void creature, overpowering strength is an easy default. While I love discovering magic, I didn't have a real need to worry about anything beyond crushing an opponent through sheer might."

"Is that something we can use against that old Void guy who escaped the cave because of Delph and Dredd?" Damien asked.

"It Who Stills the Seas? Absolutely," Henry confirmed. "Whenever he makes his move, that is. It's impossible to say how long it'll be until he does, though. We need to focus on you for now."

"Fine. So, I need some magic that's good in the middle of a fight and is either fast or difficult to avoid," Damien deduced.

"Do you have any pointers to get me started? I'm feeling a bit lost on where I should even begin."

"Well, we can start simple," Henry said. "You're looking for something that can do damage to even a powerful enemy."

"Right, and I want it to serve more purposes than just a direct attack. I need to make it harder to fight me. Something unpredictable or difficult to block. Or maybe just something nobody would expect."

"You can't rely on surprise," Henry advised. "That only works once against a powerful opponent. It's useful, but not something you should base your fighting style off."

"Yeah, that's true. So, something that serves multiple purposes would work well. Like how Devour can be both defensive by blocking and offensive by returning me or my opponents' spells."

"Best get to reading, then," Henry suggested. "There are a lot of things that could accomplish your goal. While you're at the library, pick me up a few books as well."

Damien scrunched his nose and stood. Henry mentally rubbed his hands together like a conniving child. He headed out of the room and made for the library.

A short while later, he returned to his room with a stack of books, only three of which were for him. The remainder were claimed by Henry, who dragged them to the corner and started pouring over their contents. The two got to work reading. Damien scratched notes onto the floor with chalk, taking down any spells of interest and how he might modify them to create something that would fit his needs better.

It didn't take long before a spell started to come together in his mind. Many of the schools of magic seemed to have at least one spell that focused on creating an area around the user infused with their element, either for offensive or defensive purposes.

"Could I mix multiple types of magic for this?" Damien asked, tapping several of the spells he'd taken note of. "Like if I had a domain comprised of both Dark and Space magic so I could make it do more than just one thing?"

"You could," Henry allowed. "It would be considerably harder, but if you pulled it off, it would probably be quite effective. However, before you can even think about that, you're going to need to learn how to actually see Dark Ether. It occurs to me that I haven't actually shown you how to do that yet, so we'll get started there."

Henry sank back into Damien's shadow, then sent his will out to take control of Damien's body. Damien mentally took a step back, observing carefully as Henry cast out a net of mental energy, illuminating the room with golden strands.

How is this any different than just grabbing Space? Ether is Ether.

"Not exactly. I'm most practiced with Space magic, so your vision leans toward it as well. If you want to use Dark magic, you need to find the corresponding strands of Ether," Henry said with Damien's voice.

Damien's eyes furrowed in concentration, and the Ether around him rippled. He reached out and grabbed a golden line. "This has Dark magic instead of Space. Can you tell the difference?"

Not even slightly. It's just gold.

"Look at the pattern within it," Henry said. "It's tiny."

He squinted at the line, bringing it right up before Damien's nose. Even with Henry's help, it took him a moment to spot them. Miniscule runes representing Dark flickered within the golden glow, pulsing in and out of existence.

Eight Planes, I never noticed this before. They're so small.

"That's because they weren't necessarily there," Henry said. "I'm using my mental energy to call to Ether with Dark energy in it. The runes are my own energy identifying the strand. Since my natural state would call to Space instead of Dark, you don't need to do more than you already do."

I see. So, how exactly are you using your mental energy to do that? Is it just like direct casting?

"Not really," Henry said. "You aren't actually communicating with the Ether when you do this. It's more like you're telling your own mind what to look for. It's just a matter of practice. Let me get through the whole spell, and then you can ask questions after."

Damien gave him a mental nod and Henry resumed, drawing the Dark Ether into Damien's body. The mote of energy felt clammy as it ran down Damien's arm and into his Core. It floated a short distance away from all the Space Ether, as if it didn't want to mix.

"Ether types reject each other," Henry said. "That's why casting spells with two different types is more difficult. However, with sufficient mental energy, we can force it to bend to our will."

He took the Dark Ether and a mote of Damien's normal Space Ether, then pulled them out into his palm. Henry worked the tiny sparks of energy, melding them together into a churning ball that sent jolts of lightning racing through Damien's body.

Two tiny orbs of black and purple light formed above Damien's hand. Henry's mental energy plucked and pulled at them, forcing the light together and creating a pair of inter-locked runes.

"Keep the shape in mind," Henry said. "I've forced each type of Ether into a rune, then forced them together so that neither can diffuse because it's trapped by the other. You'll obviously have to do this within yourself, I'm just showing you what to do as an example."

Henry let the magic disperse, then drew another mote of Dark Ether into him and restarted the process. This time, he left the Ether in Damien's body. It was difficult for Damien to tell when his companion finished the spell, but Henry eventually brought the magic up to Damien's palm.

He traced a line through the air. A perfect replica of Damien's arm, made up of thousands of tiny black and purple specks, followed after it a second later. Henry moved around for a few seconds, letting Damien observe the artificial shadow tracing his actions.

"I'll do it a few more times so you can try to get more of a feel for it before giving it a shot yourself," Henry said before doing just that.

He then returned Damien's body to him and let the boy take his own shot at the spell. Damien ran into difficulty almost immediately. Despite Henry's words, shifting the way he looked at the Ether proved significantly more difficult than he had expected.

It took a severe headache and over three hours of constantly trying to coax his mental Energy into identifying the Dark Ether before he finally managed to spot a flicker of a Dark rune on one of the strands of Ether.

"That's it?" Damien exclaimed, wincing as his loud voice jabbed into his head like rusty spikes. "It's so simple! Why does it work like that?"

Henry snorted. "I'm not philosophical. Don't ask me."

Damien paused, a thought pushing past the pain bouncing around his head. "Wait, *are* there gods? You would probably know about that, right? With the whole Cycle thing—"

"Don't ask that question," Henry said flatly. "I'm not answering it. You don't want the answer to it. Also, you're talking out loud again."

Damien opened his mouth to respond, then grimaced. He

scurried off to the shower, letting the healing water soothe his head for a few minutes before he tried forming coherent thought again.

He considered asking Henry why the topic was so taboo but decided against it. Henry had been honest with him for some time now. If there was something that bad about pressing that particular question, he trusted his companion enough to leave it be. Instead, Damien returned his attention to learning how to cast Wake.

Now that he could actually see the Dark Ether, it was trivial to draw it into his Core. Instead of trying to form it within himself, he copied what Henry had done the first time and brought it out over his hand so he could see what he was doing.

Mixing the two types of Ether proved significantly more difficult than Damien had expected. It was like trying to pinch two skinned grapes between his fingers. The energy slipped and warped in every manner except the one that Damien wanted it to.

"Is it actively working against me?" Damien asked in exasperation.

"You're giving it too much leeway," Henry said. "Control it with your mental energy. Don't just push in one direction. Completely enclose it and squeeze the Ether into a mold."

Damien grunted in a mixture of annoyance and understanding. Individually, he had no trouble forming both runes. The problem arose when he tried to mix them, which resulted in everything either falling apart or warping beyond usability. It took him several dozen more attempts and a little over two hours before he managed to get the Ether to begin to show semblances of following his requests.

By the time he did, his heading was pounding with such a horrible headache that he immediately headed straight back to the shower. Once the pain receded enough for him to think straight, he activated his wristband.

Damien Vale
Blackmist College
Year Three
Major: Battle Mage
Minor: Dredd's Apprentice
Companion: [Null]
Magical Strength: 15.8
Magical Control: 4.5
Magical Energy: 30.1
Physical Strength: 2.2
Endurance: 4.4

More increases across the board, but he could barely bring himself to feel smug. The exhaustion was just too strong. He finished his shower and headed back into the main room. As soon as Damien spotted his bed, he flopped into it and fell asleep.

Henry woke him several hours later with a mental poke. He groaned, not opening his eyes. His bed felt warmer and comfier than usual, and he could still feel the aftereffects of the mental exertion rattling around his head.

Eh? What is it?

"I'm pretty sure you've got people headed for your door," Henry replied. "I can't tell more than that. They aren't drawing much Ether, so I'm pretty sure it's Nolan and the others. I thought you might want to be awake before they arrived."

Damien reluctantly opened his eyes and quickly discovered the reason that his bed was more attractive than normal. Sylph shifted, looking up at him.

"Henry heard them coming?" she asked, unentangling herself from him.

"Yup," Damien said with a reluctant sigh. Now, he wanted to leave even less, but it wouldn't be fair to back out now. "Did your training go well?"

"As well as I could expect," Sylph said. "I read through Delph's book a little, but I'm going to focus on a full manifestation before I start working with that."

"Probably a good idea," Damien said. "Henry is still working on mine."

"Has anyone ever told you how unfair it is that Henry actually does half the work?" Sylph asked. "My companion tries to help, but it can't just create the full manifestation on its own."

"I'll have you know I do much more than half," Henry said indignantly, his voice emerging from a tiny mouth at the edge of Damien's shadow. Damien squished it.

They climbed out of bed, and Damien brushed his hands through his hair, trying to smooth it out a little.

No more than a second later, someone rapped on their door. Sylph pushed it open.

"I hope I'm not here too early," Nolan said. Reena peeked over his shoulder, but Nolan pushed her back down. "We can come back later if needed."

"No, now is fine," Damien said, hiding a yawn. "Sorry, I've been training a bit. Is everyone else here yet?"

"Kind of," Nolan said. "They're trying to convince Mark to come. He wants to train instead."

"Oh, this ought to be fun," Damien said with a chuckle. "Let's go, then. I want to see."

CHAPTER
EIGHT

They found Mark in his room, surrounded by the Goldsilk girls and with a dozen swords on the ground around him.

"It's just dinner," Mark said irritably, holding one of the blades up to the light to examine it. "I don't see the point of spending so much time on it. Besides, I already ate."

"When?" Elania asked, crossing her arms. "And it won't take that long."

"This morning," Mark replied. "I've been busy."

"You've been staring at a sword for the last thirty minutes," Viv pointed out, trying to hide a smile. "We won't force you to come if you don't want to, but you really shouldn't lock yourself up like this."

"If I go, dinner will end up stretching on for hours, and you'll probably decide to do something equally as pointless afterward, dragging me along with you," Mark said, setting the sword down with a grunt and picking up another one.

Eve's eyes crinkled in amusement, but she seemed content to let the others speak. As far as Damien could tell, she wasn't a woman of many words anyway.

"But Damien and Sylph are going," Elania said. "If they can

find time, why can't you? If constantly training without any breaks was that effective, you'd be winning the tournament instead of them."

Mark paused at that. His gaze shifted over to Sylph before traveling over to Damien. "You're back from training?"

"We weren't training," Damien replied. "We were on vacation, actually. Delph mandated it."

"Elania said you and Sylph were training," Mark said with a frown.

"More like we trained them," Damien corrected. "We didn't actually do much training ourselves. I did a bit in my free time, I guess. Nothing serious. The break feels like it did a lot of good, actually. It helped me recalibrate myself a little, you know?"

Mark rubbed his chin. "I take breaks, sometimes. They're called sleep."

"When's the last time you actually sat around and did nothing for a few days?" Damien asked. "And for that matter, why hasn't Delph told you to rest for a bit? You've been at this longer than I have."

"Delph mostly lets me do my own thing," Mark replied with a shrug. "He can't exactly teach me much magic I can use as I don't share any types with him. All he can do is hone my combat skills, and I show up to class for that."

"Don't you ever feel like your progress is slowing down?" Nolan asked. "There's only so hard you can push yourself."

"Eh. Progress is progress," Mark replied.

"Not if you account for what you're losing by trying too hard," Reena said. "If you get too tired and lower your potential to learn, you might spend five days figuring something out that would normally take you one."

Mark mulled over their words for a few seconds. "I see what you're getting at, but I feel like you can just push yourself past that point of worsening return until you surpass it."

"In the time we've spent arguing, we could have already gotten to a restaurant," Viv pointed out. "Just saying."

"Gah. Fine," Mark said, hopping to his feet and sheathing the sword at his side. "Let's just get it over with, then. I don't think you're going to go anywhere until I say yes."

"Glad to see you've come around," Nolan said. "We should take the opportunities we get to relax when we can. Things are only going to get busier for us from here on out."

"You mean the ranking tournament coming up?" Mark asked as they walked out of his room and headed down the mountain path.

"No, I'm talking about the strange new monsters that have been popping up all over the kingdom, seemingly out of nowhere," Nolan said. "The ranking battles are important but, at this point, I'm not even sure how much they matter."

"If they even happen," Reena said. "I've heard rumors saying that students might get called on to help suppress the monster attacks."

"Are they really getting that bad?" Damien asked. "Sylph and I have kind of been out of the loop."

"A lot of the professors are gone to help the surrounding cities," Viv said. "Although Blackmist still has a fair number of them in the area. The attacks seem random, but it's believed they're under the control of a dangerous monster that's planning something. Nobody wants the schools unprotected since a lot of them house dangerous artifacts."

"That's worrying," Damien said with a frown. Second was clearly gearing up for something, but he had no idea what it was. He doubted it was just the artifact he and Sylph had gotten from the Crypt, or Second would have just showed up at Blackmist. Whatever happened to Moon, Damien suspected the man wasn't in a position to oppose Second at the moment.

"It's not as bad as Viv makes it sound," Elania said. "Most of the attacks have been in pretty remote areas, and there are a fair number of mages that are capable of fighting them to a standstill. I know a few of them tagged along with Delph to figure out how he fought the Corruption and know how to fight them as well."

"The queen hasn't sent out any word that we should be more concerned about this than what the situation implies," Nolan said. "For now, let's leave it to the professors. If the situation was really that dangerous, they wouldn't be sending us on an expedition to the ruins of Forsad."

The others nodded, and conversation fell into a lull as they made their way through Blackmist's campus. Instead of heading to the dining hall like Damien had expected, Reena took the group over to a large, open-faced restaurant.

Several chefs manned the kitchen, making large bowls of soup while waiters dashed from table to table, delivering dishes. A set of stairs in the corner led up to a balcony that overlooked a large garden.

Reena took them up the stairs and over to a long table at the edge of the railing, where Yui and her attendants were sitting.

"I'm sorry we're late," Reena apologized. "We had to spend some time convincing Mark to come."

"It's quite all right," Yui replied with a small smile. "I only just arrived a few moments ago. I've heard good things about this restaurant."

"The Frisky Fish hardly seems like a name for an upscale joint," Gaves grumbled. "But the view is nice."

They sat down, with Damien and Sylph taking the chairs at the far end of the table. A waiter floated up over the edge of the balcony, nearly giving Damien a heart attack as the man alighted beside the table gracefully.

"Welcome to the Frisky Fish," the man said, making the name somehow sound sophisticated. "We have several fresh catches from off the coast today, and I would highly suggest them to anyone looking to experience the flavors of the sea without having to travel beyond the comforting walls of Blackmist."

He spread his hands out, summoning menus before himself and sending them flying out to land before everyone at the table. "I'll be back shortly once you've all come to a decision. Do you have any questions before I go?"

"I think we're good for now," Reena said.

The waiter inclined his head and leaned back over the balcony, flipping once as he fell over the edge. Damien resisted the urge to rush over and peer over the railing. Henry did no such thing, splitting a tendril off Damien's shadow and slithering up to the railing to look over it.

Damien tried not to glance down at his companion. He didn't need to bring any more attention to Henry than was necessary.

"So, how has training been going after your break?" Yui asked, crossing her fingers on the table.

"Surprisingly fruitful," Damien said. "I've been making a fair bit of progress, although it'll be hard to say anything for sure until a few days have passed. Delph just trounced both me and Sylph in sparring matches and told us we needed to work harder."

"Sounds about right," Nolan and Reena said simultaneously. They glanced at each other, then looked away.

Damien picked up his menu and scanned through it. There were a lot of fish dishes, which he supposed made a fair amount of sense given the name of the restaurant. They were also all reasonably expensive.

He eventually settled on one that didn't look too fancy and was mercifully only a few silver instead of a gold. The waiter returned a few minutes later as promised, bearing glasses of water for all of them. Once they'd been distributed, he took their orders.

Nobody was surprised to find that Yui ended up ordering the chef's special, which happened to be a ludicrous ten gold. Everyone else settled for more appropriately priced dishes. Both Sylph and Mark ordered the same meal Damien had.

"We haven't sparred in some time now," Mark said idly, taking a drink of water. His words sounded considerably flatter than usual, almost as if they had been rehearsed. "Now that we're all here, we should get in some practice together sometime this week. It would be a good use of our time, and I'm sure we'd all enjoy spending time together."

Out of the corner of his eye, Damien spotted Elania give Mark a discrete thumbs up.

"I want to get a better grasp of the new spells I'm working on," Damien replied, holding in a laugh. "But I'd be happy to afterward. Maybe in a week? We didn't get a chance to fight during the intermural, so it'll be interesting to see how we stack up against each other."

"Same with me," Sylph said. "I can't speak for anyone else, though."

"We'd all be happy to take some pointers from you," Viv said. "If I'm being honest, half the reason we're here is because we want to figure out how Blackmist got such a menacing group at the tournament. Sparring with you will be an excellent way to do that."

"I would love to join as well," Yui said. "But let's not talk about that for now. We do so much fighting already, it would be nice to move our attention elsewhere for a few hours."

"We don't do much other than fight and train," Mark pointed out, returning to his normal cadence. "What else would be worth talking about?"

"Well, there's the excursion coming up somewhat soon,"

Yui said. "But let's not worry about that either for the moment. Perhaps you could tell us all a little more about Blackmist? I've only been here for a short while, so I don't know much about the area."

"To be honest, I don't know that we know much more than you do," Damien muttered. "We've spent almost all our time here fighting or training. I didn't even know this restaurant existed. I normally just eat at the dining hall or cook in our kitchen."

"I remember you mentioning that," Yui said. "Your room has a kitchen?"

"Well, we had to make it," Damien replied. "We just got a tiny room to start off with. I used destructive energy to grind away the walls and make some extra rooms."

"Ah. They gave me the same thing," Yui said.

"Blackmist doesn't differentiate between nobles and normal students," Nolan said. "It's...somewhat refreshing."

"I can't say I agree," Reena said with a small frown. "But it's fine. You get used to it. Kind of."

They chatted for a few more minutes until the waiter brought their food over. He placed an enormous platter bearing the head of a fish easily large enough to feed a small family in front of Yui, then distributed much more appropriately sized meals before everyone else.

Yui eyed her fish with distaste. But, to her credit, she didn't hesitate to dig in when everyone else started to eat. She offered everyone a portion the meal, although Damien politely declined. He was pretty sure the fish was still staring at him.

The meal finished a short while later. Damien let out a relieved sigh and leaned back in his chair, stuffed beyond words.

Mark burped. "Anyone up for a spar?"

A cacophony of groans drowned him out. After paying the

waiter for their meal, they all dispersed to head back to their housing. Damien considered practicing his new spells a little more, but he dismissed the thought. The meal had been far more filling than he'd expected, and he didn't feel like regurgitating it.

His thoughts turned to Nolan, and a small frown tugged at his lips. The conversation he'd had with Yui before leaving Ardenford tugged at the back of his mind. At the very least, he'd have to tell Nolan about it. He didn't know what it really meant for the noble boy, but it wouldn't be fair to keep it from him.

Unfortunately, before Damien could pull Nolan aside, the other boy broke away from the group, saying that he had some business to take care of. Damien made a mental note to take care of it when he saw Nolan tomorrow.

He and Sylph got back to their room and exchanged a glance.

"You going to practice?" Sylph asked.

"Probably not," Damien said. "You?"

"A little," Sylph said. "My companion is starting to come around a bit, and it doesn't take too much out of me to communicate with her."

"Ah! Your companion is a she," Damien exclaimed. "That's the first hint you've given me."

"And the last one you get for now," Sylph replied with a grin. "I'll try to keep things down, though. See you tomorrow."

"See you," Damien said, watching her head into the training rooms.

"I wonder what we could accomplish if you had her training ethic," Henry mused. "We'd probably have destroyed the world a year ago."

Hey, that's hardly fair. I think I work pretty hard.

"You do," Henry admitted. "But that's not as funny."

I still don't understand how you came to develop such a horrible sense of humor.

Henry's laughter followed him into bed.

Delph woke them the following morning for his normal class. He was gone by the time they got up, of course. All that remained of him was a slip of brown paper. The class went as normal, with Delph mostly overseeing their general progress and giving suggestions on fighting strategies.

After the class finished, Damien pulled Nolan aside. He regurgitated what Yui had told him about his father getting closer to deciding on an heir. The noble boy didn't speak, but the tightening around his eyes and the worry crossing his features said more than any words could. Nolan thanked Damien and headed off, seemingly lost in thought.

Dredd was waiting for them after Nolan had left, but he only exchanged a few words with Sylph before going to dismiss them. Both he and Delph seemed distracted. Damien and Sylph had their own things to worry about, so neither complained about the classes being cut short. Still, as they started to head back, Damien paused and caught Dredd's attention.

"Why is my minor listed as your apprentice?" Damien asked. "On my wristband. Shouldn't it be magic theory or Rune Crafting or something?"

Dredd blinked. "What? I didn't do anything like that. Between us, those bands aren't doing your abilities much justice. The numbers and the strength of your companion don't add up, so I can tell he's modifying it. Don't worry—it's not noticeable, and I only noticed because of the strength you showed over the summer. But I certainly haven't been doing anything to your band. I couldn't care less about it."

Damien frowned, then his eyes narrowed. "Delph?"

"Almost certainly. I'd suggest ignoring it," Dredd said. "If you bring it up, he's almost certain to change it to something worse. If you'll excuse me, though, I have some meetings to get to."

Damien nodded absentmindedly, waving farewell and heading off together with Sylph. They both got back to training as soon as they returned to their room. Once Damien was alone, Henry peeled away from his shadow and leaned against the wall to watch him practice.

Dark Ether came to Damien easier today than it had the previous day, and it only took him a minute to bring the energy to his fingertips. He shot a triumphant glance at Henry. "Now, I can get started with the actual spell."

"And what were you thinking for it?" Henry queried.

"I want to mix the types of damage I'm doing," Damien replied. "I was thinking about Devour and how it only stops magical energy. I bet a lot of spells are meant to specifically stop one type of attack, so if I swap it up, it'll be a lot more dangerous."

"Go on."

"So, I was thinking of something like a storm of stuff flying around me. Rocks, magic, and then darkness to obscure all of it to make it harder for people to block or see where the attacks are coming from once they're near."

"That's possibly the lamest way to describe what actually sounds like it might be a fascinating spell," Henry said. "How about you call it Storm and never describe it again?"

Damien rolled his eyes. "Oh, get over it. If you think it'll work, then I need to start with telekinesis so I can pick the stones up."

"Right. It's one of the easiest Space spells to learn, so you shouldn't have trouble there."

Damien started to nod, then paused. "Wait. Why didn't you start me off with telekinesis? That feels like it would have been way easier to learn than Gravity Spheres. Probably would have been more universally applicable as well, considering I can do more than destroy things with it."

"It was boring," Henry said, sounding ever so slightly apologetic. "I did say I skipped a few fundamentals."

"No wonder Delph thought I was lying," Damien muttered. "My teacher is an idiot."

"It's your personality messing me up. This is your fault," Henry said, crossing his arms. "Now, do you want to learn the spell or not?"

"Just show me," Damien said, shaking his head. "And are there any other fundamentals you skipped that I should know?"

"Oh, dozens," Henry said, then shot back into Damien and snagged control of his body before the boy could reply.

Damien flicked him with a small blast of mental energy, then sat back to watch his companion work.

"This should really be quite simple for you," Henry said, taking a mote of Ether that already resided within his Core. "Use Space Ether and envelop it with your mental energy. Then, kind of stretch it as you release the spell, enveloping the object you want to control."

Henry extended one of Damien's hands toward a loose stone on the floor. A flicker of faint purple magic ballooned from his hand, washing over the stone and lifting it into the air.

"The only thing you have to keep in mind is that you've got to maintain connection to your mental energy the entire time," Henry continued. "The moment you let go, the spell ends. Most mortals I saw using this spell would just pick rocks up and throw them, releasing their mental energy right after so they wouldn't overstrain themselves."

He took a figurative step back and let Damien control himself once more. The boy repeated Henry's motions and was pleasantly surprised to find that the spell seemed to be just as easy as Henry suggested.

There was minimal work changing the Ether within himself, and he was able to form a disk of magic without too much difficulty. He enveloped the rock Henry had demonstrated on, then willed it to rise into the air. The rock floated up to his eye level. A faint purple sheen hummed around it.

"Huh. It actually worked," Damien said, sending the rock in circles above his head.

"It *is* a beginner spell," Henry grumbled. "I'd be worried if you couldn't get it. Just make sure not to overexert your mental energy on this spell. It's a lot of effort for a pretty basic result."

Damien nodded. The rock did a little dance around him, then shot off into the wall and broke into several pieces with a sharp *crack*.

"That's a fair bit of force," Damien observed. "I could do some damage with this."

"Not as much as a Gravity Sphere. Much lamer, too."

Damien snorted. "On to the other spell, then. I was hoping you could actually give me a suggestion for this one. I don't want to use Gravity Spheres since it'll be so close to me. I need something more accurate and difficult to see."

"I suppose I can lend a hand at this point. You've gotten most of the spell figured out anyway," Henry decided, pulling a mote of Ether from Damien's Core and bringing it out as destructive energy so Damien could watch him shape it. "This is called Tear, and I think it fits what you're looking for perfectly. It actually functions like the opposite of Warp Step but works offensively instead of for mobility. Instead of compressing space, you split it apart in a small area."

Henry worked the Ether through a series of patterns slowly enough for Damien to memorize them, then let the spell fade and drew another mote of Ether.

"Allow me to demonstrate," Henry said, pulling the Ether through Damien's arm. It burst from his fingertips, sending a dark purple crescent moon about the size of his palm shooting through the air. The spell flitted into the wall and vanished.

It didn't do anything.

Henry formed a glove of destructive energy and scooped a portion of the wall away, much to Damien's dismay. He tossed it into the air, then sent another crescent moon flying at it. Two perfectly smooth halves clattered back to the ground.

"It did do something. It cut right into the stone, but the slice is so thin you can't even see it," Henry said. "And there is a reason I didn't show you this particular spell before today. It's very easy to make a small mistake and accidentally release it inside your body or just cut limbs off on accident. It's a lot of danger for a spell that's easily blocked by any form of magical defense."

That's probably for the best. I think I would have lost a few digits if I'd tried learning this earlier. Actually, I'm not convinced I won't lose them learning it now.

"I've been observing how you control Ether," Henry said. "You've gotten passable at it, so I think you can handle this spell. It really isn't that difficult, but making a mistake will punish you very heavily. Unlike Gravity Spheres, Tear doesn't need a command to do damage. It'll cut through what it hits, be it you or anything else."

He went through the runes to imprint into the Ether one more time, with Damien occasionally interjecting to ask a question. They spent almost an hour just going over the theory before Damien tested the runes out outside himself.

It was another few hours before Henry proclaimed Damien's progress sufficient enough to let him start practicing the spell for real. Damien steadied his breathing and turned his concentration inward, repeating the pattern he'd been reviewing with careful, practiced commands.

Controlling the Ether when it was inside his body was still

significantly harder than controlling it once it had left since he couldn't see what he was doing. He finished the pattern and pushed the Ether out of his palm.

A thin blade shot from his palm and sank into the wall. The spell was considerably smaller than the one Henry had made and lacked the moon shape. Damien grinned and raised his hand to wipe the sweat from his forehead.

He paused as he spotted a thick sheen of blood flowing down his little finger. Damien swore and rushed to the shower, thrusting his hand under the water.

"Not too bad," Henry said while Damien shook his hand off. "Your pinky was too close to the spell, though. That's why I sent it out of your fingers instead of the palm."

"Noted," Damien said, letting out a small sigh as the cut sealed up. It had been so fast and clean that he hadn't even felt any pain, but the amount of blood still felt like cause for mild concern.

"Are you okay, Damien?" Sylph asked, walking up behind him.

"Yeah. I just cut my finger practicing a new spell," Damien replied, turning to show her his healing hand. "Sacrifices in the name of progress, or something like that."

Sylph rolled her eyes. "I was worried your less amiable imaginary friend was making itself known."

"Oh. No, it's been pretty silent recently," Damien said. "Can't say I mind. It's nice. How's sharing with your companion going, though? It must feel a bit weird."

"You're going to have to try harder than that if you want information about her." Sylph grinned. "But it occurs to me that neither of us could use our full strength in the tournament. It would only be fair to have another match where we didn't have to hold back."

"By the pool Delph showed us?" Damien suggested. "If I

win, you have to show me your companion and tell me everything about them."

"Hmm. That's a lot," Sylph said playfully. "And I already know a bunch about Henry. Then, if I win, we do whatever I want for a day."

"Why do I feel like that's going to be running for twelve hours?"

Sylph cocked an eyebrow. "Only one way to find out."

"Fine," Damien laughed. "Deal. But I want to get a handle on the spell I'm working on right now. Let's do it in three days."

"I was about to say the same," Sylph said. "Three days it is. I'm going to get right back to practicing, then."

"Good luck."

"I won't need it," Sylph said with a grin. She headed out of the bathroom, leaving Damien staring at her back.

"Better get to work," Henry said. "I'm not so sure you're going to get Storm under grips in three days, but I do think she might be trying to motivate you to try harder. It would be pretty funny if you lost to her for the third time, though."

Oh, shut it.

Henry cackled as Damien returned to his room and got back to work. Time flew by as he practiced, only stopping to attend Delph's classes, eat, and sleep. In between working on the new spells, Damien also practiced direct casting.

Unfortunately, Henry's prediction was more accurate than Damien had hoped. He made progress with both Tear and telekinesis, but Henry wouldn't even let him start on Storm, claiming that he wasn't nearly competent enough with Tear to risk it.

Damien wasn't about to argue. He managed to cut himself several more times with the spatial blades, nearly removing a finger more than once. If it hadn't been for the healing water, he would have garnered some nasty scars for the rest of his life.

Before he knew it, three days had passed. Damien found himself standing across from Sylph a short distance away from the healing pool. The sun had only just started to rise, and faint yellow rays poked through the trees surrounding the clearing. Dull orange hues danced in the sky overhead.

"Did you manage to get your new spell?" Sylph asked.

"No," Damien admitted. "I've gotten some new stuff, but not the one I was working on. What about you?"

"You'll get it soon enough," Sylph replied. "Unfortunately for you, I didn't have any such difficulties. I've got a full manifestation now."

"Congratulations!" Damien exclaimed. "What is it?"

"You aren't supposed to be excited for that until after the fight," Sylph said with a laugh. "And you'll see in a few moments. You're going to need a lot more magic than what you've used at the tournaments if you want to win this. I've already got tomorrow all planned out."

Damien cast out a net of mental energy, drawing Ether into his Core. "There's only one way to find out. Are you ready?"

Henry commandeered his shadow and walked over to the edge of the woods to watch. Sylph raised an eyebrow.

"You're not going to use his power?"

"That would be two versus one," Damien replied. "I'm keeping this fair."

Sylph snorted. "You better not regret that. I'm ready."

Wind whipped up around Sylph, and she shot at Damien. He threw a Gravity Sphere at Sylph, but the wind around her surged, and she launched to the side, easily avoiding its range and closing the distance between them.

Damien tried to cast Warp Step, but he was unsurprised to find the spell failed to activate. A black blade sprung into Sylph's hand, and she swung it at Damien's side. He hardened his mage armor, blocking the strike.

"Blocking my magic already? Really?" Damien asked, ducking under another attack.

Sylph kicked him in the chest, sending him stumbling back.

"Anything to win," she replied, then flicked the blade at him. Damien smirked, then vanished. Sylph's eyes widened, and she spun, narrowly blocking his kick before it connected.

A Gravity Lance leapt from Damien's hand. Wind surged to meet it, and the spells canceled out. Sylph blurred and shot back several feet.

"How are you casting magic?"

"Your anti-magic works the same way as the Corruption draws the Ether from the world, you just connect to me instead," Damien said, teleporting again and throwing a Gravity Sphere at her. "Now that I know how it works, I can break it."

Sylph jumped, wind carrying her far into the air to avoid Damien's spell.

"We'll have to do this the normal way, then," Sylph said. The wind churning around her surged in intensity, growing almost completely opaque around her feet.

Damien teleported high into the air to avoid whatever she was preparing. Sylph spun, then looked straight up at him and started sprinting in his direction.

Ripples of air ran out from every footstep she took as Sylph ran straight up through the sky. Damien's eyes widened, and he Warp-Stepped back to the ground. Sylph's form seemed to grow faster as she spun in the air and shot back toward him.

He teleported twice, trying to throw her off. It bought him a moment, but Sylph spotted him quickly. She blurred, and he barely had time to teleport before she was upon him. This time, Damien was certain she was moving faster with every passing second, and she didn't show any signs of slowing down. If he continued playing her game, she'd get lucky and catch him.

He reached out through the connection to the Ether within his mind.

"*Stop,*" Damien said. What felt like an enormous hammer slammed into Damien's back, staggering him. Sylph, who hadn't been prepared for the spell, crashed to the ground. She rolled over, groaning as she forced herself to her feet.

Damien pushed more power into the spell, bringing her to her knees. The air around them shimmered with faint purple light.

The wind around Sylph flared once more, and she started to slowly rise. Damien gritted his teeth and reached out with his mental energy. Then, he cast two more spells on the earth beside Sylph.

Two giant pieces of stone erupted in front of her and slammed together with a loud crash. Damien released them, letting the rocks *thud* back to the ground.

CHAPTER
NINE

"If you'd been between those, I think you would have been squished," Damien said, his voice shaky from speaking while trying to maintain direct casting.

Sylph inclined her head, and Damien dropped his last spell. She flopped to the ground and rolled over, staring at the sky.

"You weren't kidding about holding back," Sylph said after a moment. "Now, I honestly feel a little guilty about the tournament. I don't deserve first place."

"Sure you do," Damien replied, sitting down next to her. "The circumstances were different. If we were to repeat it, I'd lose every time. I just can't use direct casting in front of other people yet. It would raise too many questions."

"Yeah, but you've more than surpassed me in strength," Sylph. She scooted back so her head rested against Damien's thigh. "It's a bit embarrassing, to be honest. I've been training for years, and you're already stronger than I am."

"I kind of have a cheat," Damien said, nodding to Henry. "Not to mention direct casting. I didn't even learn that myself. Moon gave it to me. When I can't use my unfair advantages, you crush me."

"There's no such thing as an unfair advantage in a fight," Sylph replied. "There are only winners and losers."

Damien pursed his lips. "There's also the situation of the fight. Your skillset lends you more toward being a mobile fighter that zips in and out of a fight, while I'm more suited to an all-out slugfest. If the location or circumstances we fought in were different, you'd probably have done much better."

Sylph leaned back to look up at him. "That's actually quite insightful. You're not wrong. I'm just disappointed in my own performance. With all the training I've done and gotten, I should be able to do at least a little better against you."

"Well, I don't think any less of you for it. You'll probably figure out what you can improve on and hone it to perfection before our next fight."

Sylph's cheeks reddened a shade, and she sat up. "That's sweet of you, Damien."

Henry made a gagging noise across the clearing. Damien was actually slightly grateful for it, as he had entirely no idea what to follow that up with.

"Hey, Damien. Check your little band thing," Henry said. "I've improved it."

Damien's eyes narrowed, and he pulled his stats up immediately. Something in Henry's voice made him think that the change wasn't going to be for the better.

Damien Vale
Blackmist College
Year Three
Major: Battle Mage
Minor: Bedwetter
Companion: [Null]
Magical Strength: 16.4
Magical Control: 5.1

Magical Energy: 33.9
Physical Strength: 4
Endurance: 7.2

"Seriously?" Damien asked.

"Better than Dredd's apprentice. Besides, it's not even wrong. How many times have you bled all over a bed?"

Damien opened his mouth, then closed it again. "That's not what that word means."

Henry cackled. "Just focus on your abilities! You're growing quite quickly. Good improvements to Endurance and Strength."

"You're the one changing them half the time!" Damien complained. "I don't even have a good read on how strong I am because you modify everything the stupid band sees."

"I could let it actually read us," Henry offered. "We could see how that would go."

"No thank you," Damien said promptly. "I'm quite okay with it right now."

"Fantastic. Bedwetter it is."

Damien sighed, and Henry laughed even harder.

"Sylph, I think I might be able to help you a little. Damien was right about one thing. You aren't using the full potential of your powers. In particular, you seem to have latched onto the Corruption's ability to draw out Ether and ignored the other boons you gained from it."

"You mean this?" Sylph asked, raising her arm. A curved blade sprouted from beneath the skin just below her wrist, running parallel up to her elbow.

"That's one aspect of it," Henry agreed. "The Corruption are deadly because of their tenacity, which might seem like it wouldn't lend itself well to your fighting style, but I've seen the Corruption in other Cycles, and it can be incredibly effective if used in the right way."

"I don't see how they're much better than normal daggers aside from me being able to have a little more control over them," Sylph replied.

"I can show you," Henry said. "We'll have to see just how many of the Corruption's abilities you inherited before we can determine how far I can go."

"That doesn't sound fast. Damien also needs practice," Sylph pointed out.

Henry snorted. "He can work without me. There's only one more thing I need to teach him before he can start learning the real spell we've been practicing. I'll do that, and then see what I can do for you."

Sylph glanced at Damien. "Are you sure?"

"Of course, he is," Damien said. "I'll probably learn better without that asshole peering over my shoulder anyway."

Henry's eyes all rolled simultaneously, which was slightly nauseating to look at.

"Then I won't refuse," Sylph said. "I want to be able to get stronger. Half to fight the Corruption, and half for myself."

"We should get to it, then," Damien said. "Henry, do you think I have a good enough grasp of Tear to try to put it together and cast Storm yet?"

"You could try very, very carefully," Henry said after mulling over his words. "And only while we're next to a lot of this healing water. No using it anywhere else until I give you permission or you'll take your own head off on accident."

"I'm going to go practice a little on my own before Henry is ready," Sylph said, standing up and helping Damien to his feet. "I'll meet you back at our room."

"Hold on, what about your companion?" Damien asked, cocking an eyebrow. "I think I won a bet."

"Oh, right," Sylph said. She pursed her lips and extended her hand, palm up. Wind twisted into a tiny white sphere above it, condensing and forming into small features. It turned into a tiny woman with translucent wings and two faint red pinpricks for eyes.

Damien burst into laughter. "I— You know, that kind of makes sense. You got a sylph."

"Sylph got a sylph," she agreed with a wry grin. "I didn't have much room to get a companion with a lot of energy, so I'm lucky she showed up. Unfortunately, we're in a bit of dispute over who can use my name, so she doesn't have one."

"You both want to be called Sylph?" Damien asked. "But she *is* a sylph. That would be like you wanting to be called Human."

The tiny figure jumped up and pointed at Damien, letting out a high-pitched titter. Sylph's eye twitched slightly. "I think she's just decided on a new name."

"Oops."

The small fairy laughed, her wings fluttering as she took off and flew in a tight circle around Sylph's head before bursting into tiny streamers of wind.

"Human seems interesting," Damien hedged.

"She's a bit of a handful, but I appreciate her, nonetheless," Sylph admitted. "Her magic is also very useful. I can't quite fully understand her words yet, but I'm starting to get portions of conversation. I wish we could talk like you and Henry, though."

"I am pretty great," Henry agreed. "But not everyone can be as cool as I am."

"Just keep telling yourself that," Damien said.

Sylph shook her head, hiding a grin. "I'll actually head off this time, then. Good luck training."

"To you as well," Damien replied. Sylph headed out of the clearing, leaving him and Henry alone. The void creature melted into a pool of shadows and returned to Damien.

"Tell me exactly what your plans are for Storm so I make sure you don't accidentally feed the fishes," Henry said.

"Well," Damien started, "I want Storm to work by casting hundreds of very miniature versions of Tear, interspersed with telekinesis to throw a bunch of shit around myself. The next thing I wanted to practice was making a bunch of small Tears at once."

"Good," Henry said. "That's the best thing to work on next. You can already multicast Gravity Sphere, so you'll just have to apply that a little more and send the magic out of more spots on your body. I figure you want me to be able to help Sylph as much as possible, so I'm going to focus on the stuff you need me to show you. Just this once, since I can already tell what you're going for, I'm going to show you the final version of the spell. You've already decided on it, so this shouldn't impede your creative process much and should help you from dying on accident."

That works for me. Let's do it.

Henry took control of Damien's body. He drew a large amount of Ether from the lines surrounding them, taking equal parts Dark and Space. Working methodically but quickly, Henry took several dozen of the motes of energy and started to shape them.

It was the most Ether Damien had ever felt used for a single spell. Even though the spells Henry was forming were just Tear and the normal telekinesis, the sheer amount of Ether and mental energy he was working with was significantly higher than anything else Damien had ever done.

Henry sent the Ether out through Damien's body. Instead of just using his hands, the motes pushed out all over his skin, forming a faint haze around his body. The air around him crackled with power.

Clumps of dirt and rock tore away from the ground and floated up around Damien, starting to spin around him. Flashes of purple light tore through the air, growing in speed and intensity. At the same time, the light faded in a small sphere around him and obscured the projectiles surrounding him.

For the first time, Damien realized that he and Henry had picked a very apt name for the spell. The mixture of the impossibly sharp purple energy surrounded by hurtling stone formed a wall around him, tearing up the ground at his feet.

He walked up to a nearby tree. A series of resounding cracks split the air and the wood was simultaneously shattered and carved into tiny pieces. It tipped back, crashing to the ground with a loud bang.

Eight Planes. This is incredible.

Henry let the spell fade, dropping rocks all around Damien. The spatial magic had carved them up into tiny pebbles. "And dangerous. Imagine what would have happened if I lost concentration and you moved your hand just a bit."

That sobered him up pretty quickly. His fingers weren't any tougher than a tree. Henry let out a satisfied grunt.

"Just start by casting lots of miniature Tear spells. Once you can do that, mix in some telekinesis. This spell is too difficult to sustain far from your body, so you have to center it on yourself. Just sit really still when you start."

Henry gave Damien back control of his body.

You make that sound a lot easier than it is.

"You're the one who suggested it," Henry replied with a mental shrug. "It won't be easy, but you've got a healing pool right here. Just take things slowly and don't chop off anything too important. Do you need me to show you it again?"

Not yet. I have enough to work with, and there's no point getting overwhelmed. I'll focus on multicasting Tear for the moment. Who knows, maybe it'll take me so long that you finish up with Sylph before I get on to the actual spell.

Henry snorted. "We'll see. I'll go find her, then."

He split away, stealing Damien's shadow and shooting off into the forest in the direction Sylph had gone.

Damien watched him leave, then sat down at the waterfront. He let out a slow breath and inhaled, drawing Ether into his Core. Accessing the Dark Ether still wasn't very natural to him, but he managed it within a minute.

He sent the energy to his hand, warping it along the way, and cast Tear out over the water while making sure to keep his fingers safely out of the way. The spell shot off along the water and faded a few feet later.

Nodding to himself, Damien repeated the process, but this time made the spell smaller and tried to use less energy. The result was a similarly sized yet considerably wobblier spatial tear.

Grimacing, he repeated the process. And then he did it again. And again. The sun traced through the sky and started its downward descent. Damien didn't budge from his spot at the edge of the lake.

By the time night had fallen, Damien had lost count of the times he'd cast the spell. A powerful headache had built up multiple times throughout his practice, but the healing lake was enough to push it back into a slight annoyance instead of an insurmountable pain.

The fruits of his labor hadn't been quite as much as he'd been hoping for. He'd managed to work his way up to casting Tear without cutting himself on accident, and he was able to do as many as three at once.

Unfortunately, Henry was using dozens upon dozens when he cast Storm. Damien continued practicing well into the night before he felt weariness finally start to overcome his senses. Not wanting to seriously injure himself, he stopped for the day and headed back to his room.

Henry was at the door waiting for him. His companion

silently slipped back into his shadow after he stepped through the door. Sylph laid in his bed, sprawled out in every direction.

Any luck?

"Some," Henry said. "She's got a lot to do if she wants to get a good handle on the Corruption. The connections I made to save her weren't perfect, and I've reworked a few of them. There are more that I'll take care of tomorrow, and she'll have a lot of experimentation ahead of her. How did your practice go?"

I couldn't get past Tear, but I'm getting better. I should be able to start on Storm in a day or two, if all goes well. It just depends how fast I can learn to multicast.

Henry let out a pleased grunt and receded into the back of Damien's mind. Damien glanced at his bed, which was currently occupied, then mentally shrugged and climbed in beside Sylph as quietly as possible. She shifted in her sleep, crinkling her nose and throwing an arm over him. The endless ocean of sleep swallowed him shortly thereafter.

He trained and practiced the spell within his mindscape through that night and the next. It was two days of ceaseless practice later when Damien managed to cast Storm for the first time. The spell was about a tenth of the size of the one Henry had made and sputtered out after just a few seconds, but it didn't stop Damien from pumping his hand in the air.

Every attempt after that one slowly nudged him closer to the true spell, expanding the range it covered and the duration it lasted by small but significant increments. He managed to cut himself deeply several more times in the process, but he'd taken to practicing right beside the lake, so he avoided any lasting injury.

Damien drew on the Ether, ignoring the headache setting in after what must have been the hundredth spell in the last few hours. He distributed it throughout his body, shaping and releasing the magic before it could leave him.

Clods of dirt ripped out of the ground, already ravaged by all his practice, and whipped through the air around him as miniature scars of purple light split the air around him. Damien kept stock still as the spell expanded around him, forming a rough sphere.

He continued drawing Ether into him while casting the spell, sustaining it as long as possible. A slow grin started to stretch across his face after the one-minute mark passed. Exhaustion had already set its grips on him, but he forced it back.

Damien moved his hand through the air slowly. The destruction warped around it like he was pushing through water. A few small cuts appeared on the back of his wrist and palm, but none of them were serious.

The spell fizzled out and Damien stuck his arm into the lake. He then dunked his head in as well to fight off some of the headache. Once it had faded, he wrung his hair out and headed back to his room, a smug grin etched into his face.

It faded when he realized the door was open. Delph leaned against the wall, studying his fingernails. Sylph sat across from him, and Henry had taken up his spherical form to float beside her.

"Did I miss out on a meeting or something?" Damien asked.

"I'm just coming by to check in on your training," Delph replied. "And to share some news. I only just arrived, so you haven't missed anything. Congratulations on the spell."

"Oh, thanks," Damien said. "Wait, how did you know?"

Delph chuckled. "I'm here to let you know this year's Ranking Battles have been postponed and, in all likelihood, canceled. Yui has probably filled you in already, but the Ruins of Forsad take priority and we'll be heading there shortly. Blackmist is putting that at a higher level of importance."

"Do we have to fight for our spots to get in or something?" Damien asked.

"That would be ridiculous. You're the strongest third-years by a significant margin, although I suppose Mark might be able to give you a good fight. It's a moot point, since three students from every grade are going to the ruins. Well, every grade but first."

"For free?" Damien asked suspiciously.

"Well, Whisp is a little indebted to you, even if the artifact got stolen," Delph replied.

"I see. Is it just us from the third-years?" Sylph asked.

"And Mark," Delph said. "Anyway, that's not the only thing I'm here to talk about. The other schools that managed to buy spots in the expedition are sending their students over. We're going to be introducing everyone shortly, and there's sure to be some dick measuring."

"You're telling us not to stir up trouble?" Damien raised an eyebrow.

"On the contrary. Slap it on the table," Delph said. He paused. "Figuratively. You've already got Goldsilk and Kingsfront in your corner, but there are some pretty strong year four students from the other schools. There should be some interesting stuff in Forsad, so the last thing you want to be dealing with while you're there is people thinking they can steal from you."

"Wait, stealing? I thought we were supposed to be working together," Damien said with a frown.

Delph waggled a hand. "You're all taking the same way there and back, but the city is large and there won't be a ton of supervision. There should be a fair number of artifacts in the area, even with the amount the place has been searched. When great wealth and power comes into play, morals go out the window. I'd expect at least a few freeloaders to try and lift your work off you."

"Are they likely to try to kill us?" Sylph asked.

"If they're dumb enough, sure. But, to be honest, I'd expect them to just try to rough you up and take anything you've found. With how the frontlines are going and the Corruption intensifying its assault, everyone knows we don't have mages to spare."

"Okay, so we're just trying to be intimidating so that they don't all try to take our stuff because we're only Year Threes," Damien said.

"Pretty much," Delph agreed. "It'll be easier if you make a strong first impression, and I'm sure there'll be a fair amount of sparring going on before we leave. The last representatives from the other schools should arrive at least a week before we set off, so there'll be a fair amount of time to get to know everyone."

"Sounds good," Damien said. "And when exactly do we leave?"

"About three weeks," Delph replied. "As of now, the only groups that have arrived are Goldsilk, Kingsfront, and Mountain Hall."

Damien and Sylph both grimaced.

"Mountain Hall?" Damien asked. "Are you sure that's a good idea? Both Drew and Bartholomew were working with Second."

"It's a school, Damien," Delph said. "They aren't all working under Second. How many third- or fourth-years do you even speak to or know from Blackmist?"

"Two," Damien admitted, thinking of Sean and Don, Sean's large friend. "And I've only really spoken to one of them."

"There you go," Delph said. His expression darkened for a moment. "That being said, I did look into the representative Mountain Hall sent. She's a fourth-year and specializes in Magma magic. She's got some strength for a kid, but everything I found indicates that she has absolutely no interest in anything other than fighting and getting stronger. She reminds me of Mark."

"We'll keep an eye on her," Damien decided, sitting down on his bed. "It would probably be a good idea to get ready before we met too many of the other students, though."

"Smart," Delph said. "I'll let you get to that."

"Some supplies would probably be appropriate," Damien continued. "If only my teacher hadn't shamelessly robbed me and left me destitute."

"I unfortunately spent my entire gold supply on pastries, thinking that I would have our prize from Whisp to make up for it," Sylph added. "I sure hope Professor Delph didn't put any money on us looking impressive in any sparring matches. We're going to be on a diet of the free lunches from the dining hall."

"Oh, shut it already," Delph grumbled, drawing a gray line in the air with his finger. He reached into it, pulling a small portal open, and pulled out two large bags that he tossed onto the bed beside Damien. "It was to motivate your training. And renovate my house."

"Doesn't Whisp pay you enough to do that?" Damien asked, peering inside one of the bags. It was completely stuffed full of gold. There must have been at least one thousand, and more if Damien had to guess.

"My job takes most of the money I earn," Delph replied with a shrug. "Teachers don't get paid nearly as much as we deserve for dealing with you goblins. I need some extra sources of income every once and a while."

"And that just happens to be us?" Sylph asked.

"Glad you understand," Delph replied. "I've canceled my class tomorrow. Dredd won't be bothering you either. Go probe the students from the other school and see just how much you can figure out about them. Maybe have a sparring match with Mark or something. I know he's been waiting for that."

Delph waggled his fingers in farewell and his cloak whipped around him, swallowing the professor up. Damien rolled his eyes and handed one of the bags of gold to Sylph. "I'm pretty sure they've got about the same amount of coin."

"Thanks," Sylph said, glancing around, and then stuffing it under her bed, right next to the rest of her coin stash. Damien took a fistful of the gold out to put into his travel pack, then followed Sylph's example with the rest of it.

"How did your training end up going?" Damien asked.

"Not bad," Sylph replied. "I think."

"It's going at a decent pace," Henry said. "I've repaired most of the problems, so we're just working on Sylph's usage of her powers. Now that she's got proper access to them, there's some new magic that's actually novel to me that she should be able to develop. It's like a mix between the Corruption and what we'd consider 'normal' magic. It should be...fascinating, once we get it working."

There was a note of primal hunger, born from his incessant desire to learn new magic, within Henry's voice. It was just enough to remind them that the companion was still far from human.

The sun was already setting outside, so both of them headed to bed. Neither had the energy to get any more practice in today.

After waking the following morning, the two of them headed out to follow Delph's suggestion and find Mark. The boy still didn't have anything covering his room, so it was impossible not to peek inside as they approached.

Mark sat on his bed, inspecting one of his swords. He glanced up as Damien and Sylph stopped outside the entrance of his cave.

"Has it already been a week?" Mark asked.

"No," Damien replied. "More like five or so days. But we were thinking of checking out the people who showed up for the expedition from the other schools, and then doing some sparring to see how we match up."

"Now, that's an idea I can get behind," Mark said, hopping to his feet and grabbing a belt. He slung it around his waist and slid the sword into a sheath at its side. "We can spar with some of the older students once we finish. If they're anywhere near as disappointing as the rest of the people we met at the tournament, it'll be a joke."

"They weren't all that bad," Damien defended as they started down the mountain. "And you did tie with Bartholomew."

"A few of them were okay," Mark said after a moment. "But I want a challenge. Bartholomew was okay, but you went and killed him."

"How many people is Elania going to tell about that?" Damien asked, groaning.

"Just me and the others from Goldsilk," Mark replied with a shrug. "It's not like it matters. Fighting wasn't completely prohibited just discouraged. Nobody knows exactly what happened, so they can't prove it wasn't self-defense."

"It *was* self-defense," Sylph said. "And we didn't technically kill Bartholomew. He kind of did it to himself."

That wasn't entirely true, considering Second had been the one to land the killing blow, but Bartholomew had thrown his lot in with the Corruption, so Damien didn't find any fault in her words.

Mark took the lead when they reached the base of the mountain, setting off through the campus toward the north side.

"Wait, do you know where the other students are already?"

Damien asked. "I thought we'd have to go find someone to ask for directions."

"Yeah," Mark replied. "Elania showed me where they were all staying, and I saw some other people wearing colors that looked like they were from other schools. It's not much farther now."

Damien and Sylph exchanged a glance. They didn't say anything else and just let Mark take them to their friends—and possible competitors.

CHAPTER
TEN

Mark led them up to a mountain on the far side of the school. Damien knew there were other caves where the students lived, but he'd never actually been to one of them before. Instead of heading up the path, they walked into a large pavilion at the mountain's base.

"What's this place?" Damien asked.

"It's a training area," Mark replied as they climbed the stairs leading up to the big, open doorway at the front of the pavilion. "Only for visiting schools to use."

They reached the top of the stairwell and headed inside. The pavilion was two stories. On the bottom floor was a thick bed of sand and several training dummies on the far end, all scorched and smashed to pieces.

Above it, a balcony hung over half of the arena. It was set with tables, lounge chairs, and large crates full of weapons and armor. Yui and her entourage sat on the top floor across from Eve. In the arena below, Elania and Viv sparred. A tall, girl woman that Damien didn't recognize was laid out flat on the sand on the other side of the arena, her brilliant orange hair splayed out like a halo around her.

They walked up the staircase leading to the second floor, and Damien spotted two more students he didn't recognize. A large boy, almost as large as Bartholomew had been, sat at a table alone, watching the arena with an unreadable expression. At the edge of the balcony, a hunched form was bent over a pile of scrap.

Yui raised her hand in greeting as they approached. "How has your training been going?"

"Well enough," Damien replied. "We just wanted to see what all of you were doing. I had no idea Blackmist had a location for visiting students to stay and practice at."

"All the colleges do," Yui replied. "It's not that uncommon to have transfer students for a month or two. Many students want to specialize in something that the teachers in their college just aren't that practiced with, so they swap over to get some instruction from someone else for a little while."

"I don't think that happens at Blackmist much," Eve said, her voice a soft whisper. "Our rooms looked like they hadn't been touched in years. They're nice, though."

"C'mon," Mark said, nodding down at the arena. "You've seen them. Let's spar."

"We haven't even figured out who everyone is yet," Sylph said. "Yui, do you happen to know already?"

"I do. The large boy is from Greenvalley. His name is Teddy. The person in the cloak near the balcony is representing Flamewheel, and I've got no idea what their name is, nor do I know if they're even a boy or a girl. And the girl lying down in the sand is Mountain Hall's. Her name is Quinlan."

"How do you know where they're from but not who they are?" Damien asked, sending a glance at the hooded figure out of the corner of his eye.

Yui shrugged. "I couldn't find any information on them. I

only know they're from Flamewheel because my mother told me. I don't even know what year they're in."

"Isn't that a little concerning?" Sylph asked. "This is an important mission, should some random person really be allowed in it?"

"Oh, don't worry about that," Yui said, waving her hand. "I don't know who that person is because my mother didn't tell me, not because I can't find out. I'll know soon enough. This is just a test for me. She wouldn't actually put me at serious risk from an unknown like that."

Damien grunted and Mark shot him a pointed look as Elania and Viv finished their sparring match. They were both breathing heavily and covered in scratches, but from the expression on Elania's face, it was clear Viv had won.

A man materialized in the air beside them, washing both girls with healing magic before vanishing once more. Damien's eyebrows rose.

"You have a personal healer?"

"Just on certain days," Yui replied. "It's to encourage sparring sessions between us so we can learn from each other. It's unfortunately not working as well as I'd hoped, though."

"What? Why not?" Sylph asked.

"Well, aside from my group and the girls from Goldsilk, nobody will spar," Yui said, rolling her eyes. "They won't fight me because I'm the princess, and they keep coming up with new reasons why they won't fight everyone else."

"Well, that's lame," Damien said. "But it doesn't seem that bad. Maybe they just aren't the combative types?"

"More like they don't want to show their strength," Sylph replied softly. "It might not be a good idea for any of us to spar, either. We don't want to give anything away if they're planning something when we enter Forsad."

Damien mulled over his words, then grunted. "Nah. I'm

here to get stronger, and I already promised Mark a fight. If they want to play this like cowards, that's fine by me. Besides, I doubt I'll even have to show anything too important. Mark is going to have to put in a lot of work if he even wants to make me sweat."

"Hey!" Mark exclaimed, but the only emotion in his eyes was excitement. "You've gotten real cocky since the last time we fought. If I recall, it didn't go so well for you."

"Time and practice change a lot of things. Let's see if that sword of yours is good for anything other than cutting vegetables," Damien said, Warp Stepping and appearing on the sand. Mark leapt over the railing, landing nimbly beside him.

"Oh, hi, Mark!" Elania said, stopping at the edge of the stairs. "I didn't realize you were here. Hi to you as well, Damien."

Viv raised her hand in greeting. Damien returned it with a nod.

"We're just sparring," Mark replied. "Come on. Let's get this started. You can't taunt me, and then just chat."

"We'll talk in a few seconds," Damien said, turning back to Mark with a grin.

Stay out of this for now, Henry. Sylph is right. We shouldn't give everything away. Delph said to put on a show, but we'll keep your strength as our trump card.

"Just don't lose," Henry said. "That would be pathetic."

Damien rolled his eyes and pushed his companion back.

"Ready?" Mark asked, his skin starting to take on a faint red hue. Mist rose from his body and puffed out from his nose with every breath. Damien clearly hadn't been the only one practicing.

"Let's do this," Damien said. The sand surged, gathering around Mark's legs and launching him forward like he was surfing a wave. Damien teleported, channeling Ether and flinging two Gravity Spheres at the other boy.

He detonated the spells in quick succession, but Mark managed to launch himself into the air and out of the range of the spells. Damien grinned, grabbing Mark's clothing with telekinesis and slamming him into the ground.

He started to raise Mark again, but his connection snapped as a dozen lines of red light flashed around Mark. Sand erupted around him in a huge cloud. Damien teleported to safety instants before a brilliant flash carved through the sand where he'd been standing, turning a portion of it to glass.

Mark stepped out from the cloud, his body hissing with red energy. The glowing visage of an armored warrior overlaid his features, making it difficult to make out where one started and the other ended.

Damien reached out with his mental energy to try to cast telekinesis on Mark's clothing again, but his magic slipped off the other boy's red shell. Attempting to grab his sword gave him the same result.

With a roar, Mark bounded forward. Damien teleported to the other side of the arena, right into the path of a blast of red energy. His eyes widened, and he teleported once more, narrowly avoiding getting bisected.

"How'd you know where I was going?" Damien asked, flinging a Gravity Lance at Mark. A wall of sand erupted between them, blocking the spell.

"Tremor sense," Mark replied with a smug grin. "You're still on the ground, and I'm faster than you."

Three more arcs of red light flashed toward Damien. He gathered his Ether and teleported once more, bringing two Gravity Spheres to his palms and flinging them as quickly as they formed. Mark's sword flashed, carving the spells apart before they could detonate.

Damien didn't relent, pushing closer as he peppered his opponent with a barrage of magic that would have been foolishly wasteful if it had been done by anyone else. The sheer amount of magic hurtling at Mark forced him to fight defensively, unable to find an opportunity to break away.

Gravity Spheres detonated all around Mark, but whatever the red warrior was, it protected him from the majority of the damage Damien's magic could do. The ones that hit Mark directly only dented or cracked the armor, while the ones that went off beside him didn't even manage to pull him off his feet.

As ineffective as the barrage of spells was against Mark, he only had so much Ether to work with. The cracks in his armor spread with every second, and they both knew the fight would be over the second a single spell managed to break through it.

Mark and Damien came to the same conclusion. The red energy around Mark surged, and he darted forward, sweeping his sword out before him and sending a wave of red energy burning toward Damien.

Damien cast Devour in front of himself, absorbing the magic before it could touch him. He dismissed the dark circle, already knowing what he would find on the other side and hardening his mage armor.

Mark's sword slammed into Damien's arm, sending vibrations coursing down into his body. Damien flicked his hand, sending the prepared Tear spell straight into Mark's chest with a purple flash.

He teleported back, and Mark made to step after him. Blood trickled down the boy's chest, and he glanced down in shock as the trickle turned to a river. A healer appeared beside Mark, golden strands of energy reaching out and dismissing his magic while the healer sealed the wound shut. Once he was done, the man vanished as quickly as he'd arrived.

"What was that?" Mark exclaimed, touching his shirt. A

long slash ran down the material from the top of his shoulder to right above his hip, so thin that it was invisible until he moved it.

"A new spell," Damien replied. "It was a good fight, though."

Mark grunted. "I didn't even get to try out everything I wanted to. I didn't think you'd have such a fast spell. How deep was that cut? I didn't even feel it."

"I'm not entirely sure," Damien admitted, rubbing the back of his head. "If there hadn't been a healer here, I wouldn't have risked it."

"Damn. Next time, I'm just summoning my full manifestation right from the start," Mark grumbled. "My performance was pathetic."

"He is the second strongest student at Blackmist," Yui said, peering over the edge of the balcony. "You did underestimate him, though. That's on you. If you treated your opponents as equals, you'd do better."

Mark nodded, not looking even slightly offended at her unrequested advice. "It'll go different next time."

"You still did really good," Elania offered. She headed down the stairs and gave Mark a thumbs up. "I can't believe you managed to withstand that barrage of spells."

"Yeah, well," Mark paused, reconsidering his words. "Thanks. I'm sure you would have lasted at least a bit."

Damien fought to keep the surprise from his face. That was as much of a compliment as he'd ever seen Mark give someone weaker than him. Sylph caught his eye and waggled an eyebrow, nearly causing him to burst out in laughter.

"Your last attack almost got me," Damien said. "Even with my mage armor, my hand is still tingling. If you'd gone for my head instead of my side, I don't know if I would have been able to block it."

"It was a sparring match," Mark replied with a shrug. "We weren't trying to kill each other."

The cloaked figure at the edge of the balcony caught Damien's eye. There was a tiny flash of green from beneath their hood as they realized Damien had spotted them, and they turned away.

"Are you going to spar as well?" Mark asked Sylph.

"You just got squashed by Damien, and now you want to try your hand against Sylph?" Yui asked.

"How else do you think you get stronger?" Mark asked.

"I wouldn't waste the breath on him," Gaves advised Yui. "That one's a maniac. I don't think his brain even functions if he isn't fighting."

Mark didn't even bother refuting that statement. He just glanced around, checking if anyone would take him up on his request.

"I'll spar you," Elania offered meekly.

"Perfect," Mark said, grabbing her by the wrist and dragging her toward the far end of the arena. Damien turned to start heading back up to the second floor. Quinlan, the girl from Mountain Hall, stood as he passed her.

"You've got a lot of magical energy," she said, pulling her vibrant hair back out of her face. "What level is it at?"

"I've got some," Damien agreed. "And I don't think I'm particularly inclined to answer that. You haven't even told me your name."

"Princess Yui already told you it."

"Yup. You don't look like Princess Yui to me. If you're going to go around asking people for personal information, the least you could do is be a little cordial."

Quinlan's lip twitched up in the slightest hint of a grin, but there was something else on her face Damien couldn't read. "My name is Quinlan. I'm a fourth-year student at

Mountain Hall, and I specialize in Magma magic. How's that?"

"Better," Damien said. "I'm Damien, and I'm a third-year student at Blackmist. I specialize in Space magic."

"So, about that magical energy level..."

"Nope," Damien replied with a grin. "I'll be keeping that to myself for now, but it's nice to meet you."

Sylph hopped over the ledge, landing beside them and barely displacing the sand in the process. Quinlan's expression shifted slightly, but Damien still couldn't get a read on it.

"This is Sylph," Damien said, putting a hand on her shoulder. "The first ranked student in the second year of Blackmist."

Sylph snorted. "For now."

"I-it's nice to meet you," Quinlan said, clearing her throat. "I, uh, have to go now."

She turned and headed out of the pavilion at a brisk pace. Damien and Sylph exchanged a glance.

"What's her deal?" Damien asked quietly.

"No idea," Sylph said with a small frown. "Her expressions didn't make sense. I'm missing something."

Henry?

"Already on it," Henry said with a cackle. "Check this out."

A tiny portion of Damien's shadow, only the size of a sliver, broke away from his feet and shot off toward the wall, vanishing in an instant.

"That'll let me trail her," Henry said. "Since my senses are ruined by your human soul, I had to figure out another way to track things down. I'll take a peek at her later when nobody is staring at your shadow."

With Mark and Elania off to the side of the arena practicing, nobody else seemed particularly interested in sparring. Damien and Sylph chatted with Yui's table for a while, occasionally trying and failing to pull in the students from the other school.

When it grew late enough, they headed off to get dinner. The two grabbed a quick meal at the mess hall before setting off to their rooms.

"Mark seems to be getting along with Elania pretty well," Damien observed.

"I'm surprised he hasn't managed to insult her yet," Sylph said with a laugh. "Then again, she seems just as determined to get strong as he is, so it works."

"They do fit together," Damien agreed. Sylph nodded, but a pensive look crossed over her face. They reached their door and headed inside, sitting down.

"Do you ever wonder what it would be like if we didn't have to deal with...everything?" Sylph asked, waving her hands around. "Like if I wasn't made to be a— Well, you know. And if you didn't have Henry. If we were just normal students."

"I never would have become a combat mage if that were the case, and you probably wouldn't have come to Blackmist," Damien replied. "And I don't know if I can imagine life without Henry."

"That's true."

"Last year, I made a decision not to question or wonder about the hand I've been dealt," Damien said, moving to sit beside Sylph. "I was so out of control of my own life that I felt like I was going to shatter. I was just drifting along, doing whatever I was told. It felt like there wasn't any other option."

"So, what changed?"

"Nothing, really," Damien admitted with a wry grin. "The world is still a gentle push away from a violent end from either the Void or the Corruption, but I can't control that. I just realized that the only thing I really could control was how I dealt with the situations I was dealt, and I was done being tossed around. Even if I've only tricked myself into thinking that I've got more control, it still helps me feel better."

Sylph nodded slowly. "That's one way to look at it. I just hope that we can find some way out of this that ends well so we can finally have a chance to relax without the threat of doom hanging over us."

"That's a problem for tomorrow," Damien said. A smile flickered across Sylph's face, and she inclined her head. They stood up and started preparing for bed.

Henry, you've still got that tracker on the Quinlan, right? Do you need me to do anything to help find her?

"Nah, I've got it," Henry replied. "The Mountain Hall girl stopped walking around a few hours ago, probably in her room inside the mountain. The security in Blackmist for student housing is nonexistent, so this will be a joke. You've got no stealth abilities, so you'd just get in the way."

Good luck, then. Fill me in tomorrow, or in my dreams if it's urgent enough.

Damien laid down next to Sylph, yawning as his shadow peeled away from him, taking Henry with it as it slipped out of the room.

———

Henry flashed through the streets of Blackmist, just barely managing to hold back a gleeful laugh as the world sped by him. Traveling with Damien was fine, but nothing really beat moving around of his own volition.

Unfortunately, as far as he could tell, there weren't any goats in the vicinity. That would have really made the night more interesting. If he had a few more days with the strange little creatures, he was pretty sure he'd break his own record in goat stacking. Instead, he had to settle for following the scrap of magic he'd attached to Quinlan.

Her mountain was directly behind the pavilion that all the

other students had set up in. He spotted Yui and her two retainers sitting at the table, but the others had all left. Henry slowed, considering stopping to listen what they were talking about but decided against it. There would be more than enough time to spy on the princess later.

He flickered up the side of the mountain, along a remarkably similar path until he was nearly level with his shadow. Three rooms were inlaid into a small plateau in the side of the mountain. Each one had a carved metal door complete with runework.

Sending a pulse of mental energy out, he received a response from the room in the center. Henry slipped up to it, bypassing the runes without a second thought, and entering the room behind it.

If Damien had been there, his eyes would have popped out of his head. Quinlan's room was the size of a small building. Her bed was outfitted with a very soft-looking mattress, complete with puffy blankets and a plush Devourer Beast toy.

A fully equipped kitchen took up the left wall, and there were four doors along the wall. Her bathroom alone was nearly the size of Damien and Sylph's entire room, and it had color changing runes carved into the walls.

His magic called to him from behind a large wooden dresser behind Quinlan's bed. Henry slipped up to it, passing through the gap between the bottom of the dresser and its doors. He pushed past a large pile of clothes, nudging them out of the way to reveal a thin passageway that led downward.

"Did everyone get a secret passage?" Henry wondered, grabbing a pair of pants. He pulled them on, then summoned an eye to examine himself. "Bah. Horrendous taste."

He tossed them back into the pile and headed down the hole. The passageway was lined with runes and the dust on the floor implied that they'd either been carved recently or it had been a while since anyone had passed this way.

Considering the scrap of magic he'd sent after Quinlan was somewhere below him, Henry was pretty sure the situation was the former, but the runes made no sense. They were almost nonsensical, as if someone were simply practicing them rather than trying to actually make a coherent pattern.

The hallway wound down, stopping before an empty doorway leading into a large, circular chamber. A large rune circle had been carved into the ground surrounding a chair, where Quinlan sat, her chin in her hands. At her feet rested a thick book, but he couldn't make out its title from where he stood.

Henry melded against the wall and entered the room. The ground everywhere outside the circle was pockmarked and warped, and the room was full of residual heat. Several stone tablets had been thrown to the floor and were either melted or shattered.

Quinlan glanced up, looking at the doorway and clenching her hands. Henry followed her gaze, but there was nothing there. Henry contemplated approaching her, but he had no plans to enter any protective rune circles no matter how amateur their creator might be.

Still, there was no point taking risks. Henry extended a thin tendril, carving miniscule cuts along several of the runes. They were too small to spot with a glance but would render the circle worthless if activated.

"I know you're there," Quinlan said. Henry paused his work, turning his attention toward her. She still wasn't looking in his direction. If she was bluffing, she wasn't particularly good at it.

He continued his trek around the room, memorizing everything he saw. Quinlan was clearly trying to learn runes, but she wasn't even as good as Nolan was. Her work was sloppy and borderline dangerous. If all the damage to the floor around her was due to her shoddy work, Henry wouldn't have been surprised.

"You get one chance," Quinlan said, standing up. She had a piece of paper crumpled up in her hand. "Show yourself, or I'm going to act."

She was still staring at the door. Henry prepared a spell, wishing his senses weren't completely befuddled by the human spark. A part of him wanted to destroy Quinlan's hand and whatever she had in it, but he was pretty sure Damien wouldn't have appreciated that.

Judging by the look in Quinlan's eyes, she'd been sitting here for some time now. Henry mentally sighed. She'd probably managed to detect the tiny sliver of magic he'd left on her. Nobody else had noticed it when he'd tested it, but it was possible she was more sensitive than his previous subjects.

Quinlan leapt to her feet, and fire enveloped the paper in her hand. A ring of runes erupted from it, spreading through the air and tracing across the ceiling, carving themselves into the stone with magma. Molten rock dripped, sizzling against the ground as a wave of magic seared through the air.

Magical energy coiled around Henry, lighting him up like the window of a busy tavern. Quinlan spun toward him, her eyes wide. She thrust her other hand down and lit up the now useless rune circle at her feet.

"One move, and I rip you apart. The moment I activate it, that spell will blast you with magma, leaving nothing but a tiny pile of ash.," Quinlan warned, summoning a snake of molten energy to coil around her hand. "Now, who are you?"

"You've got to be kidding me," Henry said. "Oh, I'm so blasted mad right now. I was trying to be stealthy here, you annoying little brat. How did you see me?"

Quinlan blinked, but she narrowed her eyes and took a step

forward. Her fingers twitched, and the bands of magma around Henry started to squeeze.

"Stop blabbering. Drop that disguise and reveal yourself. Tell me who you are, and then start begging for your life. If you grovel hard enough, I might even consider letting you live."

Henry couldn't help himself. He started to laugh. Quinlan's brow furrowed in anger, and she clenched her hand. The molten bands wrapped around Henry, sending a pulse of pain through him. His laughter cut off abruptly.

He couldn't remember the last time he'd felt true pain. Quinlan's attack was barely a scratch, but it still *was*. Henry snarled, unfurling into his full form. Eyes sprouted across his body, and the molten bands snapped as he absorbed them, siphoning their magic like a refreshing drink.

Quinlan drew a rune in the air, sending a bolt of magma shooting at Henry. He flicked his hand, and a dark circle formed before the spell, swallowing it and spitting it back out at Quinlan. The magma scored across her shoulder, and she cried out in pain.

"Seriously? You don't even make yourself immune to heat when you use Magma magic?" Henry asked, his voice coming out of several mouths across him. Quinlan tripped over her chair and fell to the floor.

She quickly cast another spell, summoning a wave of magma around Henry. He teleported, appearing a few feet to the side. His ire grew with every second. "How am I supposed to explain this? I was being *stealthy*!"

"Get back!" Quinlan yelled, scrambling back to her feet. She pressed her hand over the wound on her shoulder, grimacing. "I don't know what the hell you are, but this circle will blow you apart if you step over it. I've connected it to my lifeforce so, if I die, this whole place will explode. Neither one of us will survive."

Ether started to gather behind Henry. A bolt of magma shot at the back of his head. He reached up, catching it. He had eyes on the back of his head, after all. Still, it had been a clever attack. Unfortunately, he wasn't in the right mood to praise it.

He paced around the circle, muttering to himself furiously. Quinlan stared at him, the bravado fading when she realized Henry didn't even respond to her warnings. He jerked to a halt and spun toward her.

"Wait a minute. You threatened me," Henry said. "What was it you said? To beg for my life?"

Quinlan flicked a rope of magma toward him. Henry grabbed it, ignoring the sting of the magic, and yanked her toward him. She let go, windmilling her arms and just barely managing to stay within her circle.

Henry's eyes twitched. He considered taking some deep breaths to calm himself like Damien sometimes did. Then, he decided against it. That sounded lame. He stepped over the circle. Quinlan's eyes went wide in horror, and she turned, sprinting for the doorway.

He snapped his shadowy fingers. A portal snapped open right in front of Quinlan, and she ran through it, reappearing right in front of him. Panic started to set in as she leapt back, tripping over the chair again and falling hard on her back.

A shadow leapt from Henry's hands, slamming into Quinlan as she tried to stand. It picked her up and slammed her against the wall, pinning her in place.

"What do you want with me?" Quinlan asked. "Are you an enemy of Mountain Hall? I swear, I don't know who you are."

"What to do," Henry muttered to himself. "Shit. If you go missing, I won't even have a good excuse."

"Excuse?" Quinlan asked.

Henry's eyes snapped toward her. "You never answered my question. You, a mere mortal, told me to beg for my life?"

Quinlan swallowed. "Sorry?"

"Sorry?" Henry said with a snort. "Sorry? That's what I'm going to be saying tomorrow morning, when I explain why you've gone on a permanent vacation to the Void. Ah well, you did try to attack me first."

Quinlan's eyes widened. "Wait! You can't kill me!"

"Why not?" Henry asked, cocking his head. "You're rather irritating. You've already tickled me twice, and your runework is so horrid that it makes me want to throw up. And I can't even throw up!"

"I— Didn't you want to know how I could detect you?" Quinlan asked, her eyes darting around desperately.

"Hmm. I do, actually. Okay, tell me."

"And then you'll let me go?"

"No, I'll just kill you after," Henry replied. "Whyever would I let you go? Seems pointless. I'm going to have to make a new technique if I want to wander around just because of you. Do you realize what an inconvenience that is? I'll have to waste *days*!"

"I don't want to die," Quinlan said weakly. "I can't!"

"Yes, you can. You're mortal," Henry growled. "Come on, tell me how you spotted me. I don't have all night."

"No. Why would I help you if you're going to kill me?"

"Ah. Good point. Bye, then." Magic started to gather around Henry.

"Wait!" Quinlan begged, tears building up in her eyes. "It's an artifact! Mountain Hall gave it to me. It lets me sense Ether to a much higher degree than normal. I don't pose any threat to you, I swear."

Henry cocked his head. "What use do you have for an artifact like that?"

"Mountain Hall is trying to figure out who killed two of our students in the Crypt," Quinlan stammered. "They sent people with artifacts like this to all the schools so we could figure out if someone was strong enough to kill them and why they did it. But you're way too strong to be in the Crypt, so it couldn't have been you. Please, just let me go, I swear on my life I won't tell anyone about you. It's in my pocket."

Henry reached out with a tendril, pulling a small orb dotted with green gems from Quinlan's pocket. He brought it over to himself and tucked it away. "Hmm. Well, that's good. I won't have to make my technique again. Thanks for the info."

"No! I'll do anything. I'll enter a contract. I'll be your servant. Please!"

Tears poured down her cheeks as she struggled fruitlessly against Henry's bindings. Henry groaned. He should have gotten rid of her already, but Damien's disapproving face was growing sharper and sharper in his mind.

"Shit," Henry said, ripping the bindings away from her and dropping the girl unceremoniously on her face. She scrambled upright but didn't try running for the door. Henry gave her credit for that. He was already annoyed enough.

Quinlan pressed her forehead against the ground. "Thank you. Thank you. I swear I won't tell anyone who you are."

"No," Henry agreed, tendrils extending from his body and tracing runes across the ground before her. "You won't be. I'm going to give you two choices. You offered to do anything to live, so here's your chance. Either that or die. Your choice."

"What is it?" Quinlan asked, staring at the runes uncomprehendingly.

"A contract," Henry replied. "Eight Planes, how are you doing anything with runes with this level of understanding? I'll summarize it. You do exactly what I say or the Ether I plant inside your heart will explode, ripping you apart so badly that no healer will even get a chance to save you. It'll go off the moment you even consider betraying me."

"E-even if I think about it?"

"The moment you think with intention to act. No second chances. No mistakes," Henry said. "Your choice. Blood signature, by the way. I don't have a quill on me."

Quinlan swallowed. Henry tapped a blank line at the bottom with a tendril. She bit her thumb, drawing blood, and reached out with a shaking hand to press the spot he indicated.

The runes flashed, turning black and coiling up her hand. They disappeared beneath her shirt sleeve, coiling around her chest and gathering at her heart.

"What do you want with me?" Quinlan asked, letting out a shaky breath and desperately trying to hold her composure. The quiver in her lip and her red eyes proved she wasn't doing a very good job of it, and if Henry had been human, he might have felt the slightest spark of remorse.

Still, he'd managed to find a solution that Damien wouldn't hold against him for the rest of eternity. That served to slightly assuage the sting of being spotted. As far as he was concerned, the night hadn't gone all that badly. Maybe some good could come of it yet.

ELEVEN

"Well," Henry said, drawing the word out. "I am in need of some goats."

"I— What?"

"Goats," Henry said, gesturing with his hands. "Furry, ugly little things. They've got horns and try to headbutt you. Taste like cheese."

"I know what a goat is. Wait, cheese?"

"Never mind," Henry said irritably. "I'll need more than just the goats."

"Are you sacrificing them? Do you use blood magic?" Quinlan asked, swallowing nervously.

"What? No. Actually, cut the questions. You're going to need to do more for me than just acquire a few goats."

"I understand." Quinlan nodded, her cheeks pale. It really didn't look like she did, but Henry didn't particularly care.

"First, you're going to stop looking for whoever this person Mountain Hall is seeking. If they ask, you haven't seen the slightest trace of him, and you're relatively sure Blackmist had nothing to do with any deaths you might be researching."

Quinlan's eyes widened. "So, you killed them?"

Henry let out an irritable sigh. "Considering that contract will rip you apart if you even try to share that information, yes. I might have had a bit to do with their deaths, but they had it coming."

"Are you going to kill me, too?"

"Planes, girl. Get over yourself," Henry snapped. "I couldn't care less about you. If you hadn't had that rinky little artifact, you never even would have known I was here. You'd be running around, drinking lava or whatever it is you do for fun."

Quinlan nodded despondently. "I'll do as you say."

"Good. Next, now that you've messed up my plans, I might as well get a little use out of you. You're going to do whatever my partner tells you. Some of the other students hanging around seem a little problematic, so having you in our court will make things go my way without as much bloodshed."

"Wait, it's another student?" Quinlan asked. Her eyebrows twitched, and she took a small step back. "No way. If it's one of the Blackmist students...Sylph or Damien?"

"I could tell you, but I'd rather see your reaction," Henry decided. "I'll let you know with the little bit of magic that I've marked you with. Either way, you're going to be on their side from here on out. Is there anything in Farsad that we should be aware of? And while the contract doesn't require you to do exactly as I say, I can promise that aiding me will be in your best interests."

"There were a few locations that Mountain Hall suspects libraries and weapon caches still have some more useful information." Quinlan's shoulders slumped in defeat. "I was told to investigate them. But if all of it ends up going to Blackmist, I don't think I'll be of much use to you for long."

"They'd kill you?" Henry asked.

"Success is a mandatory metric at Mountain Hall."

"Idiots. Killing all the recruits off just weakens them," Henry said, shaking his head. "Whatever. So long as you don't go against that contract, you're more or less under my protection. We won't be letting you die unless you do something really stupid."

The smallest spark of hope lit in Quinlan's eyes. "Will you let me go after the Forsad expedition?"

"Hmm. Probably not. You know too much," Henry said. "But depending on how hard you try, I might look at loosening the contract we've got. On the other hand, if you're a problem, we'll resume our activities from a few minutes ago."

Quinlan bit her lip and nodded. "I understand. I won't cause any issues."

"Good. In that case, we're done for now. Unless there's something else I should know?"

She mustered her nerves, her eyes darting about the room as if searching for anyone else to look at. "You said my runework was bad."

"Horrendous," Henry agreed. "I could do better drunk, blind, and dead."

"Can you teach me?"

"Why in the Planes would I do that?" Henry asked. "Do you think I just sit around doing nothing all day?"

He paused, realizing that was essentially what he did. Henry dismissed the stray thought with a scoff.

"I could be of more use to you if I were stronger," Quinlan said. "And I really need to learn Rune Crafting. It's vital."

"Why?"

Quinlan pressed her lips together. "Do I have to answer that?"

"Interesting. This is where you find your backbone? Does it have anything to do with Mountain Hall or Blackmist?"

"No," Quinlan replied, shaking her head. "It's personal."

"Then, I don't care," Henry said. "You're welcome to beg one of the Blackmist students or professors for tutelage, though. Some of them passable at it, and they'd probably know enough for most purposes that you'd need. I won't stop you, but I won't help you either."

"Which ones? The students. A professor won't work. I need secrecy. Anyone who might have ties to Mountain Hall or the other schools could cause me a lot of trouble if they found out I was trying to learn Rune Crafting, and that would make me a useless agent for you. Do any of the students really know enough?"

"Probably not," Henry said cheerfully. "But I don't know what you need to do, so I can't answer that. Damien and Nolan both know Rune Crafting, and they're reliable. I can't vouch for anyone else."

Quinlan nodded once. "I understand. I will seek them out tomorrow."

Henry prepared to leave, then paused. "About those goats..."

———

Damien woke the following morning feeling remarkably rested. Sylph was already up, sitting against the pillow beside him and meditating. There was barely enough room on the bed for both of them, but she'd managed to make it work.

He laid there for a few moments, not wanting to actually get up before he finally shifted upright.

How did your visit go last night, Henry?

"Fantastic," Henry said, his smug tone setting off alarm bells in Damien's head. "Quinlan is clear. Well, as clear as she's going to get. You'll also notice I nicked you a little souvenir. It's in your bag. Don't mess with it yet, though."

You stole something from her? She's going to notice if an artifact went missing!

"Trust me, she won't be talking to anybody."

You killed her, didn't you?

"Would you be mad if I did?"

Yes!

"Ah, I figured as much. Well, you'll be excited to know that I did not," Henry proclaimed.

Why do I get the feeling you're waiting for me to praise you for doing the absolute bare minimum in what would be a normal interaction?

"You'd be correct," Henry said. "I'll take that praise now."

Damien rolled his eyes and sighed.

Good job. Killing people for no reason is bad. So, what exactly happened?

"She had an annoying little artifact that made her more sensitive to the Ether," Henry said. "And she might have spotted me while I was snooping around, so we had to have a little chat."

You know what, I take it back. I do mean it when I say 'good job' this time. You're actually starting to become a decent person. The old you would have offed her without a second thought.

"Right?" Henry asked. "Your human spark is going to ruin my credibility whenever I go back to the Void. Everyone is going to think I'm a softie. Regardless, Quinlan had a side mission. She was meant to figure out if Blackmist had anything to do with Drew and Bartholomew's death. Luckily, she didn't find anything and will be reporting we're all clean."

How do you know? Couldn't she have just lied to get you to leave, then immediately tried to contact whoever it is she's working with at Mountain Hall?

"Nah. I bound her to a contract that would destroy her heart and Core the moment she tried to betray me. Real painful way to go, and there's no easy way to circumvent it since she signed it in blood."

Ah. That's more like you. That feels a bit...barbaric. Better than being dead, though.

"You aren't annoyed?" Henry asked carefully.

A few months ago, I probably would have been. Now? We can't take the risks anymore. I'm just glad you didn't kill her. So long as we don't abuse whatever contract you made and release her as soon as we can, it's not too bad.

Henry made a noise like he was clearing his throat. "Right. No abusing the contract."

What did you— Actually, don't tell me. I think I'd rather not know, so long as you actually aren't doing anything terrible to her. You aren't, are you? Slavery would be worse than killing someone. Imagine how Sylph would feel.

"Nothing like that," Henry said quickly. "I just asked her to do a little manual labor. If you feel that bad, she does have something she wants in return. She'll probably be coming around shortly to try to get it."

Damien rubbed his forehead. Sylph nudged him, and he opened his eyes. She was leaning over him, her hair draped around her head. "Are you okay?"

"Yeah," Damien said, giving her a small smile. "I was just talking with Henry. He investigated Quinlan last night, and apparently things didn't go exactly as planned. Everything should be fine, though."

"She's dead, isn't she?" Sylph asked.

One of Henry's mouths formed at the base of Damien's shadow. "Why does everyone automatically assume that?"

They both stared at him. Henry harrumphed.

"Fine. I might have done that once before, but I'm a changed...Void man-thing. She's alive."

"We'll have to bring Sylph up to speed, but we probably shouldn't do it now," Damien said. "Henry has told me there's a fair chance we're going to be having a visitor, and I don't want someone walking in on us talking or the sound ward."

Sylph nodded. She slipped out of bed and Damien followed her. Henry retreated into his shadow as the two of them got ready for the day. No more than a few minutes after they'd both finished, several muted *thuds* echoed out from the door.

"That's probably her," Damien said, pulling the door open to reveal Nolan. His hair was matted with sweat, and he was covered with small scratches.

"I need your help," Nolan said.

"She looks different than I last remember," Sylph said with a small grin. Nolan gave her a confused glance, but she just shrugged in response.

"Come inside." Damien stepped out of the way and gestured for Nolan to sit on his bed. "What's going on?"

"It's about my father," Nolan replied, rubbing his temples with the palms of his hands. "He's almost certainly going to choose me as the heir. After you warned me, I did my best to try to convince him it was too early to decide, but someone is pressuring him to finalize things."

"I think I'm missing something important." Damien frowned. "I get that becoming the heir is bad, but I'm not seeing why. Is it all the extra responsibilities or something? I recall you and Reena arguing over who would become heir in our first year, and both of you seemed to want to be selected."

"That was then." Nolan shrugged helplessly. "This is now. And you're partially right. It's the responsibility."

"Will you not be able to finish college if you're chosen?" Sylph asked.

"No, I will," Nolan said. "But I'll be expected to start taking on some roles and duties to further strengthen the Gray household. A year ago, I would have been more than happy to. But now..." He shuddered and shook his head. "I couldn't want anything less."

"So, how can we help?" Sylph asked. "I don't think anything we could do would actually convince your father of much. Neither of us are nobles."

"That's not true," Damien said, his lips pressing thin. "My dad. Stormsword is about as high as you can possibly get in nobility. If he disapproves of you, then your father probably wouldn't select you as the heir, right?"

"I was actually going to ask if you could beat the shit out of me in a sparring match so I looked pathetic," Nolan replied, scratching the back of his head. "But that would work, too, actually. I know you aren't very close with your father, so I don't want to cause needless strain."

Damien chuckled. "I couldn't care less if we're just using him to get something we want. If anything, I'd be more worried that he wouldn't bother doing it. I don't have any good way to contact him. Is there a timeframe on how long we have to make you look pathetic?"

"A month at most," Nolan said. "He's very close to selecting. I'm honestly surprised Yui isn't trying to fight against this harder than she is."

"Yui? Why would she care about you becoming the heir?" Sylph asked. "I suppose she might try to do something to help one of her people or get you in her debt, but she doesn't strike me as the type to stick her neck out for no gain."

"It's the opposite," Nolan said bitterly. "Politically speaking, this isn't my loss. It's hers as far as I can tell. In order to strengthen the Gray household, my father plans to have me wed Yui, and the queen has agreed."

As Nolan spoke, the stone door swung open, revealing Quinlan. The words died on her lips as she processed what Nolan had just said. All of them stared at her.

Within Damien's head, Henry let out a curse. "What is it with this girl and stumbling into things she isn't supposed to find?"

"I— Uh," Quinlan stammered.

Nolan's eyes flicked over her, studying and assessing the intruder in seconds. His lips thinned slightly, and a flicker of Ether traced down his arm. "I should have been more careful with where I spoke."

Henry peeled away from Damien's shadow, taking on his spherical tentacled form. Quinlan nearly jumped out of her shoes. Her cheeks went pale, eyes wide. Beside her, Nolan's eyes widened slightly.

"Is that your companion?" Nolan asked, staring at Henry.

"Oh, yeah. You haven't met him yet," Damien said. "This is Henry."

"It's a pleasure to meet you." Nolan inclined his head, Quinlan temporarily forgotten. "I'm honored to finally know what you look like."

"You should be," Henry said, bobbing once. "I'm amazing."

"Let's stay on topic," Damien suggested, indicating Quinlan.

"Don't worry about her," Henry said with a lazy yawn. "She won't be saying anything about what she just heard. Quinlan unfortunately has a talent for poking her nose into business it shouldn't be in."

"You're sure?" Nolan asked, looking from Henry to Quinlan. "This information can't get out. If my father figured out what I was doing..."

"Trust me," Henry said. "It'll go with her to her grave."

Quinlan paled even further and nodded empathetically. Nolan chewed his lower lip and let out a sigh. "I guess that's all I needed to talk about. Sorry for barging in so early in the morning, Damien, Sylph. I've got a lot of practice to get in, since there's a good chance I'll have to start earning my own way through the rest of college after all this. Please don't hesitate to find me if I can do anything to pay you back. Henry, it was a pleasure to come face to face with you."

He raised a hand and stalked out of the room, heading down the mountain and out of sight. Quinlan looked like she wished she could disappear into the wall, but Damien and Sylph were both studying her curiously.

"Henry told me you might be paying me a visit," Damien said. "What exactly is it that you need?"

"You're his partner?" Quinlan asked, looking from Henry to Damien in dismay. "But...you're a Year Three! How could you have such a powerful companion? And for it to be that strong outside your body...are you an agent for Blackmist or something? It's impossible for someone our age to have so much power."

"Aw, she's buttering me up," Henry said. "You should praise me more often."

"No. Your ego is big enough," Damien said. "And, yes, Henry is my companion, even if he goes a bit...astray at times. I don't think I'll be telling you any more about him, though. You're only here because he forced you into a contract, which I'm already not too thrilled about. The less you get involved in my business the better."

"I'll stay out of your way," Quinlan promised, not taking her eyes away from Henry.

"There's a *but* coming," Sylph said.

"But I need to learn Rune Crafting, and Henry said you could teach me."

"I said he *might* teach you," Henry corrected. "I didn't make any promises. That's his problem to deal with. You're working for us no matter what you want, you've just got the chance to ask without getting fried. I think that's pretty fair."

"It isn't," Damien grumbled. "Not even slightly. Unfortunately, there isn't anything we can do about that. Henry, you're certain she can't share anything she hears, right?"

"Nothing," Henry confirmed. "Not what she hears, sees, or any sense. Any attempts to share information we don't want her to would end very, very badly. Think Sylph when her Core was about to explode, but a hundred times faster and more painful."

Quinlan and Damien both shuddered.

"I guess I should hear you out, at the very least," Damien said with a sigh. "Why do you need to learn Rune Crafting from me? There are dozens of teachers at Blackmist who know it, and I'm certain there are similarly informed people at Mountain Hall."

"I can't let anybody know I'm learning Rune Crafting," Quinlan said, shifting nervously. "It would be very bad for me if Mountain Hall discovered it."

"Why?" Sylph asked. "Wouldn't you getting stronger be a good thing?"

Quinlan pressed her lips together. "I don't want to answer that."

"That's a problem," Damien said, holding a finger up. "How do we know you aren't just going to use that against us? It's giving an enemy to somebody that probably hates us. You not telling me the reason why you want to learn makes it even worse."

"I promise it's got nothing to do with Blackmist," Quinlan said. Her hands clenched at her sides. "But I really need to learn. I told...Henry. Yesterday, when he was in my room. He believed me."

"I couldn't really be bothered to care, actually," Henry corrected. "But so long as she remains beholden to my contract, she isn't going to be betraying anyone. Just for her sake, I'll say that you don't have to worry about that."

Damien clicked his tongue. "I guess I could probably show you a little in that case. If you're a fourth-year student, the runes should probably be pretty advanced already. Henry would do better, but something tells me he's being an insufferable ass about it."

"Hey! I'm busy helping Sylph," Henry said, crossing his tentacles. "Of course, I could stop..."

"All right, all right," Damien said, rolling his eyes. "You're busy. Can you describe what exactly it is you need to learn?"

"An array to keep an entity trapped in a location. It has to also be linked to a person and feed energy into them from the entity. If possible, I'd like to get healing and restoration runes involved as well."

Damien blinked. "That's...pretty complex, I think. I don't know a pattern to do that off the top of my head. It would vary heavily depending on what you're trapping and the strength of the person you're powering. That's also pretty nefarious. Isn't that basically just enslaving something?"

"No. The entity is willing," Quinlan said. "And how much variation would it have?"

"Again, I have no way to know without seeing it," Damien said with a shrug. He walked over to his bed and sat down, pulling a few sheets of paper out from his travel pack and grabbing a piece of chalk. "You know how to make a summoning circle, right? We can start from there."

Quinlan cleared her throat.

"She can't even draw a basic rune," Henry said cheerfully. "Utter rubbish. Nolan was better than her when he started."

"Seriously? And you want to start with some sort of trap-energy leech?" Damien asked, cocking an eyebrow. "And you won't let me see whatever or whoever it is you're trying to work on?"

Quinlan shook her head firmly. "No, I cannot."

"Then, you're making it very hard for me to help you." Damien shrugged. "You're asking for knowledge I'm not even completely certain I have. At the very minimum, it would be hours of training. With the expedition to Forsad coming up, I've got a lot of practice to do. I can't afford to spend that much effort training you. I'll fall behind."

A sharp knock on the door interrupted them.

"Seriously? Is this just the gathering place for all of Blackmist?" Damien asked, standing up and stepping past Quinlan to open it. Dredd stood on the other side, drumming his fingers on the hilt of his staff.

He ducked inside without waiting for an invitation. "Sylph. How is your progress going with the full manifestation?"

"I've got one, but there are some imbalances in my body from where... Well, stuff happened," Sylph said, sending a pointed glance at Quinlan. "I'm working on repairing it, and there are still some problems I'm having with getting full access to my companion's strength."

"With your unique situation, that doesn't surprise me," Dredd said, rubbing his chin. "I suspected you might have trouble with that, actually. I've dug through some old books, and I believe the problem should eventually stabilize, but we don't exactly have the time to waste. There's a way to expedite the process."

"What is it?" Sylph asked eagerly.

"Easier to show you," Dredd said. "I've skipped a few too many classes with both of you recently, so we can count this as one of them. I trust you aren't busy?"

Sylph glanced at Damien. He gave her a small nod.

"I'm free," Sylph said.

"Good," Dredd said, turning and heading out of the cave. He paused, holding the door open for Sylph before glancing back at Damien. "Don't get too cozy. I'll be back for you some other day."

The door swung shut, leaving Damien with Henry and Quinlan.

"Was that Captain Dredd?" Quinlan asked, staring at the door in shock.

"Professor Dredd, as far as I'm aware," Damien replied. "You know him?"

"He's a legend. How do you not?" Quinlan exclaimed. She caught sight of Henry again and deflated. "Captain Dredd is one of the best strategists on the frontlines. Why is he at Blackmist?"

"He's our professor," Damien replied. "And, honestly, at this point, I wouldn't be surprised if the entirety of Blackmist somehow happened to be some bigshot on the frontlines. It's looking like they'll take anyone."

"What do you mean?" Quinlan asked.

"Never mind." Damien shook his head. "Is there really nothing you can tell me about what you're trying to fix? With the information you've given me, it would take years to get you to a point where you could do anything."

"It's an old artifact," Quinlan finally said, forcing the words through her lips like bile. "And it's inside somebody. The artifact is falling apart and releasing something trapped inside it, but we don't have the original runes used on it. I need to repair it. It's the entire reason I volunteered to go to Forsad. I was hoping something there could help me. Please, I swear I won't betray you or Blackmist. I just need to—"

She bit her words off and stared at Damien with a mixture of desperation and fear. He pressed his lips together. "If I'm giving up time to get stronger, you're going to have to fill in for what power I could have had. I'm going to expect you to be completely working on our side."

"Your companion's contract already makes me do that."

"It keeps you from betraying us," Damien corrected. "It doesn't mean you'll actively be trying to help us. I don't want your forced assistance. I want it to be your own choice. Throw your lot in with me with the intention to do everything you can to help me and Sylph. In return, I'll set aside some time every day to teach you Rune Crafting."

To her credit, Quinlan seriously considered Damien's words for several moments before giving him a small nod. "Okay. I'll do it."

"Good," Damien said. "Come back in the evening. The later, the better. I've got to get back to training for today, and I'll need to think about where to start you. I'm hesitant to believe Henry's criticism since he's a bit apt to exaggeration, so maybe this won't be as hard as I fear it will."

"I will. Thank you," Quinlan said. She reached up to push the door open, then paused. "How long will it take to teach me?"

"Depends on how hard you work and how good you are at it," Damien replied. "But I'll do my best to try to get you the knowledge you need before we go to Forsad. If I can't, I'll continue helping you for as long as you stay at Blackmist and I still have time."

She gave him one more nod, and then slipped out of the room, letting the door swing shut behind her. Damien sighed and rubbed his forehead.

"Don't worry too much about what to do with Quinlan," Henry said. "Her real mission was to figure out what happened to Bartholomew and Drew. We can observe her during Forsad, and then try to set her loose with a much more forgiving contract later."

"That's better than nothing," Damien said with a nod. "Is there any way Mountain Hall can actually figure out what happened?"

"There's always a way, but I wouldn't be too optimistic about their chances," Henry replied. "Just train for now."

Damien sighed again.

"That's not training," Henry observed. "That looks more like pouting."

"Oh, don't you get started on me," Damien said, a laugh slipping out of his lips. "This is all your fault."

"Hey, she's a fourth-year. Her magic actually stings a little too, so she should be a useful addition for this expedition thing. Certainly more effective than anything you'll be able to learn in the few hours you spend teaching her."

"That's probably true," Damien admitted. He headed into the training room and started to gather Ether in his Core. "Is she really as bad at Rune Crafting as you're saying she is?"

Henry's only response was fading laughter as he returned to Damien's shadow. Damien shook his head. He started practicing, but his movements were largely mechanical while he pondered what to do about Quinlan.

There was no doubt in his mind that he'd have to find a way to get rid of the contract Henry had made with her. It wasn't slavery, but it was too damn close for his taste. Even if it hadn't been for Sylph, the thought filled him with revulsion. At the same time, now that she'd seen Henry, there really wasn't a good alternative other than killing her. Not yet, at least.

Magic twirled from his hands, forming into miniscule purple blades that flickered through the air around him. Damien came to a decision. He'd do his best to avoid actually triggering the contract as much as possible and let Quinlan do her own thing, training her when he had time. If a better solution came up, he'd take it. There was no point worrying about it now.

He threw himself back into his practice, working with renewed vigor now that he'd lost a portion of his day. Time flew by as magic flashed around Damien. He took a few breaks to douse his head in the healing waters of the shower, but then returned to his training.

CHAPTER
TWELVE

When the door swung open and Sylph walked in that evening carrying a large canvas bag, he was still working.

"Quinlan isn't here yet?" Sylph guessed, poking her head into the training room.

"Nope. It's for the best," Damien replied, standing up from his seated position. He followed her into the main room.

"Hopefully she doesn't show up in the middle of the night," Sylph said, setting the bag down on her bed. She ducked down, pulling a change of clothes out from below it, then headed into the bathroom, emerging a few minutes later with the dirty clothes in her hand.

"I'm not spending all night training her, so she better not," Damien replied. "I'm already exhausted enough. I don't need a lack of sleep to that. What's in the bag?"

Several sharp raps echoed through the cave as someone knocked on the door. Damien snorted and stood up, walking over to pull it open. Quinlan stood outside, wringing her hands together nervously. A small travel pack hung over her shoulder.

"We were just wondering when you'd show up," Damien said, heading back inside and waving for her to follow.

"I got food," Sylph said, pulling the pack open and taking out several small wheels of cheese, dried meat, and an assortment of fruit. "I thought you might not have eaten today."

Damien's eyes lit up. "Thank you! You're right, I haven't. Got caught up with practicing. It doesn't help that every time I think of getting food, Henry suggests goats."

He claimed some of the food for himself and started to eat. Sylph nodded to Quinlan. "You can have some as well, if you'd like."

Quinlan shifted her weight to her back foot. "I don't want to intrude too much."

"It's fine," Sylph replied. "I wheedled it out of Dredd, so it isn't my money. You're not going to make very much progress studying if you're hungry. Unless you've already eaten?"

"I haven't," Quinlan admitted reluctantly. She snagged a single grape for herself. "Thanks."

"I won't count this as part of the time I promised you," Damien said, spreading some cheese on a cracker. "And Sylph is right. We aren't going to make great progress if you don't eat. I really should be eating more myself, but it's just so damn easy to forget."

Henry slipped out from his shadow, breaking off a small piece of the cheese with a tentacle and popping it into his mouth. He chewed thoughtfully for a few moments. "Tastes like goat."

"No, it doesn't," Damien and Sylph said at the same time. Henry snickered and took a few pieces of fruit before retreating to Damien's bed. Quinlan glanced between all of them, then slowly claimed a small pile of food for herself.

They finished the food off a few minutes later. As soon as the last morsel had vanished, Henry floated over to Sylph and prodded her in the shoulder. "Right, then. Let's get to it."

Sylph nodded and rose to her feet. "Good luck. I'll be back later tonight. Henry and I are going to the pool to train."

"Likewise," Damien replied. "Thanks again for bringing dinner. I'll get it next time."

Sylph gave him a quick grin, then headed out of the room with Henry floating at her shoulder. Quinlan's shoulders slumped in relief as soon as the door swung shut behind them. Damien pushed himself to his feet and nodded at the training rooms.

"Let's move in there." He snagged a piece of chalk from his pack as they passed his bed.

"I've got paper," Quinlan said, raising her own pack. "I also have a quill and ink."

"We'll get to that in a bit. I want to see the basics first, and there's no point wasting paper when we can just wipe the chalk away. Why don't you start by going through the runes you know? You can stick to the most common ones so we don't waste too much time. I just want to know what gaps I need to fill in."

He tossed Quinlan the stick of chalk. She chewed her lower lip, then knelt on the stone and started to draw. Damien looked over her shoulder as the older girl drew. His brow creased, furrowing more with every rune she made.

Two major problems immediately stuck out to Damien. The first was that her actual drawing skills were subpar. The strokes were shaky, and her lines weren't straight. That alone would have been a significant issue.

The bigger problem was that it took Damien several seconds to recognize almost all the runes. Only a single one of them even resembled anything basic. The rest were rather advanced and only meant to be used in conjunction with other runes that would stabilize them.

Damien stopped her after she'd drawn around a dozen

runes. "Quinlan, don't you know any more simple? You're all over the place here. Only one of those runes is in the beginner's alphabet."

"What's that?" Quinlan asked. "I just learned from my book. I've never heard about a beginner's alphabet."

"What book?"

Quinlan dug around in her pack and pulled out a tome trimmed with metal. She handed it to Damien, who flipped it open and paged through it. It was full of some of the most complex rune circles he'd seen. Some of them were so detailed that he wouldn't have even considered trying them without Henry to back him up.

"Quinlan, where did you get this?" Damien asked, closing the book and handing it back to her. "You seriously learned Rune Craft from this?"

"I found it on an expedition," Quinlan replied. "And I did. Why? Is that a bad thing?"

"Well, yes," Damien said, scratching the back of his head. "I'll be blunt. You're worse than some of the little kids in my hometown at drawing runes. I don't think that's entirely your fault, considering you taught yourself using a book that was way too advanced for your level, but why didn't you start with the basics? This book is insane."

"It's the only one I had," Quinlan said, her cheeks reddening in embarrassment.

"Just buy a better one? They aren't that expensive."

"Mountain Hall wouldn't let me," Quinlan said with a sigh. "They don't even know I have that book. We're discouraged from pursuing anything other than combat magic. Strongly. This is the first time I've been away from Mountain Hall without supervision in years."

"That's just stupid." Damien shook his head. "What are

they trying to do, train a bunch of blockheads who don't do anything other than fight?"

"Yes."

"Ah. Well, they're idiots," Damien said. He pursed his lips and thought for a few moments. "Okay. I need you to forget literally everything you've learned. Your foundations are terrible, so we're starting from scratch."

"But that'll take a lot of time!" Quinlan exclaimed. "We can't do that. Can't you just skip some of the information and get to the relevant stuff?"

"No," Damien replied in a flat tone. "Runes build off each other. You're lucky you haven't blown yourself up yet. Trapping and drawing power out of something is really complex. There's no room for an error. If you make one, the best-case scenario would be killing them. Is that a risk you're willing to take?"

Quinlan shook her head. Her hands clenched at her sides.

"I'll try to go as quick as I possibly can," Damien promised. "It depends on you. If you pick things up quickly, I can accelerate. But I'm not going to help you kill yourself. We'll stick to the promise I made earlier today, but it isn't going to be easy. I'll be assigning you practice to do once you go home."

"I can handle that," Quinlan said, holding out the piece of chalk to him. "Please, start."

Damien took it and sat down beside her. He brushed some dust out of the way and a simple rune consisting of a circle with two jagged lines through its center on the ground.

"We'll start with this. Draw this rune."

Quinlan took the chalk and scratched out a jagged copy of Damien's rune just below it.

"No good," Damien said. "Your lines are too sloppy. Draw slower and concentrate harder. Rush it, and you'll just end up drawing it a second time. Even small variations in the rune can cause it to be completely useless."

Quinlan bit her lower lip and narrowed her eyes, drawing it again. Her second attempt looked considerably better than the first. The circle was a bit wobbly, and the lines weren't quite as straight as they should have been.

Damien pointed out the mistakes and had her draw it again. On the fifth attempt, he gave her a slight nod.

"That's passable. You need to keep that speed for everything you draw. Don't let yourself accelerate or get impatient. Rune Crafting is about precision. Remember what you're working for. A mistake when you're drawing a rune circle for light will either just make it fizzle or fail. A mistake when you're linking two living beings could end up killing someone."

"I understand," Quinlan said.

"Make sure that you do," Damien said. He took the chalk back from her and drew ten more runes on the floor. "Do these next."

The next hour passed by in a blur. Damien and Quinlan ground the stick of chalk down into a tiny nub and covered almost the entirety of the training room floor with drawings. Quinlan was a quick study, but they had a lot of material to cover.

When the quality of her work started to drop, Damien dragged her to the bathroom and had her hold her hand under the shower water. As soon as she could handle the chalk properly again, they went right back to work.

Damien had only planned to spend an hour or two, but nearly four had passed by the time he felt exhaustion starting to creep up on him.

"That's enough for today," Damien decided, putting a hand on her shoulder. "There's only so much your brain can absorb."

"But—"

"I also need to sleep," Damien added. "I want to help you, Quinlan. But not at the cost of everything else. Go home and practice all the runes we covered today—but do that in the morning. If you show up exhausted tomorrow, I'm sending you back home. You can't learn runes when you can't think."

She nodded reluctantly. "Okay. I'll review them in the morning. Do you have a sheet I can reference?"

Damien smacked himself in the forehead. He grabbed one of her papers and plucked the quill from her bag, quickly drawing the basic runes they'd covered onto it. After blowing on the ink to dry it, Damien handed it to her.

"Here. You can take what's left of the chalk as well."

"Thanks," Quinlan said, pocketing the nub of chalk and taking the paper gingerly from Damien. She slipped it into her travel pack. The two of them headed back into the main room. Quinlan reached for the door, then paused. "You're taking this seriously."

"Of course, I am," Damien said irritably. "I said I would."

"I know," Quinlan said. "But I didn't think you actually would. You don't have any real reason to help me."

"Aside from the fact that I promised I would?"

Quinlan studied his expression, then shook her head. "You're strange. This isn't what I was told Blackmist was like. You don't match your companion at all, either. He's...terrifying."

"And what am I?" Damien asked with a laugh.

"I'm not sure yet," Quinlan replied. "Thank you, though. I needed to learn runes very badly. I can't explain why, but thank you."

She pushed the door open and slipped into the night. Damien watched it swing shut, then turned and headed over to the bathroom to get ready for bed. Once he'd finished and was sliding under the covers, a shadow flitted across the room and Henry's presence returned to his mind.

"How'd it go?" Henry asked.

She was just as bad as you said. Where's Sylph?

The door swung open, and Sylph walked inside. Her clothes were cut up, and she was covered in dirt. She grunted a greeting and staggered over to the bathroom.

Eight Planes, what did you do?

"Training," Henry replied. "Her body really didn't take to the Corruption that well at all. All things considered, though, I don't think anything would. I'm just unraveling all the knots and optimizing all the wasted energy. It's not easy on her, but she's getting stronger."

That's good. Is it possible her low Magical Energy could be fixed?

"Probably not. That's a problem with her Core, and expanding it even further isn't realistic. There's only so many times you can break and put someone back together before the shards become too tiny. She'll just have to live with it and make up for the weakness with her other strengths."

Damn. I was hoping you could fix that somehow. I know it really bothers her. Do you think that one artifact in the Treasure Pavilion would help much? The dagger that she was looking at last year.

"It might make a tiny boost, but not anything too noticeable," Henry said with a mental shrug. "She'll be more than dangerous enough, don't you worry. Especially once she starts utilizing the Corruption properly."

Sylph trudged out of the bathroom a short while later, her hair soaked and plastered to her skin. She flopped into her own bed. Damien frowned and sat up.

"What's wrong?"

"Too tired to dry my hair," Sylph replied. "It's cold."

Damien hopped out of his bed and slid into Sylph's. She was right—her hair was cold. "I think I'll survive."

Sylph let out a small laugh. Henry grumbled and put up a barrier, blocking the two of them out. There really wasn't much need, as Damien and Sylph both fell fast asleep within minutes.

When Damien woke up the next morning, Sylph was

already gone, and Henry was missing. Damien got ready and headed out of the room in search of Delph. While the others were busy, he had to follow up on his promise to Nolan.

The campus was still waking up when he got down the mountain. A few people milled about the streets, talking in hushed tones or eating breakfast at small restaurants along the pathways. Most of the shops were still closed, although the general store's doors were wide open.

Damien was tempted to stop by and grab a snack on his way but eating right before meeting Delph felt like a terrible idea. Granted, he didn't actually know where he was supposed to find the professor, but Delph had a habit of popping up whenever someone was looking for him.

"Looking for me?" Delph asked, materializing in the air behind Damien, causing the boy to swear and spin, raising his arms defensively.

"E— Seven Planes, Professor," Damien snapped. "Why and how do you do that?"

"It's funny," Delph replied with a smirk. "And you were wandering around campus like a lost puppy. Who else could you be looking for?"

"I'm more interested in finding out exactly how you knew that was what I was doing. Are you always watching me or something?"

"Pretty much," Delph replied, his face straight. "With the amount of trouble you're consistently involved in, it's not a bad call. Whenever you head out on your own, something happens."

"Hey, that isn't true," Damien defended. "Wait, are you actually watching me all the time?"

Delph cocked an eyebrow, making no effort to answer the question. "Name one time something *hasn't* gone wrong."

"I went on vacation back to Ardenford, nothing happened."

"The princess of the kingdom chased you down, and you found out your father was Stormsword."

"The princess is your fault," Damien said.

"Never said she wasn't," Delph replied with a shrug. "But let's cut to the point. Why are you looking for me? Training?"

"Not quite," Damien said, still all too aware Delph had yet to actually tell him if he was under constant surveillance. "I need to speak with Derrod."

"Stormsword?" Delph asked. "Why not just speak to him yourself? You don't need my help there."

"I've got no idea where he is. Unlike you, I don't stalk people."

"I don't stalk *everyone*," Delph said, affronted. "Just those of importance. And as it happens, I happen to know where he is. He's also quite busy, but I think he can probably make some time for you."

"This won't take long," Damien promised.

Delph traced a circle in the air, leaving gray energy in his wake. It snapped into a portal and hummed to life, motes of magic churning within it. Damien stepped into it, and Delph followed.

They emerged onto a grassy field. The bodies of half a dozen Corrupted monsters littered the ground around them, and Derrod was leaning against his sword, which had been planted deep in the ground.

Aside from the corpses everywhere, there wasn't a single sign of a fight. Even the grass was largely undamaged by the acidic blood characteristic of the Corrupted monsters. The only burnt sections were directly under the monster's bodies.

"Dove, Damien," Derrod said, cocking his head as the portal closed behind them. "What are you doing here?"

"I'm just bringing your kid over for a chat," Delph said. His right eye twitched slightly. "And I go by Delph now."

"Right," Derrod said, waving his hand. "I'll be sure to remember that. Shouldn't you be at Blackmist, Damien?"

"I just wanted to chat with you for a moment," Damien said. "I'll keep it short."

"Go for it," Derrod said, yawning and pushing the hair out of his eyes. "I've got a minute to kill."

Damien bit down an annoyed retort. "I recently found out the queen plans to have Yui marry Nolan Gray."

"Your tone tells me you don't approve."

"I don't."

Derrod's eyes focused on him, poised like those of a snake coiled to strike. Damien's lips thinned as he met his father's gaze. "Why not? Take a fancy to Princess Yui?"

"What? No," Damien said, taken aback. "Not at all. It's more Nolan than her. He'd be a terrible match, and the kingdom needs the rulers to work together well. Nolan and Yui hate each other."

"No, they don't," Derrod said. "Nolan dislikes Princess Yui, but Yui doesn't mind him. In fact, she rather enjoys his company. He's got a powerful noble house backing him, and he's decently talented. With enough time, he'll become a good mage. He wouldn't be the strongest king we've had, but he doesn't need to be. Princess Yui will be strong enough."

"It doesn't matter if Nolan is capable if he doesn't want to be there," Damien replied. "Anyone forced into doing a job they don't want to do isn't going to be as successful as someone who actually wants to be there. I suspect he doesn't even want to lead the Grays. What would happen if it was revealed that the princess' betrothed got kicked out of his own home?"

Derrod didn't respond immediately. He studied Damien for a few moments, allowing the silence to stagnate in the air. Finally, he stood up, pushing away from his sword.

"You don't care about the kingdom."

"What?"

"It's fine," Derrod said. "You don't have to. It's not your job. But you don't care about the kingdom. You never have, especially considering your girlfriend."

Damien's eyes narrowed. "Keep Sylph out of this."

"Why?" Derrod asked. "Do you know who she was? What she's really capable of? I saw what she could do long before she arrived at Blackmist, Damien. She's not just a wronged student."

Ether flickered in Damien's Core, threatening to leap to his palms of its own volition. Damien repressed it and clenched his hands into fists. "She was raised as a slave. How can you blame her for any of that? She told me about all of that. Unlike you, she hasn't tried to hide anything, and none of that was even her fault."

Derrod snorted. "She told you what she wanted you to hear. She's a skilled manipulator. If she told you everything, then you'd know she spent some time with the kingdom's soldiers after her rebel master was killed."

"You mean you kept her prisoner," Damien snarled, his composure starting to crack.

"I did what I had to for the kingdom's safety," Derrod replied, his voice not changing from its usual tone. "She might not have had any deigns against the kingdom, but she certainly has ulterior motives."

"I think that's quite enough," Delph said.

"Stay out of this, Dove," Derrod said. "This is between me and my boy."

"Clearly not since you're bringing Sylph in," Damien said, starting to draw Ether into himself from the lines around them. "She hasn't done anything that would be even remotely bad for the kingdom. All she's done is tried to survive. What does she have to do with any of this?"

"That's what I'm keen to figure out," Derrod said. "This newfound interest you have in the kingdom's future concerns me, especially since I can tell you're hiding something. Perhaps I should go check myself."

"Stay away from Sylph," Damien said, his voice lowering. "You've done enough."

"Are you going to make me?" Derrod asked, the corner of his lip quirking up in a taunting smile. "You couldn't even scratch me when we last fought, and I wasn't even trying. The son of Stormsword, unable to keep up with his crippled roommate. I expect more than that from you."

"Is that what this is about?" Damien asked, trying and failing to keep the fury from reaching his face. "Your ego? Because I lost in a fight against her?"

"It's about the kingdom." Derrod snarled. "I keep it protected, and you galivant around like you have no responsibilities with a girl who's probably just sleeping with you to get closer to her assassination target. You—"

Damien whipped a Gravity Lance forward and teleported, driving two spheres of destructive Ether toward Derrod's back. His father spun, crackling blue light flaring around him and deflecting the spells.

Derrod flickered, and Damien teleported into the air, narrowly avoiding getting grabbed by the collar.

"Ah, you do have a backbone," Derrod said. "Unfortunately, it isn't even for something that matters."

Damien snarled, drawing on as much Ether as he could handle and shaping it as he warped toward Derrod. He grabbed the ground beneath his father with telekinesis and hurled it into the air, sending dirt and stone flying everywhere.

Derrod flickered, avoiding the attack. He appeared before Damien just as purple energy hissed to life around the boy. Dozens of miniature scars flared around Damien as he cast storm, grabbing the debris around them and whipping it around himself.

A thin line cut across Derrod's face before he blurred to safety a few feet back. Damien sent several Tears after Derrod, forcing him to dodge farther backward. As he cast, he ripped up more of his surroundings, adding them into the howling wall building around him. At the same time, he bound a small Gravity Sphere in place at his foot, keeping it readied with his mental energy.

Derrod flashed forward, shielding himself with a thin layer of blue magic and pushing through the storm. Damien teleported, yanking all the debris down on where he had been standing with all his might. It formed a stone tomb around Derrod, crushed into one single piece by the sheer pressure.

A loud *crack* split the air, and Damien's spell shattered along with his tomb. It crumbled around Derrod, and he stepped out, largely uninjured.

"That's all?" Derrod asked.

The Gravity Sphere Damien had left behind detonated. Derrod's eyes widened, and he blurred, but he wasn't fast enough to dodge the entire spell. When he reappeared, jagged cracks ran up his armor from where the Gravity Sphere had caught him.

Damien didn't give his father a chance to speak again. He tore up the ground beneath him once more, launching as much into the air as he could. Derrod blurred for him, but Damien shut his eyes and teleported several times in rapid succession.

He opened his eyes again and reached within his mind for the gate of runes that connected him directly to the Ether.

"*Shatter,*" Damien commanded. The word ripped from his lips, and the Ether thrummed in response. The grassy field erupted as hundreds of black dots flashed into being, blanketing the ground in an enormous radius around all of them.

They detonated as quickly as they had arrived, filling the air with countless loud *snaps* as stone, dirt, and the corpses of dozens of Corrupted monsters were torn to shreds. One of the spells caught Damien's left hand, nearly ripping his entire arm out of his socket and shattering the bones in several of his fingers.

He forced the pain away, blanketing the area with telekinesis and thrusting all the dust down to clear the air. Derrod stood in the same place where he'd been standing before, his sword drawn from its place in the ground. *Pops* of electricity coursed along his skin, but his armor had been shattered, and he was heavily favoring one of his legs.

A hand fell on Damien's shoulder, stopping him before he could cast again. Delph stepped up to stand beside him, his eyes stormy.

"That's quite enough, Derrod. If you push this any farther, I'm going to throw my own lot in. I've never been known for my good temper."

Derrod studied Delph for a moment. The impassive expression fell off his face, replaced by a bare-toothed smile. "That's more like it."

"What?" Damien asked, the Ether still dancing at the edge of his lips as if it were begging for release. "What in the Planes are you talking about?"

"He's testing you," Delph said, his voice level and measured. "He did it to everyone in his teams. Find out something that drives them and harp on it until they get pissed off enough to go all out. It's a tactic only used by a scumbag leader who doesn't think about anyone's feelings other than his own."

"It's effective," Derrod replied, driving his sword back into the ground and leaning on it. "I had to see how strong my son really was, and he wasn't going to show me everything unless he had sufficient motivation. Isn't it a father's right to see how his boy is growing?"

Fury welled within Damien's chest, but he tied it down and buried it. He wasn't going to give Derrod the pleasure of seeing any weakness, and the pain in his fingers was more than enough to distract him.

"What do you want, Derrod?"

"I just said," Derrod replied. "I wanted to see how strong you are, and people don't put it all on the line until they're fighting for something that matters. Wipe that expression off your face. I won't touch your girlfriend. Won't even talk to her unless she approaches me. She's off the kingdom's list."

Damien slapped his wrist, bringing up the information within it and throwing it forward so Derrod could see.

Damien Vale
Blackmist College
Year Three
Major: Battle Mage
Minor: Rune Crafting
Companion: [Null]
Magical Strength: 19.2
Magical Control: 5.4
Magical Energy: 35.1
Physical Strength: 4.3
Endurance: 7.9

"You could have just asked." Damien snarled. He idly noted that Henry had swapped his Minor to something normal but was too angry to care.

Derrod snorted. "Those numbers are just numbers. They can't read how you can truly fight or who you really are."

"That's it, then? You threatened her just to screw with me?"

"Don't take it so harshly," Derrod replied. "I might have been the first, but I won't be the last. Your control over your temper could be improved. If it helps, I'll take care of your little request. I lied about Yui liking Nolan. She tolerates him, but if he truly doesn't want to be king, we'll need a better candidate. I would have taken care of that regardless of the outcome of this fight."

"Of course, you would have," Damien said tightly. "The kingdom comes first."

"Exactly," Derrod said. "I'm glad you understand. You've done very well for yourself, Damien. The power you showed me today is incredible. More than what I wielded at your age, that's for sure. You're becoming a very powerful mage. Sorry 'bout all that bad business, but I'm sure you understand."

A small smile crossed Damien's face. "Thanks, Dad. I do."

He walked up to Derrod, extending his hands for a hug. Derrod's eyebrows twitched up, but he wrapped his arms around his son. Damien reached up, resting one of his hands just behind Derrod's neck, and drew a mote of Ether into his finger, forming it into a thin claw of destructive energy and driving it into the other man's skin and drawing blood.

"Touch someone I care about again, and I swear on the Planes I'll kill you, Derrod," Damien hissed. Within him, It Who Heralds the End of All Light shifted, allowing the faintest amount of its power to seep out. Damien pushed away from Derrod and strode over to Delph. "I'm done here."

"You deserved that," Delph informed Derrod, waving his hand and forming a portal. Damien stormed through it and Delph followed, snapping it shut behind them.

CHAPTER
THIRTEEN

They emerged in Delph's house. Damien kicked a book on the ground, sending it flying through the air. Delph flicked his hand, and a portal appeared before the book, swallowing it up and depositing it in the professor's hands.

Damien ground his teeth and flopped down on the couch, his hands clenching at his sides as he gathered himself. "Sorry. Didn't mean to throw a temper tantrum."

"If the book had feelings, I'm sure it would understand," Delph said, tossing it aside. "Derrod is an insufferable man. When I was still on the frontlines, I had my fair share of cursing sessions after dealing with him."

"I never knew how bad he was," Damien said, grinding the material of his pants in one of his hands. "He's never done something like this."

"He probably didn't consider you a threat before," Delph said. "Or worse, an opportunity. Before you joined Blackmist, you wanted to be a researcher, didn't you? That wouldn't have had any major implications to the kingdom, so it doesn't surprise me that he cared so little. For what it's worth, I'm sorry."

"It's fine," Damien replied. "He was never really my father. I just need to keep him away from everyone else."

"You might find that difficult to do while at Forsad," Delph said. "But Derrod probably won't push too hard there. He wouldn't want to risk aggravating Yui. I trust that, at the least, your goal for the meeting was accomplished?"

"If he keeps his word," Damien said bitterly.

"He will," Delph said. "Derrod is many things, but he doesn't break his word when he gives it. Well, not unless it would hurt the kingdom. He'd punt a baby into a Devourer Beast's mouth if the queen asked him to."

"Good to know my father is such an upstanding person full of admirable morals."

"Hey, at least he was a deadbeat," Delph said. "Would have been worse if he actually rubbed off on you."

Damien couldn't keep himself from laughing. "I seriously hope you never take up counseling."

"Don't worry. I won't."

A few minutes passed in silence, and Damien fully suppressed the turmoil brewing in his heart.

"I've been meaning to ask you something," Damien said. "Derrod clearly knows how to fight the Corruption, as do you and Dredd. Why did you make Yui and the other students come to me and Sylph for training? And for that matter, how come there weren't any actual adults involved? It feels like they're the ones who need to know this."

Delph cocked an eyebrow and took a book from one of his shelves, brushing it off and sitting in a chair across from Damien. "Why do you think?"

"It seems pointless. I mean, it's probably good to be able to fight back against the Corruption, but it should be the strong mages and professors who know how to do it, not a bunch of students."

"It would be quite foolish to leave the fate of the world entirely in the hands of a group of children," Delph agreed. "But why would we do that?"

"Huh? But— Wait. Did you just train the other teachers yourself?"

"For those who needed to be trained, Dredd and I taught," Delph said. "Many did not. There are a lot of very powerful and resourceful mages in the kingdom. If there weren't, we would have lost the frontlines long ago."

"So, what's the point of sending everyone over to me? You could have taught them yourself."

"I could have," Delph said. "But that would have been a massive waste of my time. I have better things to do than teach a bunch of children how to fight in my free time. I already do that for a living. It's much easier to just have someone else do it for me."

"Is that really it? You just didn't want to do it, so you sent them my way instead?"

"What do you think?"

"Part of me wants to say yes."

"That part of you is wrong," Delph said, flipping the page and glancing up at him. "Think harder."

"I'm coming up blank. Everything really just points to you being lazy."

Delph closed the book with a *snap*. He let out a weary sigh. "I suppose I can't get too peeved about that. I *am* lazy. Trying hard is for people a lot younger than I am. You'll get burnt out and exhausted with the world soon enough. Given today's events, I'll just give you this one for free. I sent them to you for training."

"That is remarkably useless," Damien said. "They told me that themselves."

"It wasn't for their training," Delph replied. "It was yours.

Evidently, you missed it. I doubt the significance was as lost on Sylph, but she's got her own problems to worry about. Derrod was right about one thing today, Damien. You're growing in strength, but there's more than one kind of power. Even the strongest living mage needs support sometimes."

"I'm not sure I follow. You think they're going to help us fight the Corruption?"

"They might. They might not." Delph shrugged. "That wasn't the point. It isn't their power that really matters. If I were some wise, mystical figure, I'd probably tell you to figure the rest of this out yourself. Unfortunately, I'm impatient. As annoying as it is, there's strength in politics. By training all of them, you indebt them to you. Since it was a favor given freely, it also makes you look better in their eyes."

"That sounds like the crap Nolan and Yui are worried about. But not all of them were nobles," Damien pointed out. "Was this just to get Yui on my side? I kind of already spent my favor."

"It's not about the petty little favors that nobles toss around," Delph said, shaking his head and standing up. "It's about how they feel toward you. You've helped them. Many people in that group already consider you a friend. Building those bonds is important, and not for fighting monsters. You need a group of people to support you. Shoulder the weight of the world on your shoulders and, eventually, something will give out. They might not be able to pick that burden up themselves, but at least the wolves won't move in for the strike when you're weak if they're there to help."

"That's awfully specific," Damien said slowly.

"Read it in a book somewhere," Delph said gruffly, his eyes narrowing. He traced a line in the air, creating a gray portal. "And I am suddenly getting the urge to have my house back to myself before nosy students start digging around. I'll see you for training tomorrow, Damien."

Damien rose from the couch. "Thanks, Professor."

"Teaching is my job."

"Not for the advice. For everything else."

He stepped through the portal, and it snapped shut, leaving Delph alone in a darkening room, his eyes unreadable.

Damien threw himself into his practice the rest of the day. Sylph got back a few hours after he did, looking thoroughly exhausted. She flopped into bed and got into a cross-legged position to meditate. Henry returned to Damien's shadow, but he didn't say anything to avoid distracting Damien. He worked until a knock on the door that night interrupted him.

Sylph opened it and let Quinlan inside. The older girl carried a small basket of food in one of her hands.

"I brought something to eat," she said, holding it out. "Since you paid for dinner last time."

"Oh, you didn't have to do that," Damien said, pushing himself upright and shaking his legs out to get the feeling back into them.

"It's appreciated, though," Sylph added.

"It only felt right," Quinlan said. She dug around in her pocket and pulled out a slip of paper covered with runes. "I did what you said I should practice, Damien. This is the latest attempt at drawing the basic runes."

He took it from her and examined the paper. The strokes had gone through significant improvement from what she'd shown him yesterday. They were much neater and more precise. There were still a few slight inconsistencies and mistakes in the drawings, but it looked as if a different person had drawn them.

"This is great progress," Damien said, handing it back to her. "If you can keep this up, we might actually have a chance of getting you to your goal. I'm just not sure if this pace can continue once we get to the more difficult parts."

"Well, there's only one way to find out," Quinlan said, revealing several new pieces of chalk.

"Food first," Damien said. Quinlan pursed her lips but nodded her understanding. All three of them ate, then Damien set about teaching her as he had promised.

Sylph watched over his shoulder as he went over some more advanced runes and some basic linking techniques. She occasionally asked a question but mostly tried to stay out of the way to avoid bothering them.

They worked well into the night before Damien called it off, once more assigning Quinlan some homework. She headed off, and the other two went to bed shortly after. Before Damien fell asleep, he brought Henry up to speed about his meeting with Derrod.

"We could always kill him," Henry suggested. "He thinks he knows the full extent of your power, but he's got no idea. If we worked together at full strength, there's a good chance I could put a blade through his heart before he realized what was happening."

Tempting. And that isn't a good thing. Can't you suggest something more peaceful? I'm not supposed to want to murder my own father.

"You should have gone to someone else if you wanted some comforting human bullshit," Henry said with a mental shrug. "I'm not that far gone. Yet. The other day, I found myself thinking that it might be fun to take a walk around Blackmist to admire the scenery. A walk! And not even to eat goats although, now that I think about it, the goats would be a good addition."

That doesn't sound like such a bad thing to me. Minus the goat part.

"Of course, it doesn't. But what kind of self-respecting Void creature goes around on peaceful walks?"

I doubt most Void creatures go around eating goats that taste like cheese either.

"Well, if they ever tasted them, they would. Speaking of goats...I'll be back tomorrow. I have a visit to make."

Wait, what?

Henry slipped out of his shadow and darted out of the room before Damien could press the matter. Damien rolled his eyes and gave up. There wasn't any way for him to chase Henry, even if he wanted to. He let sleep take him.

The next week was much of the same routine. He and Sylph trained, either at class with Delph and Dredd or on their own, then met up with Quinlan to practice Rune Crafting. Sylph sat in on some of his lessons and worked with Henry during others.

Time passed and the day of the expedition grew closer. When only three days remained before they were set to leave, Damien and Sylph took a break from their routine to return to the pavilion where the other non-Blackmist students were staying and see how everyone else was doing.

Remarkably, almost nothing had changed. Yui's group sat with the Goldsilk students at the same table overlooking the arena. Mark and Elania were busy training in the corner of the arena, while Teddy and the still unnamed hooded figure watched over them from the tables.

There were only two differences. The first was Quinlan, who was nowhere to be found. If Damien had to guess, she was probably locked up in her room, practicing runes. The other was Nolan, who sat on the sandy ground of the arena and watching Mark spar with Elania.

"Haven't seen either of you in a while," Mark said, blocking a kick and shoving Elania back, knocking her to the ground. She lashed out, trying to take the boy's legs out from under him.

Sand roiled, rising to block the attack. Golden light flowed off Elania's leg, wrapping around the sand and striking Mark in the stomach. He spun with the blow, and Elania used the opportunity to stand.

"Hi," she said. A rock pelted her in the stomach, and Mark copied the move Elania had just used, knocking her to the ground for the second time.

"Have you been training?" Mark asked.

"What do you think?" Damien replied with a bemused grin. Elania sent several cylinders of gold light flying at Mark, forcing him back.

"Hold on," Mark said, dodging Elania's attack and diving forward, tackling her. Sand wrapped around him, encasing both him and her lower half before setting itself like stone. "You lose. You need to be more mobile when fighting someone with stronger defenses than you are."

"I was doing good until Damien and Sylph showed up!" Elania complained. "I got distracted."

"Don't," Mark said, standing up and allowing the sand to slough off him. Elania scrunched her nose and stuck his hand out. Mark glanced at it, then reached out and pulled the girl to her feet.

"It looks like you're improving," Damien said. "Good job."

"Really? How can you tell?"

Mostly because Mark isn't constantly insulting you.

"Just because your movements look more fluid," Damien said. "And it looks like Mark is actually taking things seriously. He wouldn't be bothering if you weren't."

"Oh, that's true," Elania said, her face lighting up. "Mark's a good teacher."

"I just like hitting people."

"We all knew that already," Damien said with a chuckle. "Have we missed anything this last week? I haven't really left my room much."

"Not really. The professors are all busy," Mark said irritably.

"They won't tell us anything about Forsad other than some strong mage is going to be babying us."

"Figures," Damien said, keeping his face straight. "Good to know I'm not completely out of the loop."

"There has been one small thing," Nolan said, rising from his spot in the corner and brushing the sand off his legs. He gave Damien a wide smile. "It worked."

"Did it really?" Damien asked, grinning. "That's great! I was a little worried, to be honest."

"Went better than I could have expected," Nolan said cheerfully. "I owe you a lot, Damien."

"I'm just glad I could help. Don't worry about it."

Nolan smirked. "Maybe I'll do just that. I'm not going to Forsad with the rest of you, but I've just been hanging out here to watch Mark train. I've never seen him do something for someone else, so it's been quite entertaining."

"Hey!" Mark snapped. "I do things for people all the time. I'm very mag—mugh—meghnamus?"

"Magnanimous?" Sylph offered.

"That's the one," Mark said.

They all stared at him for a moment before bursting into laughter, Mark included.

"You want to see just how much stronger you've gotten?" Mark asked, nodding at Damien.

"Hold on," Sylph said, raising a hand. "This time, it's my turn. It's been too long since we fought."

"All you had to do was ask," Mark said. A grin crossed his face as the others all took a few steps back, giving them space.

They both started to gather Ether, but Mark's expression flickered, and he lowered his hands. Sylph blinked.

"What's wrong?" she asked.

Mark nodded over her shoulder. They all turned, and the air seemed to freeze as Derrod walked through the door, Quinlan and two other students in his wake. He glanced around, his eyes not even stopping on Damien, and gave them all a wide grin. Damien didn't recognize the new students, but they wore the purple and black colors of Blackmist. His hands clenched at his sides, but he didn't let the anger reach his face.

"Sorry to interrupt," Derrod said, raising a hand and giving them an easygoing grin. "Given that the excursion to Forsad will be happening in a few days, I thought it was about time I introduced myself to all of you. I hope I'm not interrupting anything important."

Nolan rose and slipped out of the room, giving Damien a small nod before he left.

"We were just doing a little practice," Yui said, standing up and starting down the stairs. "It's a pleasure to see you again, Stormsword. I'm surprised you've got enough time to take care of us on something so unimportant."

"The queen would never let you travel somewhere dangerous without the proper protection," Derrod replied with a chuckle. "And we are sending some of the top students out of several schools. It would be a tragedy if anything serious befell any of you. I will do my best to ensure all your safety."

Damien noticed Derrod didn't actually promise anything. Delph's words rang in his head, and his annoyance only grew further. Sylph nudged him with her foot, but he just shook his head.

"Now that we're all here, have you all been introduced?" Derrod asked. "We'll be working closely on this trip, so it's important that we all get to know each other. I'll start, since I'm the one asking. My name is Derrod, but I'm known by my title as Stormsword."

Admiring gazes shone on just about every student's face. The only exceptions were Damien, Sylph, and Yui. Derrod chuckled again.

"I see some questions in your eyes. You're welcome to ask me whatever you'd like after our introductions are complete. I can't guarantee I'll answer, but I'll do my best. I'm already aquatinted with a few of you, but I see some new faces."

"I'm Teddy," the large boy. His voice was surprisingly elegant, and Damien would never have matched it to his muscular body. "I'm a Year Four from Greenvalley, and I specialize in Vibration magic."

"That's a rare one," Derrod said approvingly. "Lots of applications, but difficult to use effectively. Considering you've made Year Four, you must have a rather solid grasp on it. I wouldn't be surprised if we run into each other on the frontlines in a year."

Teddy beamed at the praise. "I very much look forward to that, Sir Stormsword."

"Just Stormsword, please," Derrod said, waving his hand. "Sir makes me feel old."

"I'm Mark," Mark said, inclining his head. "I specialize in Earth magic, and I'm a Year Three at Blackmist."

"I've heard you've got a bit more than just Earth," Derrod said.

"I do," Mark said, but he didn't elaborate. Apparently, even his respect for Derrod's strength wasn't enough to get him to reveal all his secrets.

"You probably all know this already, but I'm Yui," the princess said, reaching the bottom of the stairs. "Please, don't worry about my status during this excursion. I'll just be another student. I specialize in Fire and Ice magic, and I'm a Year Three. My attendants will be coming with us, but they aren't official members of the excursion."

Gaves and Bella both nodded but didn't say anything else. Damien caught Elania making a face at them behind their backs before she wiped it clean.

"I'm Viv, and the other two are Elania and Eve," Viv said from the floor above them. "We all specialize in Light magic, although we dabble in a few other fields. We're all Year Threes."

"I'm Quinlan," the last girl said, her face unreadable. "I'm a Year Four, and I focus on Magma magic."

"That's quite impressive," Derrod said, giving her a nod. "Magma magic is very dangerous, both to you and your opponents. Not many mages have mastered it. If you can use it well, you could become one of the best mages in your generation."

Quinlan tilted her head in appreciation. "I will do my best, but there are many talented mages just in this room. Claiming the title of the strongest mage will not be something done easily by anyone."

The small, hooded figure on the second floor shifted and hopped off the table. They barely stood tall enough to peer over the railing, and their face was still hidden behind the shadows of their cloak.

"I'm Reva. I'm a Year Four at Flamewheel, and I specialize in Shadow magic."

"An effective and powerful path," Derrod said approvingly. "One well suited to assassins."

"I plan to put it to great use in the service of the kingdom."

"Then we will get along handsomely," Derrod said.

One of the students behind Derrod, a tall boy with blonde hair and green eyes, raised his hand in greeting. "Heya, all, pleased to meet you. I'm Cheese."

They all stared at him, waiting for him to elaborate. He didn't.

"What magic do you use?" Derrod prodded.

"Whoopsie. I just kind of punch things." Cheese gave them an easygoing grin. "I can't really cast magic intentionally. It works, though. I'm a Year Four, by the way."

"Excuse him," the girl beside him said. Her mouth and

lower face were covered by a heavy black scarf. "Cheese is a bit of an idiot. I'm Aven. Year Four, and I use whatever magic I'm feeling like at the time."

A few mutters passed through the students at that. Derrod raised a hand.

"I know Aven sounds like she's skirting the question, but I've actually seen her in action, and she's telling the truth. Her companion has granted her access to nearly a dozen schools of magic, and she's adept at using all of them. She's the top ranked student in Blackmist's Year Four, and Cheese is just barely behind her. That leads us to the last two students."

Sylph and Damien both introduced themselves.

"There's one more thing I should mention," Derrod said, his grin widening. "It hasn't been a widely known fact, but considering the nature of this mission, I need to come clean. Damien here is my son."

The gazes of everyone who didn't already know that particular fact snapped to Damien.

"What an asshole. He just painted a target on us," Henry growled. "At least nobody will try anything while he's watching, though. They don't want to get on his bad side."

"Now, given our relationship, I'm sure a lot of you are thinking a few things you're too polite to say out loud. Blackmist sent a lot of Year Threes to this excursion and only two Year Fours, so how do we know that Damien really deserves his spot here? He could have just been chosen because of me."

"He and Sylph both performed very well at the intermural tournament," Viv said. "They're stronger than many of the other people here."

Derrod kept talking as if he hadn't heard her.

"For that reason, I'd like to state this right now. I want to push Damien to his limits. As my son, I hold him to the highest standard possible. For that reason, if any of you wish to test just how strong he is, I implore you to do so now. Let him prove he deserves his place among the rest of us."

Henry leapt into Damien's Mage Armor, turning it black and raising it defensively around him as Teddy leapt off the railing, letting out a shrill whistle. A wave of force slammed into Damien, throwing him across the room. He teleported before he could hit the wall, appearing behind Teddy.

Henry lashed out with a tentacle, striking for the larger boy's back. Teddy spun, blocking the attack and whistling again. Invisible force drove into Damien's stomach, and Henry hardened his armor, reducing the effect of the attack so it only knocked the breath from his lungs instead of tossing him away.

Sylph darted at them, but a dark spike shot up from the ground and forced her to dodge back. Reva rose from the ground before her, jagged blades made of shadow forming around her.

"Teddy is fighting Damien right now," Reva said. "You're not part of—"

Sylph's arm flickered. A bone-colored scythe sprouted from her arm, whipping forward and burrowing itself into Reva's chest. The hooded girl let out a choked gasp as Sylph leaned forward, pressing her onto the ground. Sylph put her foot on the other girl's chest and ripped the blade free in a spray of blood.

Damien grabbed Teddy's shoe with telekinesis, ripping it out from beneath him before the other boy could react. Teddy rolled, kicking his shoe off and coming back to his feet with a grin on his face.

"Didn't realize you could do that. Haven't fought someone with Space magic before," Teddy said. He snapped his fingers, and a tremor shot through Damien's leg, followed by sudden pain. It vanished a moment later, much to Teddy's apparent surprise.

"Nullified it," Henry reported. "He's using targeted vibrations to try and cause microfractures in your bones. A layer of mental energy around your entire body can counter that strategy entirely."

"You already figured it out?" Teddy asked, surprised.

Damien's response was to try and grab his other shoe with telekinesis. Unfortunately, Teddy was just as fast of a learner as Henry was. He batted Damien's mental energy away with his own and dove at him.

Behind them, Sylph's dash was interrupted as a dark blade nearly took her arm off. She spun as Reva rose from the ground, shadows knitting the wound on her chest back together.

"If I hadn't reacted fast enough, that might have seriously hurt me," Reva said. "What kind of psycho goes for a killing blow while training?"

"You're a Year Four," Quinlan said from the sidelines. "If a Year Three offed a Year Four with a single attack, that would be pretty pathetic."

Teddy and Damien danced around each other, slinging spells and trading blows. It was apparent Teddy wasn't using his full strength, since after his targeted vibration spell failed, he didn't try any magic other than what he'd previously used. Even still, his magic was strong enough that it took all of Damien's concentration to keep up with it and avoid using Direct Casting or any of Henry's other magic.

Sylph and Reva were caught in a similar fight, but Sylph had the upper hand. However, with every passing second, Reva regained ground. Her attacks only grew faster and more accurate while Sylph heavily limited her magic usage, avoiding depleting her low stores too quickly.

"You're too distracted," Teddy grunted, driving a palm into Damien's chest. The strike sent a ripple of magic throughout his whole body, picking him up and launching him into the wall with a loud *crash*.

Damien dropped to the ground, his ears ringing. "So are you."

A Gravity Sphere he'd locked in place near Teddy's foot detonated. The large boy tried to dodge but couldn't get his whole leg out of the blast zone. With a series of loud *cracks*, several bones shattered.

Damien turned, grabbing Reva's clothes with telekinesis and picking her up. Unprepared for the spell, she didn't get a chance to negate Damien's mental grip over her, and he slammed her into the ceiling.

Reva broke Damien's hold over her with a shield of mental energy and dropped back to the ground, covered in dust. A dark gauntlet formed over Sylph's hand, and wind whipped around her. She shot forward, ducking under a shadowy blade and driving her fist into Reva stomach.

The smaller girl shot back like a rock launched from a catapult, slamming into the wall much like Damien had seconds before. Reva snarled, pushing away from it. The lights in the room started to dim.

"I'm getting in on this," Mark said with a gleeful laugh. His skin took on a reddish tint, and he slashed his hand through the air, sending a blade of red energy hurtling at Teddy. The large boy's eyes widened, but Cheese appeared before him, batting Mark's attack away with the back of his hand.

"Me, too," Cheese said gleefully, rubbing his hands together.

Mark and Cheese darted at each other. The remaining students glanced around, then seemed to share a collective shrug. Ether surged as everyone channeled magic, and the room descended into chaos.

The fight lasted for nearly five minutes. By the time it was over, almost everyone was slumped on the ground or against the wall, breathing heavily and covered in wounds. The room was in shambles. Furniture on the second floor had turned to ammunition and was broken to pieces. Large scars covered the arena walls, and large sections of sand had turned to glass.

Damien sported a jagged cut along his forehead and several of his fingers were broken from one of Teddy's attacks. The only students in the room untouched from the fight were Yui and Aven.

Mark and Cheese were leaning back-to-back, both covered in darkening bruises and panting heavily. They each sported an enormous, shit-eating grin.

FOURTEEN

"We should do that again. I had no idea my underclassmen were so fun," Cheese said, speaking with a lisp from a busted lip.

"Agreed," Mark said. He wiped the blood from his nose and rubbed it off on his shirt. "I didn't realize the higher year students at Blackmist were this much fun."

A short distance away, Reva and Sylph glared daggers at each other, neither letting their guard down. Teddy gave Damien a slight nod.

"Not bad for a Year Three. You're Stormsword's kid all right."

"He had nothing to do with my education," Damien replied flatly. "And you were holding back."

Teddy chuckled. "Course I was. I wasn't about to go all out against a kid a year behind me. Wouldn't be right. Find me again once you graduate, and maybe we'll really see how we match up."

Sylph broke away from the other girl, grabbing a waterskin from her pouch and tossing it to Damien. He grabbed it with his uninjured hand, giving her a grateful smile as he poured the healing water over his hand. His fingers snapped back into place, and he let out a relieved sigh.

"Thanks." He handed it back to her.

"You should really start carrying some around yourself," Sylph admonished. "You're the one who keeps breaking things."

"You're probably right," Damien admitted. "I'll get a waterskin once we get some free time."

"I trust you're all satisfied," Derrod said, clearing his throat. "I wasn't quite expecting an all-out brawl, but I can't fault any of you kids for wanting to get in on it. Real life doesn't throw you predictable situations anyway, so this was a good simulation of what a real battle might be like. Does anyone have any doubts or questions about the students going to Forsad?"

Nobody said anything. Derrod gave them a satisfied nod. "Good. My main goal today was just to meet everyone and take care of introductions. I've got a fair number of preparations to do before we head to Forsad, so I'll be taking my leave. We'll next meet on the day we leave—meet me at this pavilion, one hour before sunrise."

He raised a hand and turned, walking out of the destroyed building as if he wasn't responsible for all the rubble strewn across the ground. They watched Derrod go, not saying a word until he was completely out of sight.

"Sorry about your pavilion," Damien said to Yui. "We kind of wrecked it."

"It's not your fault," Yui replied with a shrug. "Blackmist will send someone to repair it soon enough anyway."

"We'll be on our way, then," Damien said. "Lots to prepare before the expedition and all that."

"I've got some work to take care of as well," Quinlan said. Yui's eyebrow twitched up, and the three of them headed out of the pavilion.

They made it about five minutes down the road before Quinlan sped up to walk side by side with Damien and Sylph.

"Are we going to be able to finish everything up today?" she asked. "I did the runes you told me to practice yesterday."

Damien chewed his lower lip. "I'm not sure. You're still making great progress, but there's only so much you can learn at once, and you're already moving at an incredible speed. You've still got a lot of material you need to cover if you want to make anything as advanced as your goal, even if I'm supervising you."

"Are we going to be able to finish before the expedition to Forsad?"

"It's hard for me to say since I really don't know much about how complex your rune circle is going to need to be," Damien replied. "It depends on the strength of whatever you're binding, the strength of the person being bound, and a bunch of other factors that I need to teach you how to recognize. You might be able to make something that works close to what you want since I've been focusing on the runes that would help you, but I wouldn't bet too much on it."

Quinlan's hands clenched. "I see. I'll have to continue research back at Mountain Hall, then."

"Well, we still have a little more time before the expedition," Sylph pointed out. "And I don't know exactly how the expedition will go, but nothing stops Damien from spending a little time continuing to teach you during our down time there. It probably won't be as much as he's spending now, but we'll still have some time."

Damien nodded. "So long as you don't mind other people seeing. Then again, if we break off in small groups, it shouldn't be an issue at all. Although I'll be honest, even with the extra time in the expedition, it's still going to be a tight call."

"It's better than any other choice I have," Quinlan said, letting out a breath. "Thank you. I'll take what I can get."

"We've got some free time now, and I don't really want to get tracked down by anyone," Damien said. "If you already did your rune practice today, why don't you show me how it went?"

"I don't actually have it on me," Quinlan said with a frown. "I've been drawing on the floor since I ran out of paper. If we head to my room, I can show you."

"I've done that a few times," Damien chuckled. "Sylph, did you have any more training planned with Henry today?"

"No, we finished up yesterday. I'm about as fixed up as I'm going to get, according to him. I can come with you."

"Wait, really?" Damien asked, pausing to turn and look at her. "That's great! Can you feel the difference?"

"Definitely," Sylph replied. "It feels a bit strange, but all my magic comes easier to me now. I still barely have any magical energy to work with, but at least the spells are almost like second nature now. I didn't realize how much I was struggling to control some of my powers before this."

"What happened to your magic?" Quinlan asked, cocking her head to the side. "I've never heard of someone getting an injury that made it difficult to access the magic they already know. There's breaking your Core, but I don't think you'd be talking about that so casually. From what I know, you can't really come back from that."

Henry scoffed, and Damien mentally shooed him away.

"I had a pretty severe injury that Henry fixed," Sylph said. "For now, that's about all I'm going to say on it. The less you know, the less Henry's spell is going to force you to keep quiet."

"That's a fair point," Quinlan said, her face falling slightly. They turned the corner and started up a mountain path toward where her room was. "I still find it hard to believe that I'm learning runes entirely because I pissed Damien's companion off."

"Stranger things have happened because of him," Damien said, shaking his head. "Just don't feed his ego. I'm just glad we were able to find a way to make up what he did to you."

"It's fine. The strong rule," Quinlan said with a one-shouldered shrug. "That's just how it is. Mountain Hall isn't any different. If someone had caught me there, things wouldn't have gone nearly as well. Granted, I never thought someone that powerful would just be sneaking around my room."

"The strong should protect the weak," Damien said with a frown. "I remember Derrod used to say that mercy was the right of the powerful. I don't like him, but he was right about that. I'm just not strong enough to do more than I already am. I really hate the deal we've got to keep you under for now, but I can't take any risks."

"It's fine," Quinlan replied with a shrug. They reached her room and headed into it. She opened her dresser and pushed the clothes out of the way, starting down into the passage behind it. "I'm getting what I wanted anyway, and the rules of the contract aren't anything that I can't deal with. They're more than fair."

A distant groan reached Damien's ears. He paused, glancing at Sylph. She gave him a slight nod, but shrugged, indicating she'd heard it as well but had no idea what it was.

Quinlan didn't seem to notice their hesitation. She got to the bottom of the pathway a few steps ahead of them and headed into a large circular room. Scribbled chalk runes covered the floor and walls, all considerably better than the chicken-scratch that she'd initially been writing.

About half of the room was taken up by an enclosure with six goats in it. Each goat had a knitted hat perched atop their heads, and there were several large bowls of food laid out for them. A goat wearing a red hat bleated loudly, answering where the noise Damien and Sylph had heard earlier was coming from.

Quinlan cleared her throat. "Oh. The goats."

"Henry?" Damien asked, trying to hold back a laugh. His shadow twitched, and Henry rose from it in his blobby, spherical form.

"What?" Henry asked.

"Are you responsible for the goats?"

"No. That's Quinlan's job," Henry replied. "Why would I bother taking care of a bunch of goats?"

Damien tried to keep himself from laughing. "I'm sorry, Quinlan. I probably should have expected this."

"It's fine," Quinlan replied. "They're kind of cute, actually. They keep me company."

The goat in the red hat bleated again. It slowly lowered its head, eating something within the bowl without taking its beady black eyes off the newcomers in its house.

"Where did the hats come from?" Sylph asked. "Is that also Henry?"

"No. I just like knitting. It helps me concentrate when I'm trying to think," Quinlan said. She pursed her lips. "I'd appreciate if you don't go around sharing that. It would ruin the persona I've built for myself among the other schools."

"We won't say a word," Damien said, walking over to the fence and examining the goats. Red hat walked up to the short fence and eyed his clothes. He took a healthy step out of chomping distance. "Henry, do you know how to knit?"

"Why in the Eight Planes would I know how to knit?" Henry asked. "I learn magic. I can knit magic. Not yarn."

"Well, you should learn," Damien said. "If I remember correctly, you stole Yui's hat and fed it to a goat."

"The goat was hungry."

"Not for a hat," Damien said. "And taking someone's stuff, especially something personal, is honestly pretty messed up. That would be like someone grabbing my scarf while I was asleep. I'd be furious, so you're technically in Yui's debt. That means I am, too, and I really don't want to be in her debt."

"Bah. Fine. Why don't you just buy a new hat for the girl?"

"Because she can buy a new hat herself. She probably didn't even notice the monetary loss. It's the thought that counts."

"More of Stormsword's teaching?" Quinlan asked.

"No. That's my mom," Damien replied, a slight grin crossing his face. "And I'm sorry—I didn't even ask you if you wanted to teach Henry how to knit. It's not part of our deal or anything, so you don't have to if you don't want to."

Quinlan eyed Henry, thinking over Damien's words. "I can teach him after I get my practice in for my runes, but I really need to get as much progress in as I can. I can't say much, but I'm on a time limit."

"And I haven't said I'm going to learn," Henry said crossly.

Damien raised an eyebrow. Henry crossed his tentacles and glared at him. After a few seconds, he threw them up and let out an exaggerated sigh.

"What is this emotion you're making me feel? I do not like it. Stop that."

"That would be guilt."

"Take it back. How do I make it go away?" Henry asked.

"By making the hat, probably," Sylph said, trying to hide a smile.

"Eight Planes, you're all on the same team," Henry complained. "Fine. I'll make the damn hat, okay? Now, teach the girl the runes so I can get this over with."

"I've got a better idea," Damien said, holding up a finger. "You're done fixing Sylph up, and you've forgotten more about runes than I've ever known. You teach Quinlan. It'll be way better and more efficient than anything I can do."

One of the goats bleated.

"You've got to be kidding me. You just want me to do your work for you," Henry complained.

"Are you saying I'm better than you at drawing runes?"

"Absolutely not."

"Am I a better teacher than you?"

"Not in this lifetime. I'm the best at everything I've ever done."

Damien cocked an eyebrow. "Then..."

"You are the lamest host I could have gotten," Henry decided. "If I'd landed Sylph instead, we would have destroyed the world a dozen times over already."

"I'll keep your complaint in mind. But, honestly, wouldn't you rather hang around the goats than me and Sylph?"

Henry paused. One of his eyes flicked over to the goats. "Hm. You are quite lame."

"Then it's settled," Damien said. "Quinlan, I hope you don't mind. Henry really is your best bet if you want to learn faster, though. He should be able to teach you more and better than I ever could. Just...don't agree to anything too crazy. Are you okay with learning from him?"

Quinlan nodded once. "I'll do it, if he's willing."

"There are goats here. Why wouldn't I be?" Henry asked, forming an eye and sending it floating toward the goats. "Now show me those runes you made. Let's see if I can salvage whatever you've learned from Damien's ham-fisted teaching."

Quinlan pointed at a section of runes at the corner of the room and Henry went over to them. He turned, glancing back at Damien and Sylph. "Why are you two still here? Get lost. I'm teaching."

"We're already gone," Damien said, raising his hands in mock surrender. "Good luck."

He and Sylph retreated up the pathway while Henry started instructing Quinlan.

"Nice one," Sylph whispered. "But what do we do now? More training?"

"We've done enough of that these last few days. How about we get some dinner instead? Henry's busy, so he can't complain if we go somewhere," Damien said with a smug grin.

Sylph shook her head. "Did you have that all planned from the start?"

"I might have gotten an idea once I saw the goats," Damien replied. "So, what kind of food are you feeling?"

They ended up settling on trying a restaurant they'd never been to before—which was most of them. After wandering around Blackmist's sprawling campus for almost half an hour, they chose a nice, two-story restaurant named the Toasted Bun.

A waiter seated them promptly, depositing a pair of menus in their hands before sweeping away to go stand at the podium near the entrance in preparation for the next pair of customers.

One quick glance around the room revealed that only around half the tables were occupied, but the low level of chatter in the room and warm light coming from a large fire-place in the center of the building gave it a comforting ambiance. A thin stream of smoke rose through a hole in the roof right above the fire, curling away and disappearing into the sky.

"I bet getting all the smoke to go straight up was a pain," Sylph said. "I doubt they'd have very many happy customers if everyone got smoked out."

"Maybe a bunch of wind generating runes around the edge of the fire," Damien said, rubbing his chin. "They'd have to be pretty weak to avoid making a bunch of noise, but that's what I would do."

"Very astute," a waiter said, inclining his head as he set a glass of water down before each of them. The light reflected off his slightly shiny, slicked back hair. "Have you ever visited the Toasted Bun before?"

"First time," Sylph said. "Any recommendations?"

"Everything on the menu is certain to meet your expectations," the waiter replied with a smile. He tapped one of the entrees. "But the fried and battered sourfin is one of our specialties. Nobody has complained about it yet, so it can't be too bad."

"Do people typically complain about your other dishes?" Damien asked, laughing.

"Oh, people will complain about anything," the waiter said with a conspiratorial wink. "Would you like some more time to look at the menu?"

"I'll go with your suggestion," Damien replied. "Sylph, do you need more time?"

"I'll get this," Sylph said, pointing to a dessert at the bottom of the menu.

"Brilliant choices," the waiter said. He collected their menus and swept away, disappearing through a rotating door at the back of the room. The scent of warm cinnamon, honey, and freshly baked bread wafted out from behind it.

"I like this place," Damien said. "It feels comfortable."

"You haven't tried the food yet." Sylph grinned. "But I agree. It's relaxing. Somehow, I don't think we're going to find much of this in Forsad."

Damien shuddered. "Let's not think about that for now. Considering the company we'll be keeping, Forsad is the last thing I want on my mind. Well, actually, scratch that. When we're there, you need to be careful."

"Careful? Of what? Do you think Second is going to cause problems?" Sylph asked, lowering her voice.

"I don't know about that, although it wouldn't surprise me," Damien said, leaning closer. "It's not him that I'm worried about. It's Derrod."

Sylph's lips thinned. "I'm always wary of him. Is there something else I should pay even more attention to about him?"

"I feel like he's trying to do something, but I don't know what," Damien said. "He hasn't bothered with me once in the past few years and, all of a sudden, he's showing up all the time."

"You've met him a total of two times now in the past month. That isn't exactly all the time."

"Three, actually," Damien corrected. "And you'd be right if it were anyone else. He doesn't do anything without a reason, but I don't know what his reason is. I don't trust him, and I'm worried he might try to do something to you."

Sylph's features softened. "I can take care of myself, Damien. Derrod was right about one thing—I'm trained. I can deal with someone gunning for me—even him. I can't take your dad in a fight, but I'm also a lot more resilient than anyone else we know, and he isn't aware of that ability as far as I'm aware. I do appreciate your concern, though. Are you sure that the one in danger isn't *you*?"

"No," Damien admitted. "I'm not. I know one thing—he only cares about the kingdom. He wouldn't do anything against its best interests, and I have no reason to ever go against them."

Sylph raised an eyebrow ever so slightly. "I know. You just can't discount anything. If he's as dedicated as you think, he might just be really making sure you're on the kingdom's side to make sure you won't turn into a threat. He's one of the most egotistical men I've ever met. He probably assumes you, as his son, have to be strong and doesn't want to risk anything."

"The sad thing is that you might be right," Damien said with a laugh. "Good point. I didn't even think about that."

They let the conversation trail off and just sat there, soaking in the atmosphere of the restaurant while they waited for their food. The waiter emerged from the kitchen a few times, each time passing right by their table but delivering the food to someone else.

Finally, after around fifteen minutes, the man finally brought them their dishes and laid them out on the table. After confirming they didn't need anything else, he swept off and the two dug in.

———

Derrod Vale leaned against his sword, enjoying the evening wind as it rustled his hair and chilled the blood cooling on his knuckles. He drew in a deep breath, savoring the smell before letting it out slowly and opening his eyes.

A lanky, humanoid monster loomed in the distance. Its limbs were thin and gangly, and its face featureless. Green liquid and strips of rotted fur covered its body, barely covering the rocky skin beneath it.

The monster approached him, covering enormous swathes of ground with every single awkward step. A keening screech ripped out from it, although from where Derrod could not tell. It reached out for him with a hand the size of a large horse.

Derrod lashed out with several dozen mental spikes. They punched into the monster's arm, turning it into a pincushion in his mind's eye. His eyes flared with blue energy, and he flickered forward, the huge sword at his side tracing a path through the air and severing several of the creature's fingers.

He drove several more spikes of energy into the monster's body around the wound. Energy rushed into the creature from the surrounding Ether, trying to repair its wound, but it faltered and failed to pass through Derrod's mental energy.

Derrod chuckled. He blurred once more, his sword falling once more and taking several fingers off the other hand. More spikes followed the wound, stopping it from healing.

"You are a waste of time," Derrod informed the beast from behind it. It spun, trying to strike him with the back of an enormous hand. A bolt of lightning leapt from Derrod's hand, striking the monster's hand and sending it flying in the opposite direction with a brilliant bang.

Green acid dripped from the monster, sealing the smoking wound. Derrod didn't stop it. He ripped his mental energy free of the monster and acid started to flow freely once more. Within seconds, its fingers had regrown.

The monster lunged at him, crashing into the ground and tearing dirt and grass away in a huge cloud. Derrod flickered back, then leapt into the air and hurled his sword down. The blade punched into one of the Corrupted monster's arms, severing the hand cleanly at its wrist.

Derrod wrapped both pieces of the limb with mental energy, then sent a thick bolt of lightning into the tall creature's head, slamming it back into the dirt before it could stand.

"Where is the one that sent you?" Derrod demanded. "You are boring me, and my time is needed elsewhere."

If the monster could respond, it didn't. It simply let out another screech. Its arm bent back at an impossible angle, swinging to strike Derrod. He raised a hand, and a powerful gale whipped around him. He caught the blow with his hand, then sent the power coursing back through the monster's body.

It bulged in a dozen places, skin splitting in miniature explosion as lightning forced its way out of the monster's body and back into the ground. Derrod sent dozens of miniature spikes into the wounds, forcing them to remain open.

"It is unfortunate that you caught me on a night where I can do nothing but wait," Derrod whispered, his eyes as cold as the moon starting to rise in the sky behind them. "You can clearly feel pain, so you're going to help me discover if your kind can speak the common tongue."

The monster struggled against him, but Derrod's sword leapt back into his hand. He stepped onto it, sending blue energy scoring through the beast's body as he walked, and drove the weapon into its chest, twisting it. He didn't stop it from healing and allowed the acid to sizzle as it tried to push the crackling blade out fruitlessly. Another furious screech filled the night.

"It'll be a long time before you use up all the Ether in the area," Derrod said, drumming his fingers on the pommel of the weapon. "And this is less boring than sitting around and doing nothing. Do you speak?"

A blur shot at Derrod from the tall grass in the distance. Small and lithe, it moved with incredible speed as it flung itself through the air, green acid dripping from jagged fangs as it went to rip the distracted mage's throat out.

Its incredible speed was such that most other mages wouldn't have even been able to spot the creature before it reached them. With Derrod's blade stuck in the other monster's back, he had no weapon to deflect its attack.

The beast's eyes widened as Derrod's head turned to look straight at it. There wasn't a single ounce of fear or surprise in his gaze. There was only hunger. Derrod twisted, driving his hand up and grabbing the blur by the throat.

He shifted his weight, swinging the monster over his shoulder and slamming it over the hilt of his sword with such force that the blunt end drove through its chest. Acid and fragments of stone sprayed everywhere.

Blue crackling energy surged around Derrod, disintegrating it before even a drop could touch him. The new monster struggled on his sword, but he drove his mental energy into it, forcing the wound to remain open. It was vaguely canine shaped, but its limbs were far too long and jutted out in all the wrong spots. Two nubs on its back looked like they had been meant to be other limbs but had been chopped or fell off somehow.

"What about you?" Derrod asked, raising an eyebrow. "Do you speak?"

"T-the Corruption will consume you," the dog monster snarled, sputtering and coughing as acid dripped into its throat and filled its lungs. "Your world will suffer for what it has done."

"Why do you attack the kingdom?"

"We care not f-for the kingdom." The monster snarled. Its taller companion tried to rise once more. Derrod sent a thick blast of lightning into it, blowing the creature's head off in a single strike. It started to repair itself, and he did nothing to stop it.

"Ah. We're just in the way, then?"

"All man will be p-purged so that we may live."

"Go on," Derrod said.

"I will say no more. Death comes for you all."

"Ah. Pity," Derrod said. His lips quirked up in a small smile. "I've never liked dogs, you know."

Several thick beams of lightning leapt from his fingers, surging into the sword pinning both monsters to the ground. The night sky lit up, and an enormous bang shook the grassy plains. A huge tree formed of lightning erupted from the monster's bodies, disintegrating them. Derrod ripped every last shred of their connection to the Ether apart with his mental energy, ensuring not a single fragment of them remained when he was done.

A purple portal carved itself into the air beside Derrod, and Dean Whisp stepped out from within it, her gauntlets soaked with blood. She glanced around, then raised an eyebrow at Derrod.

"I was told you were sent to fight a strong Corrupted monster. Where'd it go?"

"Dead," Derrod replied. "It wasn't much of a challenge."

"Figures. Learn anything?" Whisp asked, reaching for her side and grabbing a flask to take a large swig out of.

"Nothing of interest," Derrod replied. "But my boredom was assuaged slightly. Any service for the kingdom is one I am honored to do."

Whisp snorted. "Sure. Want a drink?"

"What is it?"

"Red wine."

"I'll pass," Derrod replied. "I don't drink spirits when I'm hunting."

"I don't think I've ever seen you drink," Whisp said with a laugh. She took another long drink from the flask, then turned it over and shook it. It was empty. She harrumphed and tossed it onto the ground.

"Not in the past ten years," Derrod replied with a tight smile. "But there are more important things to address. Who knows when we'll get a few moments alone again. I have some questions to ask."

Whisp cocked an eyebrow. "You about to proposition to me?"

"Don't delude yourself," Derrod replied. "Tell me about my son."

"He's your kid," Whisp snorted. "What can I tell you about

him? How he's doing in class? I don't even know that myself, but he must be passing."

"I don't care about that," Derrod said. "What about his schools of magic?"

"Geez. You don't even know that? What kind of father are you?"

"Those don't sound like schools of magic to me."

"Gah. No wonder everyone hates working with you," Whisp said. She hiccupped, then wiped her mouth with the back of her sleeve. "He's got Dark, Light, and Space."

"Interesting combination," Derrod said, rubbing his chin. "That's it?"

"Space is a very powerful school, and most people don't even have two, much less three," Whisp said. "Your kid isn't half-bad, Derrod. He's done some good work, even if he is a bit of a smartass now."

"Dark, Light, and Space," Derrod repeated. "From what Plane?"

"Darkness. Some new demon, supposedly. As expected as a child of Stormsword," Whisp replied. "Why?"

"Just curious," Derrod replied. He turned, starting toward the portal. Just before he stepped through, he paused and glanced back at her. "Has anyone ever seen his companion?"

CHAPTER
FIFTEEN

The day of departure arrived before any of them were truly ready for it. Damien and Sylph arrived at the training pavilion early in the morning. Most of the other students had already arrived and were milling about.

Blackmist had yet to fully replace the furnishings in the buildings after the carnage that they'd caused, but a few new tables had been put in on the top floor so Yui and Reva, the hooded girl, could look down on everyone.

Cheese and Mark had claimed the left corner of the arena and the Goldsilk girls sat a short distance away from them, discussing in hushed tones.

"And here I was thinking I'd get here before most people," Teddy's basso voice rumbled from behind them.

Damien turned, moving out of the way to let the larger boy past them. He inclined his head slightly, although it was difficult to tell if the motion was out of respect or if he'd simply seen something interesting on the ground.

"It's more looking like we're late," Damien observed, keeping his guard up. Cordial words or not, it wasn't lost on him that Teddy had held back a lot of his strength when they'd fought and hadn't shown an ounce of hesitation when Derrod had told them to fight.

He and Sylph wandered into the room and sat at the remains of one of the tables that had been yet to be replaced. Teddy watched them go but didn't make any move to follow. He just flopped down in a cross-legged position on the sand, leaning against the wall and watching his fellow students through half-lidded eyes.

Damien had bigger problems than the other students, though. Henry, who had gone to work with Quinlan the night before, still had yet to return. There was still no sight of Quinlan, but Damien doubted they'd have run into any serious trouble.

The last remaining students piled into the room over the next few minutes. Quinlan finally arrived, bearing a large leather bag nearly as tall as she was on her back. She spotted Damien and Sylph, making her way over to them and setting the large back beside them.

Sylph cocked an eyebrow. "Are you bringing everything you own with you?"

"No. Just a few essentials," Quinlan replied. "We don't know what's waiting for us in Forsad, and I brought some extra materials for Rune Crafting so we could continue practicing. Some other things, too. I've got your companion with me as well."

"Ah, that's good," Damien said. "I was wondering where he was when he didn't show up this morning. Nothing bad happened, right? Why is he still hiding?"

"He's finishing up a project," Quinlan replied, nodding at her bag. "In there."

The pavilion doors darkened, interrupting their conversation. All the low chatter in the room vanished as Derrod stepped in, Aven at his heels. She shot a sharp glance at Cheese, who stuck his tongue out in response.

"Everyone is here," Derrod said, nodding once. "Good. I do not appreciate tardiness. We will be setting off shortly. Due to the nature of this mission, before we leave, I will be personally inspecting all your companions. Your schools might have determined that you are strong enough for this mission, but I do not take our task lightly. I have already inspected Aven and Princess Yui's companions. We can start with Flamewheel and move on to Mountain Hall."

Damien pressed his lips together and narrowed his eyes. There was little doubt in his mind that Derrod had said that specifically because of Henry, but he didn't let his expression change in the slightest.

Reva hopped down from the second floor, landing with a puff of sand on the ground before Derrod. She straightened, extending her hands palm up. Darkness gathered in her palm, dripping to the floor at her feet.

The shadows rose, knitting together and forming into the shape of a dog with four burning coal-red eyes. It let out a woof, releasing a cloud of hazy smoke from its nostrils.

"Shadowhound." Derrod nodded approvingly. "And a full manifestation. Respectable. Next."

The monster vanished back into Reva, and she walked to the side, turning back to watch the proceedings without revealing her face. Somehow, Damien suspected she had a smug grin.

Quinlan approached Derrod. The air around her grew hazy and magma dripped from her fingertips, forming into craggy armor that covered her body. "I'm sorry, Mr. Derrod. I cannot manifest my companion safely within the confines of this building. It is a magma elemental."

"I think that's quite all right," Derrod said, a trickle of sweat beading up on his forehead. He wiped it away. "That combat manifestation is more than enough. I can feel the heat from here, and I can tell you're suppressing it. You can control the intensity, correct?"

Quinlan nodded, and the orange glow surrounding her faded until her armor was little more than glowing obsidian. "Yes, sir."

"Good," Derrod said. "Goldsilk is next."

Eve walked up to him. She extended her hands before her, and a gentle chime filled the air. A glowing orb coalesced between her and Derrod, blinking gently. He sucked in a slow breath.

"Haven't seen one of these in a long time. A warden?"

"A very young one, Stormsword." Eve's voice was little more than a whisper.

Derrod nodded. "More than sufficient. Your powers aren't the most suited to combat, but you'll be a brilliant addition to the group."

Elania and Viv went after her. Elania had a light elemental while Viv had a whisp, much to everyone from Blackmist's amusement. Damien discreetly tugged at Quinlan's bag, which had been left beside him. He could vaguely feel Henry within it, but it was sealed tight.

Teddy went after Goldsilk, revealing he had a monster from the Plane of Stars called a Ripple. It was a large, stone frog that stood half as tall as he did and was covered with jagged ridges.

"Right, then," Derrod said. "We'll finish with Blackmist. Who's first?"

"I have an exception," Mark said. "Has the school informed you about it?"

"They have," Derrod said. He examined Mark for a few moments. "Can you control it?"

"So long as I limit the amount of strength I draw," Mark said. "I don't have complete domination over its powers, but I have enough to use comfortably."

Derrod rubbed his chin. "I'd prefer to see just what you're capable of, but I've seen a few of your fights myself. I'll respect the Dean's wishes for now but know that if I even see the slightest sign of you losing control, I will take what actions are necessary to protect the group."

Mark nodded his understanding. Damien tugged more furiously at the straps, trying to untangle them.

Henry! You are not doing this to me again! Don't you remember almost missing the test ceremony when I first got to Blackmist? Come on, get out of there!

His request fell on deaf ears. Without Henry inside his mind, he didn't have a non-verbal way to communicate with his companion.

"I've got a sylph," Sylph said, noticing his struggle and walking up to summon Human and buy time.

Derrod cocked an eyebrow, and several students chuckled.

"That's a rather weak companion," Derrod said. "Its magical energy is relatively low. But you've clearly got more than enough talent if you've remained at the top of your class thus far—unless it is just that the rest of your class is disappointingly weak. Regardless, your combat skills are more than sufficient for this mission, even with a less influential companion."

Sylph's expression didn't change. She snuck a glance back at Damien just as he managed to get the straps of Quinlan's bag unfastened.

"What's the deal?" Henry asked, floating out from within it. He still wore the blobby, tentacled form that he'd taken to using while around other people. Two of his tentacles held knitting needles, while the other was wrapped around a bright pink hat bearing his likeness on the front. "Oh. Hello, everyone."

"And what is *that*?" Derrod asked, his eye twitching. "Damien, is this a joke? Where is your companion?"

"No, I'm Henry," Henry said, tossing the needles back into Quinlan's bag. "Damien hasn't told me anything about you either, so we're on the same page."

"Henry, please," Damien muttered. "We really don't need a scene here."

Henry snorted and placed the hat atop his head, adjusting it slightly.

"Damien, I can barely feel any energy coming off your companion," Derrod said, raising an eyebrow. "Are you seriously going to tell me this is what gave you Space magic? What even is it?"

"He already told you. His name is Henry," Damien said with a shrug. "New companion from the Plane of Darkness."

"Is Henry his name or his race?" Aven asked, her eyes sharper than Damien had ever seen them.

"My name, and I talk," Henry said. "You can address your Henry-related questions to Henry."

"Noted," Aven said. "What are you?"

"If you're going to insist on being pedantic, I am a greater demon from the Plane of Darkness," Henry said, forming some fingernails on the back of his tentacle and examining them. "And your mortal antics are entirely boring to me. Damien and I have come to an arrangement in which I can enjoy myself a little while spending a bit of time crushing pitiful creatures like yourself into powder."

The pavilion went silent. Aven squinted at Henry, trying to figure out if he was being serious.

"Those are bold claims," Derrod said, watching Henry closely. "What magic do you grant Damien?"

"Space, Light, and Dark," Henry replied. "But that's only when I'm not knitting. It's quite interesting, you know. The little click-clack of the needles is exciting. Almost as exciting as goats."

"I can vouch for Damien's prowess," Sylph said. "He's easily as strong as I am. His companion is just a little strange."

"As can I," Yui said.

"And I," Mark added. "Henry is powerful. At least as strong as mine. Maybe stronger. Probably not."

The Goldsilk girls all added their voices in as well. Quinlan glanced at them, but Damien shook his head slightly. He didn't know if anyone would try to cause trouble during the expedition, but the less people knew about who his allies were, the better. Granted, Quinlan had walked right over to them when she'd arrived at the pavilion, but there was no need to confirm anything else.

"Very well," Derrod said. "I've tested your skill myself. I am quite curious about your companion, though. Unknown variables can be difficult during missions. Everything that we can control should be controlled. That which we do not understand is what can undermine us."

"I've found that hitting most things with a sword hard enough tends to make the problem go away," Mark said.

Cheese nodded empathetically in agreement.

"That only works until you meet someone stronger than you," Aven said with a disapproving glare. Cheese's nod quickly changed to a shaking head.

"Then, I just have to be stronger," Mark said, crossing his arms.

"Now isn't the time to discuss philosophies," Derrod said, clapping his hands to get their attention back. "Follow after me. We'll be going to a specialist in Blackmist for the teleportation to Forsad. I'll explain more as we walk."

They all filed after Derrod as he started out the door and deeper into Blackmist's campus. The crowd drew more than a few glances from students who had gotten up early to get started with the day. Judging by their expressions, several recognized Derrod.

"When we arrive at Forsad, I will not be taking any action to direct or otherwise aid you," Derrod said. "I am there to ensure that you are safe from any threats beyond your ability to handle. Forsad is home to all sorts of monsters, and you'll be expected to be able to hold your own against the ones at your strength level. Some will be challenging or even impossible to defeat, but they will not be impossible to escape from. If you encounter any such creatures, that is where I will step in."

"So, we can do whatever we want once we get there?" Aven asked.

"Essentially," Derrod replied. "Although you are expected to act with etiquette and represent your school with honor. If you begin indiscriminately attacking your fellow students or intentionally sabotaging the mission, I will step in. Otherwise, you are free to do as you will. Train, seek out artifacts, or hunt monsters. Just push to improve your strength in any manner that you can."

"Do you have any artifact locations for us?" Teddy asked. "I was told that you were aware of a few."

"Blackmist earned some advance information that is little more than speculation," Derrod replied. "The queen detected several artifacts of interest when she opened the gateway to Forsad. That information has been given to the students of Blackmist as the other part of their reward for reward for trading in an artifact from the Crypt."

"Wait, what?" Damien asked. "We didn't get anything like that."

Derrod shrugged. "Say what you will. This is the information that the queen delivered to me."

"You could just be saying that to avoid getting people tailing you," Reva said, pulling her hood lower. "Likely story."

"It's also possible not all of the Blackmist students were told about the artifact locations," Teddy said. "If anyone, it's most likely that Aven and Cheese know about them. The weaker students could just hold the fourth-years back."

"If I recall, you were having trouble fighting one of those weaker students," Reva snipped.

"You weren't having much more luck," Teddy replied. "You were losing to a girl using a sylph as a companion. I don't think you should talk. Unless you want to try your strength against me?"

Reva looked away. "We'll see about that during the mission. I'm not wasting my strength on you now."

"That's what I thought."

Derrod didn't address their small argument. They reached the treasure pavilion, and the guards at its front nodded respectfully to him, opening the door so that the group could head inside.

The door at its back was already wide open. Auntie stood in the doorframe, tapping her foot impatiently.

"About time," she said, pointing at Derrod. "You were supposed to be here a minute ago."

"I arrived precisely on time," Derrod replied. "It is not my fault you expect everyone to be early."

"Not everyone," Auntie replied, turning on her heel and starting into the hall. "Just you."

They followed her.

"Does she know Derrod?" Sylph whispered to Damien.

He shrugged in response. "No idea. Don't know who he interacted with. Barely know the guy."

They wound down the corridor for several minutes, low excited chatter accompanying them, until they came to a stop before an archway. Heavy metal chains hung from it, coiled around the ground on either side of the entrance.

A thin layer of dust covered the gray ground leading up to a tall dais, where two huge pillars stood in the center of a raised platform.

"This is one of the entrances to Forsad," Auntie explained, taking them up the stairs and onto the platform. "Or rather, it's just a boosted teleportation array. Connecting directly to Forsad would be incredibly difficult on its own, so this helps optimize the amount of Ether the spell takes from me. Even with the queen holding open a pathway, sending things into Forsad is hard. Leaving will be much easier. Derrod can handle that part himself."

She raised her hands as she spoke. Shimmering green energy swept from her fingertips and into the pillars, crawling up them like twin snakes and lighting up runes as they went.

"Now, stand still, if you can," Auntie said. "It'll be easier for me, and I don't want to accidentally leave a few fingers behind."

That was pretty effective at getting them all to stand stock still. She smirked, then let the expression drop from her face as concentration took its place. She raised her hands, pouring more energy out and into the pillars.

Runes flared and sparked. Damien resisted the urge to look around as the air started to hum with Ether. His skin tingled and the room took on a green hue. A sudden lurch in his stomach took him by surprise, and he nearly doubled over, but he managed to remain upright. The expressions of his fellow students showed they weren't doing much better.

"Don't worry," Auntie called over the growing buzz filling the air. "It'll only be uncomfortable for a moment. Get ready. I'll be sending you over in three...two...one..."

Damien voided last night's dinner against his best attempts not to. The world went green, and his body felt like it had been crumpled up into a little ball and launched from a catapult.

Everything vanished, turning into a roaring scream and dancing colors.

Seconds stretched on as the spell tore through space, sending the group hurtling toward Forsad. Damien's lungs, which he was pretty sure were now located somewhere near his feet, ached for air.

He tried to draw a breath, but it was like trying to inhale stone. All attempts to move were equally as fruitless. Just as the panic started to set in, he struck something hard and tumbled forward, crashing into a wall and drawing in a deep, gasping breath.

Dust and stagnant air greeted him, mixed in with a hint of something sweet that he couldn't quite place. Damien groaned, not even trying to move for a few moments as his head spun.

He finally managed to force his eyes open. Students laid strewn across the floor around him. Aven was already on her feet, while Yui's retainers were struggling to help her to her feet. Everyone else was in various states of waking up. Derrod leaned against a wall, observing them idly while they struggled.

Damien pushed himself upright just as Sylph stood off to his left. He brushed some of the dust off his mage armor with a grimace. "That was less than graceful."

"It was a very difficult teleportation," Derrod said. "Everyone, do a quick check to see if you're missing anything. Auntie wasn't joking about that, and I really do mean everything."

Everyone examined themselves, then each other to make sure all was in place. Damien thought he caught the slightest smirk flicker across Derrod's face, but it was gone by the time he did a double take.

"So, what now?" Mark asked, looking around the musty room they'd arrived in. "Doesn't look like much."

"You could try going outside before making a judgement," Gaves said, brushing dust off his chest and turning his nose up.

"Is there anything else we should know before we venture into the city?" Teddy walked up to a stone door and pressed a hand against it, tilting his head as if listening to something before turning back to face them.

"It's all your decisions from here on out," Derrod said. "There are enough plants growing around the city for you to survive off, and you can also eat the monsters. Use your brains and don't eat anything that smells bad or looks poisonous. I'll be around, but you won't see me."

Aven pushed past Teddy, drawing the stone from the ground around her to form tight fitting armor that covered her body completely, not even leaving a single gap for mobility. It shifted around her like a living being, allowing the armor to have mobility despite its solid form.

She pushed the door open and poked her head out into the gray light that spilled into the room. Then, without another word, she stepped out and sank into the street, vanishing without a trace.

"The hunt is on," Cheese declared. He jogged after her, turning to stick his tongue out at everyone before bounding into the air. There wasn't a single trace of magic around the boy as he rocketed into the air, vanishing over the top of a building.

The others all turned to look at the remaining Blackmist students.

"Don't give me that expression," Damien said. "Not all of us have cool departing moves. I'm just going to walk out."

"Speak for yourself," Mark said, drawing his sword with an eager grin. He strode out the door, summoning red energy around him until two massive wings sprouted from his back. The magic forming them was so thick Damien could barely tell it apart from flesh.

They flexed, then swept down, launching Mark into the air. He cackled as he flew away in search of prey. By the time he was gone, Reva had also disappeared. Everyone else quickly followed their lead.

Damien and Sylph broke away from the rest of the group, stepping into the street and weaving into the ruins of the buildings that surrounding them as quickly as they could. Quinlan followed them but at a fair distance. The sun in Forsad was muted and weak. Even though it hung directly overhead, the light that graced them was drab and gray.

Shadows danced along the buildings, and not all of them belonged to the students. A tickle constantly sat at the back of Damien's mind as he and Sylph climbed through rubble, their magic at the ready for the slightest sign of danger.

"This place looks deserted," Damien whispered. "But it doesn't feel like it."

"I know what you mean," Sylph muttered, giving him a small nod. "I keep thinking someone is watching me. But, if they are, I've never seen cloaking like what they're using. I'm normally very good at picking up magical energy since I had to get so sensitive to Ether to actually use it."

Henry set his hat on top of Damien's head and crossed his tentacles. "I'm noticing it as well. We aren't alone. I'm picking up traces of Dark Ether, but my senses are so dulled that I can barely tell where it's coming from."

"What's the hat for?" Damien asked, pushing it out of his eyes.

"Me," Henry replied, taking it back. "I was just checking how it fit on a human head."

Quinlan picked up her pace, jogging over to join them as they made their way over the crumbling wall of a long decrepit building.

"Do you actually know where some fancy artifact is?" Quinlan asked in a low whisper.

"Nope," Damien replied. "We're kind of just wandering around. You?"

She cleared her throat. "Kind of."

Henry grew an eye on the back of his head to look at her. "Go on, then. Spill."

"Henry, she isn't technically on our team," Damien pointed out. "Mountain Hall probably expects her to get that artifact, and she could get in a lot of trouble if she doesn't."

"Those Kingsfront assholes took the last shiny bit we got," Henry complained. "I want to examine them. What if it's got some revelations about magic stored within it? The artifacts are wasted on those morons you call teachers."

"I'd actually like to get my hands on it as well," Sylph admitted. "It doesn't have to be yours, though, Quinlan."

Damien blinked. "Why? I know they're useful and can be very powerful in the right situation, but we've already got so much on our plate with figuring out our normal magic. Tossing extra artifacts into the mix seems like we could spread ourselves too thin."

"It's not that," Sylph said. "While Henry was helping me fix the imbalances in my magic, I realized that I've kind of been stuck in a rut that was partially caused by the magic tweaking with my head."

"What do you mean?" Damien gave her a worried glance. "How badly did it mess with you?"

"Oh, it wasn't messing with any decision making, if that's what you're worried about," Sylph said with a small smile. "Nothing was wrong there. It's more that I've been stuck in a rut ever since I got to Blackmist, and the constant turmoil my Core went through made it difficult for me to realize just how bad it was. Henry freed some things up."

"And?" Damien asked.

"I've been thinking about what I actually want to do," Sylph said, glancing around and sitting down beside a mostly intact wall. "After all this is done, you know."

She waved around them, letting her eyes rest on Henry for a second longer than needed.

"I know what you mean," Damien said. "Although I haven't spent much time thinking about that at all. It's hard to comprehend anything else, honestly. Especially with everything that we can't really talk about."

Quinlan cocked an eyebrow curiously, but she didn't press.

"It helps to have sight of what you're working toward," Sylph said. "Something my old teacher taught me before he met his fortunate end. He was right about that, but I lost track in trying to train and keep up with you."

"You've always been ahead of me!" Damien protested.

Sylph snorted. "At the pace you were increasing with Henry's help, it's always been a matter of time if I didn't figure out some other way to keep up with you. But that isn't the point. Once this is all done, I want to hunt for artifacts. Maybe I can find other kids like me—ones with low magical energy or other problems—and give them artifacts to try and make up for their weaknesses so they have a chance to train."

"That's a very respectable goal," Quinlan said. "I wish other people shared it. Too many just discard people who can't use magic properly."

"Are you also..." Damien trailed off and gestured.

"No," Quinlan said with a delayed chuckle. "I'm the opposite. My magic is more than sufficient. I was very lucky. It's nothing. I was just thinking of somebody else. But is it safe to stay here? We might get attacked by a monster in an enclosed space."

"I'm not really that worried about most monsters," Sylph admitted. "Anything that Derrod doesn't think is a major threat for the other students shouldn't bother us in the slightest."

"What do you mean?" Quinlan asked. "He isn't going to kill everything that isn't a threat."

Sylph smirked. "You haven't seen what we've been fighting this past year, Quinlan. If Derrod thinks the monsters are going to be a struggle the other students can handle, we aren't going to have much difficulty at all."

"That's...dangerously bold," Quinlan said slowly. "I don't want to sound cocky, but while Henry is strong, he's still just a companion. He's limited by Damien's strength, and I was still able to fight back against him a little. Some of the monsters here are sure to be dangerous enough to at least make you respect them."

"Oh, I respect everything I fight," Sylph said. "But that doesn't mean I don't know that I'm going to win."

"That's what I'd expect from a mage on the frontlines, not a student," Quinlan said, standing up and frowning. "But there's no way you've gotten this far with a foolish attitude like that and nothing to back it up."

"I'd like it to be known," Henry said, raising a tentacle, "You did not hold me off. I was trying to figure out how to take you out without killing you. Damien wasn't happy the last time I killed a meddling student, and that one actually deserved it."

"Let's not talk about that," Damien said, grimacing. "But, Quinlan, if Sylph wants to look for artifacts, I'm going to do everything I can to help her. I don't want to stop you from getting your artifact, though. Do you want to go and find it, then meet us somewhere to train for runes later?"

"That might not be a bad idea, although a part of me really wants to see what Sylph was talking about," Quinlan said. "Where should we reconvene? I should probably take care of things for Mountain Hall just to keep them off my back."

Sylph nodded up at a crooked two-story building looming over them, visible through holes in the ceiling above them.

"How about below that thing? It's tall enough that it should be easy to find, but not so big that it's an obvious meeting point."

"That works," Quinlan said with a nod. "I'll try to finish this up tonight. The artifact isn't far. Take care of yourselves. It would be very unfortunate if something were to happen to you."

"Likewise," Damien said. "Don't worry about us. Henry would be furious if he got shunted off the Mortal Plane too early."

"Damn right I would be," Henry growled.

Quinlan laughed and gave them a last nod before making her way out of the house, turning down a street and disappearing.

"So, should we go look for some artifacts?" Damien asked, glancing at Sylph. "We don't want the others to find everything before we do."

"Actually," Sylph said, a tiny grin tugging at her lips. "I was thinking we might look for some of the other students. We don't have a great way to locate artifacts, but Blackmist isn't the only one that has information sources. I bet you the others have some leads, too."

"And how do we find them?" Damien asked, raising an eyebrow.

"I figure all we'll have to do is wait for the inevitable fighting to start. It won't be long before they run into each other, and that'll be the perfect time for us to show up," Sylph said with a wicked grin. "I'd like to get artifacts normally in the future, but I don't quite have the skillset for that yet. We'll have to make do with what we're already good at."

CHAPTER
SIXTEEN

Damien and Sylph stepped out of their makeshift shelter a minute after Quinlan left and headed straight for the center of the city. They did little to mask the sound of their footfalls as they echoed through the vacant halls of the once great city.

Several times, Damien paused to marvel at the buildings. Amongst the rubble scattered everywhere were the faintest traces of what the city had once been. Half of a tower leaned against the side of another building, the rest of it already crumbled away. Across the road, the stone sign for a long-destroyed building stood tall.

The city slanted downward, granting them vision of the great walls in the distance. Massive sections of them were missing or so badly damaged that they might not have been there. The remains of a watchtower sat at the edge of the wall in front of them, the roof missing and a huge portion ripped out of its walls. Just beyond it, a purplish-gray wall of energy shimmered at the horizon. It curved up, forming a dome above the city above them.

"I wonder what happened to this place," Damien said. "It

looks like there was some sort of war, but that wouldn't explain why it got sealed off."

"Failed defensive measures with some ancient magic?" Sylph guessed. "Or perhaps it was a monster attack. The barrier might not be to keep things out—it could have been put up afterward to keep something else in."

"I thought you just said we could handle anything here," Damien accused. "Something strong enough to warrant a barrier like this seems like it might be just a little bit beyond our skillset."

"Anything of any real power is long gone." Sylph stepped under a broken bridge, slipping effortlessly over several boulders that blocked her path. Damien clambered up them with considerably less grace, then teleported to the ground beside her to avoid having to climb back down. "And Derrod is here."

"I trust him as far as I can throw him."

"Have you been doing more upper body workouts recently?"

"Not really. I just do the bare minimum," Damien admitted. "I've been more focused on magic."

"Then, you really don't trust him very much at all," Sylph said, grinning. Damien rolled his eyes.

"Are we just hoping that we'll run into someone near the center of the city?"

"Pretty much," Sylph replied. "I could try to stalk someone down, but I don't think that's your expertise. I figure it'll be easier if we wander around like idiots until someone tries to jump us. They'll all be focusing the artifacts first, so by the time we run into anyone, they should have something interesting."

"I feel a little bad about this," Damien said as they cut through a decrepit tavern. "Isn't this like...bad guy behavior? Stealing and stuff?"

"They'd all do the exact same thing," Sylph said. She reached out and grabbed Damien's hand, causing his eyebrows to rise. Their eyes met, and she flicked her gaze to an alley at their left that they were coming up on. "If you're uncomfortable with it, we don't have to. We could just go look for something normally. We might not have a special way to find anything, but we could get lucky."

"No, it's fine. Maybe we'll get lucky and it'll be Reva. She seemed pretty rude to me," Damien said. He didn't break pace as he cast out his net of mental energy, drawing both Dark and Space Ether into his Core.

Henry's eyes narrowed, and he held his hat slightly tighter.

"What do you want to do once we finish up with Forsad?" Damien asked casually, pulling more Ether just below his left knee. He doubted anyone would expect an attack from there.

"I've heard that some people like to take their girlfriends shopping," Sylph replied.

"We did get that kitchen."

"That doesn't count," Sylph replied. "It was different."

The alleyway was now almost directly to their left. A building had fallen sideways, blocking off the majority of the entrance and casting it into shadows. Damien wanted to squint at it to try and see into the darkness, but he didn't need Sylph to tell him how stupid that would be.

They passed the alley, much to Damien's discomfort. He shot a glance at Sylph, but she shook her head slightly and squeezed his hand. Damien's senses stretched to their limit as he tried to figure out who was watching them, but all he had to go off of was Sylph's warning.

He felt Henry poised to slip into his mage armor at the first sign of a fight. Another few steps went by.

"I guess we can go—"

His armor turned jet-black, and Henry shot two tendrils out, blocking a pillar dark spike before it could strike him. Sylph spun, throwing two of her green-tinged daggers before she had even finished the motion.

The blades spun once before striking a hooded form that had just barely poked out of the alley, forcing them to stagger back with a surprised gasp. Damien's attack came just a moment later, but it was so dark that it was almost impossible to see.

A thin purple blade shot from his knee, cutting his pants. He didn't see it strike the figure, but a spurt of blood shot from their side a moment later. They staggered, spinning and dashing back into the alley.

Damien gathered his magic to teleport, then stopped. He shot a glance at Sylph, who shook her head. "Good call. I don't know what's in that alley, nor do I know if that was a student. They didn't look that familiar, and it could have been a trap."

"Ugh, my heart is still racing," Damien said, shaking his head. "Good catch, Henry. And nice spot, Sylph. I had no idea that person was even there. It's too bad I missed. I'm not used to aiming much because of my Gravity Spheres. They kind of just hit everything in the area."

"Not the best ambush I've ever seen," Sylph said, taking a wide loop back to peer at the alley. "Even if that spike had hit you, I don't think it would have been fatal. I suppose it depends on the magic, though."

Henry disengaged from Damien's mage armor. "It was just basic dark magic. Very unlikely to kill unless it hit a vital spot, which was possible."

"Probably a student, then," Damien said. "Maybe they thought we'd already managed to get an artifact?"

"If that's the case, it was a pretty stupid student," Sylph said, pursing her lips. "We've only been here for a little while and aren't injured in the slightest. If we'd already found some powerful artifact, we wouldn't be completely uninjured. And, if we were, I'd be pretty concerned about attacking us."

"Nobody said brains were a requirement to coming here," Damien pointed out.

"Thank the Planes for that," Henry said. "We would have still been at home if it was."

"Oh, shut it. You almost gave us away when you hugged that dumb hat," Damien said, crossing his arms.

"Notice how you automatically assumed I was talking about you," Henry said, pointing a tentacle at him. "Telling. I could have been talking about Sylph."

They both glared at him. Henry snorted, an impressive feat without a nose, and set his hat back on his head. "If only you had half my wit. I prefer armed opponents."

Damien rolled his eyes, and they started back toward the center of the city.

"I'm holding you to that, by the way," Sylph said a few minutes later.

"To what?" Damien asked, cocking his head.

"You agreed to take me shopping," she said with a smirk.

"Oh. I didn't think that would be something typically up your alley, but sure. We have to use the gold that Whisp is giving us for something. What do you want to get? Clothes? Or weapons?"

Sylph cocked an eyebrow. "Honestly, this wasn't how I thought this was supposed to go. I read that most guys don't enjoy shopping and are supposed to complain about it."

"What? Why would I do that?" Damien asked. "Shopping is cool. I mean, I don't really care about clothes that much since I'm usually wearing my mage armor, but if it makes you happy, I don't really see a reason not to like it. It's not like it'll be boring. What have you been reading?"

Sylph reddened, and Henry glanced away. Damien narrowed his eyes. "Henry, what drivel did you give to Sylph?"

"She just happened to stumble upon some of my library acquisitions," Henry said, not looking at him.

"Which ones?" Damien pressed, unsure if he should laugh or groan. "Because all I've ever seen you get in regard to human relationships has been horrible smut."

"It was that one," Sylph confirmed, her cheeks still red. "One of them, at least. Henry told me it was good research into relationships."

"He lied."

"Yeah, I've gathered," Sylph admitted. "I'll be tossing everything I learned from that out, I think."

"It's perfectly good knowledge!" Henry complained. "I'll not stand for this slander. Show some respect."

Damien opened his mouth to retort when he felt a slight tingle toward the back of his right shoulder. His body reacted before he could even process was happening. A Tear shot from his palm, slicing through the air and passing through the wall of a nearby house.

The wall rippled, shadows fading away to reveal a hooded form clutching their neck. They pitched forward, tumbling off the building, exploding into dozens of dark streamers that shot down an alley as soon as they hit the ground.

"Seven Planes, what was that?" Sylph asked, her eyes wide. "How did you notice them?"

"I-I'm not sure," Damien said, staring at his hand as if it belonged to someone else. "I didn't even realize what I was doing until it was already done."

"That was actually somewhat impressive," Henry said. "For you, at least. I could have done that in my sleep."

"Thanks," Damien said. "I'm not so sure I got them, though.

I didn't recognize that magic they did when they hit the ground."

"Body transformation," Henry said. "High-level application of dark and shadow magic. Looks pretty similar to the stuff that the girl was doing back at Blackmist. What was her name again? Rump?"

"Reva." Sylph scrunched her nose. "But that's quite the jump in spell complexity, isn't it? She wasn't doing anything nearly that dangerous when we fought back in Blackmist, and I'm certain we wounded that other hooded figure. This one looked identical to the first, but it didn't look like they were injured when they fell."

"Could you really tell? We only saw them for a few seconds," Damien pointed out.

"Yes," Sylph replied. "They didn't favor either side and were standing too tall when you first revealed them. That person wasn't injured—not badly, at least."

"Well, it's not like we didn't hold back ourselves," Damien pointed out. They started back along the road, setting out toward the center of the city once more. "Maybe she was doing the same?"

"I guess it's possible, but isn't something like that considered near mastery of the element?"

Henry snorted. "Mastery. Mortals are so amusing. Not a single mortal has ever gotten near truly mastering a spell, much less an entire school of magic. Even my own kind have yet to truly master the magic that you yourselves have created. But for the span of your short little lives, getting to the stage where you can turn your entire body into magical energy for even a few seconds is very impressive."

"Could it be Second?" Damien asked, lowering his voice. "The last time we saw really powerful magic in the hands of people it shouldn't have been in, it was him empowering Drew and Bartholomew."

"That was still Time magic, which Second has shown he has mastery over," Henry said, bobbing from side to side as if he were shaking his head. "He's shown no signs of knowing Dark and Shadow magic. That makes me hesitant to suspect him, although it could certainly be some other Corrupted trick. I'm not going to be able to help you figure that out without fighting them more. My senses are as useless as ever."

Damien chewed his lip and raised his hand to look at the rune circle on his palm. At the same time, the shadowy designs covering the rune circles on his chest tightened and twisted, sensing his unease. "I could ask Herald."

"Do you really want to deal with it?" Sylph asked, worry creasing her brow. "Every time you do, you get hurt or it makes you do something ridiculously dangerous."

"Isn't that what we're usually doing?"

"The moment Herald is involved, things seem to get about a dozen times worse. Having it on our side feels like working together with a ball of condensed magic that is just seconds from exploding and taking us all with it to the afterlife."

"You forgot to mention how incredibly boring he was," Henry said. "Not to mention stiff. I can't believe I was ever part of that fool. All the magic it could have learned if it cooperated with us—I bet that keeps Herald up at night."

"Does Herald even sleep?" Sylph asked. "Do you?"

"No, and no," Henry replied. "But that isn't the point, is it? Look, we're almost there."

The three slowed to a stop at the edge of a large clearing. It was mostly free of rubble, and the dry water fountain in the center was in surprisingly good shape. Three statues of angels stood around it, their arms raised in rapture to the sky. The last one had fallen and laid on the ground at their feet.

Intricate runes and artwork covered the four basins that made up the fountain. They had been arranged in such a manner that water would trickle down from the top bowl to the bottom, and Damien suspected the runes would have likely delivered the water from the lowest bowl back up to the peak so it could start all over again.

"I wish we could have seen this place before it got ruined," Damien said sadly. "This fountain must have been really popular."

"We can still enjoy it now," Sylph said. "No point lamenting over what's already passed. It's a pretty rock, even if it isn't a fountain anymore. And, better for us, it looks like a great place to sit while we wait for someone to come hunting for us again."

They both approached the fountain and sat down at its edge, relaxed but ready for whoever was unlucky enough to come seeking them first.

Time passed slowly. Damien fidgeted, mentally running through his repertoire of spells and trying to figure out any ways he might improve them. In the distance, the sounds of battle picked up. Flashes lit the horizon for brief seconds, fading away only to restart on the other end of the city.

"Looks like everyone is out getting themselves into trouble," Damien said, drumming his fingers on the stone by his side. "It almost feels wrong to just sit here."

"It won't be long now," Sylph said confidently. "There's no way not a single other student mistakenly got the idea that we've got some secret information to find the fancy artifact."

Damien grunted. "It doesn't help that Derrod basically set everyone off at us. There was no reason for him to say anything. It's not like he cares about who wins this."

"More like he's just testing you more," Sylph said with a frown. "We need to try to stay away from him. I'm already looking over my shoulder constantly. Adding this in on top of everything might start causing some serious problems."

"Not arguing there," Damien said. He cracked his neck and squinted up at the muted sun beyond the barrier. It was dark enough that his eyes could actually handle staring straight at it, although it got uncomfortable enough after a few moments to force him to look away.

Sylph leaned forward, drawing a dagger seemingly from thin air and rolling it over in her hand. Damien squinted at her, but he couldn't tell where the sheath it had come from was.

"Where'd you get that?"

"I have enough knives hidden on me to fight an army of salad."

"That's...somehow actually still intimidating," Damien said. "Doesn't that get uncomfortable, though? Trip once, and you've got a pokey thing stabbing you in the side."

"It's called a sheath. And not falling," Sylph replied with a playful smirk. "But I also position them in places where they aren't going to stab me if I fall. I'll show you some other time when we aren't constantly being watched."

Damien nodded idly. Sylph's gaze flicked to his side, and he nearly spun before he managed to stop himself. Within his mind, Henry readied himself to enter the mage armor. Damien yawned, rubbing at his eyes to cover his movement as glanced at where Sylph had been watching out of the corner of his eye.

There was nothing but a surprisingly intact house and the thin, dark alleys running off alongside it. Damien drummed his fingers faster in a mixture of impatience and anxiety.

Why is this bit worse than the actual fighting? Can't whoever it is just come out and attack us already? I don't want to wait!

"Now you know how I feel," Henry said. "Imagine that, but every single second of your waking life. That's how it's like when you dally around messing with worthless things instead of studying magic or letting me get more human literature to study."

Your idea of human literature that isn't about magic is usually horrible smut.

"I take great offense to that. It's called romance not smut."

Your offense is noted and ignored.

Henry snorted. Their conversation dropped off as a shadow twitched at the end of the alley. Damien gathered Ether discreetly without taking his eyes off where he'd seen the movement.

"We know you're there," he called. "You might as well stop hiding. It's just wasting both of our times."

"Nobody is going to actually come out," Sylph said in a low tone. "We're on the defense, so that means we've got to be on guard. The longer they wait, the more likely we get tired or make a mistake. The attacker has an advantage so long as we don't know where they are."

"So, shouldn't we do something?"

"This is a waiting game. Whoever loses their concentration first loses. We only need the slightest opportunity to figure out where our opponent is and attack."

Damien scrunched his nose. "We could be here for hours, then?"

"Maybe you should have brought a deck of cards," Henry suggested. "Or a smu—romance novel."

"I think I'll just speed things up instead," Damien decided. "Sylph, I'm going to do something."

"How dumb is it going to be?"

"Pretty dumb," Damien admitted, drinking Ether in like a starving man. Sylph shook her head, but two black and green daggers snapped into her hands. She shimmered, fading into her camouflage.

If you could suspend my pain from mental energy overuse, that would be great.

"You got ten seconds. Any longer and the benefits aren't worth the cost," Henry advised. Damien gave him a mental nod, forming gravity lances and pumping them full of Ether until they overloaded. He compressed the spells with mental energy.

He walked in a circle around Sylph, creating two dozen of the spells and locking them in the air. Once he finished the circuit, Damien nodded to himself.

"You said it's all about knowing when the other person attacks, right?" Damien asked, not trying to lower his voice.

"Yes, that's—"

Sylph's sentence was cut off as Damien released every single spell at once, sending a wave of black bolts streaking through the square. They struck the walls of the crumbling buildings around them, and dark energy flared.

For an instant, there was complete stillness. Orbs of Space magic expanded like blooming flowers around them. Then, with a series of cracks so close together that they might as well have been a single, deafening blast, the world shattered.

Thick chunks of stone ripped away from the floor and walls, flying through the air and shredding through everything in their path as entire buildings collapsed as Damien's magic ripped their already weakened foundations apart.

The wall of a crumbling room off to their right disintegrated, revealing a flash of a dark cloak before flying shrapnel tore it apart. A massive cloud of dust rose into the air as Damien's ears slowly stopped ringing.

He waved his hand, tracing the runes for Devour in the air but swapping one of them. A black portal yawned open before his palm and bent inwards, drawing the dust filling the air into it.

Tiny rocks lifted off the ground, flying into the spell as well.

Within seconds, the air was clear once more. He let the magic fade, then surveyed the results of his attack.

The city around them had almost been completely flattened. What remained in the square was little more than large piles of stone and chunks of statues. A tattered cloak hung on the leftovers of a wall, covered in blood.

A young girl stepped out from behind the wall, riddled with thin cuts. She walked with the telltale limp of a broken leg, and a bump was forming on her head. Shadows twisted at her feet, forming into a brace and propping her up.

"What a ridiculous waste of Ether," Reva wheezed. Her wounds slowly pulled themselves shut, and her leg snapped back into position with a *crack*. "What did that accomplish other than forcing me to fight in an open—"

Sylph's dagger caught Reva in the throat. The girl's eyes widened, and she grabbed the handle of the blade. A second dagger thunked into Reva's right eye with such force that the girl spun, tripping over a stone and crashing to the ground.

"Huh," Damien said. "Nice shot."

She lowered her hand and shrugged. "I was aiming for her eye the first time."

"Were you really?"

"No," Sylph admitted. "Thought it sounded cooler if I said that, though."

"Another thing you read?"

"I'm not answering that," Sylph said. She nodded at Reva's body. "I'm not convinced she's dead, though."

"Probably for the best," Damien mused. "We don't want to kill her, do we? She just seems like a prickly asshole that wants power, not evil."

"I think those things are usually synonymous," Sylph observed, bringing two new daggers to her hands as she, and

Damien approached Reva's body carefully. "Henry excluded, of course."

Sylph's shadow erupted up behind her with blinding speed, punching into her back and sprouting from her chest with a shower of blood. Reva's body sank into the ground as Sylph's shadow ripped itself free.

Reva emerged a few feet away, bleeding from a line across her neck and with a cruel smirk on her face.

"Talking while you clearly suspect I'm still alive? Idiots. If you don't want your cocky girlfriend to bleed out, you'd better start crying for your dad," Reva said. "And hand the artifact over while you're at it, or I'll finish you both off before he can get here."

There was a soft *thump*. Reva blinked, glancing down at the stump of her arm. Her hand rested on the ground at her feet, not even bleeding yet. Sylph turned, toward her, the hole in her chest pulling itself shut. A jagged scythe hung over one of her shoulders, having sprouted from her back with such speed that Damien couldn't even place when it had appeared.

Reva grabbed her hand, drawing shadows up from her feet toward it. Moments before they touched the wound, the magic slammed to halt. Reva's brow tightened in frustration, then paled. She took a step back.

"What is this? What did you do to my magic?"

"Shadow magic is just a specialized form of Dark magic," Sylph said. "Unfortunately for you. It was different enough that it took me a little while to get a good grasp of it, but I've got your name now."

Damien grabbed Reva's clothes with telekinesis while she was distracted, slamming her to the ground.

"There's no need to be cruel, Damien," Sylph said. "She's lost."

"But she—"

"Fought back, even if she was the aggressor. What did you want? We aren't enemies, and she's done for unless she's really hiding something. This is supposed to be a training exercise not a slaughter."

Damien blinked. He dropped his hand, although he didn't release the Ether he'd gathered.

"I'll release your magic so you can stop yourself from bleeding out if you don't try to attack us or run," Sylph said. A tendril of wind jumped from her finger and wrapped itself around Reva's neck like a collar. "But if you try anything, I'll cut your magic off again and release this spell. You won't heal from that."

Reva swallowed and gave the smallest nod that she dared, gritting her teeth from pain. "Fine."

Shadows leapt from the ground, enveloping Reva's hand. They lifted it up to her arm and stitched it back on with a black string. The girl let out a relieved sigh as the wound sealed shut, vanishing as if it had never been there. She flexed her hand, then turned her glare on Sylph.

"How did you heal? That should have been impossible. No magic just puts you back together without any other effects. Was that some super specialized form of the healing school?"

"You seem to be under the impression that you get to ask questions," Damien said. "Where do you get off being such an asshole, anyway? You attacked us multiple times today already, didn't you?"

Reva shrugged. "It's a training exercise. It's not like your girlfriend held back when she threw a knife into my head."

"You've got some incredibly advanced form of healing magic. We've already seen it in action multiple times," Sylph replied. "I couldn't afford to assume it was weak. If you died, it would have only been your own fault."

"So, what now? You going to keep me here until someone stronger shows up to take the artifact from you?" Reva asked.

"We'll start by taking any artifacts you've gotten," Damien said. "You can think of it as payment for trying to attack us and ruining Sylph's shirt."

"Shit, I didn't think about that," Sylph said, looking down at her stomach, where there was a giant hole in her garment. She groaned. "Look at this! What if it gets windy?"

Reva's eye twitched.

"Artifacts," Damien repeated. "Sylph wants them. Don't make me search you myself."

"You'd like that, wouldn't you?" Reva asked with a sneer.

"Don't misunderstand me," Damien said. "I wouldn't touch you. I don't need to. You've already shown that you can easily heal from most wounds, so half a dozen Gravity Spheres placed in the right spots should show me everything you've got, even if it breaks you a little."

Reva's cocky expression flickered. "I'll give you one of them and promise not to attack you for the rest of the trip to Forsad. I'm not going to give up more without a fight, and I've still got some left in me. I'm certain I can hold you both off until someone else arrives to join in."

Damien glanced at Sylph, who nodded.

"That works," Sylph said. "So long as you add in that you've got to leave and not bother us at all. If we see you again, I'm not going to stop Damien from ripping you into pieces."

Reva reached into one of her pockets and threw a small wooden rod onto the ground in front of her. Sylph snapped her fingers, and the wind collar around the other girl's throat vanished. Reva sank into the earth, turning to shadow and disappearing.

Damien grabbed the stick with telekinesis and brought it over to inspect it, suspending it in the air before his eyes.

"Well, it's got some fancy runework I don't really understand," Damien said. "That probably means it's an artifact."

"That's good, but I'm not sure that should be the main thing we're concerned about right now," Sylph said slowly.

"What do you mean? This is what you wanted." Damien opened his travel pack and let the rod drop into it.

"It is, but doesn't anything else seem weird?" Sylph prodded.

Damien scratched his head, then shook it. "Nope, not really."

"Since when have you been so brutal?" Sylph asked. "Don't get me wrong, it's important to be able to suppress certain emotions when you fight, but you weren't acting normal just now. Henry, back me up here?"

"Why would he ever side with that?" Damien asked. "He's, well, you know!"

"Actually," Henry said, forming a mouth from Damien's shadow. "Sylph is right. That was out of character."

"Are you being influenced by your less friendly companion?" Sylph asked seriously.

Damien blinked. Sylph's concerned expression was more than he could dismiss. He let out a slow breath and turned his attention inward, trying to scan his mental space. Nothing seemed out of place.

He shrugged, then pulled his shirt up to check the seal he'd placed on Herald. The dark tendrils running along his skin froze as soon as the light touched them. Damien's neck prickled. The tendrils were larger. Worse, a rune in the center of the first binding circle was starting to fade away.

"Oh," Damien said. "Shit."

SEVENTEEN

"That's not good," Sylph agreed, squinting at the rune. "You might need to rebuild this."

"It doesn't work like that." Damien shook his head. "There's way too much power running through this and me. If I tried to mess with the runes at all, it could collapse completely. I have to wait until it gives out on its own, then redraw it."

"Is that safe?" Sylph asked. "That's what keeps your companion locked up, isn't it?"

"More like it keeps his gift to me locked up," Damien replied with a grimace. "It's my half of Henry's soul that was starting to merge with my mind. I don't want to know what would happen if it was completely released, but I'd imagine I'd change just as much as Henry did."

"We can't let that happen," Henry said, still using a mouth on Damien's shadow. "You'd probably try to destroy the world or something equally lame."

"I am becoming convinced you are the world's biggest hypocrite," Sylph said.

"Well, I *am* the best at everything I do," Henry allowed. "And I have decided that destroying the world is very much yesterday's thinking. Let's just kill all the Corruption so I can keep reading."

"Is that really possible?" Sylph asked.

"Honestly, I'm not sure," Henry admitted. "Some of the Corruption, sure. But Second? I don't know. We really will need to deal with them, but every passing day makes me more reluctant to take the only real steps I know that would let us do that."

"As important as this is, could we maybe figure my chest out first?" Damien asked, prodding at the rune circle. "We can't let Herald escape in any capacity. Best case, my personality gets irrevocably changed. Worst, Herald would be able to completely control my body if it managed to sneak anything into that half of its soul. That's a pretty major problem."

"What about another circle around it?" Henry suggested. "One to delay the release when the first few break, just long enough for you to redraw them."

"That could work," Damien said with a slow nod, mentally mapping out a possible circle in his mind. "But it would have to be pretty strong. The energy is all built up, so when it breaks, it'll probably explode. I don't know if I've got enough space on my body to do anything that powerful."

"An artifact might help," Sylph offered. "Something that absorbs magical energy. You could have it close, then try to use it when your rune circle breaks. Then your backup circle might be enough until you can repair the first one."

Damien opened his mouth, then blinked. He couldn't think of any problems with Sylph's plan. After running through it a few more times, he nodded slowly. "That could be it. Good idea, Sylph. I was starting to panic a little."

She gave him a small smile. "Let's deal with it before we start relaxing completely. We still have to find such an artifact, and I'm not sure where we'd get it. The chances of us stumbling into one randomly probably aren't that high."

"I'm sure there's one somewhere around here," Damien muttered. "But maybe there might be one in the treasure room at Blackmist? We've got quite a few contribution points saved up."

"Not safe betting everything on it being there," Henry said. "You're better off taking everything you can at Forsad, then sifting through it and hoping you find something. I don't believe power draining artifacts should be too hard to find—many of them need Ether, they just need different amounts for different purposes. So long as you find one that chews up a lot of energy, that could work."

Damien pulled the wooden rod that Reva had given them out of his bag and studied it again. "Do you think this thing could help?"

"No clue," Sylph said with a shrug. "I've got no real training with artifacts beyond my own experience with them."

"I'll take a look at it tonight," Henry said. "It won't take me long. Don't keep your hopes up, though. My senses are muted, but they're still enough to recognize a weak artifact. It probably just makes you smell nice or something."

Damien tossed it back into his bag and pursed his lips. "Tonight, then. What are the chances someone else attacks us, then? We've been here for a while."

"Well, there's a decent chance Reva told someone else about our fight," Sylph said. "It wouldn't technically be breaking her promise, and I doubt she's all that determined to keep her word anyway. People might be biding their time to see what else we'll do. We're here for a few days, so now that we've fought Reva off, it might be a while before someone else makes a move."

"You keep saying people," Damien said, picking a rock up and tossing it from hand to hand to keep them occupied. "Isn't it literally just Teddy? Quinlan isn't going to fight us, and everyone else is either our friends or from Blackmist."

"Don't count on anything," Sylph said. "You don't know that Goldsilk didn't order Viv or one of the others to steal from us or get an artifact at any cost. We can trust Quinlan because of Henry, but everyone else is an unknown. You don't know what someone might have over them."

"Do you really think they'd betray us like that?" Damien asked, frowning.

"I don't know, Damien," Sylph replied. "I don't think my viewpoint is the healthiest one, but it's what I've got. Maybe they will, maybe they won't. I don't trust easily. We'll just have to keep our guard up a little more than normal while we're at Forsad."

"Not a bad idea regardless," Henry said. He paused for a moment, then let out an annoyed sigh. "We do need to find Yui, though. I've got to give her the hat Damien made me make. I've been dragging the stupid thing around too long."

"I've been the one you've made wear it," Damien grumbled. He glanced up at the sky. "It's getting a little darker, I think. Maybe we should hunt around for artifacts a bit just to see if we get lucky, then head back to the house and meet Quinlan?"

"Sounds like a plan to me," Sylph said.

They headed out of the square, both keeping their Ether at the ready as they made their way through the city. Weaving through damaged buildings, the pair hunted around for anything of enough interest to catch their attention.

Damien lost count of the buildings they worked through. The drab, gray light made everything look the same, and there wasn't a single entrance or pathway to anywhere remotely interesting. There was just endless road and rubble.

Distant sounds of battle occasionally broke the monotony, but they ended as quickly as they came. Not a single monster or student made themselves known over the next few hours, and they eventually gave up and headed back to meet Quinlan.

"Well, that was disappointing beyond reason," Damien decided. "Where is everyone? I know this place is ruined or abandoned or whatever, but I expect at least something! It's practically a ghost town. How did we not run into a single monster?"

"It's pretty strange," Sylph admitted. "I did hear fighting though, but now I'm wondering if that was just other students running into each other."

"Maybe Quinlan will know something," Damien said as they arrived before their chosen meeting point. He sat down on the road in front of it, leaning against a stone fence post. "She seemed to know about an artifact, so maybe there's some sort of catacombs or sewer system below the city we just couldn't find."

"I'm sure there is," Sylph agreed. "The real question is if it's got anything in it. There has to be stuff *somewhere,* right?"

Damien snorted. "I just had a thought. What if the queen pulled a fast one on Blackmist and just tricked them into giving her the artifact for the equivalent of a horrible vacation trip for a few kids?"

"Don't even joke about that," Sylph said with a half groan. "We're wasting so much time right now. It's too dangerous to train here because we don't really know if something is lurking around, so we've just got to sit around."

"You could always hunt the other students," Henry offered. "Could be fun. A little bit of punching to brighten up the day. It's prescribed by healers all over the globe."

"We'll save that for if we get really desperate," Sylph said. "Reva clearly managed to find a few artifacts, so it's not like this place is actually barren. Things are here—we're just really, really bad at this."

"Speak for yourself," Henry said. "I'm great at it. I'm just enjoying watching you struggle."

"Right," Damien and Sylph chorused. Henry let out an affronted grunt and retreated back into Damien's shadow while the other two settled down to wait for Quinlan.

It wasn't much later when the sound of faint footsteps echoed down the city streets, coming from a rock-strewn road that led toward the center of Forsad. Damien and Sylph both watched the street, their Ether at the ready as they waited for whoever it was to arrive.

Quinlan stepped out from beneath an overhang, covered in small cuts. Her clothing had been badly damaged, and a bandage was wrapped tightly around her left arm. It was stained a dark brown, blood slipping out between gaps in the wrapping and dripping to the ground.

"Eight Planes, what happened?" Damien asked.

"There was some serious competition for the artifact I was going for," Quinlan replied with a tight smile. "Your compatriots are a lot more powerful than I expected."

"Aven? You went against her?" Damien asked, blinking. "I don't really know much about her, but are you okay? That looks like a pretty bad wound."

"I'll live," Quinlan replied. "I don't have much in the way of healing abilities, but I splinted it, and I'll get it taken care of once I can find a healer. And it wasn't Aven who did this."

"Mark?" Damien guessed, raising an eyebrow. "I didn't think he was that strong."

"No, it was Cheese," Quinlan said, scrunching her nose in annoyance. "I cannot believe I lost to someone with such a ridiculous name."

"Wait, you lost?" Sylph asked. "You didn't get the artifact?"

"No. He took it out from right in front of me after we fought," Quinlan said with a sigh. Her remaining hand tightened in anger. "I'll have to find him tomorrow, but I'm not in a shape to fight right now."

"Oh, so you managed to wound him as well," Damien hedged.

"No," Quinlan muttered. "Or rather, I don't think anything I did actually affected him. I hit him with enough magma to cook anyone else alive, but he barely even reacted. I saw his flesh burning, but it just…stopped."

"What kind of magic is that? Was he canceling it out or somehow stopping the heat?" Sylph asked.

"No," Quinlan said, leaning against the wall and sliding down with a pained frown. "I could tell he wasn't actually doing anything to my magic. I use a lot of mental energy to control my magma, and I would have felt if he messed with it. It's more like he was just…resistant to my magic. He healed just about all the damage I did within seconds."

"Now that's interesting," Henry mused, popping out of Damien's shadow to claim the knitted hat perched on Damien's head. "I wonder how he's going about it. It could be very advanced healing magic, where he's healing the damage you do before it can actually do any real harm. I've seen that before, but only in older human mages that are generally considered incredibly powerful. It seems strange for a student to have such a skill."

"I didn't feel like it was that," Quinlan said. "I didn't feel any magic at all, actually. It was just like my Ether didn't do anything to him."

"We need to find this Cheese," Henry decided. "This is vital to my research. I also need to know if he tastes like goats."

"He does not," Damien said firmly. "Nor do goats taste like cheese."

"But Cheese would taste like Cheese," Henry pointed out. "So, logically, Cheese would taste like cheese."

"I hate that I understood what you're saying," Damien replied. "And I hate the fact that you said it even more. How did you get this obsessed with cheese and goats?"

"I am *not* obsessed. It is purely scientific research."

"You did knit hats for all the goats in my room at Blackmist," Quinlan said, cracking a grin despite the pain covering her face. "I don't think most people would do that."

"They were practice. Purely scientific," Henry insisted. "And since I am now being beset upon from all angles, I will retreat to pick my future battles better."

He darted back into Damien's shadow, vanishing. Quinlan shook her head. "I wish my companion was like that."

"No, you really don't," Damien said. "Don't get me wrong, he's got his moments, but you don't know what I had to do to get him."

Quinlan nodded. "I can understand that more than you know. Do you think you can still teach me runes today?"

"Seriously?" Damien asked. "But...your arm."

"It won't impede my ability to learn," Quinlan said. "It'll just make drawing difficult. Right now, I'll take what I can get."

"I guess." Damien dug around in his pack and pulled out a stick of chalk. He brushed some of the dust away from the ground before him and started to sketch a rune circle. "Henry should have given you a lot of the knowledge you need to theoretically make a containment circle that can draw power out of something but putting it into practice is really difficult."

He drew several runes beside the circle, then pointed to the leftmost one, a wiggly circle with several lines going through it. "This one, for example, instructs the circle to siphon power from a target on its left and pass it into the rune on its right."

His chalk shifted to the rune beside it, which was identical aside from a single line having a slight curve to it. "And this one draws the power out of a target and sends it into the rune on its right."

"That sounds like the same thing," Quinlan said.

"That's the thing. They're very different," Damien replied. "The first one will slowly pull energy at a steady rate. The second one will pull it all at once. I trust you can see the problem if you use the wrong one? You could end up blowing your circle up if you use the rune on the right and try to yank too much Ether at one time."

"So, I use the one on the left?"

"Depends. The stronger something is, the harder it will be to pull Ether away from it, even if it's cooperating. The left rune might literally be too weak if your target is very powerful. You may have to use them in conjunction, using the right rune to yank the power and the left one to slowly trickle it into your circle. It depends on what your target and source are."

"I see," Quinlan said, chewing her lower lip. "I'm starting to realize why you were saying this could be hard to tailor without knowing more information. If I use that configuration and the target is too weak, it could hurt the target. If it's too strong, it could blow the rune circle up, right?"

"Pretty much," Damien said with a nod.

"How can I gauge the strength of the thing I'm drawing Ether from?"

"That's what I'll try to cover today. Henry will probably have to help me with a few things since I don't fully understand them," Damien said, starting to draw once more. Sylph and Quinlan both leaned in as he started to teach once more, the ever-present dim gray light illuminating their makeshift shelter as time ground onward.

The lesson ground well into the night. Henry took over once Damien exhausted his knowledge, but they didn't let it go so late that it ate too much into the next day. The three all went to bed and traded watches throughout the night. Night was a relative term, as the gray light never changed or relented. All they had to go off of was how tired they felt.

The following morning was much the same as it had been for the previous one. It was hard to tell if it even *was* morning. Still, they slowly got back up and readied themselves. Damien and Sylph both produced toothbrushes, much to Quinlan's amusement.

"What?" Damien asked, noticing her expression. "I'm not going to find a healer to fix my teeth if I can avoid it."

"I just burn everything away with magma," Quinlan replied. "It's much faster and feels nice."

"Seems safe," Sylph said. Quinlan shrugged. "It's fine once you hit my level of control."

Her words didn't seem to be bragging as much as a simple statement of fact.

"That makes me even more concerned about Cheese," Sylph muttered. "Just what is he using?"

"Let's hope we don't have to find out," Damien said, pausing in between brushing his teeth. "For now, Quinlan, we actually had a favor to ask of you."

She raised an eyebrow. "Me? I can't help you get that artifact from Cheese, I'm sorry. I need it for myself."

"Nothing like that." Damien shook his head. "We're actually hoping you could just point us in the direction of the sewers or catacombs or whatever it is beneath the city. Sylph and I spent all day yesterday looking for it, but we couldn't find anything. Not even a monster or the like. Just...old crusty city."

"Really?" Quinlan asked, blinking. "That's strange. I got attacked by half a dozen monsters while I was trying to get beneath the city. There are a fair number of entrances as well. I can't believe you missed them all."

Damien shrugged. "Well, we did."

"I'll show you one, then," Quinlan promised, spitting a small blob of magma out of her mouth and wiping her lips. "Follow me."

They packed their meagre belongings up, and then set off after Quinlan. She took them through a section of the city the two had already passed through the previous day. As they went, a frown grew on Quinlan's face.

"This doesn't make any sense," she said.

"What doesn't?" Sylph asked.

"The city. I know I passed an entrance to the underground somewhere in this area. It's where I went in, but I can't find it anymore."

"Could someone be hiding them from us?" Damien wondered. "That seems kind of pointless, and do Teddy or Reva even have an ability like that?"

"Teddy doesn't," Quinlan said. "I'm not sure about Reva, but I don't know much about her at all. It would be quite a waste of time for her to be following you around, making it harder to find entrances, though. She didn't strike me as stupid."

"Then, what could it be?" Damien asked, glancing around and raising his hands helplessly. "All I'm seeing is gray crap. And what about the monsters? If you ran into a bunch, and we haven't, something seems weird there, too."

"I did think we'd run into at least one by now," Quinlan admitted, sucking on her cheeks. "Huh. I don't know what magic could even do this."

"A fair number," Henry said, popping out of Damien's shadow and shaping himself into his spherical form. "Earth could do it without too much difficulty. All they'd have to do is seal the ground over wherever the entrance was and make it look somewhat believable. There are also a number of different schools of magic that can create illusions to varying degrees—it could be those as well. Furthermore, it could be a Mind mage making us unable to see something right in front of us."

"Could a Mind user really affect something like you?" Quinlan asked doubtfully.

"Nope," Henry replied with a giggle. "Absolutely not. But it's still a possible way someone could have hidden the passages."

"Henry, don't be difficult," Damien scolded.

"When is he not?" Sylph asked.

"Hey!" Henry complained. "No teaming up on me. That's no fair. Quinlan, back me up here."

"I'm staying firmly out of this one," Quinlan said, hiding a laugh. "But shouldn't we be a little more concerned about someone being able to hide this kind of thing from us? They have to be pretty strong to evade your senses."

"Eh, I'm blind as a rat," Henry said. He bobbed in a shrug. "I highly doubt something that powerful got past Stormsword, though. The man's an asshole, but he's very powerful. And frankly, none of the students here are a concern."

"None?" Quinlan raised an eyebrow. "Cheese? Aven?"

"Well, I'm curious to see what they can do," Henry admitted. "But I'll stand by what I said. They're kids. If we go all out, then we'll win. You recall what happened when we fought. That was me at less than half of my strength and separated from Damien."

Quinlan scrunched her nose at the memory. "That's not a memory I want to relive. It was pretty pathetic."

"Don't feel too bad," Henry said. "You weren't completely disappointing. I almost had a little fun, and you're great at procuring goats."

Quinlan heaved a defeated sigh. "One of the top prospects at Mountain Hall, reduced to goat herder for an egotistical floating octopus."

Henry harrumphed and darted back into Damien's shadow, vanishing and leaving them standing in the alley.

"That was remarkably useless for figuring out what in the Seven Planes is actually going on," Quinlan said.

"You'll get used to it," Sylph said. "Henry likes popping in to annoy us."

"How aren't you at least a little nervous?" Quinlan asked. "Whatever Henry says, this is still probably a powerful opponent. What if it's Aven or Cheese? If Cheese is only ranked second in Blackmist, I don't want to think what Aven is."

"We told you before," Sylph replied with a shrug. "We've dealt with a lot worse than a student. We'll handle it, although we're on a bit of a time crunch at the moment. This is starting to get a little annoying."

Damien sighed. "I'll just handle it the way I normally do. Thanks for the help, Quinlan."

"I didn't do much," Quinlan said with a frown.

"Well, you showed us where the entrance to the underground was," Damien said with a reassuring grin. "That's enough. I assume you're going after Cheese now?"

"It sounds like I'm about to dig through a restaurant's trash when you put it that way," Quinlan grumbled. She waved her injured arm. "But, yes, I am. I don't have a choice."

"Take care, then," Damien said. "Don't kill yourself over whatever that artifact is. There's always another option."

"If only that were true," Quinlan said with a sad smile. "What are you planning here, though? I'm a little concerned it might happen to me, so if you've got a solution to breaking out of whatever this is, I'd love to know it."

"I'm not so sure it would work for you," Damien replied, drawing in a slow breath as he drew Ether into his body, drinking it out of the golden strands surrounding them at an alarming rate. "But it involves a lot of magical energy."

Quinlan's eyes widened, and she took several steps back. Sylph stepped up next to Damien, standing close to him as motes of Space magic gathered on the ground around them. They spread until nearly a dozen of them had been arranged in a ring.

"You're casting them outside your body?" Sylph asked, raising an eyebrow.

"I'm using mental energy to hold them in place from the start so I can cast at longer ranges," Damien replied, his brow furrowed in concentration. "It's not easy, but now's as good a time to practice it as any. You ready?"

Sylph nodded. "Good luck, Quinlan. We'll see you tonight. Same place?"

Quinlan nodded. "To you as well. Try not to destroy too much of the city."

"No promises," Damien said with a smirk. The Gravity Spheres he'd laid out on the ground detonated as one. The ground shattered, large chunks of stone ripping away as fragments were sucked into the spells' epicenters.

He sent another wave of the destructive Space magic coursing into the damaged rock, lining the blasts up before triggering them all at once again. The ground sank under their weight, and dust rose into the air.

Damien started to gather energy for a third round, but there was no need. The rock finally gave way beneath them. Sylph grabbed onto him as they plummeted, vanishing into the hole he'd just created.

Before they could fall too far, Damien grabbed their clothes with his telekinesis. Their fall hadn't gotten a chance to accelerate much, so he managed to keep them descending at a wobbly, slow rate until they touched the ground a little less than a minute later.

"That was deeper than I expected," Sylph said, letting go of

Damien and brushing dust off her clothes. "Nice descent, though."

"Thanks," Damien said. They stood in a stone room, lit by faint golden lights embedded in the walls. Several doorways had been carved into the walls. He approached one of the lights, squinting at it. It was a miniature translucent rock, stuffed full of what he strongly suspected to be magic. However, there were no runes to be found on it. "Well, this is interesting. How is this still powered?"

"Maybe the runes are on the back?" Sylph suggested, peering at it. "Or just really small, and we can't see them because of the light?"

Damien considered prying the gem out, then dismissed the thought. Messing with unknown magic wasn't generally a great idea, and given that Henry had yet to say anything, he suspected his companion was waiting for him to get a nasty shock.

"I most certainly am not," Henry said in his mind.

I didn't say anything. I thought you said you couldn't read my mind.

"I said I got surface level thoughts, and that one was very loud," Henry replied. "But you should totally try to pull that out. It would be funny."

I'll pass.

"Don't mess with the shiny rocks," Damien said. "Henry wants me to pull it out, so we'll probably get zapped."

"Noted," Sylph replied. She examined the doors surrounding them and scrunched her nose. "Not much to go off. They all look the same."

"Then, we pick a direction and go," Damien said. "Wandering around aimlessly has yet to fail me."

"Do you do that often?"

"Well, no. But it still hasn't failed."

"You can't fail something you don't do."

"Do you have a better idea?" Damien asked, crossing his arms.

Sylph smirked. "Nope. Works for me."

Damien rolled his eyes and picked one of the corridors at random. He strode up to it, bringing a tear spell to his fingertips and carving a large chunk out of the wall. "There. Now, we'll know which way we came."

"Nice," Sylph said. "I was just going to chip it with my dagger, but that's a lot more effective."

They headed into the tunnel behind the door and descended into the darkness. The light stones still lined the walls, but they were fewer and farther in between with every passing step. Damien lit the way with the one Light magic spell he knew—he hadn't had reason to use it much before, but it came in handy now. He kept the power low, only illuminating the area immediately around them in dim light to avoid notifying anything of their presence.

Several minutes passed. Damien and Sylph kept their hands in contact, partially to make sure they knew where the other one was.

The two soon reached another room, identical to the first. Damien and Sylph exchanged a glance. Sylph shrugged, and he pointed at another door. They headed through it, then repeated the process.

Nearly an hour passed as they wandered aimlessly through the underground area of Forsad, marking their path as they went.

"Not many artifacts down here," Damien observed in a low voice.

"Well, we were told that most of the artifacts were already taken," Sylph replied. "Unless you think someone is somehow making us walk in circles or something?"

Damien shook his head. "I don't think so. I sent a miniature tear into the corner of a few doors we passed. It was really small and only took a tiny chunk off, I really doubt anyone would have noticed that if they weren't close to us, and the chunk wasn't missing when we passed through the last hall."

"Then, you're really bad at choosing where we wander," Sylph said with a laugh.

"You try it, then."

Damien felt Sylph shrug. They emerged into the next room, and she rubbed her chin before pointing at the door on the far right. Damien walked up to it and stepped out. His foot plummeted through the floor and Sylph grabbed him by the back of his mage armor, yanking him back onto solid ground.

"Eight Planes," Damien swore, his heart suddenly racing. He peered back into the hallway. What he'd taken for dark floor was actually a pit with no end in sight. The dim light from the magical stones seemed to flicker mockingly.

"Maybe you should pick them," Sylph decided.

"Maybe," Damien agreed. "Thanks for the save, though."

"Don't worry about it."

Damien gathered his nerves again and chose a different door, this time stepping out much more carefully. When he felt solid ground beneath his feet, he and Sylph set off once more.

EIGHTEEN

"You know," Sylph drawled sometime later, "I think we might be lost."

"We can't be lost. We're leaving markings behind," Damien replied. "I think the word you're looking for is confused."

"As to where in the Planes we are?" Sylph asked, cocking an eyebrow. Damien could barely even see her face in the dim light, but he recognized the changes in her tone enough to guess what she was doing.

"Pretty much," Damien admitted, letting out a sigh as they came to a stop in yet another room identical to all the others they'd just passed through. "I guess we could backtrack. Who knows how long we've been down here, but it's been hours at least. It might be night already."

"That's a possibility, but it'll take us just as long to get out," Sylph replied, drumming her fingers on her chin. "We might have made a slight mistake."

"Aren't you trained for this sort of thing?" Henry asked, popping out of Damien's shadow with a purple ripple.

"I'm not sure that's something we should be talking about, even here," Sylph reprimanded.

Henry snorted. "I'm blocking the sound waves from leaving the area. I'm not an idiot."

"Debatable," Sylph said with a smirk. "But thank you. And, no, I'm not trained for this. I'm trained to kill people and infiltrate houses, not weird maze-catacombs. I'm completely and utterly confused as to how this place is built like this. It makes no sense."

"Could someone still be messing with us somehow?" Damien asked, leaning against a wall. "Maybe the person that hid the entrance is also making us somehow circle around or remain lost?"

"It's certainly possible," Sylph replied. "But it just makes no sense to me. Who would waste so much time for literally no reward? At this point, they must realize we have no idea what we're doing."

"Maybe they're hoping we'll wear out and give up so they can attack?" Damien wondered.

"Could be. Either way, we aren't getting out today. We'll have to apologize to Quinlan," Sylph grumbled. "Damn. This entire trip is one giant waste of time."

"Should we just sleep?" Damien asked. "Maybe we'll get attacked at night and the problem will sort itself out."

"That's what I like to hear," Henry said, pumping a tentacle in the air. "Just kill everything in our way. Add in a few more visits to the library and you will become the perfect human being. Well, mostly. There are a few other small things we can change, but the murder and library hopping should cover most of it."

"You're taking first watch," Sylph informed Henry, laying her pack down on the ground and leaning her head against it. "Actually, can't you just take all of them? You don't sleep."

"He did sleep once," Damien said, setting up beside her. "For four years."

"Don't make me do it again." Henry pointed an accusatory tentacle at Damien. "But I can watch for tonight. I'm unbelievably bored after watching you waste so much time wandering around stone halls."

"Hey, look at the bright side. You're starting to get a much better grasp on how humans view time. Hours actually matter," Damien said. "Maybe you'll be able to start making your own spells soon, too. You've got half of my spark, right?"

"Hmm," Henry mused. "That's actually a good point. I'll have to do some testing tomorrow. It would be unfortunate if I accidentally blew you up and banished myself back to the Void."

"Yes," Damien drawled. "Unfortunate."

"Just sleep," Sylph said, prodding Damien in the side. Damien certainly wasn't going to argue with that, so he scooted in close to Sylph and closed his eyes, trying to ignore the cold floor digging into his back. Slowly, sleep came.

———

A tentacle prodded Damien in the nose. His eyes snapped open, and he jerked upright, nearly smacking his forehead into Sylph's. She dodged back just in time and rolled her eyes before nodding at one of the corridors.

"Company," Henry said from behind Damien. "And they aren't trying to hide their presence. Even with how horrible my senses are right now, I felt them coming from quite a distance. One humanoid."

"How strong?" Damien asked as Sylph pulled him to his feet and flicked some dust off his shoulder. "Is it the Corruption?"

"No," Henry said with a snort. "Not everything is the Corruption. I doubt I would have recognized the Corruption anyway. If I can't spot Second, I can't spot the other ones. This was much more amateur. Probably another student since it wasn't anywhere near Stormsword's strength."

"Did you catch how big?" Damien asked, rolling his shoulders and drawing Ether into himself. His reserves were still mostly full from the previous day, but a little extra never hurt.

"Bigger than you," Henry replied. "Which narrows it down a fair bit, since they were quite large."

"Teddy?" Damien guessed.

"Not bad," a voice echoed down a tunnel, immediately confirming Damien's thoughts. "How'd you know?"

"Why did you drop the noise canceling?" Damien hissed. Henry bobbed out a shrug in response.

"I got bored. It's not like the kid is a real threat. You've got to be bored, just go train on him already."

"I think I'm going to take offense to that," Teddy said, stepping out of the shadows and into the dim room. Stone snaked around him, forming a seething armor. Two long tendrils emerged from its back and hung over his shoulders.

One of them twitched, batting aside the inky dagger that Sylph launched at him. Teddy shook his head and chuckled. "Going for the kill before we even get a chance to talk. We're just students, you know. This isn't life or death."

Sylph shimmered and faded away, vanishing from view.

"It is for us," Damien said, lowering into a fighting stance. "I trust you're the reason this damn place has been so difficult to navigate?"

"Everything I've heard about you is true," Teddy said, rolling his shoulders. Particulates of stone whistled around him, forming a gale full of razor-sharp fragments to keep Sylph from getting too close. "Of course, I've been doing it. Did you really think I only had one school of magic?"

"No, we thought you'd have better things to do with your time than waste it here," Damien replied, forming a Gravity Sphere in one of his hands. "Seriously, why even bother? We don't have anything worth your time."

"I've got it on good word that you're lying," Teddy said, cracking his neck. "You've already gotten an artifact, right under everyone's noses."

"You mean the stupid thing Reva gave us?" Damien asked, squinting at Teddy.

"Of course not," Teddy snapped. "Pretending to be a moron isn't going to get you any farther, Damien. I'm onto you. I'm not foolish enough to think you'll just hand the artifact over for free, so I'm going to have to beat it out of you. Don't worry, I won't kill you. As soon as you hand it over, I'll leave you and your girlfriend alone."

A dagger flashed, and Teddy's armor shifted to catch it. A second blade flew from the darkness, drawing a thin line across the large boy's cheek.

"And what makes you so sure you can even take us?" Damien asked, forming several more Gravity Spheres. "Not that we even have the artifact you want. Two versus one is pretty dumb."

"I can handle two third-years," Teddy growled.

"Oh," Henry said, disappointment tinging his voice. "He's an idiot."

More Gravity Spheres blinked to life around Damien. He flicked a hand forward, and the black dots surged forward, rocketing toward Teddy like a miniature cosmos was being drawn in. Teddy whistled and the air shattered.

The two spells met with a loud crash. Flashes of shadow and pops filled the room as their magic warred. Damien's spells were blown away, and he yanked a Devour open moments before Teddy's magic washed into him.

The dark disk absorbed a fair amount of Teddy's magic before it touched Damien, but his bones still rattled as the magic clipped him. Damien fired several Tears out from his feet. Teddy's armor rushed to meet it, but the other boy underestimated just how dangerous the spell was.

Four purple crescents carved right through his defenses and scored lines across his body. Teddy blinked, glancing down at the blood that was suddenly flowing freely down his chest. The movement almost cost him his life as a scythe whipped out of the darkness, headed straight for his chest.

Teddy spun to the side, taking a savage cut across the side instead of straight through the heart. He snarled, and his armor lashed out in the direction of the attack, striking Sylph and shattering her camouflage as it shot her across the room.

She struck the wall hard, her wind armor dissipating. Teddy's attack had left a deep wound running from the top of her left shoulder all the way down to her hip. Not letting up on his advantage, Teddy fired off several more vibration spells.

Damien cast Devour ahead of himself and teleported, firing a Gravity Lance at Teddy before teleporting twice more, using Devour to block the majority of the damage of the other spell.

Teddy blocked the Gravity Lance with a thick shield of sand and shot a ripple of condensed air at Sylph. She raised her hand and wind surged before her, dissipating Teddy's magic before it reached her.

"Can you wrap this up?" Henry asked, yawning. "I was really hoping this would be more interesting, but this guy is just a normal mage. Let's get on with it."

"Would you shut your annoying companion up?" Teddy growled, hurling a spear of stone at Damien, who teleported to safety.

"If I could, I would," Damien replied as he appeared directly behind Teddy, casting a Gravity Sphere at the other boy's feet before teleporting once more. The stone armor whipped out, wrapping around Teddy's leg and shielding him from the magic before it could harm him. "But you really aren't going to win this. Look, you're barely holding your own."

Teddy scoffed. "Sylph took a bad blow already. She'll be out from blood loss shortly. It's just you."

Damien glanced at Sylph. Her wound had already closed, leaving only faint traces of greenish liquid and stone where the cut had been.

"You sure about that?"

Teddy glanced at her and caught a shadowy knife inches before it hit his nose. He growled, flicking it to the side. His eyes caught sight of Sylph, completely uninjured, and widened.

"You've got healing magic?"

"We aren't here to answer your questions," Sylph said, fading back into her camouflage. Teddy curled his lips and snapped his fingers. The stone armor vibrated around him as more tendrils sprouted from the ground and entered his defenses, reinforcing them.

The walls shook, and dust rained down on Damien. Thick, ropy stone vines erupted from the floor and ceiling, spreading across the room like roots.

"Fine, then," Teddy said, sinking into the ground. "You're a fair bit more competent than I expected, so you'll make me use my full manifestation again."

His head vanished beneath the stone, and several rock vines lashed out, swinging at Damien. He teleported, dodging the attack and appearing on the other side of the room.

"Again?" Damien asked. "Wait, have you been making the ground shift around us, so it looks like we're walking through the same area constantly?"

A distant chuckle echoed through the stone. Damien's eyes

narrowed. On the other side of the room, dark lines carved through the air as Sylph cut at the stone, but it didn't look like her attacks were making much headway.

"Henry, this is a serious pain," Damien complained, avoiding several vines. "He's pretty deep in the rock, isn't he?"

"Yup," Henry replied. "Not an illusion either. He's really controlling the stone. I have no idea where he is, though. Judging by the rate I feel the Ether fading, he probably won't be able to keep this up for too long. Maybe an hour."

"I really don't want to waste another hour," Damien said, tossing a Gravity Sphere into a cluster of vines. They shattered, blown to pieces, but rebuilt themselves before the debris could all even fall to the ground. "Can you get us some privacy for a few seconds?"

"I can block the area out for a moment," Henry replied. "Stormsword will know something happened if he's looking, but he won't know what it was."

"Good enough," Damien decided. "I still don't want him knowing everything I can do. Sylph, make sure you keep some distance."

Henry thrust his tentacles out, and a purple haze flooded the room. It permeated into the rock and sank deep into the ground, setting in like heavy fog.

Damien established the link to the runes in his mind, drawing on the Ether waiting for his beck and call. Power surged through his body, filling his Core and traveling through every vein.

"*Shatter*," Damien commanded. The word tore from his lips, and the Ether bent to his will. Lines of black light carved through the air, spiderwebbing out and digging deep into the earth around them.

Teddy only had time for a startled yelp before gravity

ruptured all along the lines, shattering rock and anything else unlucky enough to be caught beside it. Stone screamed and the room exploded, every single part of it tearing apart.

Damien staggered, falling to his knees as the powerful command strained his mind. Ether had poured into his body through the rune in his mind, burning through it like molten lava before spilling out and binding the world to his will.

Another cry split the din as Teddy was caught in Damien's spell. He fell from within one of the walls, his arm shattered in half a dozen locations and hanging limply at his side. The older boy caught himself with a pillar of stone that pushed him back to his feet.

He stared wide-eyed at Damien, fear stretching across his face. "What was that? How can you—"

"*Kneel.*"

Teddy's face slammed through the rock. Damien only had time for a brief smirk before the lights in his mind blinked out, and he crumbled, swallowed by unconsciousness.

Damien awoke to Sylph's face hanging right above him. He blinked up at her, and she leaned back, shaking her head.

"Whoops," Damien said, his lips feeling gummy. "I accidentally yanked the Ether out of my own body with that one."

"Not just you," Sylph replied. "The whole chamber we were in got drained for a moment. That was terrifying. If I was a little closer, I probably would have gotten knocked out, too."

"Not a bad skill if you can actually get it to do what you want," Henry commented from over Sylph's shoulder.

"Easier said than done," Damien said, sitting up with a grunt and picking a small rock out of his hair with a grimace. "I'm working on it, though. Didn't realize I could do that. Actually, I really don't know the full extent of what direct casting can do at all. But where's Teddy?"

"He ran off," Sylph replied. "I wasn't affected by your magic too much, and I think he realized he bit off more than he could chew. It's too bad, I was hoping to get the artifacts he had on him, but I didn't want to leave you here."

"Ah. Sorry," Damien said. "I'll be more careful next time."

"Just keep the dangerous risks to a manageable level," Sylph suggested. She helped him to his feet and nodded at the room around them. "But at least we can progress again. With Teddy gone, the room actually looks different. He must have literally made a maze around us, which is why carving the path we came in didn't do anything—it was new rooms."

"I never knew Earth magic could do that," Damien said, shaking his head. "That's honestly terrifying."

"All of the older students have some pretty dangerous magic," Sylph agreed. "It really is too bad he ran. I would have liked to see how we matched up against him one on one."

"I'm sure we'll get another chance," Damien said, taking his first look around the room after waking up. Like Sylph had said, it looked completely different than it had before.

The glowing stones in the walls were considerably brighter and illuminated the surroundings completely, lighting up every nook and cranny along the walls. Instead of multiple passageways, there was only a single exit and entrance on either side of the room.

One of the paths led upward, while the other descended deeper into the ground. Damien approached the latter warily and peered inside. The light extended deep into the stairwell. He couldn't see any sign of traps or missing stairs. It almost looked welcoming.

"Well, this is certainly an improvement," Damien said. "I guess we get back to it, then? Maybe we'll actually find an artifact now."

"Maybe," Sylph said, not sounding particularly convinced.

Henry snorted, and they set back off, delving deeper into the underground of Forsad.

The rooms lengthened, and the halls grew longer as they continued. Doors occasionally cropped up along the walls, some rotted away or simply just open archways. The ever present but impossible to locate drip of water echoed faintly past them.

Damien peered down one of the doors, his nose wrinkling at the smell of damp mildew that greeted him.

"These all smell like old people," he declared. "And something tells me that anything obvious has probably already been looted. How are we supposed to find an artifact without any way to point us? Henry, isn't there some magic that could help here?"

"We've already discussed that I'm not going to flat-out give you spells if you don't absolutely need them," Henry said, forming a shadowy tentacle and flicking Damien in the back of the head. "And, unfortunately for both of us, Dark and Space don't have any great tracking abilities. I had very high inherent magical sense that let me locate fluctuations in the Ether before your human spark messed it all up, but that isn't something a human can learn."

"Well, what magic does help? Could wind?" Sylph asked.

Henry grunted. "Ask your companion. I'm not a walking magic dictionary. But, in short, no. If artifacts were easy to locate, they all would have been found by now. The best way to locate them are just being really sensitive to lines of Ether or being lucky."

Damien cast his net of mental energy out, highlighting the Ether crisscrossing the room. He squinted at it, trying to see if anything was out of place, but the glimmering strands looked exactly how they normally did.

"Is there something in particular I'm looking for?" Damien asked. "It's just gold lines. Magic gold lines."

"You don't have the magical control for it," Henry replied. "It would take so long to train it that you shouldn't even bother right now. Fine control is the last of your issues. Sylph would have better luck."

"And what exactly is it I'm looking for?" Sylph asked, her brow furrowed. "I see the Ether, but it's like Damien said. It's just gold."

Henry let out an irritated sigh. "I said you'd have a better chance not a good one. Then again, your magical control is so abnormally high that you might really have a shot. Look for bends in the Ether. It should be straight, but powerful magic sources can tug it ever so slightly. The bigger the bend, the stronger the pull. Just remember that the bends are so small that you probably can't even see them with your eyes—you need to sense them with mental energy."

Sylph chewed her lower lip, narrowing her eyes in concentration. Damien didn't so much as breath to avoid distracting her. Several seconds passed in silence. Then, Sylph's eyes widened.

"I think I see one— Wait, I lost it."

Damien hid his disappointed frown. "It's okay, that's more than I can do! If you saw one for a moment, then maybe—"

"Wait, it's back. This way!" Sylph turned to a tunnel trailing off to their right side and stepped inside, bringing her wind armor to life around her.

"Huh. That was fast," Henry said. "I knew her magical control was good, but that's abnormal for a human."

She's hardly just a human with all the Corruption in her.

"Fair point," Henry allowed. Damien followed Sylph, ready to activate his mage armor at moment's notice. Their footsteps echoed through the hall as the two accelerated—but not so much as to mistakenly stumble into a possible trap.

The tunnel routed them into a clockwise stairwell that headed straight downward. It was lit by flickering magical torches that used glowing stones rather than flame for light. The stone beneath their feet turned dark and waterlogged the farther they went.

Finally, the pathway terminated before a small, unassuming metal door embedded in the stone at the end of a short room. Damien and Sylph came to a stop before it, glancing around but finding nothing else.

"Well, that was anticlimactic," Damien said.

"If you're trying to hide something important, you probably wouldn't want to make the path leading up to it really fancy or exciting," Sylph pointed out. "That would just end up calling all the looters over to your treasure."

"Good point. So...door."

"Door," Sylph agreed, touching it carefully with the back of her hand. She nodded to herself, then summoned a black gauntlet around her hand and touched the doorknob. It creaked but didn't budge.

"They locked it," Damien said helpfully. "I guess that makes sense, too."

There was a sharp crack as the knob snapped off in Sylph's gauntleted hand. She raised the knob to him and waggled an eyebrow. "Not anymore."

Damien inclined his head. "You win that one. Open it already, let's see if there's anything there."

He gathered Ether into a tear in his hand, standing at an angle so that he had a shot over Sylph's shoulder as she pulled the door open. It swung slowly, revealing a dark room devoid of lighting. It took Damien's eyes a moment to adjust.

A marble pedestal sat in the center of the room, its top

carved into the shape of a claw reaching toward the heavens. Held at the tip of its claw was a red gem. It shimmered faintly in the light coming in from the room they currently stood in.

"Trapped?" Damien wondered. "Looks expensive to me."

"Almost certainly," Sylph said, squinting around the dark room. "I wonder how extensive the trap is, though. Do you think it's just in that room, or would it have a larger area of effect? Or maybe it's on the gem itself..."

"Your guess is as good as mine if not better," Damien replied, rubbing his head. "If the trap is on the gem itself, we can avoid that by grabbing it with some cloth. I doubt it's so trapped as to just blow up on contact, since that would defeat the purpose of having an artifact in the first place. The person who originally put it there probably wanted to use it at some point."

"That's a good point," Sylph said. "So, the gem is probably safe itself, then. Now, the question is the range of the trap."

Damien squinted at the room and rubbed his chin. He and Sylph stood there for nearly a minute before he cleared his throat.

"What if I just teleported in, grabbed it, and teleported out? Then, we can run like crazy and deal with the consequences later."

"That doesn't seem like a particularly intelligent plan."

"That doesn't sound like a no."

"It isn't one," Sylph said, cracking a grin. "Just make sure I'm behind in case something explodes. I can take a hit a lot better than you can."

Damien nodded, then gathered the Ether in his Core. He flickered, appearing in the room for just long enough to pluck the red gem from the claw's grasp. Damien took care not to touch the stone, just in case it had some runes he couldn't make out.

The claws snapped shut, no longer held open by the gem. Damien vanished, having absolutely no desire to find out what that entailed. He reappeared beside Sylph, thrusting the gem into the pockets of his mage armor.

They both dashed for the exit as fast as they could. A rumble ran through the room behind them, followed by a loud groaning creak.

"Something isn't happy," Damien yelled, teleporting as they reached a corner to avoid slowing down. Sylph hopped off the wall, practically flying over his head as her wind armor accelerated her.

"You don't say. Don't let it get the gem back!"

"Keep dreaming," Damien called with a laugh, teleporting ahead of her. Magic filled the halls around them as they darted for the exit, rumbles growing louder and passing through more of the underground behind them.

Damien flickered past a falling boulder and a scythe carved through it, splitting the stone before it could hit Sylph. They turned yet another corner, but the noise gave no indication of growing weaker.

His jovial mood started to fade. Whatever they'd taken, something very clearly wanted it back.

"What did we steal?" Damien asked, risking a glance over his shoulder. "Why in the Eight Planes is the whole blasted place coming down around us?"

"Let's worry about that once we're in a better spot to fight," Sylph replied, sweat beading on her brow. "Just keep running. I think I felt a breeze. We don't want to be forced to fight in close quarters."

They accelerated once more, using all the power they had to put distance between them and the rumbles. Sylph took the lead, shooting through tunnels seemingly at random. Damien just focused on keeping up with her. They seemed to be heading up a lot of stairwells and slopes, so he was hopeful that meant they were growing near the top of the city.

More stone rained down around Damien. The noise at their heels was still growing louder, and the ground shook harder with every passing second. He gritted his teeth and grabbed Sylph by the shoulder.

"We aren't going to make it!" Damien yelled over the growing din. "Stay close to me."

He connected to the ring of runes in his mind, sending a mental command out into the Ether surrounding them.

"*Shatter.*"

Black lines erupted from Damien's chest, spiking up through the ceiling above them. With a loud explosion, they detonated. He staggered but caught himself on Sylph's shoulder. Energy drained from his body, but Damien kept his grip on reality and avoided sucking the Ether out of himself again.

Stone cascaded down around them. Huge boulders crashed to the ground, and a tiny beam of gray light pierced through the ceiling. Damien and Sylph spotted it at the same time and shot toward it without a word.

Damien teleported multiple times, avoiding falling stones until he got a clear angle to peek outside. As soon as he caught a flicker of the drab stone streets, he Warp Stepped. Sylph was right on his heels.

She'd carved clean through all the rubble in her way, bashing what remained of it to pieces with her black gauntlet. The two of them ran a short distance back, then turned to observe the growing sinkhole forming in the ground.

Buildings toppled and fell into it as the rumbling slowly stopped. Finally, the city went still once more. Dust floated in the air around them, making the gray light even darker.

"Well, that happened," Damien said, brushing himself off

and pulling the gem out. "Got it, though. I wonder what was chasing us."

Dark motes shimmered within the dust, snapping together as if pulled by an invisible force. They formed into a humanoid form, revealing Aven as she stepped out over the edge of the sinkhole.

"That would have been me."

CHAPTER
NINETEEN

"Ah," Damien said, drinking in the Ether around them. "And I don't suppose you've got a good reason for that? We're from the same school."

"Don't play games," Aven said. Lightning crackled around her, forming into a rippling cloak. "You and Sylph took an artifact I had my eye on."

"Have you considered asking politely instead of destroying half the city?" Damien asked. "It might get you farther."

"Would it have?"

"No," Damien admitted, "but it would have been nice to at least try. There are dozens of artifacts scattered around the city. Go find another one. Weren't you supposed to know the location of some super important one? Sylph and I didn't know it, so I figure you and Cheese did."

Her gaze lowered to the pocket where Damien had put the gem.

"You're kidding me," Damien said flatly. "This?"

"No," Aven replied. "I simply took a fancy to this artifact. The main target has already been secured."

"Then, you should go find an anthill and kiss it," Damien

said, binding a Devour spell in the air before him with his mental energy. "This one is ours."

A bolt of lightning ripped from Aven's cloak and streaked toward Damien. He leapt back, and his spell expanded, swallowing the bolt. Damien reversed its runes, casting Expunge and launching the bolt straight back at Aven.

She spun out of the way and stomped the ground, sending a wave of jagged stone rippling outward. Damien barely teleported out before getting impaled upon it. When he reappeared, a bolt of lightning was already streaking toward him.

He cursed, teleporting once more. Aven's reaction speed was on par with Derrod's, but she was using ranged attacks. Damien threw several Gravity Spheres at Aven, then took cover behind a building as a wave of fire scorched the streets.

It continued for several seconds before fading, leaving hazy scorch marks all over the block. Metal clashed against stone, and there was another wave of flame. Damien stepped out as soon as it faded, hurling two Gravity Lances at Aven's back.

Aven snapped her fingers and a wall of rock erupted in their path, blocking both spells. No sooner than she had moved than Sylph launched from within her camouflage, carving a dark line through the air.

A crackling fist of lightning shot from Aven's cloak, striking Sylph from her spell and sending her tumbling across the cracked, smoking ground. She sprung into the air mid-bounce, flinging a dagger at the other girl.

Aven flickered and collapsed into a puddle of shadow before reforming behind Sylph, a cold gleam in her eye. It was replaced by surprise as a silver blur shot from Sylph's back.

The older student's reaction speed was incredible. She spun, stone rushing up her body to block the blow, but Sylph had the advantage of surprise. Her scythe carved a deep cut along Aven's midsection before the other girl could escape.

Aven spat a bullet of thick, green acid at Sylph as she retreated. The spell burned clean through her shoulder and shot out the other side, punching deep into the ground. Shadows traveled down Aven's side, stitching her wound shut just enough to stop most of the bleeding.

Damien grabbed Aven's shoe with a tendril of mental energy and yanked hard on it, but she responded almost instantly, blocking out his influence.

She retaliated with a whip of hissing blue energy. Damien vaulted back, and it scored across the ground beneath him, warping and twisting the stone as it passed through. Aven yanked the whip back and dodged Sylph's scythe, only for the second one to strike her in the shoulder as Sylph unsheathed it.

Aven melted into a puddle and shot back, bouncing off a building while Sylph lunged after her, just barely falling short as the older student repositioned herself on the other side of the clearing.

"How many of those do you have?" Aven snarled, patching the new wound. "And are you seriously third-years? Or is this some test from Derrod?"

"You're the one who attacked us," Damien grunted, slinging a Gravity Sphere at her. He was tempted to use direct casting, but something told him to stop. Aven was supposed to be one of the most dangerous students on the Forsad trip, but she was barely holding her own.

She's hiding something as well. Even Quinlan would do better than this, and she lost to Cheese, who's supposedly weaker than Aven.

"None of her spells are very creative," Henry observed. "You've got the right thought. She's testing the water or trying to learn something about you. I doubt that artifact is her real goal, and I don't want to show her more than we need to. I won't be acting either unless we plan to do away with her for good."

You're sure we can handle her?

Henry snorted while Damien ducked out of the way of a screeching beam of wind that obliterated the building behind him. "Stop selling us short. I could crush her with minimal effort."

And what about Derrod?

It took Henry longer to respond to that one. "I wouldn't want to fight him if we can avoid it. Derrod is a very powerful mage. One I'd much rather have on our side when the Corruption comes knocking. If he's really dead set against us, it would be very hard for me to keep you alive while we fight."

Sylph and Aven clashed again. Sparks flew as scythes struck stone, and Sylph whipped her leg around. A blade sprouted from the bottom of her foot and slammed into Aven's collarbone, forcing her to retreat once more.

What if we have no choice?

Damien threw two Gravity Spheres at the girls. The first detonated directly behind Sylph, pulling her back as Aven lunged to grab her. The second spell shot wide, detonating just above the two of them.

"Make sure it doesn't happen," Henry said, his tone flat. "We could probably win, but at a cost you aren't willing to pay. Not yet. At the rate we're improving, a year would be enough to let me fully take over and withstand Derrod. But now? You'd be lucky to keep your limbs."

I see.

Sylph leapt up as the Gravity Sphere went off, and it pulled her high into the air faster than Aven could turn. A dagger sprouted from Aven's shoulder, and she cursed, bringing her defenses up a moment too late.

How long is she going to hold back? There's no way she's actually this weak.

"Still selling yourself short," Henry said irritably. "Not to mention Sylph. She's a killing machine. But, yes, the girl is still holding back. I wonder how much she's willing to bleed before she really starts fighting."

How about we find out? Help me with my mental energy for a moment. I'm going to press her.

Damien teleported, not needing a response from Henry to know his companion would do his part. He appeared before Aven as Sylph slashed at her back. Aven's eyes narrowed, and the stone erupted around her, encasing her in a cocoon.

Ether flickered along Damien's arms, and he fired several tears straight through Aven's spell. A cry rang out, followed by furious cursing. Damien teleported just before rock flew everywhere as Aven detonated her defenses, peppering their surroundings with shrapnel.

"Now I *know* something is wrong," Aven hissed, clutching her side, where a deep wound was seeping blood despite the stitching holding it shut. "That was not a Year Three spell."

"Then, I hope you've got a lot more to offer," Damien said, drawing Ether into him at an alarming rate. He raised his hands into the air, channeling as much as he dared to. Dozens of huge Tears formed around him, popping and hissing with purple light.

Damien let the first one fire. Aven teleported back, and he sent the next one while forming another above his hand. Every time Aven tried to gain back momentum, he attacked again. The attacks got closer to hitting every time.

"Enough!" Aven snarled, dodging the last spell and taking shelter atop a crumbling rooftop. "How much blasted Ether do you have?"

Reaching out with his mental energy, Damien formed a Gravity Sphere in the building beneath her and pumped Ether into it through his connection. It went off, and the house imploded with a loud blast, sending a huge plume of dust into the sky.

"Enough," Damien growled in reply, launching two Gravity Lances into the building. Sylph stepped up beside him and squinted at the rising cloud.

"Damn. What did she do to you?" Sylph asked. "That was a lot."

"She's holding back, trying to find something," Damien replied with a shrug. "I figured we might as well try to see what she's really capable of if she wants to fight with us. Maybe she'll drop an artifact if we beat her up hard enough."

"What do you think I am, a walking goodie bag?" Aven snarled, emerging from the ruined building atop a platform of moving stone. She was covered with small lacerations and breathing heavily.

"More like a poor excuse for a Year Four," Damien said. "I've had better competition from mindless monsters. Last chance. What do you want from us?"

"I already told you. The artifact."

Damien teleported directly in front of Aven. Then, he cast Storm.

The ground cracked, large chunks tearing away and lifting into the air around them as micro tears whipped around Damien, shredding everything into a hurricane of jagged shards. The speed of the spell caught Aven off guard, and a stone carved a line across her forehead before she could react.

She nearly lost an ear to a stray tear, only managing to save it by throwing herself out of the way at the last moment.

"What's wrong?" Damien asked. "It looks like you're running out of Ether. Spend a little too much teleporting around?"

"You're inhuman," Aven said, her form liquifying. She splashed onto the ground and slipped through the cracks, gathering back together on the other side of the clearing. "There's no way you're a Year Three."

Sylph's scythe punched through the center of Aven's chest. She materialized behind the older girl and ripped the blade free, stepping to the side.

"No," Sylph said. "You're just incredibly unimpressive. I'm pretty sure Mark is a better fighter than you, even without his demon."

Aven glanced down at the wound in her chest, then let out a heavy sigh. "Damn, you really did a number on me. I honestly thought it was all talk."

"What was?" Damien asked. All the malice had left Aven's voice, replaced by calm detachment.

"I'm not going to answer that," Aven replied, rubbing her chin. A thin crack split her finger and raced down her arm. "I've given you information. I won't risk any more. Honestly, I really am impressed. I'd love to keep this going, but I'm all out of energy. What artifact were you looking for?"

"Something to gather energy," Damien replied. "I don't suppose you're in so much awe of our talent that you're willing to give us one?"

Aven snorted. "Hardly. But I'll tell you that Quinlan is about to come into possession of one. Should she survive Cheese, you can get it off her. I trust that's sufficient reward."

The cracks spread, running up along Aven's neck and down through her feet. She shattered, crumbling apart like a brittle cookie in milk. Within an instant, all that remained of her was a small pile of smoldering ash.

"Shit," Damien muttered. "That was just some form of spell, not her?"

"Looks like a body replication technique," Henry provided, forming a mouth so Sylph could hear him as well. "A very good one. I would have noticed, but we've gone over that bit. Human spark, stinky, yadda yadda. Her real body is off somewhere else. She was just puppeteering that one. Man, I'd love to see her at full strength. I wonder what other magic she knows. Maybe there are some new techniques I haven't seen."

"We can get her autograph later," Damien said. Sylph's scythes retracted into her back, and she wiped her forehead, sitting down on a large stone and digging through her bag to find some jerky.

"I wonder what she was doing, though," Sylph said after swallowing. "Do you think...?"

"Derrod?" Damien finished. "Almost certainly. Asshole. Probably gave her something to test me, but I guess Aven couldn't be bothered to do it normally so she sent a clone."

"Lucky us," Sylph said. "A clone would only have a portion of her power. We took care of it pretty handily but imagine if it was just twenty or thirty percent. She'd be a serious menace in a real fight."

"We'll cross that bridge when we get there," Damien decided. "I'm going to have to figure out something to do with him before we're done here. I'm done with all his damn tests."

"Can we really stop him?" Sylph asked. "Even together?"

"I'll figure something out," Damien said darkly. "Until then, do you have any idea how we can find Quinlan? If Aven wasn't lying, she's got the artifact I need."

Sylph scratched her head. "Follow the explosions, probably. If she's about to fight Cheese, I'd bet it won't be long before we hear something."

"Fair enough," Damien said. He sat down next to her, and they settled in to wait.

Like the last time, it didn't take long for the sounds of battle to reach them. No more than a few minutes later, half a dozen distant rumbles shook the city. Damien and Sylph exchanged a glance.

"You think that's her?" Sylph asked.

"Can't hurt to check," Damien said as they both rose to their feet and set off in the direction of the noise. The noise hadn't been particularly close, but it was closer than some of the other fights going on around the city.

The sounds of explosions and carnage accompanied the two as more fights waxed and waned along the edges of the city. Flashes of brilliant light occasionally overtook the ever-present gray, but it always returned shortly after.

Damien slowed as he and Sylph drew up to a large section of ruined houses. The ground had been completely covered with scorched black stone. It was craggy and hazy, warping anything Damien tried to look at through it.

"Well, this looks like old lava," Damien said, squinting through the houses to try and find any sign of other people. "I don't see anyone, though."

"Hold on," Sylph said as her wind armor whipped to life around her. She took a step forward before Damien could stop her, but her foot never touched the superheated rock. A ripple swept out, and she climbed into the air, darting through the sky as easily as if it were land.

She jogged over the area, scouting it out, before running back to float before Damien atop two disks of air.

"There's a passageway underground in the middle of all the houses," she reported. "And I can hear fighting going on beneath it. They must have just gotten here."

"Let's go, then," Damien said. Sylph nodded, and he teleported into the air, spinning as he fell to get a better look at the ground.

It wasn't hard to spot the gaping hole in the center of one demolished house. A tongue of molten red light licked out from within it, further confirming their suspicions. Damien teleported again, appearing safely at the top of a section of ruined wall above the hole. Sylph ran over to join him, and they both peered inside.

This passageway looked similar to the one they'd been in previously. Every few seconds, the ground shuddered slightly, and the light coming out of the room flared in intensity. There was no direct sight of Quinlan, or Cheese, though.

"We'll just have to go in," Damien said. "Be ready. We still don't know exactly what Cheese can do."

Sylph snorted. "I was about to say the same thing. It's a good thing it doesn't look like Quinlan threw that molten stone everywhere down here or you wouldn't be able to go much farther."

"Lucky me."

They both hopped down. Damien prepared to cast Devour as they fell. The two landed lightly on the stone, and they quickly straightened, prepared to defend themselves. No attacks came.

The room they stood in was drab and gray, with only a single large doorway before them. On the other side of the door was a huge, circular room. Quinlan and Cheese stood across from each other, so locked in their fight that neither seemed to notice the newcomers.

Magma coiled around Quinlan, whipping out and lashing at Cheese in a constant barrage. Every few seconds, she'd throw in an extra blast of molten rock. Whenever her magic touched the ground, it hissed and melted away as if nothing were in her way. The sheer speed and power of her attacks was terrifying.

They were also completely useless. Cheese vaulted over a pillar of lava, laughing hysterically as his bare hands touched the lava. If it hurt him, the boy certainly didn't show it. He batted away another one of Quinlan's strikes and ducked under a searing bolt of red energy that burned a hole through the wall behind him.

"Seven Planes," Sylph muttered as they fought. Sweat trickled down her brow from the amount of heat radiating out of the room. "How is he doing that?"

"It's Matter magic," Henry said, popping out of Damien's shadow. "I've always loved it. He's changing the physical properties of the lava as soon as it gets close to him, making it as harmless as cold rock."

"That doesn't seem very reliable," Sylph observed. "He's relying on incredible reaction speed, then? What if he's half a second too late?"

"Then he cooks alive," Henry replied. "It's a very bold way to fight. Makes it a lot of fun to watch. We should keep at it."

"We do that, and Cheese will win," Damien said flatly. "We need that artifact, and we saw what happened the last time she fought him. Cheese is just going easy on her now, isn't he?"

"Oh, almost certainly," Henry said. "He could have gotten close to her half a dozen times by now, but he's just hanging back and letting her wail on him. Crazy bugger is having fun. Why don't you train like that?"

"Oh, bug off," Damien grumbled, starting toward the two and gathering Ether around himself. Before he could even step through the door, both Cheese and Quinlan faltered as they caught sight of him entering at the same time.

"Wait!" Cheese yelled, skidding to a stop and hopping a foot back. "Don't interfere."

"What are you doing here?" Quinlan asked, frowning through her grimace. Blood dripped from her forehead, and her arm hung limp at her side. The lava around her tilted as if it were an inquisitive snake. "It's not safe!"

"Forget that," Cheese snapped before Damien could answer. "I don't want my fight interrupted. I do not need help. Please, leave."

Sylph glanced between Quinlan and Cheese, then raised her

eyebrow while Damien failed to hold back a laugh. Cheese's eyes widened slightly.

"Oh, you're *with* her? That's fine, then. I suppose I could fight all three of you at once. That could be fun," Cheese mused. "Do you think it matters that we're from the same college? You wouldn't tell Derrod, would you?"

"Don't!" Quinlan said quickly. "He'll take you apart if you fight as you are. I'm barely holding him off myself."

She gave Damien a pointed look, flicking her gaze to Henry. It didn't take a genius to understand she was implying the only way he'd stand up to Cheese was with Henry's help, which wasn't something he wanted to do quite yet.

"I can't give you the artifact either," Cheese continued, ignoring all of them as he rubbed his chin. "But maybe if you took it from me when I wasn't watching, that would give me an excuse? That's a good idea, right?"

"No," all three of them chorused.

Cheese's face fell. "Damn. So, how are we supposed to fight?"

"We aren't actually here to fight you if we can avoid it," Damien hedged. "We kind of came for an artifact that Aven told us would be here. She said Quinlan would have it."

"What?" Quinlan asked. "I haven't gotten anything I can give you, I'm sorry. I'm just trying to get the one Cheese has, and I can't give it up under any circumstance."

"Well, Aven told me she'd give me a fully paid trip to every bakery in the kingdom if I got this," Cheese said, crossing his arms. "So, I'm not giving it to you. I need it more."

"Does it strike you how ridiculous this is?" Sylph asked Damien in a low whisper. He gave her a one-shouldered shrug in response.

"Better than the alternative, I guess. I have to say that I like

Cheese a lot more than Aven right now. He's yet to try to kill us."

"I could," Cheese offered. "Would you like me to?"

"No thank you, maybe another time," Damien said. "But I do really need the artifact. Not the one you're trying to keep from us, but something that gathers energy. Aven told us that we could get it from Quinlan."

"Oh," Cheese said, wiping his nose with the back of his sleeve and digging around in his pants. He pulled out a shimmering white stone. "I was supposed to give this to someone who managed to survive fighting me for five minutes straight. How long has it been?"

"More than five minutes," Quinlan said slowly. "But—"

Cheese tossed her the rock, and she caught it out of reflex, staring at it with complete befuddlement.

"I don't need this."

"Well, Aven told me to give it to you," Cheese said. "I don't want it either. It was poking my bum."

Quinlan gagged and threw the rock to Damien, who caught it with telekinesis and tucked it into his pack, trying to pretend like he knew what was going on.

"Uh, thanks. I think."

"Sure, sure," Cheese said. "Can we get back to the fun part now? I've almost been melted five times already! Five!"

"You're completely insane," Quinlan said, raising her good hand. The lava around her twitched, but then faltered and collapsed back to the ground. "Shit. I'm out of Ether."

"Seriously?" Cheese asked. "Come on. I can wait while you recover some more, then? Man, I wish I didn't break your arm last time. I didn't think you'd be so squishy. This fight would have been more fun if you moved around more."

"Gee, sorry," Quinlan said sarcastically. "I'm sorry for not being better at killing you."

"You should be," Cheese said with a sage nod. He glanced at Sylph, and his eyes brightened. "Do you want to try instead? Aven told me you were super-fast. I'm fast, too, you know."

"I— Uh, can I say no?" Sylph asked.

"Aven told me I had to listen when people said no if they were part of Blackmist," Cheese said, crestfallen. "But that wasn't you saying no, was it? That was just you asking if you could say no."

"No."

"Ah. Damn. What about you, Damien?"

"Rain check?" Damien suggested. "I might be about to explode right now, so I'd rather get that dealt with before doing anything else."

"Oh, exploding. That's fun," Cheese said. "I tend to prefer punching things, but I like watching Aven blow them up. Quinlan, when are you going to be healed? Now?"

"Uh...definitely not," Quinlan said, slowly backing away from Cheese. He followed her, not a care in the world. "I'll need at least a day and time to treat my arm if you want me to be able to do anything. Shit. I need that blasted artifact."

"Well, I'll wait," Cheese said, rubbing his chin. "You're more fun than the other guys here. Freddy was so disappointing. I broke him on accident."

"You mean Teddy?" Damien asked. "And what exactly do you mean by broke him?"

"Teddy, Freddy, same thing," Cheese said dismissively. "His name wasn't worth remembering. He didn't dodge fast enough, and he *likes* fighting close range. Look at Quinlan! She's a ranged fighter, but she didn't let me punch her chest. Isn't that smart? If Teddy were smart, I wouldn't have broken him."

The back of Damien's neck prickled. Cheese's voice rang with amusement when he spoke, but there was something cold deep beneath his eyes.

"He tried to rip my heart out," Quinlan reported, slumping against the wall and breathing heavily. "Or, at least, that's what he told me he was trying to do. For the first few minutes, he told me what he was going to do right before he did it."

"It makes things more challenging," Cheese said defensively. "Is a day over yet?"

"No," Quinlan said. "It is not."

"Oh. Well, I'll just follow you around until you're ready. It's not like you can go anywhere if you want the artifact," Cheese said with a cheerful grin. "Do you have any food?"

"You're trying to kill me and you're asking for food?"

"Yes."

Quinlan glanced at Damien and Sylph, then let out an explosive sigh. "Oh, Planes take me. I don't care anymore. If it means I get another shot at the artifact, I won't complain."

She dug around in her bag with her good hand and pulled out a small wheel of cheese. She bit back a pained laugh and turned her gaze to Cheese, holding out his namesake.

"Ooh, I love that!" Cheese said, prancing forward and plucking it from her hand. "How did you know?"

"Just a guess," Quinlan said, shaking her head. Sylph walked up to her and supported the older girl, lowering her to the ground and helping her wrap her injured arm and treat the injuries riddling her body.

"So," Cheese said, taking a bite out of the cheese and walking up to Damien. "Come here often?"

"What? No. Who comes to Forsad often? This is the first time for all of us."

"Ah," Cheese said, nodding. "Makes sense. I don't really concern myself with that stuff. I just like fighting."

"Why did you even ask it, then?"

"Aven told me it was polite to ask," Cheese replied with a shrug. "No reason not to be polite."

"That's fair enough," Damien admitted. "You're...very interesting."

"Thank you! You're quite boring yourself, but you'd be more fun if we fought," Cheese said, still chewing. "I've heard you're fun to fight against."

"Aven?"

"Nah, it was Fr— Ah, Teddy. I asked him who I should go have fun with after I was done with him, and he said you were okay."

"Good to know," Damien said, shaking his head slowly. He hated the thought, but Cheese was actually somewhat entertaining. In a strange, crazed kind of way.

"I'd be happy to fight you some other—"

Damien didn't get to finish his sentence. An enormous force picked him up and threw him across the room. He barely managed to cross his arms before he slammed into the wall.

A brilliant flash followed the shockwave, followed by a world ending explosion. The sound tore through the ground, vibrating it almost as much as the blast had. The city of Forsad let out a pained screech as what sounded like hundreds of buildings crashed down above them.

Damien groaned, pushing himself upright and trying to squint through his light-scarred eyes.

"What in the Eight Planes was that?" he asked, his words muted and distant to his own ears.

Henry formed beside him, helping Damien to his feet with a tentacle. His blobby face was cold and devoid of amusement. He staggered over to the edge of the room and looked out of the hole. The gray skies of Forsad had been completely tinted a sickly green. Damien's blood went cold as he realized he knew the answer to his own question before Henry even spoke.

"The Corruption."

CHAPTER
TWENTY

"Planes," Sylph muttered, walking up to join Damien with a grim expression on her face. "How bad is it? That's a lot of green."

Damien shook his head mutely. "I don't know. Henry?"

"Bad," Henry said. "I can feel the Corruption, even from here. The only Corrupted monster I could feel at a range like this was..."

"Second," Damien finished. "We need to move. If he's showing himself, there's something he needs here. We have to make sure he doesn't get it."

"What's going on?" Quinlan asked, limping up to join them. Her good arm was wrapped around Cheese's neck as he supported her.

"We're under attack. Forget about Forsad," Damien said. "Do you have a way to get out of here?"

"None of us do. We need Derrod," Quinlan replied. "What could possibly cause him trouble, though? He's Stormsword!"

"Is it strong?" Cheese wondered.

"Too strong for any of us," Damien said, teleporting out of the hole and onto the ground surrounding it. The molten rock surrounding them had started to cool, but it was still uncomfortably hot.

Sylph flickered up to join him. A moment later, Cheese leapt out of the hole, holding Quinlan to his chest, and landed beside them with a thud. He set her back down and squinted at the source of the light.

It originated from the east of the city, where a jagged hole hung in the gray dome in the sky.

"I think I should probably let you know that I don't actually have the artifact you were looking for," Cheese said, rubbing his chin. "Aven does. We swapped just in case someone actually beat me."

"You lied?" Quinlan exclaimed. "But I was fighting you that whole time!"

"Well, it was fun," Cheese said with a shrug. "Blame Aven. It was her idea. But...she's over in the direction of that explosion."

"Well, I figured out what Second is after," Damien said. "Let's go. We need to help her. Quinlan, you should probably stay back. You're injured."

Quinlan clenched a fist. "Damn it. You're right, I'm just a hindrance right now. I don't even have enough Ether to fight if I'm propped up against a wall."

"To be honest, I'm running a little low as well," Cheese admitted. Much of his easygoing attitude had faded with the arrival of the Corruption. "I've still got some, though. Quinlan and I will catch up with you if this Corruption doesn't kill everyone first."

"Thanks for the vote of confidence," Damien said dryly. "Let's go, Sylph."

He teleported, knowing she was only a few seconds behind him as they sped toward the east of the city.

Houses flickered by in a blur as Damien accelerated the speed of his magic, covering ground at an incredible speed. He didn't stop for more than an instant between teleports and only paused when he put a little too much distance between himself and Sylph.

His skin prickled as he grew closer to the east side of the city. Ether delicately pulled away from him and floated into the sky, following an invisible summons.

"Hold on, Damien," Sylph said, appearing beside him in a burst of wind. "I'm not so sure Second is after any artifact. If he broke in this easily, he could have taken it at any time. There was no reason to wait for us to show up."

"Then what's he doing? We don't exactly have time to sit around and figure it out."

"Considering the time he showed up, he's probably hunting. I was trained to do something similar," Sylph said, nodding up at the hole in the sky. "He's drawing attention on purpose. You only do that when you're trying to draw someone out."

"You think he's after me?"

"Could be," Sylph said with a curt nod. "But...there's another option. There's more than one person who could pose a threat to him."

"Shit. Derrod?"

Sylph gave him a small nod. "Stormsword is a deadly warrior, even if he's a terrible person. Sorry."

"Don't apologize. You aren't wrong," Damien said. "Eight Planes. He's one of the strongest mages in the kingdom. If he dies, we'll all be in trouble."

"Just be careful," Sylph said. "This is just a thought. He's after you as well, we know that."

"It's a risk we've got to take," Damien said. Sylph nodded, and they both shot off again.

Damien teleported himself into the air, getting a better vantage point of the city.

"There," Henry said, drawing Damien's gaze to a small group of people in a large, flattened clearing full of rubble.

Damien teleported again, arriving behind a building at the edge of it. He poked his head out, preparing the Ether to teleport once more at the slightest sign of trouble. Sylph appeared beside him, her face tense.

Second stood across from Derrod, the bandages covering his body twisting and churning like he was covered by a thin layer of white worms.

Four other Corrupted monsters, their flesh a sickly mix of bone white and lime green, stood around him. They were all humanoid but lacked all the defining features that made man.

The monsters' eyes were dark, sunken holes. Only two of them had mouths, but they were warped and empty, passageways into the empty black rather than a tool for survival.

Behind Derrod, Aven leaned against a building. A brutal cut ran along her chest, weeping blood despite the thick stitching holding it shut. The bodies of three Corrupted monsters laid around her, scorched and shattered.

"Who are you?" Derrod asked, his sword pointed at Second.

"Your future," Second replied. A bandage shot from his arm, reaching for the mage. Derrod's sword flashed, and the bandage split in two. The bandages on Second's face wrinkled in anger, and the severed cloth fluttered back up to his arm, reattaching itself.

"You aren't like the other Corrupted monsters I've killed," Derrod said. "You're...more. Why do you challenge the queen?"

"I don't care about your kingdom," Second said with a grating laugh. One of the monsters beside him stepped forward, letting out a keening wail.

Aven flicked her hand a bolt of black light shot from her fingertips, punching through the monster's neck. The spell wrapped back around, entangling it with a shadowy net. The net snapped taut, slicing through the monster in dozens of places. It crashed to the ground, diced.

Before the wounds could heal, Derrod pointed a finger at the creature. It shuddered, and the lines of Ether connected to it started to snap. Second snarled, and a wave of green light washed out from his chest.

Derrod summoned a cloak of storming blue energy around him, but the light washed over all of them harmlessly.

The monster that Aven had chopped reassembled itself piece by piece, strands of green acid stitching it back together.

"Did you really think I'd just let you chop my soldiers apart?" Second asked, cocking his head.

"Stormsword, we need to retreat," Aven said. "I'm losing my Ether just by standing next to him. I don't know if we can win this. We have to get out of Forsad and seek reinforcements."

"Try it," Second encouraged. "Your son was equally as apt at running away, but he's had help. You don't."

Magic stormed around Derrod, sending arcs of lightning scoring across the ground around him. Second laughed, raising a hand as Derrod's magic leapt for him. A green rune circle spiraled out in the air before his palm, stopping and absorbing the lightning before it could even touch him.

Derrod flashed forward, swinging his sword at Second's neck. The Corrupted man dodged to the side, moving just out of the way of the blow and thrusting his palm for Derrod's chest.

Lightning wrapped around Derrod, and he vanished, reappearing on Second's other side mid swing. Shimmering blue afterimages sprung up around him, all lashing out in unison. Second blocked the main attack, but two of the images drove their weapons into his chest.

Acid sprayed as Derrod unleashed a flurry of strikes into Second's back, shredding the bandages covering the man before flickering back to avoid the green liquid.

"You're just another Corrupted monster," Derrod growled, flicking his sword clean. A thin layer of his magic coated his weapon, keeping the acid from burning it. He raised a hand, sending magical energy out to stop the other man's wounds from healing.

"You aren't wrong," Second said. Stone built over his wounds, sealing them shut. Then, slowly, the green acid reached out as well, stitching his flesh shut before his bandages shifted to cover the site of the wound. "But you lack understanding of what you're talking about. There is no 'just' in this. I *am* Corrupted."

His bandages unraveled, and he lowered his arms, hiding them within the folds of his cloak, as they started to gather on the ground around him.

"Stormsword, you have to cut him off from the Ether," Aven hissed. "You're letting him heal!"

"I did," Derrod said, raising his sword once more. "He should be cut off."

Second shimmered with sickly green light that rose off him in wisps of rancid smoke. The monsters around him advanced on the two humans.

"Such a limited understanding," Second said. Two of the monsters leapt. Derrod flickered, reappearing where he had been standing a moment later. The monsters crashed to the ground on either side of him, shredded to pieces.

"You talk a lot, but I'm not seeing any real threat from you. You're just a cockroach. Difficult to kill but harmless," Derrod growled. The monsters started to piece themselves together, but Aven thrust her hands forward. One of them collapsed back to the ground, turning to stone.

"Ultimately amusing," Second said as the monster at Derrod's side stitched itself back together and took a step back. "You have some skill, but it doesn't matter. You have no idea how many other skilled men just like you float, forgotten, in the farthest reaches of the Void."

"Nor do I care. Why are you here?" Derrod demanded. "What do you have to do with the Void?"

"Everything," Second breathed. His bandages lifted into the air, hissing and popping with dark green magic. "Everything."

The bandages shot forward. Derrod's sword flashed, and he shimmered back. The ground where he had been standing vanished under a rain of blows that shook the earth. Some of the bandages fell to the ground, cut, but they pulled themselves back together only moments later.

"Stormsword!" Aven said urgently. "We need to leave!"

"Tell me what you know about the Void," Derrod said, ignoring Aven. "What is it? Why is it here? What threat does it pose to the kingdom?"

Bandages lifted Second into the air, writhing around him in a form eerily similar to Henry's tentacles. Streamers shot at Derrod in rapid succession, moving so fast Damien could barely track them.

Derrod flickered and vanished, remaining in vision for mere instants at a time. Beams of light carved through Second, but every wound Derrod inflicted on the Corrupted man healed moments later.

A brilliant blue flash lit up the clearing and Derrod reappeared on the ground only a short distance away from Damien, his brow furrowed in concentration and anger. Second sank for a moment, a thick cut weeping acid along his chest.

"You aren't immortal," Derrod snarled. Tongues of lightning stretched down his arm, wrapping around his sword.

"I am to the likes of you," Second replied. "I've fought a Blackmist teacher before. Even if you possess the ability to mildly injure me, they don't matter if you can't get close. I know what you value."

Five bandages blurred toward Aven. Her eyes widened, and she staggered back, too weakened to escape. Derrod blurred, but in Second's direction instead of Aven's.

There was no time to think. Damien cursed, teleporting and appearing before the wounded student. He arrived, Devour springing out before him just in time to block the attack. The tendrils vanished within it, and Derrod thrust his sword through Second's chest. A brilliant explosion rang out, filling the clearing with blinding blue light.

Damien raised a hand, squinting to try and see. Sylph stood beside him, her scythes poised at the ready. Derrod stood below Second, his sword still lodged in the other man's chest. Acid poured down from the wound, and the two were locked in a violent battle of mental energy.

"If you don't answer my questions, you will die," Derrod said.

"That is not possible," Second hissed, reaching down to his chest and drawing the sword from it. For a moment, the wound started to turn to stone. Then it cracked, giving way to acid as Second healed himself once more. "I am already dead. And soon, you will be part of me."

Derrod disappeared, blurring back into view behind Second. He drove a palm into the Corrupted man, knocking him away with a blast of condensed energy, and grabbed his sword from the Second's hand in the same move.

Second caught himself with his bandage tentacles, turning back toward Derrod with a low chuckle. "Damien. I had been hoping you would arrive, but I wasn't certain I'd be able to lure you out."

"We'll deal with that later," Derrod said, flashing toward Second again.

A tendril blurred, and Derrod slammed into the ground, cracking the stone beneath him.

"No," Second said. "We won't. You are enough of a bother that I will deal with all of you now. There will be no further interruptions."

Second raised his hands. Damien let out a strangled gasp as the Ether in his chest bucked. The air shimmered, tickling his skin as golden motes flooded toward Second, pouring out of everybody and everything.

Damien desperately grabbed onto what he could hold, but it took all his power just to keep his grasp over two motes of the magic. Sylph crumpled to her knees beside him, gasping for breath.

"This is but a taste," Second said, his voice a threatening whisper. "Behold what is to come. This is the fate that awaits those of us that fall into the cracks in the Void. There is nothing. Nothing but Corruption. You are nothing without your magic."

Derrod groaned, pushing himself up. His sword flickered faintly, then went out once more. Second dropped toward Derrod, a tendril sharpening to a point at his shoulder. It slammed into Derrod's chest and threw him into the ground with a loud crack. Derrod groaned and went still.

Sylph struggled to push herself upright but collapsed back to the ground with a wheeze. Her scythes retracted back into her body, and she groaned. Aven crumpled behind them, completely spent.

Damien tried to form a Gravity Sphere, but his last two motes of Ether vanished as soon as he drew them out of his body, siphoning away into Second.

Henry!

"Just run," Henry yelled. "I can't stop him like this. He's stronger than the last time we met him."

We won't make it. I don't have enough Ether to teleport, and even if I could, I can't take Sylph with me. I need your help.

Damien pulled his shirt back with shaking fingers, pushing

the mage armor out of the way. Second stopped before Derrod, reaching out with his bandages and lifting the mage into the air.

"To do what?" Henry screamed mentally.

You already know. You can read my thoughts.

Damien grabbed a rock from the ground and carved a line across his palm. Blood welled up in his hand, and he dipped a finger in it, tracing several extra lines across the runes on his chest.

It didn't take much to ruin a rune circle. With just a few strokes, runes meant to keep something in could be changed to those that keep that very same thing out. Damien's chest tingled. The tendrils of shadow swirling across his chest expanded, reaching out across his body.

Damien shuddered. The life blinked out behind his eyes, replaced by a pitch black that devoured all the light that touched it. For an instant, his shoulders slumped. Then, as if yanked upright by strings, he jerked straight.

His control of his body vanished, blown out like a candle in the wind as It Who Heralds the End of all Light took over.

Second froze. His eyes snapped to Damien, and green runes flooded the air before him, forming four rune circles between them. A column of sheer darkness leapt from Damien's hand, obliterating three of the circles and slamming into the fourth without a single noise.

The dim light faded, drawn into Damien's empty eyes. What little warmth the city had followed it, instantly casting the area around Damien into an endless night.

"You," Second breathed. "I remember you."

It Who Heralds the End of all Light didn't respond. Second flicked back just before the air around him imploded, shattering and falling away into a dark gap. Derrod threw himself to the side, narrowly avoiding getting sucked in. The hole in reality snapped shut, swallowing everything that had fallen into it.

Sylph darted over to Aven and grabbed her, pulling the other girl away from the fight. Derrod retreated as well, heading in the other direction without taking his eyes off Second and Damien.

"You're too late," Second said. One of the other corrupted monsters paced toward Damien, salivating acid. "This will be the final Cycle."

Damien snapped. The top half of the monster disappeared. Its body crashed to the ground, already turned to stone. More light leeched out of his surroundings, vanishing into him.

"Kill as many of us as you want. This cannot be stopped. Not anymore. Not even by you," Second said, letting out a crazed laugh. A bandage leapt at Damien, but a dark portal opened before it, devouring the tendril and snapping shut, severing it.

"The Cycle is already in the process of being restarted," Damien said, his voice a discordant symphony like hundreds of people speaking at once. "All that remains is to ensure that you do not slip through the cracks again."

Second snarled. Green energy erupted from his body, illuminating the clearing for an instant. Everyone froze, stuck in time. A shell of black magic formed across Damien's body, and he raised a finger toward Second.

A mote of black energy leapt out and headed for the bandaged man. Second thrust his palm toward it, and the air rippled, compressing and warping to change the spell's path. It shot past him and popped, erupting in a massive explosion that destroyed half of the block behind him.

"Your magic is nothing but an evolution of that belonging to mortals," Damien said. "Mine is perfected. You cannot defeat me in a fight, or you would have already tried. Instead, you attempt to worm your way into the flaws in this Plane to shatter it."

"I fight for all those you cast away," Second hissed clapping his hands. When he pulled them apart, thick ropes of acid hung between them. He whipped them toward Damien, who flickered and vanished.

He reappeared directly in front of Second and reached out to touch the other man on the shoulder. Second moved faster, driving his knee into Damien's chest. Magic rippled around where his knee touched Damien, absorbing the impact completely.

Second collapsed into a puddle of acid and slithered between Damien's feet, stabbing up at him with a green spike. Dozens of miniature Tears carved the attack into pieces before it could reach Damien.

"I have not even used Void yet. Even for you, this is substantially weaker than it should be," Damien said. Second clawed the air, and Damien's lips slowed, as if he were trying to move through molasses. An instant later, the effect vanished, and he returned to normal speed. "As I said. Weak."

"Damn Moon. If you hadn't destroyed my staff," Second cursed, sending a barrage of magic at Damien.

Hundreds of openings into an endless darkness formed around Damien, absorbing the spells before they could touch him. Sweat started to trickle down Damien's forehead. Three huge tentacles erupted from his back and swung at Second, nearly clipping Sylph and Aven as they filled the makeshift arena.

The ground erupted around Second, forming a dripping bone cage. It buckled under the weight of the attack as the tentacles slammed into it but managed to hold strong. Damien staggered slightly, though didn't fall.

Second's eyes narrowed. "Running low on Ether, are we?"

A thrum rippled through the air as Second plucked a line of Ether beside him, ripping the magic out of it. He inhaled deeply, drawing the magic into himself with a laugh. "You can't do this, can you?"

"You are a perversion of nature that will be blotted out," Damien said, gathering a dozen black spears in the air around him. They fired as one, and the bandaged man danced through them, cloth rippling in his wake. Several spells clipped him, drawing green acid forth, but none hit anything vital.

Second arrived before Damien and narrowly hopped back in time to avoid a collapsing ball of shadows. It ripped the ground between them up, shredding it into fine dust.

"How many more of those can you do?" Second asked. A green glaive formed between his hands, and he pointed it at Sylph. "How much of the boy is still left? Or have you ripped his psyche apart already? Would he even care if I kill that girl?"

Lines of shadow stretched out from Damien's feet, bursting free from the ground around Second and spearing him in a dozen spots. Second reared back and threw the glaive, ignoring the wounds riddling him.

A tendril shot out of Damien's back, grabbing the glaive before it could strike Sylph. He whipped it around, bringing the huge blade down on Second's shoulder. It splashed apart as soon as it touched him, turning to acid that burned Damien's magic away.

"You can't hurt me with my own weapon," Second laughed, splashing into a puddle and gathering himself atop a building. "Now, I wonder if you were protecting her. It Who Heralds the End of all Light, beholden to a mortal? Surely not."

Second raised his hands, and energy burst forth. A thick cloud of green magic formed over all of them, roiling and crackling with energy. Droplets of acid formed within it.

Damien snapped his fingers, and a huge maw appeared

above the cloud, snapping shut around it. More sweat built on Damien's face, and his hands started to tremble from exertion.

"Do you really have the Ether to be wasting like that?" Second asked, every word more confident than the last. "You showed yourself too early, didn't you? You can't defeat me. Especially not with the boy fighting you. No Void creature would ever waste effort over a few mortal souls. I'd know that, wouldn't I?"

More magic gathered around Second's hand. He brought it down, casting a huge crescent moon of green energy down upon the people standing below. Black lightning leapt from Damien's hands, obliterating Second's spell and carrying through to him.

Second screamed in pain as the magic ravaged his body, following him even as he collapsed into a puddle to try to escape.

Damien staggered, the magic falling from his fingertips. Second reformed, his bandages blackened and smoke rising from his body. He braced himself against the wall as portions of his wrapping fell off, revealing charred gray skin.

"You...can't kill me," Second wheezed. He jumped down from the building and paced toward Damien. "I exist because you do, and you are weak within this form. It's over. This Cycle will not restart, no matter what you do. The rest of the Void is sealed or in hiding. You are alone, as you always are. This time, I win."

Damien struggled upright, his body fighting for breath. He raised a shaking hand, but Second batted it away and grabbed him by the collar.

"I'm not," Damien hissed.

His mage armor turned jet-black. Tendrils erupted from behind it, wrapping around Second and piercing into the other man's back. Second stiffened, then his eyes widened in horror.

"How? You have no power over the Corruption. How are you stopping my magic?"

Sylph let out a relieved breath from behind them. Her brows were furrowed in concentration, and her hands shook with exertion, but she walked up to stand behind Damien.

"Get shit on, asshole," Henry said, his blobby form emerging from behind Sylph. "Now, if I were you, I'd be getting out of here as fast as possible before I find out just how unkill-able you are."

The tendrils started to pull, tearing Second's body apart. He roared in pain, but no magic formed around him. Sylph gritted her teeth, focusing all her energy.

A tendril whipped out from Second's foot, striking Sylph in the leg. She staggered but didn't fall, and the wound started to seal.

"Impossible," Second stammered. "I didn't make you."

"That's because I did," Henry said cheerfully, still pulling Second apart. A large hole formed in the Corrupted man's chest, but he seemed to be beyond pain.

"The Void cannot do anything new," Second insisted. "You are an echo. A repetition of a forgotten age. I am more. I am evolved!"

"You're dead," Henry corrected, ripping him in half.

The two pieces of Second crumpled to the ground. Then, one of their eyes turned, focusing up at Damien.

"I already told you this. You cannot kill what is not alive."

A tendril shot out from his body. Sylph twisted, managing to avoid taking the blow through the throat and instead catching it with her shoulder. She flew back, bouncing once on the ground before slamming into a building. It collapsed around her with a rumble.

Strands of acid shot out, reconnecting Second's halves. He pulled himself together with a snarl, then rose before Damien while Henry's tendrils carved at him fruitlessly. Without Sylph, every wound just healed a few seconds later.

"How curious," Second breathed. "Damien Vale. I wonder if you'll remain after this Cycle finally ends. Is any part of you even left?"

A flicker of anger washed over Damien's face.

"Ah. There is some," Second said. "But fading fast, it looks. It Who Heralds the End of all Light is devouring you. If you can hear me, know that I respect your attempt to sacrifice yourself for your friends. It was pointless, of course, but such things can only be learned through experience. If only you could have known what I did, perhaps you would have chosen your side better. You see their mortal live, but I fight for their eternity."

The dark void behind Damien's eyes grew deeper. Damien's mage armor turned back blue, and Sylph froze in place as Henry shot back into Damien.

Magic flickered behind his eyes. Second cocked an eyebrow and took a step back.

"Damien!" Henry yelled within the boy's mind. "Come on! Use the artifact!"

Damien's hand twitched, but nothing else happened. Henry snarled, reaching for the mental controls of the boy. It Who Heralds the End of all Light fought back, and the two Void creatures were locked in a violent fight.

Outside, Second watched them with undisguised curiosity. "Truly fascinating. However, I'm afraid I can't let this play out. If you lose, Damien, I might have some trouble. I'll find your soul if it survives what is to come and make this all up to you."

He extended his hand, and a glaive formed within it. He raised it into the air and brought it down toward Damien's neck. It slammed to a stop with a loud *clang*.

Sylph stood between them, trembling from exertion. Her

open palm, covered in the black gauntlet, had stopped Second's blow right before it could connect.

"You can move?" Second asked, blinking.

A scythe split his head from his shoulders. Sylph kicked him in the chest, and he fell back, dropping into a roll and rising back to his feet, grabbing his head along the way. Second put it back in its proper place and let out an aggravated sigh. "Impeded by a perversion of my own form. You cannot stop me, girl."

"I won't let you kill him," Sylph said, her second scythe rising from behind her back.

"Impressive. Such conviction," Second said. "Very well. I see myself in your eyes, girl. Let us try our convictions against each other, then."

They dashed at each other while Damien stood before them, helpless. The inside of his mind was a warzone. It was impossible to tell what was Henry, what was Herald, and what was him. Fragments of his mind spun in a violent vortex that crackled with furious energy.

If his soul hadn't already been damaged so many times, it probably would have been snuffed out by the fight. Instead, it teetered on the edge of extinction, the stands of his desire stretching and twisting in a last-ditch attempt to maintain his hold on life.

Metal sparked on stone all around him, but Damien was barely aware of it. Flashes of the fight trickled into his struggling consciousness, but he could do nothing to help her. It was all he could do to keep his fraying consciousness together.

CHAPTER
TWENTY-ONE

Second drove a fist through Sylph's shoulder. She stood her ground, cutting a deep line across his chest with one of her scythes. The other whipped at Second's neck, but he dashed back before it could hit him.

Sylph's wound started to seal, but it wasn't anywhere near the pace that Second's did. However, with Sylph suppressing his magic, the acid trickling from Second's wound showed no signs of stopping.

They dashed at each other again, trading a rain of blows. Cuts sprouted along Sylph's body like weeds. Despite the number of wounds Sylph did to Second, the man didn't seem to be letting up.

"You are but an imitation of me," Second hissed, dodging one of Sylph's scythes and driving his knee into her chin. She flipped with the blow, landing on her feet several feet and thrusting a hand at his chest.

A blade erupted from her palm, but Second caught it with his bare hands. He jerked it to the side, cutting his own palm open in the process, and threw Sylph into a building. Damien's hand twitched, and a flicker of anger crossed his face.

Second glanced at the rubble where Sylph had fallen, then turned toward Damien and raised his glaive once more. A dark blur shot from the building and slammed into Second.

Acid sprayed through the air as Sylph's weapons carved deep gouges through Second's flesh.

"Get off me, you mangy animal," Second roared, grabbing Sylph with a bandage and ripping her away. He slammed her into the ground with such force that the stone cracked—along with several of her bones.

Second raised her into the air, his features twisting in anger as Sylph's body started repairing itself. He steadied himself with his bandages and brought her closer. One of Sylph's scythes shot out, darting past the tendrils Second raised to block it, and cut deep into his right leg.

Second snarled and drove Sylph into the ground once again. He lifted her, then did it twice more. Her limbs slumped, but her eyes fluttered open, and she pierced him with a bloody, defiant glare.

Second spat a glob of acid onto the ground. "Your powers are interesting. You've done more damage to me than anyone other than Moon, but it will all go away once you die. You should have run. If you were stronger, you might have actually been the only one to have a chance to defeat me."

Sylph weakly flexed her fingers. A dagger materialized in her hand, and she flicked it at Second, catching him off guard. The weapon buried itself deep into his shoulder. "You can't take all the Ether away as long as I'm alive."

"Which won't be for much longer," Second said, ripping the dagger free. It vanished as soon as it left his body, and he brought Sylph closer while lifting his glaive toward Sylph's neck. One of her scythes met it, pressing back as hard as she could, but the glaive slowly inched toward her. "You may have stolen my power, but you're just a mortal. You will die just like everyone else when your head is severed. You were an interesting opponent. We will meet again once the Cycle has ended forever."

Damien's hand clenched into a fist. The shadows behind his eyes receded, and they returned to normal.

"This isn't perfect," Henry said in Damien's mind, his words laden with exhaustion. "You've only got a few seconds. Use the artifact and seal Herald."

Damien reached out and grabbed some of the faint Ether at the edges of his senses, yanking it into his body. There was barely anything to work with, but he didn't have time for more. Sylph was trembling with exertion, and Second's weapon was nearly at her throat.

He weaved a Devour spell, but not one that he'd ever done before. Almost instinctively, Damien changed the runes that made up the circle. He didn't have time to double check his work. He couldn't afford to be wrong the first time around because there wouldn't be a second chance.

"Damien, what are you doing?" Henry asked, letting out a groan. "Seal Herald! I can't hold it like this forever!"

What I have to.

Damien cast the spell out and burst into motion. A black disk sprang open behind Second, using every last drop of Ether Damien had. The Corrupted man turned to Damien, surprise flickering across his covered features.

With a yell, Damien drove his shoulder into Second's chest. Wounded and bleeding acid all over, he took a single step back. That was enough.

He pitched into the darkness. His hand shot out and grabbed Damien's wrist, pulling on him with incredible force. His other hand caught the edge of the circle, pushing back as it struggled to close.

Time slowed for Damien. Two futures seemed to stretch out

before him. The first, where he resisted a few seconds longer and Second climbed out of the spell, killing everyone there. And the second...

Henry. I need your help.

"No. We aren't doing that," Henry said. "Stop. I can't take control of your body right now. Herald is fighting me!"

Not me. Please.

There was no more time for talk, but nothing else needed to be said. Second's face started to emerge from the shadows of the disk as he pulled himself free. Damien dove forward, slamming into the man for the second time that day.

Henry shot out of his back, slipping free just before Damien and Second plummeted into the darkness. Second lost his grip on the edge of the spell, and the circle snapped shut behind them, severing all the bandages caught in it. The world warped around Damien, shifting and stretching as it shunted him and Second through space.

The two were torn apart and sent careening through the dark.

It was impossible to tell how long Damien plummeted in his endless fall. He lost track of time, and his mind seemed incapable of forming coherent thought as he spun in the nothingness.

But, eventually, it ended. Gray bloomed in the black, and Damien gently floated down, coming to a rest upon a flat plane of featureless, smooth rock. It stretched on as far as he could see, vanishing into the darkness all around him.

He lay there for several minutes, his mind slowly kicking back into gear. He groaned and pushed himself upright.

"Where am I?"

His words vanished into the void around him. And then he knew.

"Oh, no."

The air around Damien warped, miniature stars blinking to life. They grew more numerous, forming into a humanoid form beside him.

"And so, I return to where I started," It Who Heralds the End of all Light said. "We have returned to the Void."

"But so has Second. Not the worst result. It will buy more time for It Who Stills the Seas."

"This is the Void?" Damien asked, glancing around. "It's...empty."

"It is the Void."

"Fair enough," Damien grumbled. "How do I get out of here?"

"You do not. There is no Ether in the Void. You cannot cast magic," Herald replied. "You will die here, and I will be freed from your body."

The words sent a shard of ice through Damien's heart, but he didn't let it show on his face. He was pretty sure Herald could tell he was scared anyway, but he wasn't about to show it.

"There's always another option," Damien said. "Surely, you can realize that by now. Didn't we beat Second my way?"

"You postponed a problem you caused," Herald replied. "You have proven nothing."

"What about Henry?" Damien asked, coughing. He wiped his mouth with the back of his hand and stood up. "You're all about learning new magic. He's new. Isn't that good?"

"He will persist beyond your death. There will be time to discover the extent of what this change has done to him once the Cycle has been restarted."

"Stop being a hardass," Damien said, trying to force confidence into his voice. He glanced around for literally anything, but there was only endless gray rock. "There has to be some way out of here. Haven't you enjoyed everything on the Mortal

Plane at least a little? Learning while you're right next to someone has to be better than watching them from here."

Herald didn't respond. It just watched Damien silently, the stars that made up its eyes twinkling.

"How did I get here, anyway?" Damien asked, changing his strategy. "I just meant to make the Devour spell send objects to somewhere very far."

"I aided while you were making the spell," Herald replied. "It suited my needs, and I was not confident we could defeat Second while limited to your weak mortal body. You cast Void magic—the Void version of what you call the Devour spell."

"So, if I could do that again, I could get out of here?"

"You cannot. Attempt to reach the Ether if you wish."

Damien reached out with his mental energy, casting the net out like he had thousands of times before. Nothing appeared. Damien frowned, trying it again. There was no response. No golden lines of light met him. He swallowed, then tried to activate the rune circle within his mind to attempt direct casting. It too found nothing.

"Oh," Damien said in a small voice. "There's really no Ether."

"None."

"Then, help me cast the Void magic again."

"I cannot."

"Cannot or will not?"

"You used Ether to fuel that spell. I simply twisted it with Void magic. Mortals cannot access the Void directly. Not even with your portion of my—Henry's—soul. It will tear you apart."

"That isn't what Henry told me. He said I wasn't ready, but it was possible."

"Henry believed many things that were incorrect. Your human spark corrupted him. Still, he likely meant that you could cast Void magic together with normal magic, not on its own. This is why you are trapped here. There is no way for you to leave."

"What if you just cast the spell on your own instead of doing it through me?"

"We are bound. Until you die or the contract is broken, I cannot."

"I'm not breaking the contract. You'll just destroy the world."

"That is correct. I understand this much of you after being trapped within your mind. This is what led me to my conclusion. You will die. When you do, I will consume your soul to ensure it does not become one of the Corrupted. This is the only service I can offer you unless you change the contract to free me before your death."

"I won't," Damien said, steeling his nerves. "I'm not going to destroy the Mortal Plane."

"You would not. I would."

"Same thing."

"Even if you don't, It Who Stills the Seas will," Herald said. "The Cycle will be restarted. You may feel pride that it lasted as long as it did."

"Henry and Sylph are still there. They won't let it happen."

"Henry's senses are gone. The mortal lacks the ability to locate one of my kind. There is nothing they can do. Henry also lacks access to your magic, so he cannot reach you. Every factor has already been accounted for, Damien Vale."

Damien slumped down, crossing his legs. His stomach knotted s he fought down the fear that the rest of life would be spent starving to death in the Void. Damien tried to access the Ether several more times, straining his mind to its limits and bringing on a violent headache in the process. He found nothing.

Slowly, he closed his eyes and fell into a dreamless sleep. There was nothing else he could do.

———

It was hard to keep track of time in the Void. There was no sun, no wind. There was nothing. His mind buzzed with boredom, and he occupied himself by running in circles or fiddling with the ring Sylph had given him back in Ardenford. He suspected he would have gone insane long ago—if such a concept even existed here—had Herald not been standing with him.

The Void creature wasn't much for conversation, but at least he wasn't alone.

"How long has it been?" Damien asked. "I don't feel very dead."

"You are not dead," Herald replied, its voice coming out in a slightly higher tone than usual. After a moment, he realized what the emotion it felt was. It was confusion.

"How long has it been?" Damien repeated.

"Eight days, by your mortal terms."

Damien blinked in surprise. "Eight days? That's not possible. I'm not even thirsty."

"There has not been an observed mortal in the Void before, only your soul. It appears that you might not experience the passage of time while you are outside of the Planes."

"Then..."

"You will be trapped here. For eternity," Herald said. "Until you are killed. Or until you change my contract."

"Well, I'm not changing the contract."

"Then, we will remain here until the end of time," Herald said. "We have all the time in the Planes. Eventually, your mortal mind will break, and you will free me—or another of my kind will find us and end you for me."

"Ah. I forgot there were more of you," Damien said, pressing his lips together. Somehow, his new situation didn't feel much better than the old one. "Is there at least anything to do here? How do you watch the Mortal Plane?"

"Void magic and a viewing well," Herald replied. "One surrounded by my kind. You're welcome to seek them out if you are prepared to die."

"Why are you telling me this?" Damien asked. "I would have thought it would be smarter to just not warn me, then let me die when we showed up."

Herald took several seconds before replying. "I have not studied any life form as extensively as I have you. I will admit a degree of interest in your activities. Not enough to betray my role, just as you would not betray yours, but enough to allow you death on your own terms."

"Huh. Thanks, I think," Damien said. "If I ever do feel like there's absolutely no way out of here, I'll let myself get offed, then. But, until then, I'm not going to give up."

"There is no point. You cannot escape the Void without Void magic, and you have no Ether."

"Then, you can keep me company until I figure that out myself," Damien replied. "Now, how does one get anywhere within the Void?"

"You walk," Herald replied. "My kind can fly, but you cannot. Once you have visited a place in the Void, you may return to it by visualizing it. However, you have not been anywhere here, so you cannot go anywhere you cannot walk to. I believe Henry would say that you are torturing yourself."

"You aren't Henry. I don't want to hear what he would have said from you," Damien replied. He picked a direction and started off. Herald walked with him.

Damien's thoughts drifted as they continued through the Void. They went to Second. Then, to his mother, and to all the other students at Blackmist. A smile flickered across his face at the idea of Mark being stuck in the Void. He probably would have tried to cut his way out of it.

But, mostly, his thoughts went to Sylph. Damien's chest ached, and he clenched his hand around the ring on his finger. In the endless chill of the Void, it was a tiny mote of warmth.

"How long has it been?" Damien asked, an indeterminate amount of time later.

"Two weeks."

"It doesn't feel like two weeks."

"Time does not flow in the Void as it does in the Planes. Or, more accurately, your mind is simply incapable of comprehending it."

"What about Moon?" Damien asked. "He somehow survived more than one Cycle, so he must have been outside of the Mortal Plane, right?"

"Moon was not merely a mortal. He was more, and I do not know where he was. He would have been destroyed if we did. The Void is endless, so it is possible he hid within it."

The snowy mountain Moon had met Damien on drifted through his memories. What he would have done to find the strange man now. If anyone knew how to escape the Void, it was probably him.

There was a sharp tug at Damien's chest. The breath caught in his throat, and a violent gale howled past him. Something cold trickled into his shoes, and he glanced down to see a field of white beneath him.

He stood atop a snowy mountain. Clouds drifted far below him, and he shivered, his breath coming out in white clouds.

"Eight Planes," Damien breathed, teeth chattering. "Well, that solves one thing."

"It does. So, this is where he took you when he blocked me

and Henry out," Herald said, materializing beside him. "You will freeze to death here. Is this where you wish to die?"

"Is that concern I hear in your voice?" Damien asked, forcing humor through his rapidly chilling lips. He squinted down the mountain, trying to see if there was anything beyond the snow to be found.

"No. Simply a statement of the inevitable."

A dark speck caught Damien's eye. It was halfway down the mountain, along what was nearly a sheer cliff. Herald followed his gaze but said nothing. Damien set off toward it carefully, choosing each step meticulously.

Snow shifted precariously beneath his feet, threatening to give out and send him tumbling down the mountain. He lost count of the times that he fell, managing to catch himself on protruding rocks just moments before he went over an edge.

Slowly but surely, Damien continued toward the dot. It grew in size, soon becoming a stone outcropping positioned over a small plateau.

"So much for nothing being here," Damien said.

Herald neglected to respond once more. He dropped the final few feet to the plateau, nearly slipping at the edge before he caught his balance. The outcropping ran into the mountain, turning into a tunnel. Faint orange light glowed from its depths.

"Would you look at that," Damien said, sending a smug glance at Herald.

"This should not be here," Herald said.

It was Damien's turn to ignore his companion. He scurried into the tunnel, trying to temper his expectations. He didn't know how long it had been since he'd arrived at the mountain, but if this proved fruitless, he wasn't sure how much more he had left in him.

The tunnel curved, depositing him before a circular room. It was a little larger than his room at Blackmist, with a single bed at the side. Across from it was a basin and a pedestal, both made of black stone.

Opposite the entrance was a thick metal door that had been completely covered in runes. The only empty spot on it was a small, hand-sized circle at its center.

Damien approached the pedestal. An old, weathered ring rested atop it. The basin beside it was full of dark, murky water.

"What is this?" Damien wondered, glancing back at Herald.

Herald peered down at the basin, its starry face twisting in surprise. "A viewing pool. Not the one we use, but of the same make."

They both looked at the ring resting on the pedestal. Damien picked it up carefully, examining it. Whatever the ring had once been, it was so worn down now that it was little more than a metal band. He chewed his lip, then glanced at his own hand. He worked the ring off his finger and set it on the pedestal.

The basin rippled, the dark water taking on color as a scene painted itself in perfect detail. Sylph sat in their training room, Henry floating beside her. Books were strewn across the floor around them, and she was pouring through them.

"Sylph!" Damien exclaimed, almost reaching for her before he stopped himself, worried he'd break the magical item. They didn't respond.

"It is one way," Herald said. "They cannot hear you."

Damien stared at Sylph and Henry, trying to memorize the sight of them. "Will this ever run out of magic?"

"No. It is Void magic," Herald replied.

He took the ring back, and the image vanished. Damien tested the basin once more before returning the ring to his finger. He didn't want to risk somehow losing it to something when he wasn't watching.

He examined the door and put his hand against it, but nothing happened. He didn't recognize the runes on it either. The rest of the room didn't provide much of interest.

"There's got to be more," Damien muttered.

"It is likely behind the door," Herald said. "The runes are a magical lock tuned to Moon. Only he can open it. I could do it as well, with sufficient time. Some of those runes reset to deliver a magical charge to whatever is behind the door, destroying it if the door is damaged. I cannot brute force it.

Damien ran his hand along the door, tracing the runes with his fingers. He glanced back at the stone basin, then shook the bed.

"This can't be it. He wouldn't have left all of this here for no reason, right? It doesn't look like anyone has been here in a long time."

"According to your memories and what I saw of the fight with the Corruption, Moon is likely dead," Herald said. "He was more than mortal, but not enough. You are seeking solace where there is nothing to be found. There is no gain from the suffering that you are putting yourself through."

"I'll be the one to decide that," Damien said, striding over to the bed and pulling back the covers. He peeked under the pillow and shuffled around the sheets.

"Moon was an interesting creature, but he was not dumb enough to hide the key to something as clearly important as this room in his bed," Herald said, cocking it's head to the side. "Do not ruin the information stored within this room. It would be a waste."

"I'm not ruining anything," Damien replied, squatting to look under the bed. He reached underneath it and felt around on the ground. His fingers met a smooth, cold piece of metal. A grin stretched across Damien's face, and he pulled his prize out.

It was a small, metal disk covered in runes smeared with a

brownish red substance that could have only been blood. Damien sent a pointed glance at Herald. "Waste, huh?"

"He was a bigger fool than I suspected."

Damien ignored Herald and walked up to the door, placing the rune circle against it. A second passed. His smile wavered, and he pulled away. As the circle broke contact with the door, the runes covering it lit with faint purple light.

A hiss of air escaped from behind the large door, and it swung inward, revealing a small room. Disappointment struck Damien like a hammer. Aside from a single desk bearing a thin metal spike and a large, sealed pot, the room was empty.

"What is this?" Damien asked, walking over and picking the spike up. It was vaguely shaped like a thorn, with an incredibly sharp tip and knobby end.

"It appears to be made of the body of a Corrupted monster," Herald observed. "Beyond that, it does not seem to have any magic. The pot also appears to lack magical properties."

"Why would be leave something like this behind a sealed door?" Damien asked, turning the thorn over in his hand and doing another glance around the room. There was nothing else. He popped the top of the pot open, revealing a thick black liquid. "And what is this?"

"Distilled blood from a Corrupted monster," Herald said. "Poisonous to mortal bodies."

Damien resealed the pot and set it back on the table beside the thorn.

"You didn't answer why he kept this sealed."

"I don't know. I study mortal magic. Your quirks are of no consequence to me if they do not directly aide my studies."

With a final look at the table, Damien headed back into the main room. He took the ring off his finger and set it on the pedestal, bringing forth the image of Sylph once more.

She was in the arena, sparring against Delph. The two

danced across the sand with incredible speed, Sylph's scythes clashing against the professor's cloak. In the corner, Whisp watched them, a dangerous expression on her face.

A flash of silver at Sylph's arm caught his eye. His eyes narrowed. She was wearing runed cuffs of some sort, but she was moving so fast that it was difficult to make out exactly what they were.

"Help me out here," Damien said, nodding at the image. "I need to figure out what those runes do."

"They will not help you."

"That wasn't a request."

Herald stared at Damien for a second, then approached the pool. It raised a finger, tracing runes in the air. They remained there, glimmering with faint starlight. As it drew, Damien's chest tightened. He recognized a fair number of them from parts of a summoning circle, and the rest weren't hard to extrapolate.

"Magic seals. They must be deactivated since she's fighting Delph, but why?"

"It is likely that the mortals discovered her association with the Corruption or Henry," Herald replied. "From my understanding of mortals, they are likely to terminate the threat."

"No. They can't," Damien said, his hands tightening around the basin until it cut into his palms. "Delph wouldn't let them."

"I do not know or care about what they will do. It no longer affects you," Herald said flatly. "The Corruption will do irreparable damage to all the Planes. She will just be one of the many souls to suffer the consequences of your inaction. The best thing you can do for her is to die so that I may aide in the fight, unless you plan to release me from our contract."

"Shut up," Damien said, staring down into the basin. His blood trickled down the sides of the bowl and mixed with the water. The image of Sylph flickered and faded away, turning to a black slate. He yanked his hands back and cursed.

He picked the ring off the pedestal and slipped it back onto his finger. "Why does it show me Sylph? How are these controlled?"

"The viewing well that I have used follows our will, but it functions with Void magic. This one uses some sort of focal crutch," Herald replied. "The ring is tied to her."

Damien blinked. He extended a tendril of mental energy to the ring, gently brushing against it. A tiny mote of Dark Ether responded to his touch, stored within the center of the ring. It was so small that he could barely feel it, but it was still there.

"I've got Ether," Damien breathed. He thrust his hand toward Herald. "Can't you use this?"

"There is not enough Ether there to do anything other than temporarily amuse yourself," Herald said, shaking its head. "I could not even begin to work with that."

Damien's face fell. He studied his hands, somewhat relieved by the stinging pain that came from the cuts along his palms. It almost helped take his mind off the situation. Almost.

"Can you give me some time alone?" Damien asked.

"That will change nothing."

"Just...do it. Please."

Herald silently walked out of the cave and vanished into the snow. Damien clenched his hands and turned back to the basin, leaning on it and staring into the murky water. He set Sylph's ring back on the pedestal, but nothing happened. There was too much blood in the water now.

"Damn it all. Did I break the stupid thing?" Damien asked, resisting the urge to slam his fists onto the magical scrying bowl. Frustration built up in his chest, and his palms felt slick with blood.

He dipped them into the water, washing the blood off

before drying his palms on his shirt. If he'd broken it, at least it would have some use. He turned to head over to the sealed room, but a flicker in the bowl caught his eye.

The water was growing darker. Damien stepped back over to it, hoping for another glance of Sylph. Instead, the water just kept growing blacker. Then, color started to spiral out from its center.

The image was muted and fuzzy, as if a distant memory. A man, wearing long, streaming robes, stood surrounded by an army of monsters and men. Jagged black tattoos covered the parts of his skin that were visible, and magic roared at his fingertips, giving all those who stood against him pause.

A dream from long ago resurfaced in Damien's mind. The image in the pool wasn't the exact some as the one he'd had, but the runes...

Damien staggered back from the bowl and sprinted into the sealed room, desperation flooding his thoughts. But deep within that desperation, there was something else. An idea, grounded in nothing but hope.

He slammed the huge door shut behind him. Runes flared along it, as if it had been waiting for this exact scenario. With a loud *crack*, the seams along the door sealed themselves shut. Four rune circles formed over the door, transposing themselves into it.

Damien grabbed the thorn and popped the top of the bottle off. The runes from the basin still floated in his head, as familiar as an old friend.

Something gave him pause. Damien turned the thorn over, trying to scan for anything he had missed. There was nothing. Extending a thread of mental energy, he brushed the thorn. It felt...empty.

Damien's gaze traveled to his ring. He swallowed, then coaxed the tiny spark of Ether out from within it. Instead of drawing it into his body, he sent it into the thorn. The Ether vanished within it, and the tool grew slightly warmer in his hand.

Taking the thorn in his left hand, Damien dipped it into the pot of ink. Then he raised it over his palm and gritted his teeth. With a swift jab, he brought it down through his skin. Agony pierced through his body, and he yanked the thorn out, staring at his work. A tiny dot of black color remained beneath his skin. He rubbed at it, but the dot didn't budge.

Damien swallowed, then raised the thorn again. The image of the runes was still firm within his mind. Almost all of them were foreign to him, but they felt strangely familiar at the same time. He steadied his mind, and then got back to work. He had a lot of runes to carve.

CHAPTER
TWENTY-TWO

Wind whipped through Damien's hair, drying the liquid on his cheeks. He blinked, reaching up uncomprehendingly. His hand came away stained red. The sides of his eyes felt wet as if he had been crying, and there was no sign of the cave that he had been sitting in.

A small pile of snow had built up on Damien's shoulders. He had no idea how long he had been sitting there, nor how long ago he had started carving the runes into his body. He glanced at his hands, but they were unblemished and unmarked.

"They aren't there," a voice said from behind him.

Damien turned, but he already knew who he would find waiting for him. Moon sat on a throne of snow, his features still covered by the heavy cloak. The runes covering his body twisted and squirmed whenever Damien tried to look closer at them.

"Why? I need them," Damien said. "Please. I have to get back to the Mortal Plane."

"I know," Moon said. "But you can't do it on your own. You know how much precision runes need. There's no way for you to copy my work with such little preparation."

"Then, what am I to do? I have nobody else to help me, and something tells me this isn't even real."

Damien swiped his hand across the snow, focusing his senses. It passed through it, and the mound flickered, vanishing as if it had never been there.

"This is very real," Moon promised. "The word you are looking for is physical. Your body remains within the room inside my chambers, but your soul is very much here."

"And where is here?"

"In my mindscape," Moon replied. "Or what is left of it, at least. Second's power has grown too much this Cycle. I cannot stand against him any longer."

"We were doing pretty well against him in Forsad," Damien said, starting to stand. Moon flicked a hand and a heavy weight slammed into Damien's shoulders, pushing him back down.

"He was limited by the location. There was no Corruption to draw on there, but there will be in the rest of the Mortal Plane," Moon said, shaking his head. "His true strength is that he controls all the Corruption completely. Without access to the other monsters, he is weakened greatly. And, even still, you were barely able to fight him to a standstill while using the best surprise you had. He will be prepared for it, now."

"You didn't bring me here to tell me it was hopeless."

"I didn't bring you here at all. You brought yourself," Moon said. "But you are correct. I'm not here to warn you off. On the contrary, Second must be stopped."

"So, you can help me get out of here? We need your help, Moon. I really don't understand you, but you can fight against Second. We need that."

Moon let out a dark chuckle. "I can aid you in escaping the Void, but I am afraid my fight against Second is almost concluded. I have perhaps a single action left in me, and it will not be against him."

Moon pushed his cloak back, revealing a jagged hole in the side of his chest. The edges were scarred a sickly gray, and they seemed to be slowly spreading across his body. Moon let the cloak fall once more.

"I am just what remains of Moon. My true body departed to do what it could to protect the Mortal Plane, but it is not long for this Cycle either."

"But...you beat him," Damien muttered. "Back in the Crypt. He was losing!"

"He is Corruption. I am just a man," Moon replied with a grimace. "But you have powerful allies. Delph is an apt warrior with great strength, many of the other mortals you know will aide you, not to mention your companion."

"Which one?" Damien asked bitterly. "Herald is determined to just watch me die."

"The Void are little better than the Corruption," Moon said, leaning forward and putting a hand on one of his knees. "The Cycle is flawed. I have seen countless mortals consumed within the Void and eventually join the Corruption. They are not without point, but if Second achieves his goals, the universe will collapse. The Planes must remain separate."

"So, what am I supposed to do?"

"If I knew, I would have already done it," Moon replied. "Now, that burden falls onto your shoulders. There is very little I can still do for you with the meager power this memory of me possesses, but I left enough to do what was needed. I wish I could give you more advice."

"How can't you?" Damien demanded. "You've been around for Cycles! You might not be as old as Henry, but surely you know at least something I can work with!"

"I know much, but little that will be of true help to you. Much of my knowledge will be mere distraction. All but this: You must focus. Second is an emotional creature. He cannot reason like we can, but he cannot be defeated by mortal means. He may not even be your true foe. This problem must be ripped out at its roots. Do you understand?"

"Conceptually, sure. That doesn't help me actually do it."

Moon gave him a wry smile. "I know. Much good all these years have done me, but you are in a position to bring this all to an end. You must trust me."

"How can I trust you? I mean, I know you're on my side or whatever, but you've given me nothing but mysteries!"

"The years have not been kind to my ability to speak with those younger than me," Moon said wearily. "This is what I meant. There is not much I can tell you that will make any sense to your mind. It would simply distract or even harm you. Recall how looking into Henry's mind for the first time affected you."

"How do you know about that?" Damien asked, his eyes narrowing.

Shadows condensed around Moon, forming into black tentacles. "You have already determined the answer to that. I have been watching you for some time. This Cycle is a turning point. We cannot fail."

"You were really the one who made me summon Henry?" Damien asked, fighting back against the magic holding him down. It broke, and he rose to his feet. "Why? How much else have you affected?"

"I have done what I needed to. You will understand because you will do the same. The Corruption must be stopped. Has my interference really caused you such difficulty? Would you prefer not to have Henry as a companion? Would you have even met Sylph if you did not?"

"I— Probably?"

"And would she have survived when her Core shattered?"

"How long have you been watching me?" Damien demanded. "Have you seen every second of my life?"

"Every last one," Moon confirmed. "I wanted to act more, but I could not. Over-interference would destroy you."

"How do you know? Who are you, really? You aren't Void. You aren't Corruption. Why do you care?"

Moon stood, his cloak whipping around his body as the wind picked up around them. "You will understand. This is my last chance, but it is your first. Unfortunately, you will not have the same amount of tries that I did. I leave you the rubble of my failings, but a glimmer of hope remains. Stop the Corruption. Fix the Cycle. Save the people you care about, Damien. If you do not, it will haunt you until the Planes collapse forever."

"Is there really nothing more you can tell me? Some weakness of the Corruption? Who controls the Void? Anything?"

"I have failed countless times. There is no information I can give you that will aide you. I have tried before. It always leads to the same result. I will influence you no further. You must deal with this in the way that you see best, for Moon has no more place in the sky. The stars have blinked out around me, one by one. Each failing—my fault. Some knowledge will come to you through the runes. They are the only remaining thing I can give. Do not ask for more."

Moon drifted across the snow, stopping before Damien and placing a hand on his shoulder. "I will guide your body. Once you have the runes, you will understand how to return to the Mortal Plane."

Damien desperately wanted to ask him more, but he slowly closed his mouth and nodded. Moon let out a slow sigh, and the dark tentacles reached out, pressing into Damien's chest.

Moon hissed. Fragments of his cloak started to burn away, turning into motes of light and vanishing in the snowfall. His body started to fade as well, but at a slower rate. Damien's body tingled, but he felt no pain.

To his surprise, he found he could still move. He raised a

hand to Moon's hood and, desperate for at least one answer, pushed it back.

Damien's own face, weathered by years and scars, stared back at him. A tiny smile tugged on Moon's lips, and he inclined his head. Then, he was gone. The snowy mountaintop vanished, and Damien was back in his own body.

Black lines surged across his body. Rune circles traced themselves across his skin, covering every spare inch. The thorn dropped from Damien's numb fingertips and shattered against the ground.

Then, as soon as the last rune had been drawn, the lines faded, becoming nearly invisible. Damien stared at his hands, his head pulsing. Something was there, just at the edge of his mind. He reached for it...and then he knew.

The rune circle on his chest had been worked into the intricate designs now covering him. Runes meant to contain instead now directed and channeled, using the power to every last bit of its potential while protecting him from the worst of its effects.

Damien rose to his feet, visions flickering through his mind. Flashes of a life that he had never lived danced through his memory and vanished into oblivion, leaving only the faintest traces of their passing.

Ideas for spells graced his mind, but the exact methodology of casting them was completely beyond him. They writhed and seethed, slipping free of his grasp as well. Many were so complex he couldn't even begin to figure out what they did, much less how to actually cast them. They had a mind of their own, almost like living beings more than just runes.

But not everything was lost. With every miniscule fragment of knowledge that was left behind from Moon's passing, Damien became more. The tiny remnants of the man who had lived beyond time joined with him, and Damien drew on their knowledge like a parched man at a lake.

And then, finally, it was over. Damien placed a hand against the sealed door. It slid open of its own volition, revealing Herald standing behind it.

Damien stepped past his companion without a word. He paused, taking the tarnished ring that Moon had kept on the bracer and slipping it over his finger beside Sylph's. Its exact meaning had been lost to him, but it had been important to the man. At some point, it had belonged to someone whom Moon had cared about. They were no more—that much, Damien was certain. But the least he could do was ensure that it saw everything through until the end.

"It's time for us to go," Damien said.

"You are changed," Herald said. "Your mind is clouded to me. How is this possible?"

"Sylph needs my help. The Mortal Plane needs our help. Enough asking questions. We need to act."

"You think the meager amount of power you have gained is enough to defeat Second?"

"I think you misunderstood me," Damien said. "That was not a question. I don't give a shit what you are or if you've got questions. Sylph might need my help, and the Mortal Plane is at risk. I will not waste any more time here."

"You will die. A mortal cannot channel the Void without Ether."

"Then, you'll be pleased. Teach me. I can access the Void. I know it."

Herald shook its head. "For reasons that I find myself unsure of, I will not teach you now. If you wish to arrive on the Mortal Plane within any amount of time considered short to humans, you will not have time. Instead, let us arrive at the moment of your death."

Raising a starry hand, a rune circle formed in the air before Herald. The runes were all twisted and warped, jagged in the parts where they should have been smooth and broken where they should have been whole.

"This is a crutch. A spell I have already created that will do all the work for you, so long as you can provide the Void energy. However, you are a mortal. You will not survive. It will be an agonizing, slow death. The fragments of your soul will burn for as long as this Cycle continues. I believe Henry would say it a mercy if you chose death instead."

Damien scanned the rune circle, then reached out. It floated to his hand and hovered above his palm. "We will determine exactly what Henry would say when we meet him."

"At least this will be an interesting experiment," Herald said, cocking its head to the side. "How long will you last in contact with the Void, I wonder?"

He ignored the eldritch creature and reached out to the runes with a strand of mental energy, gently brushing his senses over them. Cold ice spiked into his mind, but Damien suppressed it.

The runes covering his body darkened. Tendrils of magic emerged from the circle on his chest, wrapping around his arm and covering it completely. Miniature tears in reality the size of a fingernail started to split open around Damien's hand.

Utter darkness slipped out from them, coursing around his palm and flowing into Herald's rune circle as if it knew where it belonged. As it touched Damien's wreathed arm, agony spiked straight into his soul.

It was unlike anything he had ever felt. It was not true pain but rather the lack of everything. Apathy, greater than any he could ever describe, threatened to consume him completely. The complete lack of not just emotion, but also life.

Damien let out a strangled gasp, fighting back against it

with everything he could gather. He couldn't even muster the care to cry out. Slowly, his arm started to droop.

"I warned you," Herald said. "A mortal cannot channel Void."

Damien's fingers twitched. The bracelet on his wrist shattered, the metal raining to the ground in smoldering fragments. Runes pulsated along his body, and he gritted his teeth, forcing his hand to raise slightly. "And I told you. I. Am. More. Than. Mortal."

Void flared around Damien, searing up his arms and wreathing his head. He accepted it all, drawing it in like Ether and sending it out through his palm, into the rune circle.

"*Open!*"

A pitch-black maw stretched out before him, consuming all the light that touched it. Damien jerked his hand back and the rune circle dissipated, returning to Herald. The endless apathy abated, but it did not leave. It settled at the back of Damien's mind, building up like an ocean held back by a thin log dam.

Herald stared silently at Damien for an instant, then dissolved into a streamer of stars and shot back into his chest. Damien stepped into the portal, and it snapped shut behind him, leaving the snowy mountain peak desolate once more.

———

The story will continue in Downfall.

THANK YOU FOR READING VOIDWALKER

We hope you enjoyed it as much as we enjoyed bringing it to you. We just wanted to take a moment to encourage you to review the book. Follow this link: Voidwalker to be directed to the book's Amazon product page to leave your review.

Every review helps further the author's reach and, ultimately, helps them continue writing fantastic books for us all to enjoy.

—————

Also in series:

Blackmist
Greenblood
Duskbringer
Voidwalker
Downfall

—————

Want to discuss our books with other readers and even the authors like Shirtaloon, Zogarth, Cale Plamann, Noret Flood (Puddles4263) and so many more?

Join our Discord server today and be a part of the Aethon community.

Facebook | Instagram | Twitter | Website

You can also join our non-spam mailing list by visiting www.subscribepage.com/AethonReadersGroup and never miss out on future releases. You'll also receive three full books completely Free as our thanks to you.

———

Want to own your very own Eldritch Horror?

Looking for more great books from Actus?

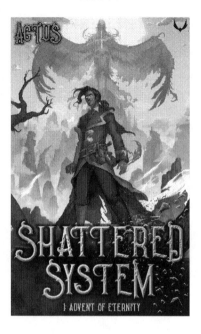

A ruthless tactician. A pantheon of traitor gods. A quest for revenge.

The Gods were believed to be immortal. To exist so far outside the natural laws of the universe that their crimes were unpunishable. Countless had tried to break free of their rule, but all were left broken.

A clock hung over the head of every mortal, counting down from their birth to the inescapable day that the Goddess of Death claimed them.

Knell Coda was never born. He came into the world outside the reaches of the gods, to a family who had committed the cardinal sin of defying their rule. Had they left him alone, perhaps the world would have remained as it was.

Instead, their meddling wound the hands on a new clock – one that hung above the heads of the gods rather than mortals. Because of their blunder, Knell learns the one secret that they desperately wanted to keep.

The Gods can be tricked. They can be defeated. They can die.

To most, seeking the head of a goddess would be the actions of a madman. To Knell, it is an inevitability. Together with his loyal crew, he will use his deadly cunning and grow strong enough to claim his revenge – no matter the cost.

Don't miss the next action-packed, strategic LitRPG Series from Actus, bestselling author of Blackmist and Cleaver's Edge, about a tactician with access to a System, his crew, and his quest for mortal revenge.

Advent of Eternity

Adventurers seek dungeons for riches. Heroes storm great fortresses. Gods clash far above. Arek cooks lasagna and tops it with a dash of finely chopped basil. An orc who has seen more than his fair amount of fighting, Arek wants nothing more than to spend the rest of his days cooking and away from the chaos of combat. However, when Ming and her group of adventurers hire him as their full-time chef, his plans of avoiding violence crumble. He longs to leave his blood-soaked mistakes in his past, but old friends and foes have different ideas. **Cleaver's Edge is the first book in a Fantasy / LitRPG lite series with a cooking element that's perfect for the Holiday Season. It contains status windows and other RPG elements, but it is not set within a videogame. It will appeal to anyone that enjoys reading a slice-of-life fantasy about a group of adventurers as well as fans of Food Wars!**

Get Cleaver's Edge Now!

Ancient Magic brought the world to its knees. Now, Angel is bringing it back. In the time that passed, society rebuilt, mixing machinery and magic to form something new. Great blimps took to the sky, belching steam and smoke as metal city-states sprouted like weeds below. Angel, a daring adventurer, scours the desert endlessly in search of ancient magic. When he's given an offer he can't refuse, he finds out that he's not the only one seeking lost knowledge. His opponents wield magic that the world has forgotten, and their methods leave cities razed and the innocent in their wake. In a race against a group who has lived in the shadows since the Great War, Angel will have to determine just how far he's willing to go to accomplish his goals. **Experience the start of a Magitech LitRPG Series by Actus, the author of Cleaver's Edge. Set in a Steampunk Fantasy world, it's perfect for fans of Arcane, Final Fantasy, and lovers of all things Gamelit, LitRPG, & Progression Fantasy.**

Get Steamforged Sorcery Now!

For all our LitRPG books, visit our website.